NOTHING TO LOSE

By

JIMMIE TOMS

Publisher: Blue Skies Press
ISBN: 978-1986320580

To contact Jimmie Toms, email him at jtoms8667@gmail.com

Dedicated to the most beautiful and patient person in my world — my wife.

Prologue

One pleasantly cool Saturday night in May, Clayton Giles Matthews put a .22 caliber automatic pistol in his side pocket and a .38 caliber revolver in his belt. He drove out to the suburbs and parked behind the adult bookshop frequented by the selected victim. The man always left the bookshop at the same time according to a surveillance report. The theory put forth by the investigator was that he probably had a favorite television program because he always drove directly home.

Clay spotted his prey's car and parked a few spaces further down the same row. While he waited, Clay reviewed the situation in his mind. Was he really willing to murder this man? Had his offense been so serious that it justified taking the man's life? The answer was yes in both cases. The answer was yes because the alternative was to do nothing. And to do nothing was not acceptable to Clay.

The man marked for death was an insurance adjuster named Jerry Nagel. Together with another insurance company employee, Nagel had cheated Clay and his wife out of half of their insurance claim – some $150,000. He maneuvered them into a situation of vulnerability and presented them with a choice – accept half of the claim or be tied up in the courts forever. So, was it justice to take this man's life for the $150,000 that he had cheated Clay's family of or not? But part of the equation is this man has cheated many other people and he will go on cheating. So, yes, Nagel would die tonight.

When he saw Nagel exit the shop, Clay Matthews got out of his car. He timed his walk so that he met Nagel at the door of his car. It was dark and the parking lot was poorly lit. Probably the regular customers did not want anybody recognizing them. Clay pulled the revolver from his belt. He jabbed Nagel in the ribs and scared him. Nagel had opened the car door and Clay told him to get inside and slide over.

Nagel was too scared to object. He was shaking and seemed to be drooling. Clay had slipped on a pair of dark leather gloves before he left his car. Nagel seemed fixated on the gloves and the gun.

When he closed the door of Nagel's car behind him, Clay realized that Nagel didn't recognize him. Clay simply stared at him for a few minutes to see if Nagel would register his identity. There was no recognition in his eyes. Nagel started to settle down and get control of his breathing.

"Is this a robbery?" Nagel stuttered out the question.

"You can have my wallet! And my car if you want it! I won't yell or anything and I'll never identify you. I won't even make a complaint. Okay?" He reached for his wallet and handed it over. Clay took the money and threw the billfold on the floor. He nodded his head towards Nagel and looked at his watch. Nagel gave it to him.

"There's good news and bad news." Clay said. "The good news is that you won't be around to cheat anyone else. The bad news is that I'll have to throw away one of my favorite guns after I kill you."

"Wait! Wait! I recognize you. Look, I'm sorry you were cheated on the settlement for your house. It wasn't my idea. Wait! Don't do anything, okay? Let me explain. It was Walter's idea. He fingered you as someone who wouldn't put up an argument about being cheated. We get a bonus from the company if there's a settlement without any legal challenge. Okay?" Now he was shaking and drooling again.

Clayton Matthews was calm and deliberate as he extended the revolver so that it touched Nagel's chest. He pulled the trigger. The explosion was loud inside the car but hardly registered outside. Anyway, there was no one around to hear it. Nagel died instantly. Clay exited the car and walked calmly back to his vehicle.

Page two of the morning edition of the Washington Post Metro section reported the robbery/homicide of Mr. Jeremiah Nagel. The police were investigating and urged any citizen with information to call the police hotline.

1 - The Present

Clayton Giles Matthews was an ordinary, hardworking guy who lived a quiet life in the suburbs of Washington, D.C. Over the years, several events had occurred that brought an incredible amount of pain into his life. In each case, he shook his broad shoulders and picked himself up to continue his life.

For instance, he and his wife of many years returned home from a rare night out for dinner and found their house in flames. It was a total loss. The insurance company investigators dragged their feet and asked a million questions. First, they would not consider settlement of his claim until the fire investigation was complete. Then they suggested that culpability on his part might delay the claim for years. They questioned him about his hobby shop in the basement. Had he ever modified the wiring? Was he a licensed electrician? Was there a smoke detector in the hobby shop? Was it connected to a monitored alarm system?

Unless, of course, he was willing to reduce the claim considerably? And Clayton agreed because his wife had been diagnosed with breast cancer. He wanted to establish a new home to ease her mind.

As an interim measure, they had rented a house in a nearby neighborhood. The landlord had demanded two months deposit for the short-term rental. When they moved from the rental home, he refused to return any part of the deposit. Clayton decided not to press the issue because his wife's illness and treatment consumed all of his time and energy.

Clayton's hobby was electronics and he enjoyed working with new ideas in his home workshop.

During his tinkering, he designed a new approach to remote control of high voltage systems. He refined the design and looked into filing for a patent. The attorney wanted one thousand dollars for the initial search and a five thousand-dollar retainer for writing the application. Clayton did not have the money to file for a patent. He knew he had a moneymaking winner but he did not know how to capitalize on the idea. A friend of a friend introduced him to a sales manager of a large corporation. Clayton supplied them with samples for evaluation. They assured him that, if the ideas worked, they would return to negotiate an exclusive license. Clayton was no fool so he encapsulated his idea in a hard-epoxy case before shipping it to them. Three months later, they returned his samples. They had been dismantled and copied. When he protested, the sales manager suggested that Clayton have his attorney contact their legal office. The company was a thirty million dollar per year subsidiary of a three hundred million dollar international conglomerate. Clayton folded and lost his interest in tinkering around with new ideas.

Clayton's daughter had been fired from her job a year ago. The boss fired her publicly and ordered her from the premises. She was embarrassed and deeply hurt. As a result, she fled to California vowing never to return to the area.

Clayton's wife died three months after their twenty-sixth anniversary. He couldn't find his daughter to notify her of her mother's death. She had moved to a new apartment and had not written to them. After the funeral, he didn't bother to locate her.

In the new home purchased after the fire, they barely knew the neighbors so he was alone with his grief. He didn't return to work until he received a suspension notice from the personnel office. They wanted to know if he wanted his pension paid in a lump sum or over a specified period of time. He called them to explain that he needed some compassionate leave. He did not want to terminate his employment. He needed his job in order to meet living expenses and pay off some bills associated with his wife's illness.

"I'm sorry, Mr. Matthews," said the counselor in human

resources. "If you had notified the company of your wife's death and requested leave on Form 1556, you would have been paid for three days compassionate leave. Any time in excess of three days could have been charged to vacation if you had any accrued time in your account or taken as leave without pay. Form 1556 would have alerted our department for the need to order flowers on behalf of the company. We are authorized to send a $25.00 wreath in the event of the loss of an immediate family member."

"Well, I've never heard of Form 1556. I tried to call my supervisor but I got his voice mail so I left a message. I did not receive a return call. The wreath was not necessary but I fail to see why my employment is terminated." Clay tried to curb the anger and frustration in his voice. He knew it wasn't the fault of the person on the telephone but surely someone had to be able to take some initiative.

"I have spoken to your supervisor and he reviewed the situation with the Assistant Vice President. They feel that your extended absence and failure to request leave is grounds for dismissal. In general, the company is reducing the work force due to the shift of manufacturing work to Mexico. The NAFTA – North American Free Trade Agreement - re-defined the workplace in our industry. I hope you realize it is not a personal criticism of you or your work." She spoke in such a calm, impersonal tone of voice that she might have been discussing the recent rise in gasoline prices.

"So, Mr. Matthews, unless you have further questions, I would like to forward the paperwork to you for completion. There are several forms. Please be accurate and complete in your answers and we will be able to forward your final check in a prompt manner. Have a good day." She hung up the telephone.

Clayton sat in the darkened living room until the early hours of a new day. Finally, he stirred in order to start the daily routine of living and continuing a life.

He was alone. His wife was gone. She had passed over a barrier of no return. He had no one else in his life and, in fact, did not want any one. These were the facts.

So why live?

And the answer was that he had no intention of living.

He would settle his affairs and arrange for his funeral. He would take a lump sum settlement on his pension. He would sell the house. He had a cemetery plot next to his wife and he would prepay the other necessities – the vault, casket and transportation. There was no need for a service or flowers or music. Since he would not be filling out a Form 1556, the company would not be sending flowers.

Clay estimated ninety days to settle on the house sale and convert his estate to cash. By that time, he would have a new address for his daughter. He would send her the money as an inheritance. There would be no need for her to return to the area. In the meantime, he would plan his final exit. He was not afraid of pain but he wanted to avoid a mess. He was a tidy person. And he did not like embarrassment. He remembered reading that the body released all control of its functions upon death. Involuntary urination and defecation was the result. It would be a mess and not satisfactory. What about outdoors in an uninhabited area? What about using a bathtub? Using a motel bathtub would be the best arrangement.

Hmmm. Ninety days. What would he do for ninety days? He was not a heavy drinker. Getting drunk did not appeal to him. He had no interest in spending time with a woman. He had been faithful to his wife. He would not break his vows now. The thought of a cruise crossed his mind and rapidly disappeared. He wouldn't enjoy a cruise without Lydia beside him. Well, he would sleep tonight and start winding up affairs tomorrow. Maybe something would occur to him.

At 4 AM, Clay sat up in bed wide-awake. He knew what he wanted to do with the last few months of his life. He wanted to even up the scoreboard. He hadn't been treated fairly. In fact, he had been cheated and lied to, and stolen from, and and and…….. He wasn't going to just bow out and leave the bastards laughing at him. No! Absolutely not!

Before I go, he thought, I want justice. There will be a reckoning.

Clay got up and went into the kitchen to start a pot of coffee. While the pot was perking, he topped off the bird feeders and put out a new suet cake for the woodpecker that visited every morning. Then he returned to the house to settle down with a cup of coffee and watch the morning feeding.

Mr. and Mrs. Cardinal dropped by for a snack. They did not stay long but they were regulars – the first ones in the morning and the last ones at night. The woodpecker found the new cake and he went to work on it. Two wrens came by for breakfast. They were newcomers. The goldfinches were landing on their feeder. It was designed for them. They would land on the perch and pivot upside down to extract the thistle seed from the hole below the perch. It was funny to see the other birds try to emulate their maneuver to tap into the seed.

And, in the background of his mind, Clay Matthews started his plan to get even for some of the inequities and pain in his life. He understood the difference between pain caused by God and pain caused by man. No one can control the path of a tornado or a flood. But why would one person create pain in another person's life for money or greed?

Because they thought they could get away with it. They thought they were rich enough or strong enough or politically-connected enough that the pissant they crapped on had no recourse.

Well, there would be a price to pay. And he would collect the payment. He had nothing to lose.

And then he would depart their world and leave the confusion to those who might care to continue their greedy, pointless, shallow existence.

Clayton knew the seriousness of his thoughts. He was considering the murder of people who had hurt him and his family. He would be breaking one of the most serious of God's commandments. He would be violating several state and federal laws with harsh punishments. The words leaped into his mind as if they were burned by a branding iron.

Payback! Murder! Killer!

And, at the time, he could not dream that he would be so

successful as an assassin that he would be a professional killer for hire even before his personal vendettas were settled.

2 – The Beginning

When Clayton Giles Matthews was born in 1942, the world was deeply involved in World War II. Clay's father was an aircraft mechanic in the Army Air Force. He was stationed in the Pacific area in the midst of the action. There was no hope of an emergency leave to attend the birth of his son.

In the summer of 1943, his father was severely wounded during an attack on his airfield. Clay's father was decorated for bravery above and beyond the call of duty. When the enemy rushed the airfield in an attempt to overrun the perimeter guard and seize the airplanes, Clay's father manned a machine gun and held them off until help arrived. He refused medical aid until the airfield was safe. He was promoted two ranks to Technical Sergeant and, after discharge from the hospital, given thirty days convalescent leave.

Clayton was a year old before his father saw him and held him in his arms. Clayton was too young to remember the big event but he had heard the story many times. And there were plenty of pictures of the big event.

And he was too young to remember the telegram from the War Department. But he heard the story many times as he grew up. Clayton's father was a mechanic but he started flying combat missions as a gunner on the airplanes he maintained. On one of the missions, the aircraft was shot down. Clayton's father was missing in action and presumed dead.

Apparently Mom collapsed. When she regained consciousness, she wailed and wailed. Eventually she was hospitalized and Clayton was cared for by his grandparents. Mom was still in the hospital when the second telegram arrived. It advised her of the rescue. Dad had been wounded again. But he was recovering and would be given convalescent leave as soon as possible. Mom didn't understand. She was still under sedation.

At the end of the war, Clay's father was a Master Sergeant with a chest full of ribbons. All of the brass suggested that he consider a career in the military. A peacetime army would have to be built from the survivors. Josef Stalin was making waves and Russia looked like the next threat to world peace. The powers in Washington wanted a strong deterrent to Russia's rapidly expanding military might.

When the Air Force was split from the Army as a separate service, Clayton's father stayed with the Air Force. He was one of the pioneers. They were stationed at Andrews Air Force Base in the southeast section of the nation's capital. Mom was in the military hospital a lot of the time. She could not gain control of her life long enough to maintain a stable home. Fortunately, the paternal grandparents were able to live with them and provide some semblance of normalcy for Clayton.

The Korean War erupted in 1950 and his father was one of the first ones to leave for Japan. From Japan, he was transferred to Kempo Air Field in Korea – on the front lines again. In 1953, Clay's father returned home – unwounded but very tired and emotionally exhausted. He was assigned to light administrative duties and remained in the D.C. area as a compassionate assignment due to his wife's illness.

To fill the lonely evenings and weekends, he worked with Clayton on his homework assignments and indulged his hobby of guns and ammunition. Every time he had returned to the states, he had brought home some guns. By 1955, he had an extensive collection of pistols and rifles. All of the guns were unregistered. He was an expert in hand-loading his ammunition. He visited the firing range frequently with Clayton at his side.

Clayton was not the gun enthusiast that his father was but he enjoyed the companionship. Also, he was a fast learner. By the time he graduated from high school, he was an expert marksman with every pistol and rifle in his father's collection.

He was proficient in loading ammunition and had read every book in his father's collection on guns.

From high school, Clayton enlisted in the Air Force. After completion of basic training in New York, he was transferred to Lowry Air Force Base in Denver, Colorado. He was assigned to electronics school. No one asked him if he wanted to attend electronics school or even if he were interested in electronics. The tests indicated an aptitude for math and abstract thought. The Air Force needed bodies in the career field so here he was.

He attended electronics school six hours a day six days a week. At Christmas, he received a week's leave and returned home for a visit. On January 2, he was back in the saddle at the training command. In May, he graduated from the basics level on Friday and reported to systems training school on Monday. He received training in search radar systems and navigation systems. He was slated to be an electronics technician on the flight line.

On evaluations, the instructors noted that Clayton was a quiet, competent, unflappable sort of individual. He was not overly ambitious so he did not attain promotions and rank quite as fast as some others in his classes. In fairness, the reports indicated a unique ability to focus on problems and solutions. He had located a phantom fault in the G series of the navigation radar on the tanker aircraft used in the Strategic Air Command. At random times, the computer would jump to a bogus location. It was disconcerting, to say the very least, for the radar system to jump to a new location thousands of miles away as the tanker was about to hookup with a thirsty bomber on a cloudy night. Clayton focused on the problem during his off-hours for months. He discovered that a signal lead from one black box to another black box was not shielded. Immediately prior to a mid-air refueling, the boom operator would exercise his system in preparation for the fuel transfer. Clayton discovered the initial movement of the boom from the stowed position introduced an electrical spike across the unshielded lead. The spurious signal caused the system's computer to jump to an erroneous position. The solution was twofold and simple to implement.

The unshielded lead was replaced with a shielded wire. A filter was installed on the boom drive system to eliminate spurious signals.

The Maintenance Officer received a commendation. The field representative for the manufacturer of the navigation radar system received a bonus for reporting the solution. The field representative for the aircraft manufacturer received a meritorious raise and promotion for writing up the field modification to the boom system. There was a boisterous party at the Officer's Club on Friday night to celebrate the career advances of the individuals.

Clay Matthews was not an officer so he could not attend the party. It was explained to him that since he was close to the end of his enlistment, it seemed pointless to waste a promotion on a soon-to-be civilian. No one asked him if he intended to re-enlist.

So Clay took his discharge and re-entered civilian life. The tankers continued flying and the bombers received the precious fuel. The difference was that the whole operation was a little safer now due to Clayton's solution to the phantom problem. And three other guys enjoyed the rewards of his work.

3 – Civilian World

Visorex Systems, Incorporated, was a huge government contractor in the Maryland suburbs near the I-495 Beltway that encircles Washington, D. C. There were many companies of their ilk that were commonly referred to as "Beltway Bandits." VSI was among the most successful bandits. The employee benefits were typical and competitive for the area. The paperwork signed by new employees was more strict than most of the other bandits. The part that referred to new inventions and patents was very strict. All inventions and patents were the sole property of VSI – whether developed on company time or home time. Even if the new product or idea was in a completely different field, it belonged to VSI. Failure to report new ideas and inventions was cause for dismissal and legal action by the company.

Two weeks after starting his job at VSI, Clay met his future wife. Lydia Rathbun was everything Clay had always dreamed about when he thought about a wife. In his eyes, she was beautiful. She wore a beautiful pony tail hairdo during the day at work. In the evening, she combed out long hair that hung below her shoulders. Lydia's dark hazel eyes could laugh with happiness or darken when encountering a problem. The top of her head was even with Clay's shoulders so he estimated her height at five foot four inches. He could talk to her and she seemed to hang on his every word. She asked intelligent questions and prompted new ideas on his part. He could remember every conversation they ever had during their courtship.

"Gosh, Lydia, I could talk to you all night." Clayton looked at her as if she were the only person in the world.

"I feel the same way but both of us have to work tomorrow." Lydia was sensible and responsible.

"May I kiss you good night?" Clayton held his breath.

"I hope you will." She closed her eyes and leaned in his direction.

A month later they were sitting in Clayton's car in front of her parent's house in Bethesda, Maryland. They had gone out to dinner and talked so long that the restaurant closed up around them.

Now it was time to say good night again and he did not want to leave her.

While he was kissing her, his hands began to wander. When the kiss ended, they were both feeling a little giddy. They were positive that no one else had ever felt this way.

"I've never been touched like that before tonight. Did you enjoy it?" She asked him.

"Oh, honey, I liked it very much and I don't want to stop. Did you like it?" He was trying to take short breaths and control his pulse.

"I do like it and I don't want to stop either. I'll do anything you want me to do."

"Would that include marrying me?"

"Yes! Absolutely yes!"

"We could leave work early on Friday. We could drive over to the courthouse in Rockville and get married. Then we could drive up to West Virginia to a place I saw in a magazine. What do you think?"

"I'll be ready." She promised.

On a warm, sunshiny, August afternoon, Clayton Giles Matthews and Lydia Ann Rathbun swore to love and cherish each other until death did them part.

4 - Marriage

Clayton was very good with math but he could not seem to stretch his paycheck to cover their needs and wants. The birth of their daughter had interrupted Lydia's work. So the loss of the second income for an indefinite period required some serious juggling of the books. They had purchased a house on their first anniversary and it was difficult to budget necessary items like a washer and dryer, television, stereo system, and a dozen other "wants." Finally, the "wants" list went into the drawer and life settled down to the needs and careening from paycheck to paycheck.

In the fall, Clayton submitted his first idea to the company for review by the "From the Inventors" committee. He had worked out a way to reduce the number of signal filters in the navigation radar in production by VSI. The savings amounted to over $100 in parts per system and several hours of labor in assembly and test. The Engineering Department verified the change and his idea was implemented in production.

Clayton received a letter of commendation and $250.

Clayton took a second job at the local radio-television repair shop.

Lydia started preparing their lives for her return to work. There was a lot more laundry and housework and food preparation with the baby in their lives. They would have to play catch-up on the weekends and depend on family for day care of the baby.

Both of them were fascinated with the little, bright-eyed, living doll in their lives. They would play with her for hours on the weekends. And she quickly learned how to demand their attention.

With two jobs and the extra housework, Clayton did not have much time for tinkering around in his hobby shop. When the few hours spent in the wee hours of the morning yielded an idea, Clayton filed it away for future use. VSI had received their last idea from him.

When Clayton went to work for Joe Colissimo at his Radio/ TV repair shop, he completed and submitted Form 2102 at VSI requesting permission to work part-time for another company. Since it was in a different field, he received permission in the form of an endorsement to Form 2102.

Within a few weeks, Joe Colissimo realized that he had a treasure in Clayton. Within a few months, Clayton had revolutionized the way Joe's shop repaired electronic devices. Clayton set up a checklist for isolating the trouble to a particular section. It was much like a paramedic approaches an unconscious victim – check pulse, then blood pressure, then pupils, and so forth.

Clayton proceeded to make some special test equipment that quickly pinned down a problem to a particular component. Joe was amazed. Then he realized that he could manufacture the test sets and sell them to other shops. When he explained to Clayton what he wanted to do, he was surprised that Clayton had no reaction. Then he realized that Clayton did not understand that he intended to share the profits. To Joe, it was a simple equation – they would split the profits equally. Joe would supply the parts and do the selling. Clayton would do the assembly and test.

Clayton was ecstatic. He had a new best friend. Within the first year, Clayton was making more money from his part-time job than he was at VSI. Lydia was able to quit her job and stay home with the baby.

5 – Losses

In the early spring of the year, Clayton's mother died. She passed away in her sleep. She had been under sedation, sometimes heavy, for a lot of years. She rarely recognized her husband during his dutiful visits. She never recognized her son or even knew about her daughter-in-law or granddaughter.

Everyone said that her death was a blessing – a relief from the suffering of many years.

It didn't feel like a blessing or a relief to Clayton or his father. Neither of them had ever given up hope that she would recover. They had been looking forward to having her home someday for Sunday cookouts and ice cream crankings. They knew she would enjoy the early spring cherry blossoms along the tidal basin and the colors of the dogwood trees.

But death came and collected the life of their tormented, loved one. And the survivors mourned their loss and arranged for the traditional steps to the final resting place. Clayton's grandfather had purchased a large number of adjacent plots in Frederick, Maryland many years ago. It was the Matthews family burial ground.

Resthaven Memorial Gardens is a beautiful place located just north of Frederick, Maryland and 20 miles south of the Pennsylvania State line. The grounds are professionally maintained. A perpetual care fund provided by the initial organization of the cemetery guarantees the eternal beauty so comforting to the survivors.

In 1975, Clayton's father died. Like his mother, he died in his sleep. Clayton arranged for the funeral with a heavy heart. He hoped that his father was passing to a happier place. He could not ever remember seeing his father laugh. A smile sometimes emerged to recognize an accomplishment or an event but never a laugh. Life for his father had been one of war and pain and death. Now he lay next to his wife for eternity hopefully at rest and peace.

Clayton was the sole and uncontested heir to the estate. There was not a lot of money. The bills were paid to date and the filing of the records was meticulous as Clay expected. There was a small checking account and a four-figure savings account. His father had lived on his military pension from month to month. The funeral home director suggested that the clothes could be picked up by a local charity and a consignment shop would take the furniture.

Clay packed up the guns and reloading equipment. He was not exactly surprised at the size of the arsenal because he had fired all of the guns many times with his father. But he had never really tallied up the number of pistols and rifles at one time. What was surprising was the amount of reloading supplies – the gunpowder, shell cases, and fuses. Maybe Dad thought the next war would be fought in Maryland. Well, anyhow, he packed up the guns and equipment and, in several loads, moved the heavy boxes to his basement.

6 - Special Feelings

The financial plan for the Matthews family was succeeding as Clay and Lydia envisioned. They had a college fund started for their daughter. Their two-year old car was paid for in full. The house payments were made on time and they had a modest savings account.

What they did not have was enough time to enjoy the fruits of Clay's two jobs. By the time he came home from a full day at Visorex, ate dinner and departed for Joe's Radio/Television repair shop, the sun was setting. By the time he got home, the baby was asleep and Clay was exhausted.

On Saturdays, Clay mowed the lawn and did some repair jobs around the house. Lydia went grocery shopping in the afternoon and Clay did the babysitting. It was the only time during the week that he spent any time with his daughter. The bright-eyed little doll looked at him as if he were a stranger.

But Lydia was happy with their life and he was happy with her. She was always next to him during the night. If the togetherness time seemed short, they remembered that they were still young. There was lots of time left in life. It was important to be established and secure. They wanted their daughter to attend college. Who knows? She might be the very first female president. Or invent a new lifesaving medical technique. She was very intelligent – anyone could tell that by looking into her eyes. She was the most special little girl they had ever encountered. They may not be completely objective in their opinions but close enough.

Clayton was in awe of his wife. She was the only woman he had ever "been with" as the saying goes. And he knew that he was the only man Lydia had ever "been with." So it amazed him that, given their collective lack of experience, everything had gone so well in the sex department. He'd heard enough stories from other guys to know that sexual compatibility was not a guarantee in marriage.

Lydia was a tigress in bed. She was eager to try anything he could dream up and she was rather imaginative in her own right. In their physical exploration of each other, they acknowledged mutual explorations of masturbation techniques during their teen years. They knew the feelings of climax. But neither of them was prepared for the pinnacles of delight reached through the efforts of a partner in sex. Now all of the lyrics in all of the love songs made sense. Phrases like "take me to the moon" and "rocket's delight" were perfect descriptions of the rapturous feelings experienced in the privacy of their bedroom.

After the lovemaking sessions, both of them were sleepy and satisfied. Lydia could not keep her eyes open and slipped into a peaceful sleep. Clay was relaxed and mellow. He admired her feminine beauty from head to toe.

He looked at her sleeping body and realized how much he loved her. The magnitude of his love scared him. Omigod, what if something happened to her? Well, it just couldn't. He wouldn't let anything happen. He would protect her from everything and everybody.

Clayton reached out to touch her but he stopped. He wanted to enjoy the beautiful picture before him a little longer. She was amazing. How in the world did he find her? And when he did find her, what made her love him? Hundreds of millions of people in the world and they found each other. How did that work? Was there some sort of internal electronic circuit buried inside our bodies that worked kind of like a search radar system? It kept looking until it found the one right mate? No, that wasn't it because some couples got a divorce so – well, maybe the radar malfunctioned in some cases. But there was no malfunction with him and Lydia. Thank God. Then a thought popped into his mind - maybe he should be thanking God and not worrying about radar systems.

7 - Mutiny

"Dad, I don't want to go to college. I'm tired of school." Kathryn Ann voiced her feelings and tossed her auburn pony tail from side to side.

"It's just a little while longer. College will be a lot more fun than high school. Please, honey?" Clay reached out to touch her small hands but she stood up and stretched her full five foot two inches to the maximum in frustration.

"It's four years, Dad. I can't do it." The voice of Kathryn Ann, their only child, seemed like that of a stranger a million miles away. Why did they work so hard to establish the college fund if she didn't want to go to college? And, if she didn't want to go, why didn't she say so when she was born? Well, okay, maybe he was being a little extreme but, damn it.

"So what are you going to do if you don't go to college?" Clay tried to calm his voice and reason with her. Reasoning with Kathryn Ann was not an easy thing to do since he had never understood her. Love her, yes. Understand her, no. She had the strongest will and the widest streak of stubbornness of any person he had ever encountered. Thank God for the closeness of Kathryn and Lydia. They seemed to communicate in a way that baffled Clay. He felt like he was the only man in the world who did not understand the women in his life.

"I would like to go business school, Dad." She sat down and clasped her hands in her lap. She forced herself to control her voice. "There is a good one in Northern Virginia. The course is about one year. The cost is about $10,000. At the completion, I would be an executive secretary. I would be able to get a job anywhere in the United States – maybe even in the world." She stopped and looked at him.

Clay shook his head sadly, whoever heard of an executive secretary being the President or inventing a medical technique?

"Mom and I visited the school last week. She thinks it is okay. Don't you, Mom?" Kathryn swung her glance around the room seeking out her mother's support.

Clay looked at his wife. Was he to be sandbagged again? Was it fair to be forever outnumbered in his own house?

"Clay, it is a good alternative for her at this point. It doesn't rule out college at a later date. It gives her a good, marketable skill. She's an adult and we must face up to it." Lydia looked at him with eyes that pleaded for understanding.

"Mom's right, Dad. I am an adult. My generation is older at eighteen than your generation. I already....." She stopped as Clay held up his hands.

"Stop! Too much information. I surrender." Clay escaped to his hobby shop area.

"Too bad she might not ever be President," Clay muttered to himself as he descended the stairs to the basement. "The government deserves her."

Later, Clay was admitting to himself that he was proud of Kathryn for figuring out an alternative to college if she had no intentions of attending college. And it sounded as if she intended to live at home while she attended business school. That was good. He had been worrying about her leaving for college.

He had to leave for Joe's repair shop in a few minutes. He was meeting Joe Colissimo to discuss the business. The shop work had fallen off dramatically over the last year. It was clear that they had to come up with some alternatives or the shop would be history. Clay felt like a partner in the shop after all the years. Joe had said that he considered him a partner but he couldn't make him a part owner because the business was owned by Joe's extended family. Whatever that meant.

He was glad that he had not left his day job but he hated VSI. It was an unfriendly place. "Chickenshit" was the term used in the military service. Maybe he should have stayed in the military service. He would be retiring now with a nice pension. No! If he had stayed in service, he might not have met Lydia. God that was a close call. It was a good thing he got screwed on that discovery he made about the navigation radar or he might have re-enlisted. He shook his head to clear his thinking about these crazy thoughts. He wondered if he was getting old. He seemed to be muttering to himself a lot these days.

8 - Patents Are Expensive

Clayton sat in the audience next to Lydia. On the other side of Lydia sat Joe Colissimo and his wife, Sylvia. Both of their daughters were graduating from business school tonight. They would be honored for their grades and perfect attendance.

Clayton had to admit that he was impressed with the work ethic Kathryn had shown during the last year. The school was strict. She had to dress each morning as she would have to dress on a future job. She had to comport herself as if she were an executive secretary at all times during class. Each night after school and every morning before school, Kathryn had completed an enormous amount of homework.

Joe's daughter, Josephine, and Kathryn carpooled to school each day. They were best friends and it pleased Clayton very much.

Clay's thoughts were on another subject as he listened to the various speakers during the ceremony. A year ago, he and Joe had discussed the declining business. Sales of appliances such as radios and televisions were being taken over by the large chain stores. They were doing their own repair service. Some of the stores offered to subcontract some of their repair business but only at ridiculous prices. Clay had offered one idea for their survival. In his hobby shop at home, he had devised a special high-voltage, switching network to cope with the limited power available to a residential home. He needed to switch the power from the 220-volt appliances such as the dryer, stove, furnace, and hot water heater in such a way that the other occupants were not deprived of comforts and necessities but allowed him to use 220 volts as required. It was a careful design of selective time-sharing of an energy source.

Now the design was complete and he was anxious to demonstrate the product to Joe. They would have to figure out the merit and how to market the idea. Clay had done some market research by looking up manufacturers of similar products. However, his design was unique. It would probably obsolete some of the other products on the market.

On Monday, Kathryn Ann would start work for a software company. It was a small outfit but it probably had a good future in what promised to be a booming industry. Josephine Colissimo was slated to work for an attorney in a nearby building. The two girls could share the carpooling as they did for school.

The graduation ceremony was impressive and Clay was proud of his daughter. She was as beautiful as her mother. She was intelligent and had a good sense of humor. She was a good person and it was a pleasure to be around her.

Josephine and Kathryn were leaving for a weekend trip to Hershey, Pennsylvania after the graduation ceremony. They would return Sunday night. On the way home, Lydia whispered in his ear that she would like to have a visit with "him."

Monday evening, after a long, boring day at VSI, Clayton drove over to the repair shop to meet with Joe Colissimo. He carried several samples of the high voltage control circuit board with him plus a test circuit to demonstrate the product. Together, the two men spent several hours discussing and demonstrating the product. Despite the long session, the net result was that neither of them knew what to do next. One thing occurred to Clayton – legal protection of his new design with a patent. How do you go about getting a patent? Getting an attorney was the first step. However, he did not want VSI to get wind of the product or the filing for a patent. Between him and Joe, they decided that they would apply for the patent in Joe's name with Clayton's name listed as a co-inventor. They intended to share the profits anyway so this procedure sort of legitimized their intent.

Two weeks later, they met in the offices of Howitt, Howitt, and Levits, Attorneys-at-Law. They had been told that the first visit was an interview to make sure there was no conflict of interest with any other client and to define the task. There would be no charge for the initial visit.

Alfred Levits was a trim, mustachioed, Caucasian with a broad Massachusetts accent. He emphasized his degree from Harvard Law School augmented by a degree in Electronic Engineering from Harvard School of Engineering.

Levits reviewed the procedure for filing for a patent. The first step was to search the patent office files for patents issued for similar products. He would compare the description and determine if their product was sufficiently different to qualify for a patent. The search would cost $1,000. The fee would be due in advance and was non-refundable for any reason. The second step would be writing the application and filing it with the U. S. Patent Office located in Crystal City, Virginia in the suburbs of Washington, D.C. The cost of the second step would be a minimum of $5,000. One-half of the fee would be due before the start of the second step. The second half of the fee would be due when the draft of the application was finished and presented to them for review.

Clayton and Joe were stunned. They had no idea that the fees would be so high. They mumbled something about reviewing the situation and exited the office as quickly as possible. They agreed to meet each other during the following week and discuss their options.

Clayton knew that Joe would discuss the situation with his extended family. If they recommended the patent, they would provide Joe's portion of the fee. The only place Clayton knew to find his $3,000 half of the fee was the remainder of Kathryn's college fund. He was reluctant to entertain the thought even though it appeared that the fund would not be used for her college. He could tap their savings account but it would make a big dent in their retirement plans.

At the next meeting, Joe was upbeat. Apparently, Joe's youngest cousin lived close to a regional sales manager of a large electronics company. The cousin had posed the question to him. The sales manager assured him that his company was always on the lookout for new products. They had an evaluation process in place. If the product was good, they would negotiate a license deal. He knew of some inventors that made millions on some simple ideas.

Clayton was skeptical and had a few questions. What about a patent? Well, if the product were patentable, the company would pay for the patent application. The patent would be in their names but it would be assigned to the company.

Clayton and Joe agreed to submit three samples of the product for evaluation. To be on the safe side, Clayton decided to encapsulate the samples in hard epoxy. The epoxy was opaque and would provide some degree of protection against piracy of their product. It was not impossible to remove the epoxy but it was damn difficult.

Two months later, the samples were ready. Clayton prepared a receipt for the sales manager to sign acknowledging the transfer. The sales manager signed the receipt with a flourish – Jonathan P. Claggett. Clayton hoped that the "P" didn't stand for pirate.

9 – Disappointment

Clayton was apprehensive. It had been several months since they submitted their product for evaluation. He had called Jonathan P. Claggett several times and left messages. The calls had not been returned.

On this occasion, Claggett took his call. He was rather brusque as he informed Clayton that the evaluation was complete. The company was ready to return the samples and render their decision. If he would visit the company office at 4 P. M. to sign a receipt, he would be briefed on the evaluation. The tone of the voice was a significant tip-off that the news was not good.

Joe and Clayton appeared on time and were ushered into Claggett's office. A receipt was produced and a box containing the samples. Clayton signed the receipt before he opened the box. He had no reason to mistrust Claggett or the company on such a simple matter.

After retrieving the receipt, Claggett informed them that the company had no interest in their product. Claggett professed ignorance about the reason for the rejection. He informed them that the company was under no obligation to provide any test results or any reason for the rejection. Furthermore, he was very busy. If they would excuse him, he was scheduled to leave on a trip.

As Claggett left the room, Clayton opened the box. All of the samples were in the box. They had been stripped of the epoxy and the circuit cards were laid bare. Their product had been copied.

"Hey! Come back here!" Clay hollered.

A secretary came into the room. She asked him to leave the building or she would call security. Mr. Claggett had left the message that, if they had any further business with the company, it should be done through their attorneys.

Joe and Clayton left the building and drove back to the shop. Not a word was spoken during the trip. At the repair shop, they stared at the floor dejectedly.

"What are we going to do, Clay?" Joe Colissimo had never felt so empty.

"I don't know, Joe." Clay answered. "I guess their message is that we can accept the situation or sue them. We didn't have the money for a patent attorney. How are we going to sue a corporation worth millions of dollars?"

"You mean, that's it? We just walk away?" Joe asked indignantly.

"Isn't it always the way, Joe? The little guy gets screwed. The wheels get richer. I don't know what else to say." Clay stared at the floor wondering what he was going to say to Lydia.

10 - Moving On With Life

Clayton continued his day job at VSI. He was still demoralized from the piracy of his product. He plodded through each day with a heavy heart. Lydia understood and tried to lift his depression. Finally she booked an Alaskan Cruise with the Holland American Line. She took the money from their savings account and told him they were going. That was an order.

Clay had not seen Joe Colissimo for over a year. The repair shop was forced to close. There wasn't enough business left over from the large chain stores to support a small local business. Joe had mumbled something about "other options" than going to court. Clay didn't want to hear it. They had been screwed because they were stupid. He had seen it many times in the military service. Some guy would lose his entire paycheck because he was too stupid to understand the odds at poker or dice. Don't roll the dice if you can't pay the price. He and Joe had lost. It was plain and simple. It was time to get over it and move on.

The summer cruise to Alaska in the summer of 1990 was a cure. Lydia was spectacular. They enjoyed the ship and the service. They walked the promenade deck together holding hands like newlyweds. And the nights were as exquisite as their honeymoon. Clayton realized how lucky he was. He had a wonderful wife and a beautiful daughter. He loved them and they loved him. That was what life was all about - love. And he was a millionaire in the game of life. He was a winner. He held his head high and looked forward to tomorrow.

When the boat docked at Ketchikan, they took a side excursion to see the Otters and were rewarded with a sighting of whales.

A Momma Otter was floating on her back with her baby lying on her stomach. They were enjoying the sun. In the evening, they attended a salmon dinner at the local picnic grounds and enjoyed the 60-foot waterfall. As they went to bed, the ship's crew was preparing the ship for their departure towards Juneau.

They walked the streets of Juneau and enjoyed the sights. They bought souvenirs for Kathryn and several friends including the Colissimos. On the second day in Juneau, they boarded a seaplane for an aerial tour of the glaciers. Nature proved its strength every day in this rugged country. Only the strong could survive here. But wasn't it also true in other locales? You had to be strong to survive. Clayton was strong as long as he had Lydia.

From Juneau, the ship journeyed to Sitka. The ancient city of Russian origin was delightful. The colorful past was a reminder of the rugged individualists who settled our country. Clay felt like a pioneer. He could conquer frontiers as long as Lydia was there to hold his hand.

When the boat docked at Vancouver signaling the end of the cruise, they decided on the spur of the moment to spend the weekend at The Four Seasons Hotel and enjoy the city. This was their trip of a lifetime. They wanted to savor every second.

By the time they returned to their suburban home, their spirits were as high as any eagle could ever hope to soar. On the first weekend, they invited the Colissimos to dinner. Both of their daughters joined them. Josephine Colissimo and Kathryn Matthews were fast friends who saw each other nearly every day.

After a delicious dinner of Veal accompanied by Lydia's version of a light Fettuccine Alfredo and salad, they lingered and talked and remembered old times over coffee and a dish of Neapolitan ice cream. When the ladies started the cleanup without ever missing a word in their dialogue, Clay and Joe eased out to the screened-in porch so that Joe could enjoy a cigar. As always, he offered one to Clay. As always, Clay declined politely. The smoke nauseated Clay so he was careful to station himself upwind.

They stood on the porch quietly as Joe enjoyed his cigar. Each of them was deep in thought. Finally Joe broke the silence.

"Sylvia made me promise to give up smoking as a birthday present to her. This is my last week of using the stogies. Sure will seem strange. I've been smoking them since I was sixteen. I used to take them out of my old man's office." Joe recounted the story sadly.

"Well, she's probably concerned for your health. You're not getting any younger." Clay said the words automatically.

"She says they stink and that if I don't stop smoking, she's moving to the spare bedroom. I guess my sex life will move with her. Women are kind of manipulative, you know?" Joe shook his head as if he had just discovered a new thought.

Clay didn't respond. He could not even imagine Lydia threatening to move out of his bed. Women must be as different in their makeup as men are. He glanced at the stars and wondered which one he should thank for his luck in life.

"The family is pissed off at me." Joe confided.

"What do you mean?" Clay was puzzled.

"You know, about the product piracy and all."

"Why? We were the ones who were screwed. What do they expect us to do? Shit happens." Clayton shrugged his shoulders. This was old history for him. He was past it.

"They got screwed, too. My family operates out of a fund. Everybody puts in and everybody takes out. We share everything. My half would have helped the family. To rub it in, they showed me a new product announcement from the company. The assholes are making a mint from our idea." Joe was steaming now.

"Joe, take it easy. We'll find a new idea. We'll start tomorrow. After this cruise, I am some kind of renewed. I am a new man. We'll come up with a new idea. You'll see. We're partners." Clay clapped him on the back.

"I don't think so, Buddy. You've been a good friend and honest partner but this is where we part ways. I have to do something about the piracy or my family will banish me from the rolls." Joe was speaking so sincerely that there was no doubting his resolve.

"I'm sorry, Joe. I don't think I can be a part of what you're thinking about doing."

"Does that mean you won't build a megaton ball-buster in your basement for me?" Joe laughed and stuck out his hand. "Let's go inside. Sylvia promised me some action tonight and I want to get home early."

Clay shook his hand and laughed with him.

11 – Christmas Party

5 PM Friday – December 21 was the start of a holiday weekend. It was a chance to finish shopping and enjoy the Christmas music.

At the annual Christmas party in the main conference room of Kathryn Ann's company, the drinks were flowing freely. The music was loud and lively. Everyone was dancing. Most of the dancers were clinging to each other closely. Kathryn's boss had danced with her several times and she was having a hard time maintaining a respectful distance. Over the last month, he had made several suggestive remarks and told a lot of off-color jokes. She tried to maintain some kind of composure and politely smile.

Because of the alcohol, she had asked Josephine to swing by the office and pick her up so she wasn't driving with alcohol on her breath. Now she was glad to have her as a chaperone. It didn't faze the boss a bit. He had enough to drink that he suggested a threesome. As the two girls collected their coats and purses in preparation for leaving, he became angry and loud.

"Don't make a mistake tonight, honey. I'm tired of the teasing. It's time for you to put out if you want to keep your job. Understand?" He was drooling and weaving slightly from side to side. Everybody in the room heard him. The music died down and everybody was silent watching the confrontation.

"Please, Mr. Nolan, it's been a long day and everyone has had a lot to drink. Let's just say good night and forget about this. Okay?" Kathryn pleaded with him. She was mortified that all of her co-workers were witnessing this scene.

"No way, darling. You've been teasing me for a month leading up to this party. Tonight is the night. Your friend can watch or participate - I don't care which. I got enough for both of you. Let's go into my office." He grabbed her arm and started dragging her out of the room.

Kathryn wrenched away from him and ran for the door. Josephine was right on her heels. They didn't wait for the elevator. They ran down the stairs and out into the parking lot looking over their shoulders. Josephine got the car started and careened out of the parking lot. Kathryn's ears were still ringing with the last shout from her boss. "You're fired, bitch!"

Driving towards home on the 495 beltway, Josephine was trying to think about what to do. She pulled onto an exit ramp and found a fast food drive-thru to get some coffee for them. Kathryn was still sobbing and leaning against the door. It took an hour of patting and sipping to get Kathryn calmed down. Finally, she took her home and walked her into the house. Lydia met them at the door. One of the other employees had called and related the story. Kathryn was popular at the office and had friends who were worried about her.

Lydia took over the consoling and Josephine went to the kitchen to make some more coffee. Clay stayed in the background because he didn't know what to do or say. His little girl had been grievously hurt and he didn't know what to do. He thought about the arsenal in the basement but quickly dismissed the idea as being unrealistic. Even if he were able to find the guy and kill him, he would be arrested in a matter of hours. Then his wife and daughter would really suffer as the case played out in the newspapers and courts. This looked like another case of the bad guys winning and the good people losing again. Someday enough would be enough. He went to his desk and found the business card for Alfred Levits, attorney-at-law. He dialed the emergency number and Alfred answered. Clayton described the problem to him. Levits told Clay to meet him in the office at 9 AM. In the meantime, he would give the matter some thought and recommend a plan of action.

At 9 AM on a cold, blustery Saturday, Clay was sitting in the reception area when Alfred Levits beckoned him into his office. They shook hands and Alfred led him to a sitting area in the corner. There was a coffee thermos and pastries on a small plate. Then Alfred Levits began to talk.

He wanted Clay to return home after their conference and work with Kathryn Ann. He wanted her to make a list of everybody present at the party. He wanted their position in the company and everything that Kathryn knew about them. He wanted their age, marital status, relationship to Kathryn, relationship to the supervisor, and seniority with the company, education, everything she could remember including any gossip or rumor.

Most importantly, he wanted Kathryn under psychiatric care immediately. He said that it was not just a matter of preparing for the legal attack. He had experience with similar cases. He emphasized that Kathryn would need the medical attention.

"Clay, make no mistake. This will alter your lives forever. Whether or not you sue them for damages, Kathryn will never forget the attack as long as she lives. She deserves compensation and they deserve punishment. Let's do this. Let's teach them a lesson." Levits was pounding on the desktop when he finished and looked at Clay.

"I don't know. I have to talk to Lydia and Kathryn. Let me get back to you." Clayton waffled and he didn't like the sound of his own voice. But he hated to drag his family through the mess.

"Clay, Kathryn is not to blame for this attack. She is the victim. Your entire family has been attacked. You will regret it for the rest of your lives if you do not pursue this. Your wife and daughter will follow your lead. If you're in doubt, they will hesitate."

Levits had already started researching the company. As it turned out, he knew the Chief Executive Officer. They belonged to the same country club and he had played a few rounds of golf with him. The company had substantial assets and Levits intended to upset their profitable apple cart in federal court. He was as angry as Clayton was.

As he left Levits' office, Clay was beginning to realize that he could not retreat from this situation. He couldn't hide or delay. He resented the attack and the laying bare of his family's defenses. Dammit, what kind of man was this that pressured young girls for sexual favors? He must be a predator. And he must be stopped.

Clay pulled the car into the driveway and killed the engine. He sat there for several minutes collecting his thoughts. He knew he must remain calm but firm in front of his wife and daughter. Levits was right in that they would follow his lead. But he had no illusions about the opposition that he would face from them. He knew them well. They would prefer to cry a little then go on with life. He would prefer that approach too. But it could not be. And he realized that Levits was right about the doctor. Kathryn would need professional help to set her on the path of the rest of her life. He remembered his mother and how one event sent her into a world of darkness.

He entered the house with a heavy heart.

Both of the women in his life were sitting in the living room as if waiting for him. Kathryn's eyes were red but she was not crying and sobbing as before. He sat down and began to make the case for their action.

"No, Dad, I don't want to do this. I just want to get on with my life. It's just a job. I'll get another job." Kathryn paused to take a breath and Clay jumped in.

"As soon as you apply for a job, they will want to know where you worked and why you left. They'll call to verify your employment and salary. They'll hear the story. Honey, I'm sorry but we have to deal with this problem. It's not going to go away." He sat back to give them a chance to digest the import of his words.

He watched their faces and could see the reasoning process flow through each of them. Before either of them had a chance to start up, he spoke again.

"Okay, how about we do this? Let's take the first step and make a list of everyone at the party. Lydia, grab a tablet and ballpoint." Clay wanted to get them started on a project.

The telephone rang and Clay grabbed the receiver. It was Alfred Levits.

"Clay, I took the liberty of contacting an associate of mine – a

Dr. Jacobs. He is a Psychiatrist. He is willing to see Kathryn this afternoon. Please tell me that you'll take her over there. Write down this address and telephone number. He's expecting you. And Clay? Go with her. Don't let her drive alone for awhile. She is in a greater shock than she shows."

"Okay, Alfred, Thanks." Clay hung the phone and turned to the women.

It took nearly an hour for Clay to convince Kathryn that she should go to the doctor. The argument that he kept reiterating was – what would it hurt? Wouldn't it be better to be sure? We don't know so doesn't it make sense to get some professional help? Finally, Kathryn relented. Clayton was relieved and Lydia showed some relief in her face along with the apprehension.

When they arrived at Dr. Jacobs' office, a nurse in the reception area greeted them. She ushered all of them into the doctor's office. He stood up as they entered. He offered his hand in introduction – first to Kathryn, then Lydia, and then Clayton.

Dr. Jacobs was a tall, slender man about sixty years of age. His hair was gray and he wore glasses. He looked like an older uncle and made a good impression. He opened the conversation by telling them a little bit about himself. As he talked, he would inject questions about one or the other of them. At the end of a half-hour or so, he said that he wanted to examine Kathryn in his medical office. He asked Kathryn if she would like to have her mother with her. Kathryn said yes, she would.

In the examining room, Dr. Jacobs gestured towards a side chair for Lydia. She would be able to see everything. He placed Kathryn in a chair much like the ones found in a Dentist's office. He reclined her slightly and took her pulse. Then he measured her blood pressure and examined the pupils of her eyes. He was talking to her all of the time. He was telling her everything he was doing and why he wanted to do it. Kathryn began to relax. Then he said he wanted to administer a light sedative to calm her pulse. He said it was erratic. He asked her and Lydia if she had any known allergies. The answer was no and he prepared the syringe. Kathryn hardly felt the sting of the needle in her upper arm.

Dr. Jacobs continued to talk being sure to include both of the women in the conversation. He explained that it was natural for someone to ask herself if they were to blame. Could they have done something to trigger their assailant? Again and again, he identified the supervisor as the assailant and Kathryn Ann as the victim.

Finally, he straightened the chair so that Kathryn was sitting upright. Dr. Jacobs sat down next to Lydia and addressed both women.

"I would like to admit Kathryn to a hospital for a night or two just to play it safe. There are a couple of choices. We can use Holy Cross hospital or there is a private clinic within a few blocks of Holy Cross. The clinic has the advantage of having two room suites in case you or your husband wanted to spend the night close to Kathryn." He waited to judge their reaction.

Clearly, the hospitalization suggestion was a shock to both women. The struggle to understand and find the right questions to ask was evident in their eyes. Dr. Jacobs tried to help them.

"We have found over the years, slowly but surely, that our mental health is every bit as important as our physical health. Many of us in the field of psychiatry believe it is more important in terms of maintaining a high quality of life. The body is amazingly adept at compensating for the loss of a sense such as hearing or sight or the loss of a limb. It is much less forgiving if subjected to a mental trauma. If you were exposed to a contagious disease, you would not hesitate to seek medical treatment. That is the case here. Kathryn has been exposed to a mental health hazard. She may not need medical treatment. Her mind and body may be able to cope with the trauma. Unfortunately, we may not know for years. Rather than look back in hindsight, I propose to extend treatment now in the hope of prevention." Dr. Jacobs felt that he had said everything possible. The decision was for them to make. "I'll leave you alone for a few minutes to discuss the situation. Should I send your husband in?"

"Yes." Both women spoke simultaneously.

Two minutes later, Clay entered the room and the three family members hugged each other. Lydia brought him up-to-date on what Dr. Jacobs wanted to do. Clay turned to Kathryn.

"What do you think, honey?"

"I know I was reluctant to come over here, Dad, but I see now that it was the right thing to do. I think we should follow Dr. Jacob's suggestions." Kathryn looked better now that she had made a decision.

Clay left the room to find the Doctor. He told him they preferred the clinic so that either Lydia or he could be with her. He asked about what financial arrangements the doctor wanted to make. Dr. Jacobs smiled. "I don't think there will be a financial problem. Even if her insurance company balks, Mr. Levits has assured me of unlimited financial sources."

While Clay was in the outer office, he called Alfred Levits. He told him about the latest developments. He told him to proceed with the legal action. The list of the other attendees at the party would be on his desk in a matter of hours.

"Clay, I'm going to call the Fairfax County Sheriff and swear out a warrant. I want that sonofabitch arrested. He started this fight by attacking Kathryn. Let's see how he likes to be on the receiving end. Things are going to get hot from now on but we will prevail. We'll take a predator out of the work force and we'll take a big step towards restoring Kathryn."

As soon as he finished talking to Clay, Levits called the County Sheriff's office and started the paperwork for the warrant. He made a call to The Washington Post and made contact with a reporter he knew from past cases. He briefed him on the situation. Next he called Fox News and tipped them about the impending arrest. Levits wanted news coverage. He intended to spotlight the Christmas Party to the nation. He glanced at his watch. It was now 4 PM on a Saturday afternoon before Christmas. The Christmas party had started at 5 PM the previous night. A lot had happened in twenty-four hours.

The 11 PM news showed the supervisor being led from his home in Vienna, Virginia in handcuffs. He was wearing a T-shirt despite the chilly temperatures and cursing the police and the reporters. He was obviously drunk – either still drunk from the party or drunk again.

12 - Meeting The Enemy

On Sunday, Alfred Levits was in his office preparing the court papers for the Matthews case when his telephone rang. He answered brusquely. The voice on the other end identified himself as Marvin Forrester, Attorney for Byte Technology, Inc. He asked if he and the CEO of the company could meet with him. They wanted to come to his office now.

"I really do not think the meeting would be productive and it may be counterproductive." Levits responded. "However, I am reluctant to deny any opportunity to communicate. Are you sure this is in the best interests of your client, counselor?"

"I do, Mr. Levits. I have spoken with him in detail and I believe you will be interested in hearing what he has to say." Marvin Forrester sounded young as he spoke to the veteran Levits.

"Okay, Mr. Forrester, come on over. I'll wait for you." Levits hung up the telephone.

In less than half an hour, Alfred Levits heard the front door of his office open. He stood up to greet his visitors. The first man through the door was Larry Hoskins, the CEO of Byte Technology, Inc. and a fellow member of the Bethesda-Chevy Chase Country Club. He stuck out his hand in greeting.

"Alfred, thank you for seeing us. I'm sorry it had to be under these circumstances. I wish we were meeting on the first tee at the club." Hoskins sounded sincere.

"Mr. Levits, thanks for seeing us. It's a pleasure to meet you, sir. I've heard a lot of good things about you from mutual friends. Like Mr. Hoskins, I wish our meeting was under different circumstances." Marvin Forrester not only sounded young - he was young.

"Please sit down, gentlemen." Levits responded.

"Alfred, let me open the conversation. I've heard about the party and I am appalled. I intend to take action immediately. I wanted to meet with you and see what we can do to make this right with the girl." Hoskins waited to see what Levits response might be to his first move.

"What have you heard about the party, Larry?" Levits asked with a poker face.

"Well, I guess there was quite a bit of drinking at an impromptu office Christmas party. Combining alcohol, men, and women can be explosive. Sounds to me like things got out of hand. I'm still looking into it, of course. I need some more details. I have an open mind." Hoskins paused because he didn't like the expression he could see starting to form on Levits' face and in his eyes.

"If that's what you've heard so far, Larry, then this meeting is premature. I suggest we adjourn until you've had time to complete your investigation." Levits started to stand up.

"Wait a minute, Alfred. I came over here to hear your side of the story. As CEO, I don't always get the whole truth and nothing but the truth. Please! I'd like to hear the girl's side of the story." Hoskins kept his seat.

"Larry, your supervisor planned the party and ordered the alcohol and food two weeks in advance. There was a notice on the department bulletin board. It was not an impromptu party. During the party, your supervisor sexually harassed, physically abused, and attempted to rape my client. There were over twenty witnesses. When she didn't submit, he fired her. He made an indecent proposal to my client's friend who came over to give her a ride home. My client is in the hospital in shock and under psychiatric care." Levits sat back to judge the reaction.

Marvin Forrester sat back in his chair. Levits thought he might faint. He looked like a novice swimmer who had just found out the depth of the water.

Larry Hoskins was the first one to recover and find his voice. "My God, Alfred! It was only a Christmas party. No one was raped. There was a bunch of playing around. If he said she was fired, it was a mistake. I certainly wouldn't tolerate anything like that by one of my supervisors. This whole thing sounds like a nightmare. "

"You're absolutely right. It is a nightmare. Your company has no right to countenance such an atmosphere. We send our young people into the marketplace to work not be harassed. And I won't stand for it. The law won't stand for it. You, the supervisor, and the company must answer for your crimes." Levits tried to maintain control as his voice started to rise.

"Alfred, please stop. This is getting out of hand. I agree that the supervisor was wrong. We will correct the wrong. But let's keep this in proportion." Hoskins was visibly sweating now.

"Let me ask you some questions. It is your choice about whether you wish to answer." Levits leaned back in his chair and looked at the ceiling.

"How many women do you have on your Board of Directors?"

"How many of your corporate officers are women?"

"How many of your department managers are women?"

"During the twelve years of Mr. Nolan's employment with your firm, how many other complaints have there been against him?"

"What kind of program do you have set up in your company for harassment complaints?"

"What kind of training do the managers receive?"

"Does your company actively address harassment issues?"

"Do you personally condemn harassment? Have you ever told an off-color joke to your managers that could be construed as a wink of the eye to sex harassment?"

"Should I continue?" Levits paused.

"Alfred, my company is engaged in a very important program for the Department of Defense. Our performance will affect the safety of our nation. I don't want this case to derail our focus. If you proceed in this manner, it will be the most distracting thing on our horizon. Isn't there some way we can come to an agreement?" Hoskins was red in the face and sitting on the edge of his chair.

"Larry, I told Mr. Forrester that I thought this meeting was premature. I believe that discussing a settlement is premature at this time. I suggest you consult with your counsel and complete your investigation." He started to stand up again.

Marvin Forrester was sitting back against his chair with compressed lips. He was witnessing a violent encounter between two giants. He could not have opened his mouth and uttered a word even to save his life.

"Alfred, please tell me the scope of the problem. I need to keep my company focused."

"I believe that this matter will be the most disastrous event that ever occurred in or to your company. Criminal charges have been brought against your supervisor. Your company will be turned inside out during the investigation that will ensue in the following months. Frankly, I will be surprised if your company survives." Levits paused. And now he was angry at the failure of his visitors to comprehend the enormity of the situation. He raised his voice. "What does it matter if our country's shores are safe if we have confined ourselves to a jungle? You don't understand the problem." This time he stood up to close the meeting.

The two men left in a dejected mood. Their hopes of containing the problem had been crushed. Hoskins realized that his company was in a fight for survival. Forrester realized that he was out of his depth. The sinking feeling in his stomach was probably what it felt like to jump out of an airplane without a parachute.

13 - Memories

10 PM. Sunday – December 23, 1990.

Alfred Levits leaned back into the comfortable desk chair and swiveled around to look out the window. The view was spectacular from the eleventh floor on a clear winter night with many stars. Levits saw neither the view nor the stars. He was looking inward and remembering an earlier time in his life.

Clay Matthews had asked him if this case was really in his area of expertise. After all, he was a patent attorney. Levits responded that he was an attorney – which was the operative word. Furthermore he was fully up-to-date on this area of the law. It was a part of the law that interested him the most because it gave him a chance to help a victim. It was a chance to right a wrong. Clay was satisfied and did not speak of the matter again.

Levits remembered his final year of law school. He was studying day and night. He was tired and impervious to everything around him. One night he stumbled home from the law library and found his dad and uncle in the family room. They were crying. When his father looked at him, he motioned for him to come into the room.

Alfred's cousin had committed suicide earlier in the evening. She had taken a bottle of pills and swallowed a pint of vodka. She had left a note. Apparently, she had been having an affair with the owner of the company where she worked. He was married with kids. She became pregnant. He insisted on an abortion. He gave her a check for $10,000.

In the late sixties, there was little justice for this type of victim. Most of the population was fixated on the rapidly changing political scene. The Vietnam War was expanding. The Kennedy brothers and Dr. King had been assassinated. Equal rights for women were way down the list of America's wants. "Victims' Rights" was simply a phrase.

Alfred Levits remembered. And he vowed that the Matthews case would have a different ending.

14 - Christmas Eve

10 AM Monday - Levits filed the papers in Federal court suing Byte Technology, Inc., for twenty-five million dollars damages and punitive damages to be determined by a jury. A separate suit was filed in the name of Josephine Colissimo for five million dollars damages and punitive damages to be determined by a jury.

The morning newspapers and the TV morning programs had reported and shown pictures of the arrest of Hugh Nolan. They reported that Byte Technology had placed Nolan on suspension without pay pending a resolution of the case. The company spokesperson condemned sexual harassment and discrimination in the workplace.

Shortly before noon, Levits received a letter by courier from Marvin Forrester. Until further notice and resolution of the case, Byte Technology was placing Kathryn Matthews on administrative leave with full pay and full benefits. Levits was positive that the letter would be leaked to the press. Hoskins was fighting to save his company. Levits wasn't impressed.

5 PM – Kathryn came home for a four hour visit from the hospital to open gifts with her family and friends. The Colissimo family came over and the evening was a huge success.

9 PM - Kathryn was driven back to the hospital by her father. They talked for an hour or so revisiting other Christmases.

10 PM - Kathryn went to bed.

2 AM – Kathryn woke up screaming and disoriented. The doctor was called and he ordered a sedative.

Clayton spent the rest of the night awake and in turmoil.

There was no doubt now that Levits and Dr. Jacobs were right. Kathryn, his little girl, had been grievously assaulted. The results would be with them for the rest of their lives.

Dr. Jacobs indicated that Kathryn would be in the clinic for an extended stay. Although she could come home for short visits of a few hours, he insisted that anything that could be used as a weapon be removed from the house. All guns, knives, and sharp-pointed objects should be completely removed from the house not merely put out of sight. Kathryn had lived at home all of her life. She probably knew more about any hiding places than they did. Clayton spent several hours packing up his gun collection, ammunition, re-loading equipment and supplies, and knives. He rented a small van and moved the stuff to a secure storage facility a few miles from the house. He bought a heavy-duty combination lock to use and set in their wedding anniversary as the combination.

15 - Preparing The Case

The remainder of the Christmas season was a nightmare for Clayton and Lydia. On Wednesday, January 2, 1991, Clayton had to return to work. He hated it. Despite his vow to forget the past in reference to the pirated invention, he could not help thinking that he would have been able to leave his day job.

Alfred Levits was taking depositions from the other people at the Christmas party. There was not one dissenter. Twenty-three people, men and women, all races, all ages, agreed on the sequence of events.

Levits had been interviewing other employees in other departments. The results were chilling. There were several stories of harassment and discrimination. The company was living in the Stone Age. All of the managers were long time male employees who helped start the firm. In the early days, they worked long hours into the night. Inevitably, they sent out for pizza and beer. Many jokes were told. Levits had a file folder full of examples.

By March, Levits had built a damning case against Byte Technology. Forrester and Hoskins were well aware of the evidence. Forrester had attended the depositions and he reported back to Hoskins.

Hugh Nolan was a classic example of what not to have in a manager. He had a long history of alcohol abuse. Many employees had requested a transfer after working in his department a short time. The management had ignored all of the signs. Now they would pay. Levits knew it. Hoskins and Forrester knew it.

In the meantime, Hugh Nolan had pleaded guilty to one count

of assault and battery. He was awaiting sentence that would be pronounced on April 15.

As the trial date for the *Matthews vs. Byte Technology et al* approached, Kathryn became more withdrawn during the day and suffered nightmares every night. Finally, Dr. Jacobs recommended that the trial be delayed or a settlement negotiated.

Levits petitioned the court for a postponement of the Matthews trial due to the physical condition of his client. Levits wanted the Colissimo trial to follow the Matthews trial. The Judge set up a meeting in his chambers to hear arguments from both sides. A stenographer was on hand to record the proceedings. During the meeting, Marvin Forrester did not oppose the request for delay but he asked the court to mediate a settlement. The Judge was opposed to delays because it played havoc with his calendar. He turned to Levits and asked him why a settlement could not be negotiated? Had both sides, in good faith, tried to reach a settlement?

"Your Honor, we feel that this is a case that should be decided by a jury. The defendants have caused grievous harm to my client and the entire community for many years. As the world grew up around them, they maintained a jungle of predators preying on the young and defenseless persons in need of a job." Levits responded passionately.

"Mr. Levits." The Judge was a grumpy individual given to clearing his throat before uttering any words, "If I grant your petition for a delay, can you assure me that your client will be ready to appear on the new date? It has been my experience that these medical matters are rather open-ended."

"In good conscience, Your Honor, I cannot give you an iron-clad guarantee. The Doctor is doing his best. She is receiving the best medical care and she is responding. I can only ask for your indulgence." Levits spread his arms in a plea before the massive desk in the Judge's chambers.

The Judge gave a long harrumph and stared at the ceiling for a few minutes. Finally he turned to the two attorneys. Larry Hoskins and Clayton Matthews were seated behind their attorneys and the Judge studiously ignored them.

"Mr. Levits, you have brought suit for twenty-five million dollars and an additional amount to be determined by a jury. A jury might decide in your favor and award you the full amount plus one dollar in punitive damages. Correct?" The Judge waited for a reply.

"Yes, Your Honor, that is correct but I don't feel it is completely realistic. If the jury finds the defendant guilty and awards our claim for twenty-five million dollars, they will probably set punitive damages at an amount equal to or in excess of twenty-five million dollars. I guess, to answer your basic question, that we would consider a settlement of fifty million dollars. However, we would consider the offer with some reluctance. The main point is to expose the evil practices within this company." Levits was getting wound up.

Marvin Forrester was content to let the Judge negotiate with Levits. The depositions and other evidence were so damning that his client had no chance of anything other than a lynching in a public trial.

"Mr. Levits, I have copies of the financial statements of the company and the individuals, a fifty million dollar settlement would put the company out of business and destitute the individuals." The Judge was trying to sound reasonable but it was not his basic nature.

"So be it, Your Honor. The community would be rid of a cancerous growth in its midst." Levits did not give an inch.

"Mr. Forrester," the Judge turned to him. "How do you feel about this?"

"Your Honor, we are prepared to enter into a reasonable agreement but destroying the company and bankrupting Mr. Hoskins is not reasonable. For one thing, the community would lose a number of jobs. A large number of innocent employees would be unjustly punished." Forrester sat back feeling rather proud of his argument.

"Not true, Your Honor." Levits countered. "The company's major contracts would be awarded to another local company immediately by the Department of Defense. In all probability, the same employees would simply migrate to a new address."

"Your Honor, the shareholders of Byte Technology would lose their savings." Forrester cried.

"As they should," argued Levits. "They are the ones who elected the Board of Directors and tolerated the management of the company."

Larry Hoskins squirmed uncomfortably in his chair. Forrester felt like he had used the wrong argument. He wished that the Judge would do the negotiating.

"Mr. Levits, you're not being realistic. Let's take a twenty-minute break. Please use the time to formulate a workable arrangement for both cases. Let me add that I am not convinced that granting your request for a delay is reasonable." The Judge turned away from the attorneys.

In the outer chambers, the two parties retreated to opposite corners and began to whisper.

"What do you think, Clay?" Levits asked.

"I think we need to settle this case. Kathryn is not up to a public trial. If we get a public acknowledgment of wrongdoing combined with any amount of financial compensation, we will have accomplished our goal. Kathryn will be publicly vindicated. The doctor can use these facts in his therapy session with her. " Clay had been thinking long and hard on the matter.

"Okay, let's see what we can do." Levits stood up and closed his briefcase. He straightened his tie and buttoned his coat. He was prepared to re-engage the enemy on the field of battle.

On the opposite side of the room, Forrester and Hoskins were engaged in an intense discussion. Marvin wanted to know if his client was prepared for a settlement approaching the magnitude under consideration.

"Marvin, we need to settle. As it is, our stock has plummeted and employees are seeking other jobs. If this thing delays any longer, we'll be out of business anyway. No one is going to give us any new contracts as long as this sword is dangling over our necks. Let's get it done." Hoskins was sweating and looked ill.

The Judge looked up as the parties re-entered his chambers. He nodded for them to be seated.

"What do you have, Mr. Levits?" The Judge looked at him

with some impatience.

"Your Honor, we will settle for the following consideration. We want twenty million dollars in damages and an equal amount of punitive damages. We want five million dollars from Mr. Hoskins in damages and an equal amount of punitive damages. In addition, we want Mr. Hoskins and the Board of Directors to resign. The new Board of Directors should be directed to set up training in harassment and discrimination sensitivity. Every employee of the company should complete the training within six months." Levits sat back. Then he added, "On the Colissimo matter, we will settle for four million dollars in damages and an equal amount of punitive damages."

The Judge turned to Marvin Forrester and saw Larry Hoskins whispering in his ear. He cleared his throat and directed him to reply.

"Your Honor, we appreciate the offer to settle. It would allow the company to move ahead and stabilize their position for their customers and employees. We are prepared to agree to the training and the replacement of the Board of Directors. Mr. Hoskins is prepared to resign as Chief Executive Officer and assume a lesser role in the company. I am authorized to offer four million dollars damages and four million dollars punitive damages from the company. Mr. Hoskins will agree to one million dollars damages and one million dollars punitive damages." Forrester was trying hard not to be sick on the Judge's carpet. "For the Colissimo case, we offer one million dollars in damages and one million dollars punitive damages from the company.

"Your Honor, our position on Mr. Hoskins' resignation is firm. If we cannot resolve this issue, we are at an impasse." Levits clamped his mouth shut and glared at the Judge.

"Mr. Hoskins founded the firm. It is his life. Please do not take this from him." Forrester was almost crying.

"Mr. Forrester, would you like a few minutes to consult with your client? I don't think you have considered what will happen to Mr. Hoskins' position in the event of an adverse jury decision." The Judge looked at him shrewdly. He could barely remember being as young as Forrester.

"It won't be necessary, Your Honor. We accept the condition." Forrester responded.

"Mr. Levits, do we have a deal on the financial figures?" The Judge looked at him sternly. Alfred had the impression that the Judge was out of patience. Under the terms offered, Kathryn would receive a total of ten million dollars less his fee of thirty percent and miscellaneous expenses. Josephine Colissimo would receive two million dollars less thirty percent and miscellaneous expenses.

"If the plaintiffs will agree to pay all legal fees and expenses, we have a deal, Your Honor." Levits figured it wouldn't hurt to ask.

"My client has advised me that the terms are agreeable, Your Honor." Forrester responded to the proposal.

"Very well, gentlemen. Each of you will submit a brief to me within ten days. The brief should contain your agreement to the terms and a plan to implement the actions required. I will issue a final judgment within ten days of the receipt of your briefs." The Judge stood up and the parties filed out of his chambers in silence. Everyone seemed stunned.

Hoskins hung his head in defeat. He had lost his life's work over one incident at a Christmas party. The most devastating part of the whole mess was that he realized Levits was right. He had failed in the leadership role at his company. It was time for him to step aside. He would have to sell his home to meet the demands of the settlement but he had substantial retirement funds. In the few minutes since agreeing to the stringent terms, he was already restructuring his life. He intended to move to the West Coast. The Silicon Valley region would welcome his talents. He would start a new company and incorporate the lessons he had learned.

Hoskins intended to type up a letter of resignation to the country club as soon as he got home. He did not want to encounter Alfred Levits again in his lifetime.

16 – The Settlement

Both attorneys submitted their briefs and acknowledged acceptance of the terms discussed in the meeting. Of primary importance to Levits was the time scale proposed for payment of the moneys.

Forrester had structured the proposal so that Byte Technology would pay the legal fees and expenses for both cases. He proposed the full payment of approximately four million dollars in four equal payments spaced thirty days apart and starting in thirty days.

Hoskins would pay Kathryn Matthews two million dollars at the time of settlement on the sale of his house. The property was already listed with a real estate agent.

Further, Byte Technology would pay eight million dollars to Kathryn Matthews and two million dollars to Josephine Colissimo over a four year period with interest paid on the outstanding balance at 8% per annum.

Levits rejected the payment terms on behalf of Kathryn and Josephine. The payment terms of the legal fees and expenses were accepted. He argued in a responding brief that one of the purposes of accepting a negotiated settlement was to seek closure for the victim. He enclosed a statement from Dr. Jacobs that emphasized the importance of finishing the matter. Levits suggested that Byte Technology should borrow the money from normal financial channels and pay the money due within sixty days.

Forrester accepted the counter-proposal on behalf of Byte Technology and Hoskins.

By the end of June, the case was over and settled.

The Matthews family was struggling to regain some normalcy in their lives. The money had been put into a trust. It was to be used for health expenses and "any reasonable outlay that would maintain or upgrade the quality of life for Kathryn Ann Matthews." Alfred Levits, Clayton Matthews, and Joe Colissimo agreed to serve as directors without compensation. A similar arrangement was made for Josephine.

Over the Fourth of July weekend, Kathryn called a family meeting with Dr. Jacobs and the Colissimo family in attendance. They met in Dr. Jacobs' office. She and Josephine Colissimo wanted to move to California. Kathryn was on medication to calm her nerves and frustration plus a mild sleeping sedative at night. She had been released from the clinic and was seeing Dr. Jacobs twice per week.

Kathryn wanted to return to work but not in this area. She wanted a fresh start. Dr. Jacobs was inclined to agree with her and he had a referral psychiatrist for her to visit in California. What did Clayton and Lydia think of the proposal?

They were shocked. The proposal came out of the blue. It caught them unawares and unprepared. Their initial reaction was negative. Everything would be new to her all at once – new area, job, friends, Doctor, just everything. Wouldn't it be better to stay closer to home? How about moving to Frederick or Baltimore or Annapolis?

"No, Dad. I don't want to stay in this area." Kathryn spoke in her familiar stubborn manner with her mind made up. "I want a fresh start. In California, the companies are new and young. The state has the strongest laws in the nation for employee protection."

Well, she would be 26 in September. Basically, she was an adult and certainly financially independent. Clayton and Lydia had no way to deny her the freedom. They could only provide input and attempt to persuade her.

In early August the two girls were packed up and ready to go. North American Van Lines had combined their possessions and would deliver them in California. They were flying to San

Francisco via United Airlines leaving from Dulles Airport. On arrival, they would rent a car and check into the Cupertino Inn on the peninsula area south of San Francisco – Silicon Valley. From there they would look for an apartment to share and each of them intended to buy a car. They were excited and happy and giggly. It was the first time they had seen her so happy since the Christmas party.

Clayton and Lydia were saddened and depressed. They felt lonely and old. They were almost fifty years old – the half century mark. Clayton's hair was salted with a lot of gray and his waistline was expanding. There were wrinkles at the corners of his eyes and the beginnings of bags under his eyes. Lydia had started dyeing her hair several years ago and was fighting the battle of the bulge, too. She was much too proud and practical to even consider a face-lift but the wrinkles could no longer be covered with the normal amount of make-up.

In September, Lydia went to the doctor for a checkup. She was feeling tired most of the time. Initially, she thought it was depression caused by Kathryn's move to California. The only way she could have moved any further away was to go to Hawaii. Well, it would be best not to mention it or she might consider Hawaii. Kids were so unpredictable. Maybe on the next go-around – the next life – she just wouldn't have any kids. The pain and heartache were more than equal to the pleasure and love.

The next life?

It was the first time Lydia had ever thought about death. She was familiar with the concept and the pain. Her parents were dead and several friends had passed away or, as some said, passed over. Over what? Over to where? And suddenly she was terrified. That night she clung to Clayton and whispered, "Hold me. Please hold me."

Clayton felt helpless and confused – familiar feelings for him when he was around the women in his life.

17 - The Diagnosis

Dr. Allen Winters was Lydia's gynecologist and primary care physician. She had been going to him for years. She was comfortable with him and she trusted him. She was a little bit surprised when he mentioned that it had been a long time since he'd seen her. Hmm. Well, maybe it had been.... three years, he said. It didn't seem that long but lately, time seemed to be flying by in a big rush.

Dr. Winters went through the whole physical – poking, probing, and asking questions. Does this hurt? No. Is it sensitive here? No. Do you check your breasts regularly for lumps? Yes, of course, she replied.

"I see by the records that I gave you a lab order for a mammogram during your last visit. Did you get it done? I don't have any record of the results." Dr. Winters was peering at her over his reading glasses.

"I guess I forgot it," she confessed.

"Hmm. Well, I guess we'd better get it done now, don't you think? I'm also ordering a complete blood work-up. Let's get you back on schedule, Lydia. You're not getting any younger, you know." The doctor seemed to be uttering the words automatically. He must say them a dozen times a day.

"Everything looks okay as far as I can tell, Lydia. Let's wait for the blood tests and the mammogram. I'll give you a call. You seem apprehensive. Is everything else all right? Is there anything you want to tell me?" He looked at her.

"No, no. Everything is okay, as far as I know. I just started feeling uneasy recently but I don't know why." She shook her head in frustration. "I've been feeling very tired, as I mentioned. Or maybe I'm depressed. Or both. I don't know."

On Wednesday, the receptionist called from Dr. Winters' office. The doctor wanted to see her. Could she come in? At 4 PM this afternoon? Good. See you then.

At the doctor's office, she was shown in without any wait. That was unusual. And she wasn't taken to the examining room. She was taken into his office. Dr. Winters came in with a bunch of charts and files under his arm. He looked very serious.

"Lydia, I am concerned with the results of the mammogram and the blood tests. Let me show you what I mean." He was talking to her but he wasn't looking at her. Strange. Then he began to talk about masses on the mammogram that looked like shadows to her. Then he showed her a chart with the blood test results. "Here on the left is the normal range and your tests are considerably outside the normal range. I want to repeat the blood tests and I want a biopsy from this area of your right breast. I've called the lab. They will do the biopsy as soon as you can get over there. I'll have the results tomorrow and I'll call you."

Lydia drove the few blocks to the lab but she didn't remember stopping at any signs or parking. But she must have parked because when she came out of the lab, her car was parked in front of the building.

By the time Clay came home from work, she had started dinner preparations. She fixed a small steak for each of them on the Jennair grill that they had added two years ago. A small salad with vinegar and oil dressing plus a side dish of fresh green beans rounded out the meal. Clay was happy.

"What did you do today?" Clay asked. "Did you talk to Sylvia to see if they've heard from Josephine?"

"No, I forgot to call." She started the dishwasher loading and kitchen cleanup. Clay read the papers. Everything was normal.

On Thursday morning, Dr. Winters called her. He wanted her to come over to the office. He wanted her to bring Clayton.

Reluctantly, she called Clayton at work. She didn't do that very often. He wanted to know what was wrong. She didn't know what to say. Finally, she said the doctor wanted to review her recent medical tests with both of them. Clayton said he would come by the house to pick her up. Lydia asked him to meet her at the office. She didn't want to spend any time answering questions before they met with the doctor.

Once again, the receptionist took them directly to Dr. Winters' office. He was waiting for them. One look at his face and Lydia knew the truth. The final clock was ticking for her. Her thoughts turned to Clayton and she knew she must prepare him. Whatever time she had left must be used to comfort him.

Dr. Winters set an example for them. He was calm and serious. He showed them the mammogram and explained the results. He reviewed the first blood test and then compared it to the second test. The results were almost identical. Finally, he showed them the site of the biopsy. And the final step was to review the results of the biopsy. There was little doubt about the diagnosis. What was needed now was to find out how far the cancer had spread and how fast it was spreading. Dr. Winters wanted to do three things – (1) he wanted to bring in an Oncologist and (2) he wanted to schedule a Lumpectomy. And (3), since it would take several days to get the Lumpectomy done and analyzed, he wanted to start an aggressive program of chemotherapy immediately. The Oncologist that he recommended was in the adjacent building. He was on his way over now and Dr. Winters wanted them to meet him. If they were uncomfortable with him or preferred someone else for any reason, it would be okay. They were in for a battle and they needed to be comfortable with the team.

They left Lydia's car in the parking lot so they could be together. It was a time that they needed to be touching each other. At home, they sat in the living room and discussed their situation. They forgot to turn on the lights at dusk and their eyes became accustomed to the light. Soon they were sitting in the dark. But they were together and they were in their home away from the cruelties of the outside world.

Lydia did not want to tell anyone for awhile – and especially not Kathryn. Her reasoning was that Kathryn had enough on her plate with the relocation, job hunting, apartment hunting, car purchase, and a new doctor. Besides, she would surely plan to come home for Christmas. They would know more about Lydia's situation by Christmas.

Their approach sounded reasonable at the time. And later, when he was able to remember, he realized how naive they were – babes in the woods.

The telephone rang the next night as they were preparing for bed. "Mom? Dad? It's me! How are you?" And without waiting for an answer, she plunged on with her bubbly enthusiasm.

"There are so many things going on out here. It is so beautiful. Everyone is so young and full of energy and life. I ordered a new car today. The sunsets are so colorful. I think we must be closer to the sun out here. Did I tell you I bought a Volkswagen Jetta? It is so cool. Josephine decided to buy a Ford Taurus. I think it was because she liked the salesman at the Ford dealership. Did I tell you that my car is a bright red? It is so cool. I'll be picking it up tomorrow afternoon. I had a job interview today. It was okay but I think I'm going to look around a little bit. Salaries are a lot higher out here but so are the prices of apartments and other things. We've looked at two apartments in the vicinity but I think we're going to see where we end up working before we commit to an apartment. Did I tell you that the traffic is horrendous? We're going to a movie tonight and Josephine is making signs that we need to leave. It was nice talking to you but you sure didn't say much. I'll call you next week. Okay? Love you. Bye." And she hung up.

On Saturday, they went out to dinner. There was a new Italian restaurant in a nearby mall and they wanted to try it. Clayton loved veal cutlets. They had the small antipasto and a bottle of Chianti wine. They had a garden salad on the side with, what else, Italian dressing. They ordered Spumoni ice cream for dessert and lingered over a cup of coffee. The owner came by the table and welcomed them. He asked if they would sign the guest book when they left. Clayton would remember the evening as being the last carefree moments left to them. Over the next few weeks, they would realize that the clock was really running fast for them.

Two blocks before their home, they had to pull over and yield the right of way to a fire truck with a blaring siren and bright red lights. When they turned the next corner, they had a sinking feeling that was soon confirmed. It was their house ablaze. There were three fire trucks around the house pouring water into it. Clayton could see that the entire house was involved. He reported into a policeman standing on the perimeter to keep the rubberneckers away. He told him that he was going to check into the Holiday Inn for the night. He said that his wife was sick and he wanted to get her to bed for some rest. The policeman made a note of the conversation and nodded a curt goodnight. Clayton and Lydia left the scene with a heavy heart.

The next three days were hectic as Clayton dealt with the insurance company and the Fire Department. The firemen would not let anybody on the premises until they completed their investigation. The insurance people were being close-mouthed. They were not making any commitments. They grunted a lot and asked a few questions. The fire department had determined that the fire started in the basement. The insurance company started zeroing in on his hobby shop.

The house was insured for full replacement value in the event of a fire. They were entitled to living expenses for thirty days. The house was estimated at $280,000 – a modest amount for the Washington suburbs. Their motel and meals were averaging almost $150 per day. The claim would be for $4500. The agent that sent them Christmas cards and collected the premiums said that the matter was out of his hands. The claims department was a separate, arms-length activity.

Clayton found a rental house listed on the bulletin board at VSI. It was smaller than their house but it was furnished. The rent was $1200 per month in advance if rented on a month to month basis. For short-term rentals, the owner required a two-month deposit.

It took two weeks to find a replacement house in the same sector of town. It was still a mile or so from their old house. It was a little smaller but the owner was willing to take back a first mortgage if they had a twenty-five percent down payment. Under this arrangement, they could close on the sale immediately. They would only be in the rental house for one month. However, when they told the rental owner about their plans, he refused to return their deposit. He claimed that there was a three-month minimum.

The insurance company adjuster came by one evening. He apologized for the intrusion but he had heard of their house purchase. He guessed that they were in a hurry to get their settlement check from them. He apologized for the delay but the insurance company investigators were concerned about the cause of the fire. They thought that faulty wiring might have caused it. There would be a full investigation before a settlement was made. He hated to see such nice folks as they were inconvenienced so he had asked his boss if the company would be willing to make a discounted settlement. The Matthews family would get their money immediately and the company wouldn't have to spend a lot of time and money on the investigation. So there was good news and bad news. The good news was that the company was willing to settle. The bad news was that they would only offer 50% of the value. Oh, yeah, they would not cover their living expenses under this arrangement. The adjuster thought it was a good deal considering all of the facts. If the company determined that the fire was caused by faulty wiring installed by the homeowner, they would deny the claim in its entirety.

Clayton agreed to the settlement.

By mid-October, Clay was nearly incoherent. He was working during the day and sitting up with Lydia during the night. She was in and out of the hospital – mostly in. The side effects of the chemotherapy were devastating. She was scheduled for a radical mastectomy on Thursday November 10, 1991. She had lost an enormous amount of weight. She seemed so fragile that Clay was afraid she would break when he held her.

Clay had been trying to call Kathryn but they had found a new apartment according to the young female desk clerk at the Cupertino Inn. No, she didn't know the address or if they had a telephone. Yes, she would take a message for them if they returned. Yes, she understood it was an emergency. Thank you for calling the Cupertino Inn.

On Wednesday night, the surgeon said that she was too weak for the operation. Lydia's pulse was erratic and she seemed to be floating in and out of consciousness. Most of the time, she did not recognize Clay.

By Friday morning, Clay could not remember the last time he had eaten or slept. It didn't matter. He wouldn't leave her side. He wanted every minute he could get with her. She was on morphine now and slept most of the time. Clay held her hand and talked to her constantly.

Did she remember the time he used too much soap in the washing machine? What a mess! And what about the time she scraped the side of the car on the garage door and tried to rub out the scratch with her hankie? Clay was watching from the bedroom window and laughing all of the time. When she came in and sheepishly confessed, he kissed her and said it just an old car – what the heck? He loved her. Did she remember that? Or the time she threw away his favorite bedroom slippers and he found them in the trash? He rescued them and put them under the driver's seat in the car. When they got stuck in the mud and his shoes were a mess, he pulled out the bedroom slippers. The look on Lydia's face was priceless. He bet that she remembered that! And, oh yeah, he loved her. But, heck, she must have known that.

By Sunday night, Lydia was in a coma.

By Monday night, she was gone. He didn't know where she had gone. Or why she had gone. Or who took her. But it wasn't Lydia lying in the bed now. It was just something that looked like Lydia.

"I'm sorry for your loss, Mr. Matthews. I've never seen such fast-growing cancer," said Dr. Winters who had been in attendance at the time of death.

"I'm sorry for your loss, Mr. Matthews. I've never seen such fast-growing cancer," said the Oncologist who came by the room an hour after Lydia's death.

"I'm sorry for your loss, Mr. Matthews. I've never seen such fast-growing cancer," said the surgeon who spoke to Clay as he and the Colissimos were leaving the hospital.

Joe and Sylvia Colissimo were at the hospital with him. They cared for him and took him to their home. They went to the funeral home with him and helped him make the arrangements.

Both families got a letter from their daughter. The girls had found an apartment but they were not sure of the exact mailing address. A telephone installation was scheduled for the next week and they would call. They were driving up the coast to see the redwoods and tour the area for a while. They wanted to see the sights before they buckled down to work at their new job.

On the day of the funeral, Josephine Colissimo called her parents and gave them a new address and telephone number. Sylvia told her that she was coming out to California tomorrow morning. She would call later and give her the flight number. She asked Josephine to meet her at the airport. Sylvia would break the news to Kathryn.

18 – The Awakening

On the day after the funeral, Clayton spent the day around the house catching up on chores. After the morning routine of coffee and bird watching, he tackled the work. The laundry had stacked up and there was an accumulation of dust on every surface. The dishwasher had to be unloaded before the accumulated load could be run.

He had unplugged the telephone at 4 AM this morning.

He wanted some time to think about this new thought that had occurred to him about correcting some wrongs. At noon, Clay suddenly cried out in anger! He fell to his knees and screamed. He raised his head and fists to the heavens and cursed. At one point, he accused Lydia of wanting to leave him. As soon as he uttered the words, he realized how wrong he was. It was just that – that – well, surely somebody or something was to blame.

About 2 PM, Joe Colissimo dropped by to see how he was doing.

"Hey, how you doing, partner? Sylvia's out of town so I thought I'd see if you wanted to go out for dinner?" Joe looked at him closely to see if Clay was aware of his surroundings. Clay had really been out of it for awhile – for good reason, of course.

"Sure, Joe, it sounds like a good idea. Come on in and let's talk a little bit until it's time for dinner. Maybe I can find us something to drink." He invited Joe into the house with his arm.

"What's up, Clay? If I can do anything for you, just ask." Joe sounded so eager that Clay was ashamed of himself.

"I wanted to ask you about a conversation we had a few months ago. Do you remember when you told me that you had to do something about the product piracy or your family would disown you?" Clay was bent over looking in a cupboard for a bottle of wine. He didn't see the look on Joe's face.

"Uh, yeah. I remember. What about it?" Big Joe asked suspiciously.

"Did you take any action?" Clayton stood up and rummaged in a drawer for a corkscrew.

"Not exactly." Joe hedged.

"Look, Joe, either you did something about it or you didn't. Which is it?" Clay's voice was impatient and rather demanding.

"I haven't moved on the guy yet. My cousins have him mapped to a gnat's ass. I know every move the asshole makes. He's a man of habit – our Mr. Jonathan P. Claggett." Joe bristled. He was irritated at the question. What was Clay trying to do? Make him feel like a washout for not moving on the guy?

"So what do you intend to do?" Clayton asked.

"What do you care? You bowed out, remember?" Joe remembered real well.

"Well, now I've changed my mind. I'm in!" Clay was amused at the look of surprise on Joe's face.

"No shit?" Joe had to sit down.

"No shit!" Clayton countered. "So what do you want to do?"

"I'm gonna whack him!" Joe said and slammed his fist into his palm. "He's a dead asshole!"

"Then what?" Clay countered.

"What do you mean?" Joe was puzzled.

"Well, Claggett didn't do this alone. He had help from a few other people. And what about some money? Don't you figure they owe us some money?" It seemed reasonable to Clay.

"Well, yeah, sure I do but I don't see any way to get any money out of them. And you can't kill everyone in the company. That's why I didn't intend to do anything. It didn't seem like the risk was worth it. Then my family started leaning on me and I had to say I would whack the guy." Joe shrugged his broad shoulders as if to say, "What could I do?"

"Well, let's give it some thought. Let's define what we want and then figure out how to get it. Okay?" Clay had a faraway but determined look in his eye. The wheels were already turning.

"Okay!" Joe grinned.

"How much do you weigh, Joe?"

"Up yours, pal! None of your business."

"How long since you fired a gun, Joe?"

"I don't know. I guess it's been awhile." Joe was getting defensive.

"Look, I'm not trying to give you a hard time. But if we're going to war, let's get into shape. My waistline has been expanding and I'd bust a gut if I had to run 100 yards. I haven't fired any of my guns for almost a year." Clayton looked at him with a question in his eyes.

"Yeah, I see what you mean. Whadda you got in mind?"

"Let's go on a training program just like boxers do before a fight or like soldiers do. It would be embarrassing if they won the second round, too. Wouldn't it?"

"Yeah, you got that right!" Joe agreed.

"Let's fire some weapons every day and get proficient. We'll also get accustomed to the noise. A gunshot can be a shock if you're not used to the noise."

"This could be interesting." Joe mused.

"We'll go on an exercise and diet program. We'll include some strength workouts. It wouldn't hurt us to drop about forty pounds of flab."

"We can't do all of that in a short time." Joe protested.

"Who says we have to do it in a short time?" Clay countered. "You got an appointment to do something else?"

"Okay, you've got my attention. Now what?"

"Let's define what we want." Clay said. "Then we'll get it. Or die trying. Are you up for this?"

"Damn right, man! Give me five!" Joe slammed his hand into the air to meet Clay's hand.

"Aw right! What do we want?" Clay kept on him.

"I want that son of a bitch dead!" Joe stated his case flatly.

"What else?" Clay kept pushing.

"A ton of money!" Joe yelled it. He was caught up in the moment.

"How about a million dollars? We'll split it fifty-fifty!" Clay screamed the question.

"Fine by me. I'd be happy with half a mil." Joe's eyes were big.

"I want some more payback." Clay looked at him soberly. They were coming back to earth now. "Claggett didn't do it alone. He should have some company when he crosses the river."

"Who do you mean?" Joe had not thought it out this far. As usual, Clay was two steps ahead of him.

"The company president. His ass is going down." Clay was serious. Joe could not doubt the look in his eye.

"I'm with you, partner! Play the music!" Joe would have followed him anywhere.

"Where have you been getting your Intel on Claggett?" Clay wanted to know.

"One of my brothers is a retired cop. He runs a detective agency."

"Will he be willing to expand his activities and get some more info?"

"I think so. Whadda you want?"

"I want an organization chart of the company. I want the names, addresses, and backgrounds of the president and company officers. How long will it take?" Clay stood back prepared to protest if the time was too long.

"Tomorrow afternoon."

"What? How is he going to do that?" Clay was incredulous.

"We'll send one man to the Securities Exchange Commission in D. C. to pick up their financial reports and have someone else call the company. He will say he is from a newspaper or a financial magazine and wants a profile of the company. Simple!" Joe looked at him smugly.

"Okay, let's have a good meal and some drinks tonight. Tomorrow we start our diet and exercise. First thing we'll do is retrieve my guns from the storage locker. Let's try to figure out a place to shoot that is private. Shooting ranges tend to have video surveillance and some cops hanging around." Clay was thinking furiously.

"We'll have to drive a few miles but I have a cousin with a farm east of the city towards Annapolis?" Joe offered.

"How many cousins do you have? " Clay asked.

"A whole bunch of them. Dad comes from a clan of seven and Mom had four brothers. I have three brothers. My oldest brother heads up the family now that Dad is dead." Joe tried to explain his family to the only child of an only child.

"Will they help us?" Clay still seemed a little doubtful.

"You bet! Just tell me what we need!" Joe was eager.

"We're going to need some more ammunition for one thing. I'm not going to have time to do our reloading. I have a few boxes of everything to get us started and I want to make the ammo for the hits but we need a lot of ammo for practice."

The two men continued to talk over dinner in hushed tones. Joe wanted to know how many men would be whacked? Clay figured two at a minimum, maybe three. Joe grunted assent. Clay asked him if he had ever done anything like this before now. Joe said he would have to take the fifth. Clay said he just wanted to know how it felt.

"It ain't easy, pal!" Joe lamented. "Just take it slow and it will be over soon."

"Not for me, Joe. I'm going to even out all of the books. I'm not stopping with Claggett and Signal Control Technology. I want some payback for every time I've been cheated."

"Wow! " Joe stared at him. "Uh, Clay? Have I done anything to piss you off?"

"Don't be ridiculous. We're partners."

"What about Kathryn, Clay?"

"She's gone, buddy. I had a long talk with Dr. Jacobs, the psychiatrist. There's a lot of technical mumbo-jumbo but the bottom line is that down deep Kathryn figures I failed to protect her. That's the underlying reason for the California move." Clay looked sad.

"That's bullshit! There's nothing you could have done! You weren't at the Christmas party!!" Joe protested.

"I know that and you know that but Kathryn is in a mental jungle according to the Doc. She has to blame someone so she won't blame herself. If she starts to blame herself, she might become suicidal. He used the example of a robbery victim blaming the police not the crook. Apparently, she asked the doctor about changing her name. She's gone, Joe. And the best thing I can do for her is to let her go. It's probably the last thing I can do for her as a father." There were tears in Clay's eyes.

"Jesus, Clay. I'm really sorry."

"Thanks, Joe! You know the saying – Shit rolls downhill! If you're at the bottom of the hill, plan on a big load. Let's head home. I'm beat and we have a big day tomorrow."

After he dropped Clay off at his house, Joe drove around for a few miles to clear his head and calm down. Sylvia was still in California so he would be alone tonight. Many thoughts were swirling around in his mind. Clay had asked him if he had ever done anything like this before now. Joe had jokingly said that he had to plead the Fifth Amendment. The truth was that he had a lot of experience – too much experience.

Joe grew up in the suburbs of Newark, New Jersey. He was one of four very tough sons of a very tough father. Joe's father was an established part of organized crime during a time when there were very few controls over their activities. There were many teenage gangs around the city and Joe was a part of one of the most violent ones. Mostly, they did stupid crimes that yielded thrills but very little money. One night they were arrested in the possession of two stolen cars. Six of the gang members were passed out drunk. The cops simply slipped on the handcuffs and called for the drunk wagon.

Joe's father intervened and got him off with a suspended sentence but he was furious with the young man. He tried to hold his temper and decided to wait a few days before meting out punishment – not for stealing the car or drinking but for stupidity.

Unfortunately, another incident occurred in Joe's life during the next few days that would cost him dearly. There was a fight in the gymnasium. When a teacher tried to break up the wild battle, he was hit by a thrown object. It took twenty stitches to close the wound on the teacher's forehead. During questioning, one of the students fingered Joe as the culprit who threw the object.

The school sent a letter to his parents notifying them of Joe's permanent expulsion from the New Jersey school system.

After a monumental ass chewing, Joe's father announced that he was being sent into the city to work for a major crime family. Since he was no longer a student, he was expected to get a full time job and he was no longer welcome at home.

Joe packed a suitcase and went by Sylvia's house to say goodbye. They had been going steady for two years. He had known her since before they learned to walk. She promised to wait for him and walked him to the train station.

Joe debarked at Grand Central station and headed for a taxi stand. He handed a piece of paper to the driver that his father had jammed into his shirt pocket. His father had thrown a handful of bills toward him and left the room. Joe left the bills lying on the floor. He arrived in New York City with $39 of his own money in his pocket. He was seventeen years old but looked older due to his size and dark complexion.

During the next two years, Joe worked long hours as a soldier in a major crime family. He knew that he had to do exactly as he was ordered. There were no deviations. He was on call twenty-four hours a day. He shared an apartment with two other soldiers who, at the end of two years, were good friends. He was assigned training tasks as well as work tasks. He spent time on a firing range and many hours at the gym. He honed his knife fighting skills on the streets of New York. Joe participated in every type of armed robbery and many street fights staged to break up demonstrations.

Every time she had an opportunity, Sylvia would ride the train to New York and meet Joe. He had to explain to his boss who he was meeting and where.

Joe's mother wrote to him every week. She mourned the loss of her son to the family but was unable to reason with the father. Six months after his move to the city, Joe's mother died after a debilitating stroke. When Joe attended the funeral service, his father ignored him.

On a damp, gray day in February, Joe was ordered to report to his boss for a lunch meeting. During the two years of servitude, Joe had been paid a minimum salary. He knew from conversations with other soldiers that he could expect an envelope of cash when he was promoted to a higher position of trust. He would also receive a private apartment. He hoped that this would be the day of his elevation.

When the drinks were served, Joe was informed that his father was dead of a heart attack. The years of smoking, drinking, and overeating had shortened his life. His older brother, John, was in charge of the family now and he wanted Joe to return to the family. Joe was handed an envelope that contained ten thousand dollars. They told him that he had done a good job. If he wanted to return, he was welcome. They shook hands all around and Joe headed for his apartment to pack. By 4 PM, he was on a train to Newark.

After his father's funeral, John talked to him about a future with the family. Joe listened attentively and then outlined his own ideas for a future career. He wanted to marry Sylvia and attend a trade school to complete his education.

It took a week of discussions with John to complete the plan. Joe would remain a part of the family and enjoy their support but he would not participate in the day to day activities. He never told John that Sylvia had issued an ultimatum. She would not marry him if he intended to work for the family and live in New Jersey.

As Joe turned into the driveway of their modest home in the Maryland part of the DC suburbs, he was glad that Clay had not persisted in his questions about his past experiences. He would have had to say that, yeah, he knew how it felt to whack someone and he was good at the job – but he didn't like it.

19 – The Preparation

Joe arrived at Clay's house about 7 AM as arranged dressed in exercise clothes. The first step was to get onto the scales and write down their weights. Then Clay fixed them a bowl of oatmeal and one piece of dry toast. They had one glass of water and one cup of coffee. Then they went on a brisk, one-mile walk.

Back at the house, they did some exercises in the backyard and went into the house to unpack Clay's arsenal of guns. Joe was amazed at the collection of weapons, equipment, and books. Clay told him about his father and how the weapons and knowledge had been accumulated over two wars and a lot of years. While they talked, Clay began cleaning and checking each weapon.

For lunch, they had boiled chicken over a bed of lettuce and two glasses of water. Joe looked around to see if Clay had forgotten the pasta but he didn't ask.

"When does Sylvia get back from California, Joe?"

"She's coming into Dulles tonight. Do you want to go out and meet her with me?" Joe's offer was sincere.

"No, you guys should have an opportunity to talk alone. Maybe she can come over for breakfast tomorrow and tell me about the visit with the girls. Also, I've been intending to ask you how much Sylvia knows about your family and activities. And how much will you tell her about our plans?" Clay was concerned about these points. It could be a major weak spot.

"Sylvia knows everything about me and the family, Clay. We grew up together. I can't hide anything from her. I want to tell her everything and she'll help us any way she can. Is that a problem?"

"No, no. I just wasn't sure. Come on! Let's walk another mile. This time we'll jog a little bit."

"I jogged once about ten years ago but it made my beer foam up so I didn't try it again." Joe tried a little joke but Clay was off into serious thought - never-never land. He didn't register the comment.

Clay had awakened at 5 AM this morning and reached over for Lydia but she wasn't in her place. Then he remembered and the pain welled up in his chest.

And she would never be there again! Ever!

Sylvia came over for breakfast the next morning. Clay served a poached egg, dry toast, and orange juice to everyone. While they ate and cleaned up, Sylvia described her visit to California.

"The girls have a lovely, small apartment in San Mateo. Both of them are working for the same company about a mile from their apartment. They take turns driving to work. They seem to be happy. They're talking about taking some evening classes. I told Kathryn about her mother. I emphasized that neither of you knew about the cancer when she left for California and then Lydia didn't want to say anything to anybody for awhile. She seemed to understand. Apparently, it was just bad timing that all of us missed each other on the telephone calls. They didn't realize anything was wrong so they didn't worry when nobody answered."

"Did Kathryn cry?" Clay asked. He thought he knew the answer because Dr. Jacobs had prepared him.

"No. I think it will take a little while for the enormity of the loss to sink in, Clay."

"Right." He turned towards the door to conclude the conversation. "Are you going jogging with us?"

"Sure! I might as well lose a few pounds, too!" Sylvia tried to smile. Her heart was aching for the Matthews family.

Over the next few weeks, they started each morning by weighing and eating a Spartan breakfast. Then they went on a brisk walk with intermittent jogging spells of a few blocks. In the late morning, they had an exercise period and lifted some weights.

Everyday Joe and Clay studied the intelligence information on Jonathan Claggett, Company President Jack Carter, and Signal Control Technology, Inc. After each session, Clay spent a few minutes in thought and asked for something new. Joe would call his brother and the file would be larger for the next day's study period. Clay was starting to put together a plan in his mind but it wasn't complete yet.

In the meantime, Clay gave Joe's cousin a new assignment and told him to send a bill for his services. It was a separate matter and had nothing to do with Joe or the family. He wanted some information on a Mr. Jerry Nagel, insurance adjuster, and Walter Farthington, insurance agent. Both men worked for the Washington area office of Eastern Mutual Insurance Company.

The days rolled past at a fast pace. They had started driving out to Anne Arundel County for target practice every other day. On the off days, they cleaned the weapons and reloaded some ammo. And each day they studied the files on their targets. Now Clay started to make a list of equipment they would need.

In the evening when he was alone, Clay studied the files on the two insurance men. Jerry Nagel was thirty-two years old. He had worked for the insurance company for seven years. He lived alone and had few friends. On weekends, Nagel visited an adult bookshop located in the Maryland suburbs. Apparently, he did not eat in restaurants or entertain in his apartment.

Walter Farthington was married with four kids. He lived in a modest neighborhood of colonial style homes outside the Washington beltway. Farthington's wife seemed to be consumed with raising the kids whose ages ranged from seven to twelve years old. She drove the two youngest kids to school each day and picked them up in the afternoon. The two older kids rode a school bus. Walter worked in a satellite office with two secretaries and three other agents. Each Friday, Walter took a long lunch hour with one of the secretaries. They had a standing reservation at a local motel. Walter would run into the office. He paid cash and picked up a key. The desk clerk knew him and didn't require a registration. He pocketed the cash.

On Tuesday's, Walter's wife would meet some neighborhood

women for a round of bridge, coffee and neighborhood gossip. On Thursdays, she would drop off the younger kids and drive up to Columbia. She had a boyfriend who lived alone in a townhouse. After three hours with him, she would walk wobbly-kneed towards the car and drive home to fix dinner for Walter.

The exercise and diet programs were working for Sylvia, Joe, and Clay. The pounds were melting away. Each of them felt better than they had felt for years. Clay had gone through a period of sleeplessness but the doctor gave him a prescription for Ambien. The powerful sleeping medication did the trick. The doctor warned of addiction and Clay smiled. He wouldn't be around long enough for it to be a problem.

Occasionally, Clay would drive up to Frederick and put some flowers on Lydia's grave. He didn't talk to her because he didn't feel she was in the grave. It would have been nice to confide his plans but he had a feeling Lydia would not approve.

20 - The First Murder

One cool Saturday night in May, Clay put a .22 caliber automatic pistol in his side pocket and a .38 caliber revolver in his belt. He drove out to the suburbs and parked behind the adult bookshop frequented by the insurance adjuster. Jerry Nagel always left the bookshop about the same time according to the report. The theory put forth by the investigator was that he probably had a favorite television program because he always drove directly home.

Clay spotted his prey's car and parked a few spaces further down the same row. While he waited, Clay reviewed the situation in his mind. Was he really willing to murder this man? Had the offense been so serious that it justified taking the man's life? The answer was yes in both cases. Because the alternative was to do nothing. And that was not acceptable.

Clay and his father had frequently discussed World War II. Both of them read every book and saw every movie on the subject. Among the groups they discussed were the guerrillas or freedom fighters in the occupied European countries like Poland. They were small bands of very tough men. They were independent and were resistant to command influence. The commanders tended to be draconian in their disciplinary measures. Since there was no brig or stockade because they were on the move and no pay, there were few methods of punishment. In fact, there was only one punishment meted out – death. If a member did anything to endanger the group or betrayed his friends, he was put to death. Sleeping on guard duty or even neglecting guard duty was a reason for death. If it wasn't a serious enough infraction to warrant the death penalty, the crime was ignored. Clay was in such a situation now. Either Nagel's offense was worth the death penalty or it was nothing. So, was it justice to take this man's life for the $150,000 or not? But this man had cheated many people and he would go on cheating. So, yes, Nagel would die tonight.

When he saw Nagel exit the shop, Clay got out of his car. He timed his walk so that he met Nagel at the door of his car. It was dark and the parking lot was poorly lit. Probably the regular customers did not want anybody recognizing them. Clay pulled the revolver from his belt. He jabbed Nagel in the ribs and scared him. Nagel had opened the car door and Clay told him to get inside and slide over.

Nagel was too scared to object. He was shaking and seemed to be drooling. Clay had slipped on a pair of dark leather gloves before he left his car. Nagel seemed to be fixated on the gloved hands holding the gun. He did not want to look at his assailant.

When he closed the door of Nagel's car behind him, Clay realized that Nagel didn't recognize him. Clay simply stared at him for a few minutes to see if Nagel would register his identity. There was no recognition in his eyes. Nagel started to settle down and get control of his breathing.

"Is this a robbery? You can have my wallet! And my car if you want it! I won't yell or anything and I'll never identify you! I won't even make a complaint! Okay?" He reached for his wallet and handed it over. Clay took the money and threw the billfold on the floor. He nodded his head towards Nagel and looked at his watch. Nagel gave it to him.

"There's good news and bad news." Clay said. "The good news is that you won't be around to cheat anyone else in your insurance schemes. The bad news is that I'll have to throw away one of my favorite guns after I kill you."

"Wait! Wait! I recognize you! Look, I'm sorry you were cheated on the settlement for your house. It wasn't my idea! Wait! Don't do anything, okay? Let me explain! It was Walter's idea. He fingered you as someone who wouldn't put up an argument about being cheated. We get a bonus from the company if there's a settlement without any legal challenge. Okay? " Now he was shaking and drooling again.

Clayton Matthews was calm and deliberate as he extended the revolver so that it touched Nagel's chest. He pulled the trigger. The explosion was loud inside the car but hardly registered outside. Anyway, there was no one around to hear it. Nagel died instantly. Clay exited the car and walked calmly back to his vehicle.

The morning edition of the Washington Post reported the robbery/homicide of Mr. Jeremiah Nagel on page two of the Metro section. The police were investigating and urged any citizen with information to call the police hotline.

Clay threw his shoes and socks in the trash. Monday was the weekly pickup for his area. He dropped his clothes off at the laundry/cleaners. The young girl said they would be ready on Thursday. Have a nice day.

On the way to the farm for target practice, Clay said he would buy lunch at The Crab Shack across the Bay Bridge if Joe didn't mind the extra drive. Joe agreed. Halfway across the bridge, Clay looked around to see that there were no cars immediately behind him. He rolled down the window and threw the revolver and Nagel's watch across the rail into the Chesapeake Bay. The two men agreed that lunch was good and that they would have to do it again real soon.

21 – Planning For The Attack

Four weeks later, the scales showed that Joe had lost twenty-one pounds. Clay had lost eighteen pounds and Sylvia was down to a sleek-looking 125-pound size 7 figure. Everyone felt good and seemed pleased.

Clay was distracted as he reviewed the information file on Signal Control Technology, Inc. There was something nagging at him. He continued his studies and requests for more information.

Six months had passed since Lydia's death. He had exchanged a few letters with Kathryn but they were bland notes of information. Kathryn did not indicate any desire to visit home and she didn't invite Clay to California. Clay understood and, in fact, he was relieved. Kathryn was an adult and she was financially secure. There was nothing more that he could do for her. He was free to grieve in his own way and proceed with his plans. Clay had his memories of Lydia to keep him company in the evening and in his dreams. He relived the twenty-six years of their marriage. Life was not good but it was okay.

Two weeks ago, Clay had received the files on Steve Johnson and Arthur Goodman. Steve was Clay's old supervisor at Visorex. Arthur Goodman was the Assistant Vice President. He located their addresses in the ADC map atlas for Montgomery County, Maryland and began to plan. These two individuals plus the larcenous landlord were affronts that Clay intended to redress before he exited the world of pain and strife. Even though the product theft was the primary focus of their planning, he did not want to neglect the research required for the other acts.

The files on the two men included press releases of the

company and business reports from trade publications. Both men had received favorable reports on their acumen in maximizing profit by re-organizing the production work to the new Mexican facility. Goodman, the Assistant Vice President, was named Employee of the Year. The local Gazette reported a reduction in the work force at Visorex in excess of 25%. When asked to comment, a company official said, "a large part of the reduction was due to retirement and natural attrition."

On Saturday, Joe and Clay drove past the local headquarters for Signal Control Technology, Inc. It was a large building located in Montgomery County along the 270 Technology corridor between the Washington beltway and Frederick, MD. According to the information accumulated by Joe's cousin, the building accommodated over 300 employees on a normal workday. SCT reported annual sales of $32 Million dollars during the past year. The figure represented an increase of 8% over the previous year. Jack Carter had a large corner office with a balcony on the top floor of the three-story building. Jonathan Claggett, the Vice President of Sales, had a similar corner office with a balcony.

According to the information filed with the SEC, Jack Carter owned 24% of the outstanding stock of the company. The Sales Manager, Claggett, owned 6% of the stock. Various other employees owned an aggregate of 8%. The remaining stock was owned by International Systems, Inc. located in Munich, Germany. Jon Claggett had been elevated to Vice President – Sales in a recent management realignment. He had received a salary increase and a stock option plan. Insiders viewed Claggett as the heir apparent to the CEO spot when Carter retired in a few years.

Surveillance indicated that Jack Carter, CEO, came into the office every Monday morning about 2 AM. He stayed about two hours and returned home. Sometimes he returned in the late morning or, if he had a lunch appointment, he returned in the afternoon. It was a puzzling piece of the information until it was discovered that he was having a weekly satellite video teleconference with the German home office. Apparently, they reviewed their sales forecasts and production output every week

Once each quarter, Jack Carter would fly to Munich for a meeting with the home office. Once each year, the German managers would travel to the United States. One of the investigators assigned to the Carter surveillance did a database search on the company. It listed every article ever published on SCT. One of the articles dated three years ago noted the purchase of the Satellite video equipment and detailed the use of the equipment. Interesting.

The daily actions of the Chief Financial Officer had changed recently. He used to exit the side door of the building at 4:45 PM with two heavy thick briefcases. He placed them in the trunk of his new company-furnished Cadillac Brougham and drove to the bank. He entered the front door of the bank with the briefcases after ringing the night bell and being recognized. He left the bank about ten minutes later without the briefcases. At 7:30 AM the next morning, he drove to the bank, rang the night bell and entered. He reappeared with the briefcases and proceeded to the company. Recently, he was working until 6 or 7 PM and skipped the bank stop. He still had the briefcases but, apparently, he left them in the car at night. Fascinating stuff.

Clayton thought he knew what was in the briefcases but he needed to be sure. He asked the investigators to find out about the central computer system at SCT. Three days later, he received a thick report listing the model number and description of the mainframe computer, the main operating system, software modules, and the serial numbers of every piece of computer hardware in the SCT building. Clay shook his head in amazement. How in the world did they do it?

Joe's brother told him that they had researched the annual reports from the past ten years. Four years ago, SCT had allocated $42,000 for a study of computer systems. A Company in Princeton, New Jersey performed the study. A cousin burglarized the offices of the Princeton Company. He didn't steal anything but he did make a copy of the report. It described the computer needs of SCT in detail and listed the hardware equipment and software modules required to perform the tasks. It identified two companies best equipped to supply, install, and maintain the recommended equipment. One was located in Burlingame, California. The other one was located in Greenbelt, Maryland.

They scouted the offices in Greenbelt in preparation for another burglary. However, during the stakeout, they spotted a familiar face. The guy was a former Newark resident who had worked for AT&T. He used to do side work for the family to keep on top of his gambling debts. He had skipped out on a wife and two kids a couple of years ago. When he left, he owed the family a few thousand dollars. It wasn't a big deal and no one spent any time looking for him. But now they had found him.

Joe's brother Gino followed him home to a new wife and a young baby. A day later, they were waiting for him when he left for work. He was shaken to the core of his soul. Moreover, he was frightened to the core. He had visions of being killed and buried in a New Jersey swamp. He was willing to do anything or tell anything for a chance to live and continue his suburban dream with the new wife and baby. They asked him for a copy of every invoice sent out by his company in the last three years. It took him two nights of working late to make the copies. The cousin picked out the one invoice to SCT and threw the others in the dumpster. It was a five-page invoice listing the equipment and software delivered to SCT. A tape recorder was listed as a method of data backup for the system in the event of a catastrophic failure. The briefcase carried out nightly by the CFO contained the reels of data.

22 – The Second Murder

According to the surveillance report on Walter Farthington, he would leave the insurance office at 11:30 AM each Friday. He drove to a deli located two blocks from the motel and stocked up on snacks and drinks. He put them into a large briefcase while he was parked in front of the deli. He drove to the motel and rushed into the office. The clerk handed him a key and Walter passed him the cash. He would drive around to the back of the motel to Room 138 and enter the room with the large briefcase in hand. About 12 Noon, the secretary would drive to the motel and proceed directly to room 138. She would park beside Walter's car and walk through the unlocked door.

Just before 1 PM, the secretary would leave the room in a hurry. She had to scramble back to the office. Walter would linger in the motel room and take a shower. After leisurely dressing, he would exit the motel leaving the key in the room for the maid. The secretary always looked hassled and worried. She was looking around and checking her dress and buttons. Walter always looked relaxed and carried a smile on his face when he left.

It was eight months since Lydia had died. Clay always thought of events as how long before Lydia died or how long after she died. He wasn't happy but he was calm now. He had a routine with Joe and Sylvia. They had many meals together and compared results of the diet and exercise programs. Their weights had stabilized and they felt good. Clay and Joe went to the farm two times a week to practice with the guns. Three months ago, Joe introduced him to a friend of a cousin that owned a gym in Lanham, Maryland. It wasn't far from their houses. The owner recommended a trainer for them and it worked out very well. He brought a professional approach to their workouts and increased their strength training. He started teaching them some street fighting techniques. It was basic but lethal stuff. It wasn't kid gloves either. Clay and Joe showed up with some bruises and cuts. Joe needed some stitches after one workout. The trainer introduced them to pain. How to take it and how to give it. Both of them felt the lessons might prove valuable. They learned to keep fighting even though hurt and bleeding.

One Friday afternoon in August of 1992, Clay drove over to the strip mall next to the motel used by Walter Farthington for his afternoon rendezvous. He parked near the mall corner closest to the motel. At a few minutes before 1 PM, he walked around to the back of the mall and crossed the grassy knoll to the rear of the motel. The secretary was just coming out of the motel. She started her car and drove away. Clay looked around for any witnesses and walked up to the door of room 138. He twisted the knob and walked through the unlocked door. He could hear the shower running and Walter was singing. He was a happy man.

Clay opened the bathroom door very quietly. He stood in the doorway of the bathroom and looked out over the room. It looked like a lively session had taken place. The sheets were twisted around and half on the floor. There were snacks and dirty glasses on the low table by the bed.

Walter finished his shower and turned off the water. He pulled the shower curtain and jumped when he saw the man standing there looking at him.

"Who the hell are you? What are you doing here?" Walter screamed in anger. Then he quieted as recognition set into his mind. "Matthews? Clayton Matthews? What are you doing here?"

Clayton pulled the small .22 caliber automatic pistol from his jacket pocket. He had selected the small caliber pistol because he didn't want the bullets penetrating the walls into another room. He had scored the head of the slugs so that the bullet would mushroom on impact.

"Hey! Wait a minute! I didn't have anything to do with your settlement! It was all Jerry's idea! Ask him! He'll tell you! Wait! Are you the one who killed Jerry Nagel? Oh, Jesus! Oh, God! Please don't kill me! It was only money!" Farthington was screaming and crying. He tried to cross his legs to protect his groin.

Clayton Giles Matthews extended his arm full length and triggered three shots into the chest of Walter Farthington. He turned and left the motel room. He had killed his second person. Clay walked around to his car and drove home.

"Hey, how are you doing, old buddy?" Joe was in good spirits. "I got your message to meet you here for lunch. Did you pick up something at the deli? The cupboard is bare."

"I thought we might drive over the Bay Bridge and have lunch at The Crab Shack."

"Oh."

The 11 PM news reported the murder of Walter Farthington and showed shots of the motel. The police interviewed the clerk and he admitted that Walter had been coming there for a long time. He didn't know the name of the woman. Neither did the police until they compared the fingerprints found in the room to the secretary in the office.

The Saturday morning edition of The Washington Post reported the story on the front page below the fold. It was continued on page A12. In the article, they included an interview with the hysterical widow. She protested that Walter would never cheat on her. They loved each other. They had been married over twelve years. They had a perfect marriage and were true to each other. True love was the reason he left the large insurance policies for her.

Neither the TV nor newspaper reported that it was the second death of an Eastern Mutual Insurance Company employee.

23 – The Third Murder

Clay received a short letter from Kathryn. They had not talked on the telephone for months. She had met a young man and they were engaged. She didn't mention his name. They hadn't set an exact date as yet but it would be a small wedding. Maybe they would be able to swing through Maryland on their honeymoon if they could get enough time off from their jobs. She didn't invite Clayton to the wedding to perform the traditional role of the father of the bride.

Clayton drove to Frederick, Maryland on Sunday. He took some flowers to the gravesite. It was a peaceful place. He could see some other families scattered around the cemetery visiting their family members who had passed on. Clay stood around for awhile and didn't know what to do or say. He hated to leave within a few minutes. After all, it was a long drive to Frederick. Finally, he spoke towards the marker that listed Lydia's name, birth date, and date of death. He told her about the letter from Kathryn. And his voice broke. And he cried. He asked for her forgiveness for not protecting her from cancer and not protecting Kathryn!

When the tears dried and he opened his eyes, he saw that he was alone in the cemetery. The sun was setting in the west. He remembered that President Clinton was in Camp David this weekend. He thought it was located within a few miles of the cemetery. What a strange world. Would the next world be as strange? Would he see Lydia? According to the marriage vows, it was doubtful. According to the ceremony, the marriage would last "until death do us part." But the bible said something about reuniting, didn't it? The whole thing was confusing. Why did Lydia have to leave? He didn't understand.

On Monday, Joe and Sylvia came over for breakfast. Sylvia brought some fresh strawberries. Joe carried in several boxes.

"The video cameras that you wanted came to my house. What do you want them for?" Joe was puzzled as usual.

"Well, let's unpack them and learn how to use them. Let's start filming and find out about light requirements and all of the other jazz." Clay was thinking furiously. It was almost time to deal with Claggett and SCT. It would be their biggest score but he had a few details to clear up before the big one. In the meantime, he asked Joe to find out how to enter the trunk of a 1992 Cadillac Brougham without using a crow bar.

On Wednesday, Clayton drove out to Damascus, Maryland. The rolling hills were an unbroken expanse of single family homes on one-acre lots. The farmland had disappeared years ago. The only tractors in this part of Maryland were for lawn care.

The surveillance reports on Steve Johnson, his supervisor at Visorex Systems, Inc. for many years, indicated that he lived in a ranch style house on 1.1 acres about one mile east of the city of Damascus. The driveway was readily identifiable by the unusual mailbox fixture that used a wheelbarrow as a base. The driveway wound around to the house that faced the East. On the rear or West Side of the house, there was an in-ground swimming pool with a waterfall opposite the diving board. Apparently, Steve enjoyed reading the morning newspaper at poolside every morning even if the weather was cool. Even if it was raining, he sat out there under the umbrella sipping coffee and reading the paper. Before 7 AM, he would walk around the side of the house to the garage and drive to Visorex. The wife and kids slept until the last minute before they had to get up for school. Steve enjoyed the privacy. He prided himself on punctuality and reliability of reporting to work before any of his underlings.

Clay drove up to the garage on the side of the house and turned off the engine. He left the car quietly collecting his equipment from the seat beside him. He left the door open and keys in the switch. He walked around the corner of the house towards the pool. Steve had his back towards him. The noise of the swimming pool waterfall masked his footsteps. Steve was engrossed in the newspaper and mumbling to himself as if reading aloud. He was reaching for his coffee cup when Clayton dropped the garrote rope around his neck. Steve didn't have time to make a sound but he twisted around far enough to see and recognize Clayton Matthews. With the recognition came panic. Steve tried to raise his arms and escape the rope but he had no strength in his arms. And the rest of his body felt like melted butter. Besides, it was getting dark so it was easier to go to sleep. He was dead in less than two minutes without a sound.

Steve Johnson's wife woke early this morning and looked out the window towards the pool. She saw Clayton turn away from the body but she had never met him before in her life. The Matthews family had never been invited to the Johnson's home for a picnic or a swim. She thought it was strange for Steve to have a visitor so early in the morning. It was also strange that he had his head down on the table. She thought she better go check on him even if it was his private time. Normally he would be gone by the time she got out of bed and she didn't have to cope with him.

By the time she got to the poolside, Clayton was driving out of the driveway and turning towards Washington. He joined the commuters on their daily trek.

By the time the police arrived and the ambulance crew pronounced Steve Johnson dead at the scene, Mrs. Johnson's hysterics were starting to subside. She tried to remember everything she had seen and heard. She felt she had enough details that the police would apprehend the killer within hours.

"It was a man!" She said.

"He was about medium height!"

"He was about medium weight!"

"I don't know what color! He was either black or white!"

"Yes, I saw his car! It was big! I think it was a dark color – black or blue or something like that!"

"No, I didn't get the license plate number! It might have been a Maryland plate!"

"Why are you asking about whether we were planning a vacation? We weren't going anywhere. We never go on vacation. And I don't know why he had a Visorex Form 1556 in his shirt pocket. He didn't say anything to me about requesting leave."

"Well, I don't know why you weren't here to prevent this murder. Isn't that why we pay taxes?" She flounced away to collect the kids and go to her mother's house in the city. It was too dangerous in the suburbs.

Channel 4 reported the murder immediately as "Breaking News" with camera footage because one of their cameramen lived nearby. The other channels were scooped so they didn't report it at all. The Washington Post was already on the streets so their story was a day later. They concluded their story by reporting that despite this murder, the statistics indicated a decrease in crime for the year-to-date.

Joe Colissimo drove up to Clayton's house before lunch with a long face.

"Are we going to The Crab Shack for lunch?" He asked.

"Why would we do that?" Clayton wanted to know. "Let's pick something up from the deli."

24 - The Fourth Murder

On Saturday morning, two men and a woman walked through the US Air terminal at Reagan National Airport near Washington D.C. They presented their tickets and boarded a flight for Newark, New Jersey. The names on the tickets were Sylvia Colissimo, Joe Colissimo, and Clayton Matthews. The tickets had been purchased via telephone direct from the airline and charged to their credit cards.

The three people registered at the Sheraton Hotel under the same names and attended a Colissimo family reunion in the ballroom on Saturday night. They slept late on Sunday morning and chatted with family members all day. On Monday afternoon, they took the motel shuttle to Newark Airport and returned to Washington arriving around 5 PM. There were family members and hotel waiters prepared to testify that the three people were in Newark at the reunion if it were ever necessary.

As the dark night turned from Sunday into Monday, Clay and Joe and Sylvia stood in a circle facing each other with their arms around each other. There were tears in Sylvia's eyes. It was time to take action against SCT. This was the night.

"It'll be okay, Sylvia." Clayton assured her. "You'll see."

"Come on, Honey. We've got a good plan. We know what we're doing. Those assholes gotta pay. They got no right going around screwing people. Especially eye-talians like us. That was their big mistake and we're going to teach them a lesson." Joe was worked up.

"Clayton's no eye–talian, you dumb guinea. Maybe we better think this over. Please?" Sylvia was having doubts. If they failed, it would mean the end of her family. If they succeeded, all it would mean was some money. Suddenly it wasn't worth the risk. Now she understood why some people screwed other people over and over. They got away with it because revenge wasn't worth the risk. Why had she agreed with Clay and Joe? Why had she encouraged them? She was so scared she was shaking.

"Clay's a guinea same as us. We adopted him. All of the cousins voted and he's in." Joe gave them a big smile. "Come on, sweet stuff, get your pretty ass in the car. We got work to do."

It was 1 AM in the morning. They had loaded all of the equipment before they went to bed. They had set four alarms to wake them up. None of them thought they would go to sleep when they lay down at the Colissimo house about 8 PM. But the last two days had been so hectic that they went to sleep almost immediately.

Clay drove his car with the equipment in the trunk. Joe and Sylvia followed him. They entered the outer loop of the I-495 Washington Beltway and proceeded west. They exited onto the I-270 spur headed towards Frederick, Maryland. Clay kept the speed at 60 mph with the cruise control. He didn't want to be stopped for speeding but he didn't want to attract attention by driving too slow.

They exited 270 at Rockville on Route 28 and headed towards Research Boulevard with the high tech buildings hidden in the trees. SCT was set back from the road enough that the building wasn't visible from the local street or 270. Clay followed the road around to the SCT entrance. He pulled in far enough to see the lone car in the parking lot. He stopped and pumped his brakes several times to signal Joe. He saw Joe blink his headlights and make a U-turn. Joe and Sylvia left to do their job.

Clay coasted down the hill and into the SCT parking lot next to the lone car. He checked the license plate number and verified that it was Jack Carter's vehicle. The CEO was in the building on the transatlantic hookup for the weekly teleconference meeting with his German partners.

There were no guards at the building but the security system was sophisticated. Clay had a complete description of the system that he had studied for weeks. Each of the employees, including the CEO, had an identification badge. To enter the building, an employee had to swipe the card through a reader much like a credit card. The computer checked the name and the hours of authorization for the individual. Not every employee was authorized after-hours access. In fact, only three employees, Carter and Claggett and the Chief Financial Officer, were authorized 24-hour access. The computer registered the time and date of each entry and exit.

Clay chuckled as he parked next to Carter's vehicle. The CEO could have pulled up next to the curb adjacent to the entry but he had parked in his reserved spot – one of the perks of being the boss. Carter had several vehicles – a Mercedes Sedan, a Porsche, and a Chevrolet Suburban. Inevitably, he drove the huge, lumbering Suburban to his early morning Monday meeting. It made sense during the winter. At other times, it made him feel big, like a boss.

Clay pulled up beside the big SUV on the side away from the entrance door. Carter wouldn't see Clay's car unless he knelt down and took a good look. Not likely. Clay removed two heavy duffel bags of equipment from the trunk and walked towards the entry door. He was not concerned that Carter would see him. Carter's office was on the opposite corner of the building.

The entry door and several panels on each side of the door were solid, heavy glass. The glass extended down to within twelve inches or so from the mulched flowerbed with the low shrubs. Clay stashed the bags on the ground next to the hinged side of the entry door. He pushed them down flat so they wouldn't be spotted with a casual glance. Clay stretched out flat on his stomach in the flowerbed. He was on the swing side of the door. Clay was wearing a black windbreaker and dark pants. When he buried his face in his arms, he was almost invisible against the mulch background. He had a few minutes to wait for Carter.

*   *   *

When Joe flashed his headlights at Clay in the driveway, he started a U-turn. Sylvia picked up the cellular phone and hit a preset number button. After one ring, a gruff voice answered, "Pronto!"

"It's a go! Start digging!" She hung up. The call took five seconds.

Joe drove towards Potomac, Maryland. He knew the route through the most exclusive neighborhood of the Washington area. He had made over a dozen practice runs in the past few weeks. Tonight he was driving a Cadillac Seville with Maryland plates. It would fit into the neighborhood. The high rollers that lived in Potomac enjoyed more police protection than the ordinary citizens in the lower cost areas did. He didn't want to be noticed by a wandering police cruiser.

Joe pulled into the driveway of a large, two-story colonial house. He turned off his headlights and slowed the car to a crawl. He scanned the cars in the driveway carefully. The owner of the house had four teenage daughters. He didn't want to drive up on one of the cars with a couple of lovers saying goodnight. 2 AM was just late enough to be safe – probably! The big house had a four-car garage – standard for the Potomac area houses. In this case, however, each of the daughters had a car. The wife had a car and the husband had a Jaguar. For daily commuting to the office, the owner had a company car – a 1992 Cadillac Brougham. It was this vehicle that Joe wanted to see – the car driven by the Chief Financial Officer of Signal Control Technology, Inc.

Joe thought the big Cadillac might be inside a garage stall. He was prepared for it. Each stall had an individual, paneled wood door. Joe had a battery-powered Dremel tool on the floor with a sawblade attachment. It would cut through the decorative wood panels quietly in a flash.

Joe was lucky tonight. The Cadillac was outside. The CFO had not arrived home early enough to win an inside parking spot. Joe chuckled as he left Sylvia in the car and headed towards the Cadillac. He had a ring with ten keys on it. The third one opened the trunk of the CFO's car. Joe grabbed the two briefcases and closed the trunk lid. He walked back to his car where Sylvia opened a rear door for him. As he exited the driveway, he was glad it hadn't been necessary to use the pistol in his shoulder holster. Joe headed for the SCT building to join Clay.

The mulch in the flowerbed had a pleasant smell and Clay had dozed off as he waited for Jack Carter. He woke with a start as he heard footsteps approaching the inside of the door. As the door swung open, Clay jumped up and stuck a big, 45 automatic pistol in Carter's face. He caught the door before it closed.

Carter's eyes were big and his mouth hung open. He was having trouble getting his breath as he stared up the barrel of the pistol. He hadn't even looked at Clay. All he could see was the big hole staring at him. Clay held the door with his foot and grabbed Carter by the collar with his free hand.

"Get inside!" He swatted him hard with the gun barrel to get his attention. The gunsight on the end of the barrel tore a jagged path on Carter's forehead. It began to bleed. And hurt. Clay reached out and grabbed the identification badge from Carter's shirt pocket. He threw it on top of the duffel bags outside the door. Then he motioned Carter towards the inside of the building. The whole thing took sixty seconds. Carter was dazed and in shock.

When Carter hesitated, Clay pushed him roughly. When he hesitated a second time, he knocked him to the floor.

"There's no money in the building!" Carter cried. "This isn't a 7-11 store! You can have my money but that's all there is!"

"Get up and walk to the computer room! If you stop again, I'll shoot you in the leg!" Clay threatened.

"You wouldn't dare! Someone would hear the noise!" Carter thought he was bluffing.

Clay fired a shot that narrowly missed Carter. The gunshot was unbelievably loud in the hallway. Carter had never been in military service. He had never fired a gun. Other than television, he had never been near a gunshot. The big .45 automatic was louder than anything he could imagine. He was terrified! Now he believed truly that the man would shoot him. Now he would do anything the man wanted him to do. Anything at all!

They entered the computer room and Clay looked around the equipment carefully. It was exactly as he expected. He gestured for Carter to sit down at a desk.

"What do you want?" Carter stammered.

"Shut up!" Clay simply stared at him. "Walk over here and empty your pockets on top of this desk. Then go sit down over there."

The two men sat still for thirty minutes till they heard the noise in the hallway.

Joe and Sylvia pulled into the SCT parking lot and pulled in next to Clay's car. Joe got the two briefcases from the rear seat and they walked up to the entry door.

Sylvia leaned over and picked up Carter's identification badge from the ground. She swiped the card through the reader and opened the door. Joe set the two briefcases inside and turned around to get the two duffel bags on the ground. He moved them inside and nodded towards the briefcases.

"I'll come back for them." Joe said.

"Don't be silly. I can carry them. Why do you think I've been exercising all these months?" Sylvia smiled. She followed him down the hall.

Joe and Sylvia entered the computer room with the duffel bags of equipment and the briefcases. Joe smiled at Clay. "Everything went like clockwork." As he spoke, he glanced over at the desk with Carter's things on it. He moved over towards the desk and slipped the car keys into his pocket. Clay was brilliant. He thought of everything.

Clay turned to Jack Carter and issued a terse command. "Pick up the telephone and call Jonathan Claggett. Speak in a normal tone of voice. Tell him you want him to come over here and meet you in the computer room. Tell him there were some questions during your weekly teleconference with Germany and you need his help. Tell him to hurry."

Carter hesitated and Clay backhanded him across the face. "Make up your mind about how you want this to turn out. You can live and pay out a little bit of money. Or you can die. Which is it?"

"I want to live! I'll give you anything I have!" Carter was crying. He had everything in life he had ever wanted. He had money, wife, girlfriend, nice house, cars, a good job, security, good health, youth, looks, - absolutely everything. He wanted for nothing. And now this madman was about to kill him. He vowed not to hesitate again. He would do anything to live. Just, please, God, let me live! Suddenly Carter was a devout Christian.

Clay handed him a piece of paper with Claggett's telephone number written on it. The madman knew everything. He dialed the number and listened to the ringing.

Clay moved in position behind him so that he could listen. He cocked the gun and put the barrel so that it touched Carter's other ear.

Finally, after many rings, a sleepy voice answered the telephone.

"Hello."

"Jon, this is Jack. Are you awake enough to understand me?"

"Yeah. What's up?"

"I'm at the office. I just got off the satellite videophone with the Germans. We've got a big flap and I need your help. I want you to come down here as soon as possible. Okay?"

"Yeah, Okay! I'll be there as soon as possible."

"Jon, I mean it. As soon as possible. Just slip on some pants and shoes and get on the road. Meet me in the computer room."

"Yeah, yeah, I got it. See you in a few minutes." Jonathan Claggett hung up the phone and started moving. Carter was a no-nonsense boss. When he said something, he meant it.

Claggett was glad he lived close to the office. It was less than fifteen minutes when he pulled into the parking lot. He was puzzled to see two other cars parked beside Carter's Chevrolet Suburban but he shrugged his shoulders. It was probably some other lucky people pulled out of bed in the middle of the night.

He rushed over to the front door and swiped his card through the reader.

Claggett pushed open the door to the computer room and walked in. He was startled to see Carter sitting in a chair holding his head. He was bleeding and his eyes looked like he had been crying. Then he looked around and saw two faces that he recognized - - Clayton Matthews and Joe Colissimo. They were holding guns. The guns were pointed at him. He was speechless.

Claggett didn't see Sylvia standing in the shadows behind the floodlights. During the wait for Claggett, Sylvia had done her assigned job. She unpacked the duffel bags. She had set up three bright floodlights on folding legs and pointed them towards the center of the room. Then she stayed in the shadows and set up the rest of the equipment. There were three video cameras prepared to record the events as they developed.

"What do you want?" Claggett said angrily. "I told you to contact our attorneys if you had a beef. What part of those instructions don't you understand?"

Claggett turned towards Carter. "I'm sorry, boss. These are the two yahoos with the Model 900 Switch design. I'll get rid of them."

Joe Colissimo laid his gun on the desk and stepped towards Claggett. He hit him in the stomach with everything he had. The punch represented almost a year of exercise and training and frustration and anger. When Claggett fell to the floor, he kicked him in the gut and the kidneys. Claggett vomited and screamed.

"Get up and shut up!" Colissimo told him. "Sit down in this chair!"

Claggett struggled up from the floor and sat in the chair. Colissimo moved in behind him and pulled his arms behind the chair. He snapped on a pair of handcuffs. Then he knelt down to tie his legs to the chair.

Carter had watched the whole scene with an inner feeling of terror. He was glad it wasn't him receiving the blows. But now he knew who these people were. He knew why they were here. Claggett had come to him with the story of their invention. They were too dumb to file for a patent or even ask for a nondisclosure agreement. Claggett proposed copying their design. Carter recognized the potential of the invention and knew it would make a lot of money. They could take credit for it and look good to the Germans. If the yokels raised a fuss, let the attorneys take care of it. To hell with 'em!

Now he knew it had been a mistake. It was probably the worst mistake of his life. He hoped it didn't cost him his life. Damn Claggett! It was his entire fault. If he got out of this mess, he would fire Claggett.

While they had waited for Claggett, Carter watched Joe Colissimo attach some sort of device to every piece of computer equipment in the room. Then Colissimo took every computer tape reel and disk from the shelves and made a big pile in the middle of the room. He placed two more devices on top of the pile.

Clayton turned to Carter and outlined the deal.

"When we leave, we're going to pull the pins on the incendiary grenades. They have a ninety-second fuse. They'll burn everything in the room. I know it will set off the fire alarms and the fire department will be here in minutes. It won't be fast enough to save your computer and software." He moved over to the two briefcases that Joe had taken from the trunk of the CFO's car. He opened the flaps and showed the tape reels to Carter.

"These are the backup tape reels that your CFO takes home every night to preserve your financial records and technical data in the event of a catastrophe. We're taking these reels with us. You can buy them back by wiring ten million dollars into an overseas account."

"We're setting you free so you can carry out our instructions. Let the firemen do their job. Deny all knowledge of what happened. Understand?" Clayton paused and looked at Carter. He nodded vigorously. He understood everything. In particular he understood the part about setting him free. He was going to live. He was going to live! Oh, sweet Jesus!

"Claggett is going to die here tonight." He turned towards Claggett and looked at him. The man had a terrified look on his face. Colissimo stepped up and put a black hood over Claggett's head like an executioner sealing his fate. Clay turned back to Carter.

"You have twenty-four hours to get the money into the account or we'll destroy the tapes. Also, we'll come after you. It may take a while but some day or some night, I'll step up and put a bullet in your ear. Do you remember the sound of the shot?" Clay waited for a response.

Carter started sobbing again as he remembered the loudness of the gunshot in the hallway. He had no doubt that they intended to kill Claggett. They were killers. But he had a chance. He would do everything he could to eliminate any danger to himself. But wait! What if he couldn't do it through no fault of his own? His confusion showed on his face.

Clay was watching him.

"What?" Clay asked him.

"Well, I may have trouble getting ten million dollars together in twenty-four hours." Carter stammered fearfully.

"How much can you get in twenty-four hours?" Clay asked. Everything was developing as he had planned.

"Well, I know I can get a million dollars maybe even two million." Carter said. "I'll get it all for you in time, please believe me. I'm not trying to stiff you. Not again. I've learned my lesson."

"I'll tell you what. I'll let you off for two million dollars if you do me a favor. Are you willing to do a favor for me and save yourself eight million dollars?" Clay looked at him.

"I told you. I'll do anything. Just tell me. I promise I'll get the two million dollars for you. What else do you want?" He was sweating and breathing hard. It was the most important negotiation of his life.

Clay continued to hold the cocked .45 caliber automatic pistol leveled at Carter. Now he reached into his side pocket and pulled out a .38 caliber revolver. It was a standard issue with four-inch barrel and six-shot cylinder. He laid it on the table close to Carter. Then he backed into the shadows. Behind him, Sylvia started the cameras.

"There's one bullet in the gun in front of you. Pick it up and kill Claggett. If you even start to point it towards us, I'll kill you.

I'm an expert shot as you've seen. If you kill him in one shot, I'll let you off for two million dollars if you can get it into the account within twenty-four hours. That's the deal. Are you interested?" Clay waited for his answer but he knew what it would be.

Carter took less than sixty seconds to make up his mind. He nodded his head in assent.

"Don't touch the pistol. Walk over and remove the hood." Clay instructed.

Carter moved like a jerky robot. He walked over and removed the hood. He didn't look his friend in the eye. Claggett was terrified and moaning. He had wet his pants and the smell of urine filled the room. The video cameras were running.

"Now pick up the pistol and keep it pointed towards Claggett." Clay waited for him to obey.

Carter picked up the pistol and pointed it towards Claggett.

"Now cock the hammer." Clay spoke in a level tone of voice.

Carter looked at the pistol and reached out with his other hand to cock the pistol. He kept it pointed towards Claggett.

"Now do it." Clay spoke to him and leveled his own pistol towards Carter.

Carter pulled the trigger. The sound of the shot in the computer room was deafening. The bullet struck Claggett in the head. He was dead instantly. Carter looked at the pistol as if to ask it what had happened.

"Put the pistol down on the table and sit down. Do it now." Clay's voice was louder.

Carter complied. He buried his face in his hands.

Clay turned to Sylvia and nodded. She turned off the cameras.

Joe Colissimo swung into action. He untied Claggett's body and unlocked the handcuffs. Then he swung the body over his shoulder like a sack of flour. He reached over and picked up the pistol by sticking a pencil into the barrel. He inserted it into a plastic bag very carefully to preserve the fingerprints and headed for the parking lot. When he got to the ground floor, he looked out towards the parking lot carefully. It wouldn't do for someone to see him carrying a body out of the building.

Everything looked clear so he exited the building. He carried

Claggett's body to the Chevrolet Suburban. He threw the body in the back seat and got into the vehicle. He started the engine and drove out of the lot quickly.

Joe drove directly to Jack Carter's house. Carter had a large five-acre spread less than five miles from the SCT building. Earlier in the night, Sylvia had placed a cell phone call to one of Joe's cousins. She had told him it was a "Go" and that he should start digging. The cousin had dug a deep grave on Carter's property. Joe intended to bury Claggett in the grave. Driving the body to the site in Carter's vehicle was sure to leave some hair and blood in the event of future investigation.

At the gravesite, Joe removed the body and threw it into the hole. He threw the pistol in on top of the body. He used the shovel left by the cousin to fill the hole. Then he tamped it down and replaced the sod on top. In a few weeks, it would be invisible except to a trained dog or some determined investigator. Joe took the shovel with him and drove back to the SCT building in the Suburban. He parked in the same spot.

Joe threw the shovel into his car and started for the front door. He used Carter's identification badge to gain entry. He walked rapidly to the computer room. He looked at Clay and nodded. He laid the Suburban keys back on the table.

"Come on." He jerked Carter to his feet. "Pick up your stuff and let's get you out to your car. You don't want to be here when the fire trucks arrive." He propelled him from the room.

Joe started pulling pins on the incendiary grenades. The clock was running. Sylvia had packed up the equipment.

Clay picked up one briefcase and steered Carter with the other hand. Sylvia picked up the second briefcase full of computer tapes. Joe picked up the two duffel bags and looked around carefully to see if they had overlooked anything.

The group left the building and headed for the vehicles. Clay put Carter into the Suburban and handed him his keys.

"Remember! Wire two million dollars into the account on this piece of paper." He stuffed the paper into Carter's shirt pocket. "I'll send the backup tapes to you. You'll be back in business in no time. Insurance will cover most of the loss. Claggett will be missing but the cops won't find his body. You might want to suggest that he started the fire because of a grudge against the company. It's up to you. If you ever tell anyone what happened tonight, I swear I'll find you and kill you. By the way, here's a present for you. A little gift for you because you did so well." He thrust a videotape into Carter's hands.

"The whole scene was recorded on three cameras. Here's your copy. We have two other copies. It sure would be hard to explain to the cops. Don't you think? Now take off!" Clay slammed the door.

Clay walked over to his car and started up. He exited the parking lot with Joe and Sylvia behind him. Carter was pulling out in front of him.

They returned to the Colissimo house. Sylvia told them to sit down at the kitchen table. She quickly set out dishes and utensils. She took some sausage and bread from the refrigerator. She served a bottle of Chianti from the side cupboard. It was standard Italian fare served at all hours to soothe the nerves and comfort the body.

Everyone was quiet as they ate. Finally Joe looked up.

"Clay, a couple of weeks ago, you asked me to call my cousin in New Jersey and have him set up the offshore bank account. How did you know I had a cousin in the financial services racket? "

"It was just a wild guess, pal. Just a wild guess."

They laughed.

25 - Review And Resolve

Clay didn't know what was happening to him. He was changing in some basic, massive way. The revenge was not as satisfying as he thought it would be. He hadn't expected the world to turn rosy or for all wrongs to be righted as if they never happened. He did define his actions as justice. It was justice demanded and taken from the perpetrator.

Before Lydia's death - there it is again, marking events as either before or after Lydia's death – he was an honest, law-abiding citizen. He did not threaten people. Certainly, he did not hurt people. If someone had told him that he would kill people, he would have scoffed at them.

He realized that the training, dieting, and weapons training were mental conditioning as well as physical conditioning. He prepared himself for the tasks that he had deemed to be necessary. Certainly the things he did were not unjust to the targets of his resolve. They deserved the punishment. They were guilty. That was a fact. The problem seemed to be that the retribution did not undo the crime. Because the crime could not be undone, the victim was never completely satisfied. The punishment was never enough in the eyes of the victim.

The perpetrator always had an excuse. Things got out of hand they would say. They never intended for things to go so far. They were sorry. If they had known then what they know now – blah, blah, blah. For the perpetrator, any punishment was too much. And, of course, the perpetrators had friends and families. When the criminal received punishment, it hurt everyone around them. So the law allowed some extra mercy for the peripheral damage. Then the judge slammed the gavel down and called it justice. Case closed. The scholars said our system isn't perfect but it's the best in the world. Oh, yeah? Clay figured the world had some serious problems.

Clay was beginning to realize that he hadn't solved anything with the murders. Lydia was still dead. Kathryn was still estranged from him. He was lonely. Joe and Sylvia Colissimo were good friends but when the lights were turned out at night, he was alone.

Well, the original intent was to get even and then check out. He never intended to create a new life for himself. He knew in the beginning that he couldn't undo the pain or the injustice. He knew he could only exact payment.

There were two more issues to be resolved and then it would be time to check out.

Arthur Goodman, the Assistant Vice-President at Visorex Systems, and William Taylor, the landlord who cheated them out of their rental deposit, were still alive.

He turned out the light and fell into a deep sleep.

26 - The Fifth Murder

Jack Carter had wired the money into the offshore account within twenty-four hours. Joe's cousin had instructions in place for the dispersal of the money. Joe had put his money into the family pot. Clay had a million dollars and no idea about what to do with it.

After receipt of the money, Joe drove the computer tapes to Union Station in Washington, D. C. He placed them in a locker and mailed the key to Jack Carter. They had been careful about fingerprints all along during the action. Returning the computer tapes was no exception.

Clay knew that Jack Carter was a potential danger in the future. He knew their names. He could find them with very little trouble. In a month or a year, Carter might forget the terror he had felt and seek some justice of his own. He might forget that it was his act of piracy that started the whole problem.

Their biggest protection from Jack Carter was the man's own intelligence. He had the videotape that showed him killing Jon Claggett. And he knew they had copies. He knew they had the gun that he used to kill Claggett. It had his fingerprints on it. Carter would remember that they had disposed of Claggett's body. And he would wonder about the significance of why they had hidden the body.

Carter might be that rare individual – one who could say, "I deserved that. I did wrong and I was punished. It's a wash." Or he might not.

The Washington Post did a series of articles on SCT. They covered the fire and the mysterious disappearance of the Vice-

President of Sales, Jonathan Claggett. They noted the quick recovery from the fire that destroyed their computer system and all of their data records. Jack Carter credited the Chief Financial Officer with the foresight of implementing a plan that included offsite storage of backup files. There was never a mention of the theft of the tapes from the trunk of the CFO's car.

On Friday, Joe Colissimo drove into the driveway. Clay noted the arrival through the living room window and got up to put on a pot of coffee. When he returned to the front of the house, he was surprised to find that Joe had not come inside as yet. They had dispensed with the formality of ringing the doorbell at each other's house months ago. When he looked out, he saw Joe filling a pan with water from the outside faucet. Then he walked back to his car and knelt down behind it. Puzzled, Clay walked outside to see what was going on.

Joe was kneeling down and petting a dog that was lapping at the water. Joe looked up and shrugged his shoulders. Then he stood up and explained.

"There's an older couple in our neighborhood. You've probably seen them walking their dog. The Hanrahans. Nice people. Mrs. Hanrahan is in the hospital. She's real sick and Mr. Hanrahan is not in good shape either. They can't take care of the dog anymore. He asked if I would take the dog to the vet and have him put to sleep. The dog is not young either but I hate to do it. I'm going to ask Sylvia if we can keep him but it's going to take a few days for me to butter her up. She doesn't like animals – except me, of course." He smiled from ear to ear. "Would you keep the dog for me? Just for a couple of days?"

"Yeah, I guess so." Clay looked at him skeptically. "Are you sure it's just for a couple of days?"

"Honest to God, Clay." He crossed his heart with his fingers. "Would I shit you? I really want the little guy. I pet him all the time. He's a friendly little guy."

"What's his name?"

"Stanley." Joe said with relief. He hadn't known how Clay would react.

"What kind of dog is he?" Clay was looking at the dog. The dog was staring back at him sort of quizzically.

"Ah, hell, I don't know. He looks like that dog in the kids' movies – Benji. So I just call him a Benji dog. What do I know about dogs?"

"So what do I have to do for him?" He and the dog were still staring at each other.

"Just feed and water him. When he scratches at the door, let him out to take a whiz." Joe made it sound simple.

"What do I feed him?" The ever practical Clay asked.

"I brought a sack of canned food and a bag of dry food. Give him a can in the morning and another one at night. Put some dry food in a bowl for him to snack on. Okay?" Joe handed the leash to Clay.

"Where does he sleep? "

"Oh, I forgot. Glad you asked. I've got his bed in the trunk. I'll get it." Joe started for the rear of the car.

"Does he stay in the house at night? "

"Yeah, sure, but he won't be any trouble." Joe was getting in his car. He was in a hurry to leave.

Clay and Stanley looked at each other. They were both skeptical.

On Saturday, Clay loaded two magazines for his Walthers P-38 double-action automatic pistol. It was one of his favorite weapons. It was beautifully balanced and had a light recoil for the size of bullet. He loaded one magazine in the handle of the pistol and slipped the other spare magazine into his left coat pocket. He knew he wouldn't need the spare magazine but Clay was a careful man. Better safe etc, etc.

William Taylor was the next target.

Taylor had rented the small, furnished house to Clay and Lydia when their house burned down. Taylor knew about the fire and knew that they were staying in a motel until they could find a place. He had demanded one month's rent and two months deposit before he released the keys to them. When he and Lydia located the replacement house they wanted to purchase, Taylor wouldn't return their deposit. Clay had written him a check for $3600. The net result was that Taylor received $3600 for one month's rent of a house that should have rented for $800 per month.

Clay had received and paid for a surveillance report on William Taylor. He had him cold. Every Saturday morning, Taylor would go to his office for two or three hours to catch up on his work after visiting an apartment building. Taylor was retired from the government – he had been an IRS auditor. Now he had a small tax service business. He prepared tax returns for a small but growing list of clients. He owned two rental houses, two duplex units, and a small apartment building with eight units. He wasn't too proud of the larger unit. It was in a poor section of town and kind of rundown but it got the highest rent. The tenants were the poorest and paid their rent weekly in cash. It was a pain to go by and collect the rent every Saturday morning but it was profitable. And the cash was tax-free. He knew how to cover it up.

Taylor's office was on the second floor of a strip mall above an insurance office. They were closed on Saturday. The only store in the mall that was open on the weekends was the convenience store but it was located on the opposite end.

The door to the stairway leading to the second floor was on the backside of the building. On this Saturday, Taylor pulled up close to the building and parked. There wasn't another car in sight. He locked his car with a push of the button on the remote. He used his key to open the entry door and headed upstairs.

There was a large floor safe in his office. A client had given it to him on condition that he remove it from the original office within twenty-four hours. Taylor got another of his clients to move it for him. Then they had a devil of a time getting it up the stairs. Fortunately, the stairway was wide. Four of them grunted and pushed until the brute was at the top. Then they wheeled it into the office.

Taylor was amused every time he entered the office and saw the safe. He used it for his ledgers and a small amount of cash. The funny thing was that he kept the bulk of his cash in a secret drawer of his desk. The desk was an old-fashioned roll-top model built in the 1800s. It was a real antique. Taylor had bought the thing at an auction. While he was cleaning it up and polishing it, he found the secret compartment. It was difficult to remove but the whole idea of a secret stash thrilled him. Every Saturday morning, he locked his office door and pulled the blinds. He removed the secret drawer and counted the contents. He added the weekly collection to it and made a careful note on the journal page. He didn't know what he was going to do with the money but he enjoyed having it. He wasn't a real big spender. Taylor received a good retirement check from Uncle Sam every month. He earned a good income from his tax service. He had a nice car – an Audi. He dressed well. He ate out frequently. He dated a little bit. His wife had left him years ago and he had no desire to re-marry. When he wanted sex, there was a telephone number that he called. The dating service would send over one of his favorites for a quickie. It was okay. He enjoyed it. But it wasn't as satisfying as his Saturday morning visit to the office to count the stash in the secret compartment!

He was just completing his count when he heard the door open in the outer office. What the hell? He knew he had locked it. He was positive.

He hastily pushed the money into the drawer and closed the secret compartment. He straightened up in time to see Clayton open his office door.

They stared at each other for a minute.

"How did you get in here? What do you want?" Taylor felt a little shiver of fear go up his spine. He was a small man - smaller than Clay.

"Do you remember me?" Clay asked.

"Yeah, I remember you. Look, if you have a beef, see an attorney. Okay? You don't have a receipt showing that the money was a deposit. My story is that it was for three months rent. If you elected to move early, that's on you. You can leave now. I'm busy." Taylor pointed towards the door.

Clay removed the pistol from his pocket.

Taylor's mouth opened wide and his eyes kind of bugged out. "You can't carry a pistol like that! It's against the law!"

"Really? I didn't know that." Clay was amused.

"What are you going to do?" Taylor demanded.

"Collect my money. With interest." The pistol didn't waver a bit.

"Okay! I'll give you a check for the deposit but I won't pay interest." He really wanted to get this guy out of his office. He didn't like the idea of having a gun pointed at him.

"I don't take checks." Clay said. "People can cancel checks. They can call the police, too. Like you said, my pistol is against the law."

"I won't call the police. It's just that I don't have much cash here. Only what's in the safe. Okay?" Now Taylor was starting to get alarmed.

"I'll bet you know exactly how much is in there." Clay smiled at him.

"Well, yeah, I do. There's nine hundred and twenty dollars. But, I'll tell you what. I'll get the money together and have it for you in cash next Saturday. Okay?" Taylor didn't like the calmness about Matthews. He remembered Clay's name.

"I don't think so. You may have the police waiting for me." Clay smiled at him.

"Look, let's work something out. I'm willing to bend over backwards to make things right with you. I'm sorry we had that misunderstanding about the deposit." Taylor was shaking.

"What would you suggest?" Clay sat down in one of the chairs and relaxed.

"I'm not a wealthy man, despite what you may think. I have a modest income from my tax service and the rent from the house, that's all." Taylor lied.

"Really? What about your retirement pay as a GS-14 from the government?" Clay was amused even more at this little weasel.

"Well, yeah, I have my monthly retirement check." Taylor

was shaking now.

"What about the income from the duplexes and the apartment building?" Clay threw the question at him. "And what do you do with the cash you receive each Saturday morning just before you come up here?"

"I'm willing to give it all to you if you'll leave me alone!" Taylor tried to bargain. Now he was really scared. "You'll never find it if I don't show you. It's not in the safe."

Taylor rushed over to the safe and dialed in the combination. When the final tumbler clicked into place, he threw open the door. He pulled out the cash drawer and showed Clay the small pile of bills that represented the $920.

"Looks like you're right. Okay, give me the rest of the money and I'll leave." Clay lowered the pistol slightly.

"Do you promise?" Taylor begged for assurance and the hope that he might survive.

"Cross my heart and hope to die." Clay quietly intoned the childhood oath.

Taylor crossed over to the desk and started to remove the drawer. His mind was in a blur. What was he going to do? He couldn't lose all of his money. If Matthews put the gun in his pocket when he handed him the money, he might rush him. The problem was that Matthews was bigger than he was. Matthews also looked trimmer than he remembered. He seemed so damn confident. He wished he had hidden a gun in the money drawer. He had seen that done in the movies. If he had a gun, he wouldn't be talking. He'd be shooting.

"This isn't fair!" Taylor cried out as he handed over the money.

"I know just how you feel." Clay said sadly. "I know exactly how you feel."

Clay extended his arm and shot Taylor in the face. Then he picked up the money and left. He had promised Taylor that he would leave if he got the money. He hadn't promised to let him live. Clay knew that it was a fine distinction in detail but figured it was something that an IRS auditor would appreciate.

Clay drove home. It was time to take Stanley for a walk. The little dog was kind of cute. When he went to bed last night,

Stanley was in his own bed on the floor of the laundry room. When he woke up this morning, Stanley was in bed with him. Clay had laughed and got up to feed him.

After he took Stanley for a walk, he would have to make a trip over to the Chesapeake Bay and dispose of the gun. He would call Joe and see if he wanted to have lunch at The Crab Shack. No, he shouldn't call him on Saturday. Sylvia took him shopping on Saturday mornings. He wondered if Stanley liked to ride in the car.

Later, he counted the money. There was $242,650 in the stack. Why was that little weasel keeping that kind of money in the office? Clay made a mental note to have Joe give it to a cousin for transport to the offshore account.

27 - The Police

On Monday morning, Clay was surprised to hear the doorbell. It wasn't Joe. Who could it be? Probably a salesman.

When he opened the door, there was no doubt in his mind that the stranger was a cop. They stared at each other kind of sizing up each other.

Clay saw a tall, lean man approximately thirty years old. He was well-groomed in a coat and tie but the clothes were worn and rumpled. The cop looked tired and a little worn in his facial features. There were squint wrinkles around his eyes and brows. He looked as if he had faced problems in the past and did not lack confidence in his ability to handle future problems.

"Mr. Matthews? Mr. Clayton Matthews?" The cop asked the question in a neutral voice as his eyes scanned the house interior over Clay's shoulders,

"That's me. What can I do for you?"

"I'm Lieutenant John Higgins, Homicide Department of the Montgomery County Police. I'd like to talk to you for a few minutes. Would you mind if I come in?" Higgins held up his badge for inspection.

"What's it about?" Clay tried not to be belligerent but he resented the police presence.

"Mind if I come in? It's awkward out here." Higgins tried a smile.

"I'm about to take the dog for a walk. You can come along." Clay reluctantly extended the invitation.

"Okay. Then we'll go inside to talk or you can come down to

the station." Higgins decided to tighten up the slack.

"Not voluntarily, Lieutenant. You'll have to arrest me." Clay drew the line in the sand.

"That can be arranged." Higgins met the challenge.

"Fine. I'll call my attorney while you go get some help."

"When I arrest you, I won't need any help, Mr. Matthews. Now back up. I came here to ask a few questions on an investigation. Why would you have a problem answering a few questions?" Higgins tried to give him some slack.

"I asked you what it was about and you gave me a ration of shit. If you're ready to quit playing your little police games, ask away."

"Sounds like you've had some problems with the police. Have you been arrested before?" Higgins knew that Matthews had never been arrested; he had checked before he came over here. The belligerence was puzzling.

"No. No problems. No arrests. No help either. Just another tax sponge."

"We're not getting off to a real good start here. I'm sorry if my sudden appearance on your doorstep startled you. As I mentioned earlier, we're conducting an investigation and your name came up. I just have a few questions. Okay?" Higgins knew that Matthews' reaction to him was not that unusual. It was a defense mechanism.

"Okay." Clay forced himself to relax.

"We're looking into the death of a Mr. Jerry Nagel. Did you know him?"

"No – can't say that I do. How did my name get associated with your investigation?" Clay looked at Higgins curiously.

"The records show that your insurance claim was one of his cases. He was an adjuster for Eastern Mutual Insurance Company." Higgins watched him closely.

""I had a claim with them when my house burned down. I don't remember the adjuster's name. I had a few other problems about that time. I settled with them as quickly as I could." Clay shrugged his shoulders.

"I had a look at the file. They weren't too generous with the settlement, were they?" Higgins considered himself a skilled interrogator. He would remember these conversations word for word.

"I guess it depends on how you look at it. I think I screwed up on some electrical wiring in my hobby room at the old house. They probably could have denied my claim completely. The adjuster —whatever his name was – was good enough to intervene between the company and me. I guess that's his job, isn't it? I mean to be the middleman and get the claim settled?" Clay looked Higgins in the eye.

"So he really did you a favor? And you don't feel cheated?" Higgins asked.

"Yeah, I think he probably did me a favor. I was disappointed at the time because I wanted the full claim. But my wife was sick and I didn't want the distraction of arguing with an insurance company. They have more attorneys than I have gray hairs. You know? And I knew they had a good point about the wiring. What the hell?" They had stopped so that Stanley could mark a telephone pole. Clay kicked some dirt around with his foot and looked at the ground.

"Yeah, I know what you mean." Higgins studied the man as he agreed with him. The guy seemed to be straightforward and sincere. Matthews came across as an honest, guileless individual.

"Are you employed now, Mr. Matthews?" Higgins inquired.

"No, not really, I'm not employed full-time. I received my pension plan benefits from my old employer in a lump sum. I had over twenty-eight years of service with them. Also, I received some insurance from my wife's death. I work about halftime at TV/Radio service work in a local shop owned by a friend of mine. It seems to be sufficient for my modest needs." Clay answered the question completely.

Actually, Clay had prepared for this part of the investigation as carefully as he had planned the assault on SCT. The offshore account provided a modest monthly income to Joe's Repair Shop. The shop paid a salary to Joe and Clay. The normal deductions were paid. Income tax, social security, and state taxes were paid.

The tax forms were issued and the tax returns would be filed. Joe and Clay were careful not to display a sudden increase in wealth. Both men continued making monthly payments on their home mortgages. Clay still drove the same car. He had one suit for weddings and funerals. They did not make any unusual purchases.

"Well, thanks for your time." Higgins started to turn away. "Oh, I wanted to ask you about Walter Farthington. You knew him, didn't you?"

"Yeah, I knew him. He had been our agent for a lot of years. I read about him in the newspaper. It sounds like the guy was a real playboy. He sure didn't look like a swinger. He was always so serious when I talked to him."

"Serious, huh?" Higgins looked at him thoughtfully.

"Yeah, the last time I saw him, he was very serious. We were talking about insurance and it seemed to me that he was very dedicated to his profession." Clay sparred.

"Okay. That'll be all, Mr. Matthews. Thanks for your time." Higgins walked away.

Clay and Stanley continued their walk.

Later, he fed Stanley and they watched some television together. Stanley curled up next to him on the couch. At bedtime, Stanley sat in the doorway and looked at him.

"Okay, get up here. But it's just for the night. Tomorrow you're going back to Joe. Got it?" He patted the bed beside him and Stanley settled in for the night.

Clay slept late the next morning. It was the first real good night's sleep for him in a long while. The first thing he saw when he opened his eyes was Stanley. He was in the same spot on the bed as when Clay went to sleep.

"Hey, pal, you did a real good job of guard duty. I'll tell Joe you're a keeper. You'll enjoy him." Clay reached out and patted his head. "Ready for some breakfast?"

The telephone rang just as he was getting out of the shower. Clay danced across the room trying to dry his feet and not fall on his face.

"Clay, this is Joe. I'm sorry to call at the last minute. Sylvia reminded me last night that we're supposed to go to New Jersey today. It's a birthday party for one of her cousins. We'll just be gone a day or two. Would you mind keeping Stanley for me? "

"How are you doing on getting her agreement to keep Stanley?" Clay got right down to the nitty-gritty.

"She's warming up to the idea. This will give me a couple of more days to set the hook. I think it'll be a go. Hey, thanks a lot, pal. I gotta run. I'll see you at the end of the week." Joe hung up. Clay listened to the dial tone for a minute thinking about the tone of Joe's voice. Stanley was sitting at his feet and looking up. His tail was wagging.

Clay looked at the little dog. He looked like he could understand every word. Stanley was really intelligent. Clay wondered how the little guy was coping with the loss of the Hanrahans. That evening he turned on the television and got involved in one of the programs. He found himself talking to Stanley and felt foolish.

On Thursday, he drove up to Frederick to put some flowers on Lydia's gravesite. It was easier to take Stanley with him than to worry about what time he would be returning to the house. Besides, Stanley seemed to enjoy riding in the car. He looked out the side window and kept his thoughts to himself.

At the gravesite, he placed the flowers on the ground tenderly. He hadn't been out here for awhile and a lot had happened. He didn't intend to review the events with her. He knew she would disapprove. It felt strange having Stanley along and looking at him. The little dog seemed to be asking if he could help in any way. Just to kind of let the little guy know that he appreciated the offer, he introduced Stanley to Lydia. Then he looked around to see if anybody was watching. He felt like he was losing it.

"Come on, Stanley. Let's hit the road before the traffic gets too heavy." Stanley whipped around on a dime and headed for the car. Clay laughed but he was amazed at how much the little charmer understood.

Clay watched a rerun of "Midway" that night. He liked World War II movies because they reminded him of his Dad. He patted the couch and invited Stanley to come sit with him. "It's our last night together, pal. Joe will be picking you up tomorrow." Stanley moved up beside him slowly and laid his head on Clay's lap.

"Hey, come on, don't be sad. You're going to like living with Joe and Sylvia. They're good people. They have a normal, happy home. It's a better place for you to live. Now perk up and watch the movie." Stanley grunted and closed his eyes. He wasn't having any part of what sounded like a snow job to him.

Joe called early the next day and the conversation was not good.

"I know what I said, Clay, but she won't have any part of it. She's allergic to animals and she says she has enough housework to do without having a pet around the house. What can I say? Look, if you can hang on to him until Monday, I'll be by to pick him up early to take him to the vet." Joe started to hang up.

"What do you mean "take him to the vet?" Clay was asking him.

"Well, I promised the Hanrihans that he wouldn't suffer or be turned loose on the street. The vet will put him to sleep. It's just a shot. It takes a couple of seconds. It's the best thing for him." Joe hung up the phone. He thought he heard some curses.

When the doorbell rang on Monday morning, Clay figured it was Joe playing it cautious about walking in unannounced. He planned to give the sorry asshole a good going-over.

He jerked the door open and started to cut loose.

It was Lieutenant John Higgins. Again.

"You look like you were expecting someone else. Sorry if I'm interrupting."

"It's okay. What's up? Did you solve your murder mystery? Excuse me, mysteries." Clay asked.

"May I come in?" Higgins asked politely.

"Yeah, I guess so. Act like a gentleman though or my attack dog will tear you apart." Clay answered the question with a chuckle.

Clay unhooked the screen door and John Higgins entered.

Like a typical cop, he looked all around the room very carefully. He was looking at and cataloging everything in sight.

"Have a seat, Lieutenant. Would you like some coffee or something cold?" Clay asked him automatically.

"No thanks. I'm okay. I had my daily allotment of caffeine at the office. I have a few more questions for you."

"Knock yourself out, Lieutenant. Stanley and I are innocent." Clay reached over and patted the dog. The tail wag speeded up.

"I understand that you used to work for Visorex Systems, Inc? Is that right?"

"Yeah, I worked there for about a hundred years. Why?"

"Sounds like it was not a happy experience?"

"Ah, you know, long and boring. A drudge job. What can I say? They're probably no different than any other beltway bandit."

"And you worked for Steve Johnson? Is that right?"

"Yep. You got it right."

"Did you read about his murder?"

"No, I didn't. I try to keep up on the news but well, you know. . . . ? If you don't work at a place anymore, you don't have the same interest. You said murder? Another gunshot victim like those two insurance guys?" Clay looked at him innocently.

"Actually, it was .... " Lieutenant Higgins stopped in mid-sentence and looked down at his pager on his belt. Clay saw him blanch. Then he stood up and seemed flustered. "I'll have to come back some other time, Mr. Matthews. I have a personal emergency." He turned for the door.

"Is there anything I can do, Lieutenant?" Clay was apprehensive. The man was very upset.

"No, but thank you, anyway. I should be used to this by now but it doesn't get any easier. I'll try to get back over tomorrow or the next day." Higgins opened the door and left.

An hour later, Joe came through the door. Clearly, he was not a man at ease. He was expecting a firestorm and Clay gave it to him.

"You sorry asshole! How can you take Stanley to the vet for

such a procedure? I thought you liked animals? I thought you liked Stanley?" Clay paused for breath.

"I do like animals and I like Stanley. But between the Hanrihans and Sylvia, I got myself in a box. What the hell do you expect me to do?" Joe spread his arms and pulled his shoulders up high in a typical Italian gesture.

"Well, you're not taking him! Even if you want him and Sylvia changes her mind, you're not taking him. Lydia and I are keeping him. You got that?" Clay was thoroughly pissed. All the more so because, down deep, he wondered if he had been conned.

"Lydia?" Joe asked.

"I took Stanley to Frederick with me over the weekend. He's so damn smart that I had to explain about Lydia. Then I told Lydia about Stanley. Aw, shit, Joe, I think I'm going batty." Clay shook his head.

"I understand, partner. I'm glad you're keeping him. You'll do each other a lot of good. Are you going to be okay?" Joe put his arm around Clay's shoulders.

"Yeah, I'm okay. What are you up to today?" Clay wanted to change the subject.

"I'm on my way to National Airport to pick up my brother. He's the one handling our offshore bank accounts for us. He's got some investment advice for us. We'd like for you to come over for dinner tonight. You're welcome to come to the airport with me, if you'd like to get out of the house for awhile." Joe was concerned for his friend.

"No, thanks. I think I'll stick around here. I'll take Stanley for a walk in a little bit. I'll see you at dinner though. About seven okay?"

"Yep. I'll see you then." Joe turned and left. Clay looked around for Stanley and saw him coming out from under the bed. He had been hiding.

Two days later, Lieutenant John Higgins of Homicide returned to complete the interview with Clay Matthews. It had taken most of one day to get his ailing son settled into the hospital for another round of treatment for Multiple Sclerosis. Every step of the way through the various hospital procedures, he ended up waiting an hour or two in some lobby or reception area while his son was tested in some way. In order to divert his thinking and worrying, Higgins turned his attention to his outstanding cases.

He was the primary police officer on three homicides in Montgomery County, Maryland. Those were the current ones. He had other cases that were older. At the morning staff meeting, he barely escaped receipt of yet another new one. This one was the shooting death of a tax accountant – a retired IRS government employee. One of the officers who had been audited during the last year wondered aloud if it were against the law to kill a tax auditor. The general opinion was that there should be a bounty on certain species to control the population growth. Everyone laughed.

Higgins thought about his contacts with Clay Matthews. He had a line to each of the three victims. From one viewpoint, it could be construed that he was cheated by each of the deceased persons. According to Matthews, he had no beef with any of them. The man sounded credible but coincidences were against the religion of any police investigator.

A background report on Matthews showed that his wife had died of cancer about a year ago. Well, cancer was a natural death. On the surface, there appeared to be no relationship to the subsequent deaths of three individuals on the periphery of their world. He was not finished with his investigation so he would have another interview with Mr. Matthews.

Clay opened the door after the first summons of the doorbell.

"Come in, Lieutenant. Believe it or not, I'm glad to see you." Clay closed the door behind him and gestured towards a chair for Higgins. "You seemed very upset when you left the other day. Is everything okay now?"

"Yeah, it's okay. My son is very sick and it's a long-term thing. He's had several emergencies. I keep reminding myself that I don't have a monopoly on problems. I realize you lost your wife last year. I'm sorry for your loss." Higgins extended his hand.

"Thank you. It seems that there is no shortage of problems. There's enough for everyone. I'll bet that you see enough of them in your everyday work." Clay paused to invite a response.

"Well, the situations that I deal with during the day are a little different. They are problems caused by people that end up harming other people. Things like cancer, multiple sclerosis, heart disease, floods, tornadoes, and some fires are acts of God. The police can't help with them." Higgins stopped before he got too far away from the subject of his visit.

"Interesting distinction, Lieutenant. But can the police really help with the problems caused by man? I'll agree that you can arrest the perpetrator – sometimes. And you can punish the perpetrator – sometimes. Can you prevent crime? Can you undo the results of a crime?" Clay told himself to shut up. The last thing he needed to be doing was having a debate with a police officer.

"I share your frustration, Mr. Matthews. The police try to establish a protective blanket over the populace using the laws of the land. We try to be visible and use punishment as a deterrent. Sometimes it works, sometimes it doesn't. It sounds to me like you have experienced some frustrations. Want to share? I have some doozies." Higgins smiled.

"I'd like that but why don't we finish your questions first and see where we stand? You were about to tell me about Steve Johnson's murder, weren't you?" Clay countered with a smile.

"Yes, I was. You asked if Johnson was a gunshot victim like Nagel and Farthington. He wasn't. He was strangled with a rope. It's known as a garrote. Did you see "The Godfather" movie?" Higgins asked.

"Yeah, I did see the movie. Sounds gruesome. Do you have many of those?" Clay asked.

"Not in this area. It's still popular in New York." Higgins replied. "Were you ever at Mr. Johnson's house? You know - a visit or a picnic or anything? Maybe delivered some papers?"

"Nope. Steve and I were not personal friends. I was never at his house for any reason. Why?"

"So there is no reason for your fingerprints to be anywhere

around or in the house?"

"No reason at all." Clay agreed.

"Would you be willing to give us a set of fingerprints, a DNA sample, and stand in a lineup? It would clear you of any involvement in Johnson's murder once and for all." Higgins played a trump card.

"You know, the offer is tempting. Like everyone, I want to see instant results. But, in real life, I know that entering the lion's den without weapons is foolish. If you're making an official request, I'll call my lawyer and follow his advice. But, I'll tell you what. Let's have a beer and if you want to sneak a glass into your pocket when you leave, I won't object. How's that?" Clay countered.

"Well, the beer part sounds good, at least. I'm finished for the day so it's time for a happy hour. Are you sure I'm not keeping you from anything?" Higgins was suddenly unsure that this was a good idea.

"Nah, not a bit. It's kind of lonely around here in the evening. I have Stanley now and he's great. The problem is that he doesn't talk much. Know what I mean? What about you? Are you going to be in the doghouse for being late?" Clay inquired.

"No, I'm not married. I've been divorced for a long time. My wife couldn't handle Billy's affliction. She tried but it just wasn't possible. One day, she wrote a note and took off. Probably for the best. We get along okay. He's a great kid. It isn't his fault, you know?" Higgins was staring into his beer.

"That's still tough. But you have your job and I gather that you like being a police officer?" Clay asked.

"I like being a cop very much. I wanted to be a cop for as long as I can remember. And the homicide department was my goal. I'm exactly where I want to be career-wise. At least for a little while. I've pretty much decided to resign. I have a chance at a much higher salary in industry and I need the money for Billy." Higgins found himself being completely honest with Matthews. The guy was easy and open. He was talking to a beer-drinking buddy now not a potential suspect.

"I thought the civil service insurance was a lot better than industry in most cases. Doesn't it cover the treatment costs?" Clay was very interested. This was the type of stuff he had gone through with Lydia.

"The insurance covers the treatment. Things like the doctor bills and hospital stays. It covers most of the medications but not all of them. It doesn't cover the home nursing, the extra housekeeping and a lot of things we need because I don't have a wife and Billy doesn't have a mother. My work hours are erratic and I can't leave him alone. He wanted a computer recently and I couldn't get him one. It broke my heart." Higgins remembered the bitter feeling in his heart.

"I gotta get out of the job." Higgins continued. "If I don't, I'll be tempted to start knocking down extra income like those two insurance assholes."

"You mean the adjuster and Farthington? How were they getting extra income?" Clay knew the answer but he wondered if Higgins had figured it out.

"They were knocking down some extra commissions on settlements. They would squeeze homeowners into a short settlement. In your case, you admitted that the company had a legitimate concern about the electrical wiring but, in most cases, the homeowners are entitled to a full settlement. I don't think they deserved to be executed but they should have been prosecuted. The police didn't know about the scam because no one complained." Higgins explained.

"Do you ever run into a case where someone really does deserve to be executed? A case where a victim is faced with a choice of either executing the swindler or letting it go?" This was hitting close to home but Clay would never again have a chance to discuss this subject with someone like a homicide detective.

"Yeah, I suppose so. In fact, several situations come to mind since you mention it. I know of a case right now of spousal abuse. The husband beats up on his wife every few months. He really hurts her. She won't press charges or leave him. She's a classic case. The wife's father is very wealthy. He wishes the CIA had an outside services department. He'd pay big money to have someone eliminate his son-in-law. I agree with him. It's the only way the problem will ever be solved. Otherwise, he'll be burying his daughter someday." They were into the second six-pack of beer now and the conversation was on a different plane.

"So why doesn't the father do the job himself?" Clay asked.

"He wouldn't have a chance of getting away with it. He'd be arrested in two minutes. Then his wife and daughter would be put through the wringer. He's better off hiring someone if he can." It seemed so clear and obvious to Higgins.

"So why don't you do it? Sounds like it would solve some of your money problems." Clay was amazed at the turn of the conversation.

"In this case, I could be tempted. I think the son-in-law will surely kill the daughter in the near future. But I have to think about Billy. I'm all that he's got." Higgins was staring off into space. Obviously, he had considered the proposition. Clay had a feeling that the father had propositioned Higgins.

Higgins looked at his watch and stood up. "I gotta hit the road. Billy is expecting me to come by the hospital tonight. Thanks for the beer. I hope I don't have to bother you anymore with questions about my cases."

Clay stood up and offered his hand in friendship. "I agree about the questions part but I enjoyed the beer and the conversation. Hey, I'm having some friends, Joe and Sylvia Colissimo, over for steaks on Sunday. You're invited to join us. They're good people and they helped me a lot when my wife was sick. How about it?"

"Well, yeah, if you're sure. I could come over between visiting periods at the hospital if that's okay?" Higgins was truly touched and very surprised.

"Sure, that's fine. By the way, where will you be working in industry? One of the beltway bandits? Not Visorex, I hope?" Clay laughed.

"No, not Visorex. It's a company called Signal Control Technology, Inc. – SCT. They had a big flap over there and the CEO is re-doing their whole security setup. I've been offered the top security spot because of my investigative background. He wants me to find the perpetrators of the damage at the plant. I guess it cost them a ton of money. Talk about wanting some payback? This guy really wants some payback." Higgins waved and started for his car. "See you on Sunday!"

After Higgins left, Clay went over to the Colissimo house and told them about the strange evening. Everyone agreed to sleep on it and try to figure out a solution to the SCT problem. Clearly, Jack Carter had decided to be a problem. He had not learned his lesson.

28 – A New Plan

On Sunday John Higgins came to Clay's house for a steak cookout. He met the Colissimos and played with Stanley. It was a very friendly atmosphere and everyone was comfortable. When he left, Higgins thanked everyone and said he could not remember a more enjoyable Sunday.

After Higgins' departure, Clay huddled with his old friends to find a solution to their new situation. Clearly, they would have to deal with Jack Carter, the CEO of Signal Control Technology, Inc. He had been warned and given an opportunity to keep his life. Since he chose to ignore the warning, he would have to pay the price.

Clay wanted to come up with a plan that solved Higgins' financial problems along with their problem. If they eliminated Jack Carter, they would probably eliminate Higgins' new job. Besides, Clay thought that Montgomery County, Maryland was better served with Higgins on the police force. And lastly, Clay was remembering the story of the abused wife with the rich father.

On Wednesday, Higgins was back at Clay's front door with more questions. Apparently, in a review of the records of William Taylor, the retired government tax auditor, the police discovered that he had rented a house to the Matthews family. The only reason for questioning the routine transaction was that Clay's name was in the computer as having a link to three other victims. After all, Taylor was a landlord with several rental properties. Since Higgins had interviewed Clay Matthews on the earlier occasions, he was assigned to question him about the Taylor case.

"How did you leave it with Taylor?" Higgins asked. "And how did you happen to meet Taylor? Did he advertise the house for rent?"

"Our house burned down, as you know. My wife was sick. We had just found out that she had breast cancer. We went to The Holiday Inn after the fire but it was expensive and we weren't comfortable. There was a notice on the bulletin board at Visorex about a house for rent. I called him and we made an appointment to see the house. That was the first time I had ever met him. We rented the house. End of story." Clay answered the question.

"The records show that you gave him a check for $3600 and lived there for one month. That's pretty steep rent, isn't it?" Higgins was giving him a chance to explain everything.

"Yeah, it was. But, at the time, we didn't know we would only be there for one month. Taylor was willing to rent it to us for $1200 per month if we guaranteed him a three-month minimum. That was pretty reasonable rent for a furnished, single family house in that neighborhood. We didn't know we would find this house in so short of a time. This house was ideal for us. It was close to our old house – less than a mile. The owner was willing to hold the mortgage so we were able to settle quickly. I was in a hurry to move while my wife had the strength to enjoy decorating this house. The only downside was that we had prepaid for three months at Taylor's house. I thought it was worth the money at the time. I still think it was a good deal."

"Still," Higgins reasoned, "it was a good deal of money. Did you ask Taylor for a refund or try to compromise in any way?"

"No. I didn't bother. Taylor struck me as a typical landlord. I didn't think he would budge an inch. Why should he? We made an agreement and he lived up to his end of the deal. If I lost $2400, it was my problem, not his problem." Clay watched Higgins closely to see if he was buying this story.

"Okay. I'll write it up. It sounds plausible to me." Higgins closed his notebook and stood up. He put out his hand to shake and prepared to leave. He turned to Stanley and said, "See you later, pal!"

"How's your son doing, John? Does he get to leave the hospital at all for home visits?" Clay was sincere in his interest.

"Sure, he can come home for several hours at a time. A lot of the time he prefers to stay at the hospital. He's pretty comfortable and they have a computer in the patient's lounge. We play monopoly or some game while he waits for a turn on the computer. Then I do paperwork while he takes his turn. It works out pretty good." Higgins appreciated Clay's interest.

"Where do you stand with your new job? Have you decided to take the offer?" Clay asked.

"Yeah, I guess I'll take it. The CEO upped his salary offer and tailored some benefits for me that will be good for Billy. He's sending me a letter. I have to give thirty days notice to the county." Higgins' attitude made it plain that it wasn't his preference but that it seemed to be the best thing to do.

"Why not bring Billy over here for a visit? He can meet Stanley and I have a computer. He can use it as long as he wants." Clay offered.

"Jeez, Clay, are you sure? I mean, I know Billy would enjoy it very much. So would I but do you know what you'd be letting yourself in for? He's in a wheelchair and needs help with all of his functions." Higgins was torn between wanting to accept the invitation and hesitating about sharing his problems.

"I'm sure, John. Bring him over. It'll be good for everyone. You'll see!" Clay clapped him on the shoulder.

Clay spent the evening in deep thought. Several times he consulted the calendar and scribbled some indecipherable notes. One of the unfinished details in his mind was the problem of Arthur Goodman, the Assistant Vice President at Visorex Systems, Inc. It would stretch credibility too far if something happened to Goodman – another acquaintance of Clayton Matthews.

Three days later, John Higgins received permission to leave work two hours earlier than normal. He drove by the hospital and loaded Billy into the van. He loaded Billy's wheelchair in the cargo area. They struck out for the Matthews house.

Clay saw them drive up so he went out to greet them. Higgins made the introductions and unloaded the wheelchair. As soon as they entered the house, Stanley came running up to see what was going on in "his" house. When he saw Billy, he gave a big "aarf" of greeting. When Stanley nuzzled his hand, Billy fell in love. He had never had a pet and it was magic to watch the bond between the boy and the dog grow during the afternoon.

Clay had fixed a casserole of chopped meat, pasta, tomato paste, cheese, onion, and Parmesan cheese on top. It was an old family recipe. It was easy to fix and everyone liked it. Within the family it was called the Queen's Goulash. After cooking the meat and preparing the pasta, the ingredients were mixed together and baked in the oven. The grated Parmesan cheese was served with each portion. There was a salad on the side and soft drinks for everyone.

Before dinner, Billy logged an hour on the computer. He visited two chatrooms on the Internet to say hello to some pen pals. Then he checked the sites for multiple sclerosis to check on developments. He opened the word processing program and typed a letter to his grandmother in California. After dinner, he played games. He was amazed that Clay, an "older" adult, would have all of the games on his computer. In short, Billy had a great afternoon. Although reluctant to leave, he was a good sport about it – particularly when Clay invited him to return as soon as his Dad could get an afternoon off. Billy's only question was to ask if Stanley would be there. The little dog had stayed by Billy's side for the entire afternoon.

When the van was loaded and they were ready to leave, Clay asked Higgins if he would have time to stop over in the evening. Although a little bit puzzled, Higgins agreed to return after he left the hospital.

Shortly after 7 PM, Higgins arrived at the Matthews house. He rang the doorbell and heard Clay's holler of welcome. When Clay came out of the kitchen, he was holding two cold beers. He handed one to Higgins and invited him to sit down.

"John, I've been thinking about all of the things we have discussed over the past few weeks. We've covered a lot of ground on a lot of subjects. Would you agree?" Clay looked at him seriously.

"Yeah, I guess so. Were you thinking about anything in particular or just everything?" Higgins was a little apprehensive.

"John, we can stop this conversation and still be friends. I enjoyed having Billy over here this afternoon. I would like to have him return. So would Stanley. If we go further, we'll cross a line that cannot be uncrossed. It will change our relationship. The change might be good or it might be bad." Clay paused to gauge the effect of his words.

"Well, you've got something big on your mind. I don't think it is possible to stop so you might as well spit it out." Higgins believed in the straight approach to problems.

"I've been thinking about the father of the abused daughter/ wife." Clay said.

"Really?" Higgins looked at him strangely. "And?"

"Would you help him if you could?" Clay asked.

After a long pause and thinking over his words very carefully, Higgins answered, "In this case, I would. The way it's going now, the asshole will surely kill the daughter sooner or later. We'll put him away but it won't bring the old man's only daughter back to him. But the law is helpless until a crime is committed and she won't press charges. She's terrified and traumatized. You can't believe the effect that such a trauma can have on a young girl."

"Actually, I can. I'll tell you a long story someday. But you're saying that you would help him if you could. You can't implement a solution directly because of Billy, right?"

"Right! I've worked the son-in-law over a couple of times and warned him. The last time I tuned him up, he filed a complaint on me. Nothing came of it but the boss told me to back off." Higgins remembered the conversation vividly.

"The problem in a situation like this is that the father doesn't know anyone he can trust. He might be set up by an undercover cop or ripped off by a crook. Right?" Clay looked at him for confirmation. Receiving a nod, he continued.

"The problem that someone able to help the father has is that he might be set up by the cops or ripped off. Agreed?" Clay paused and Higgins nodded again. He was fascinated and Clay could see the wheels turning.

"So what both parties need is a middle man that both parties can trust. Don't you think?" Clay presented his case reasonably.

Higgins nodded and swallowed hard. He knew exactly where this was headed.

They looked at each other.

The line had been crossed. There was no turning back for either of them. It was up to Higgins. The proposition was on the table.

"Will you be that middle man?" Clay forced the issue. There was no point in further delay. Like a parachutist leaving the airplane, there were only two possibilities. Either the parachute would open or it wouldn't. Higgins would say yes or no.

"Yes. I will." Higgins heard his own words hang in the air as if a stranger had spoken.

"Good! Let's get into some details. How much will the father pay?" Clay asked.

"As much as you ask." Higgins responded promptly.

"Let me put it another way. I understand his desperation and the fact that he is willing to pay anything to save his daughter's life. What can he afford?" Clay approached the issue from a different direction. And with the question, Higgins felt better about the whole situation. This wasn't a cold-blooded assassin in front of him. He was looking at a man who knew what it felt like to be desperate. He felt that Clay sincerely wanted to help someone.

"The father has made a lot of money on several business ventures. He owns a string of dry-cleaners and two service stations. He bought two McDonald's franchises in the early days. I don't have any idea how many businesses he owns a part of – he's wealthy. But let me do my part here as the middleman. What would you think of a half million dollars?" Now they were partners.

"That's fine with me." Clay responded. "Check with the father."

"I'll go see him tonight." Higgins seemed a little dazed.

"If he's absolutely sure he wants to go ahead, I'll give you instructions for him about how to pay the money. Okay?" Clay felt a little sorry for Higgins. His life had taken a major change tonight.

Higgins nodded. He stood up and left.

At midnight, the doorbell rang. It was Higgins. He had come from the visit with the father. Clay had fallen asleep so he was a little groggy. Stanley woke up and recognized Higgins as a friend so he laid his head down on the blanket.

Clay steered Higgins into the kitchen and poured them a glass of milk. He was glad to see that Higgins was calm.

"The father wants to proceed. He can have the money ready in cash within two days. I emphasized that you wanted to help him. I told him that if he couldn't afford the full amount, you would work with him. He was adamant that he could afford it. He kissed my hand and thanked me a million times. He made me promise to kiss your hand. Do you want your kiss now?" Higgins smiled.

"I'll take an IOU on the kisses. Are you convinced that he knows what he's doing?" Clay smiled at him.

"Yeah, he knows what he's doing. He's saving his daughter's life." Higgins responded strongly. "He offered to give you everything he owns and estimated his worth at twenty million dollars. It took me a half-hour to get him down to giving you two McDonald's franchises. For a while, I was afraid I'd be cooking hamburgers for you after work every night. Finally, I got him down to five hundred thousand dollars and he wouldn't go any lower."

"Okay, let's start moving. Tell me everything you know about the son-in-law. Where he works, lives, and plays. Give me an address and telephone number for him. I need a description. If you have a photo, get it to me ASAP. I want to move on this quickly. We'd all feel bad if we missed our chance to save the daughter by a day. When can you have the stuff for me?" Clay asked.

"I have it now. I picked up a picture at the old man's house. The rest of the stuff I can recite from memory. Ready to start?" Higgins smiled. "I thought of the same thing about the possibility of missing by a day."

They worked for the next three hours. Higgins recited everything he knew about Michael J. Sandford. Clay took notes in his own personal, strange shorthand that he had used since high school. When they finished, both men were exhausted. Stanley was still sleeping.

"Have the old man book a cruise for him and his wife. Have him call his daughter and invite her on the cruise. Tell him to offer her a $100,000 advance on her inheritance if she'll go with them. He should remind her of their age and say that it's a last cruise for them. Chances are that the husband will let her go along with them if he sees a chance to get some advance money. Tell him to go on the cruise whether or not the daughter can go. Got it?" Clay looked at him. It was important that all instructions be followed exactly.

Higgins nodded. He understood completely. He was committed. There was no hesitation or doubt in his eyes or his actions.

"Also, tell him that the money will be transferred to an offshore account. Here's the number and routing instructions for the money. I don't want cash. Suggest that he should wire the money from as many different accounts as possible. If Sandford wants the 100K up front before the cruise, have him suggest to Sandford that the money be paid into an offshore account. If the old man is questioned later about the transfer of the large amounts of cash, he can say he was ransoming his daughter from her abusive husband." Clayton paused. He was reviewing everything in his mind to make sure that nothing was overlooked.

"Okay!" Higgins acknowledged and left. It had been a big night for him.

Despite the hour, Clay picked up the telephone and called

Joe's brother. He gave him the details on Sandford and arranged surveillance on him. He turned out the light and went to sleep at 4 AM.

At 7 AM, Joe Colissimo came over for breakfast and a briefing on the Higgins meeting. After a discussion of the Sandford contract, they turned their attentions to Jack Carter and Signal Control Technology, Inc. Clay outlined a plan for Joe. At the end of the discussion, Joe looked at him in amazement. For the first attack on SCT, Clay had laid out a plan that resembled a movie script. He anticipated the dialogue and even predicted the look on Jack Carter's face when he was faced with the necessity of wiring a large sum of money within twenty-four hours with his own life on the line. But this plan was a masterpiece that solved all of the outstanding problems.

29 - Execution

Because of the high priority placed on the surveillance of Mike Sandford by Clay and Joe, an entire team of investigators went to work within hours of the telephone call. Sandford was followed when he left his house the next morning. A telephone center was set up to receive hourly reports on his actions and whereabouts.

Sandford's father-in-law called his daughter and made the invitation for the cruise. When she hesitated, he offered the $100,000 inheritance advance. He suggested to her that she mention the money to Sandford. She was to say that her father would explain if Sandford would call him.

Sandford knew he had the family over a barrel. The wife was terrified of him and he intended to keep her that way. When the old people died off, he was looking at millions. He had been wondering if there was some way to accelerate their departure from this world. This offer of the $100,000 was a gift out of the blue. He planned to call the old man and find out how many strings were attached to the offer. He knew one thing for sure – Mike Sandford always got his money up front.

When Sandford called the old man, the conversation was not friendly. The old man offered to pay the money when they returned. Bullshit! Mike wanted the money now. The old man suggested an alternative and said to take it or leave it. That pissed him off but there was little he could do about it now. Daddy-in-law said he would deposit the money in an offshore bank account. He would give him the account number and password when his daughter showed up at the dock. He asked Mike if he was familiar with an offshore account and, of course, Mike had to say he was. Actually, he didn't know anything about them except for some mystery novels. However, he had a bookie that was tuned in on all sorts of the high finance shit. He'd get the word from him and make the old man dance to his tune.

At Fran's Bar, Mike had to wait at the bar for over an hour before he got in to see the bookie. When he explained the deal, the bookie laughed at him. Mike gritted his teeth. The bookie explained that an offshore account was solid gold. The reason for going offshore was to evade taxes. If the old man gave him more than $10,000, it would have to be declared as income. Now he would be able to transfer the money out of the account in $10,000 chunks without any tax liability. The bookie told Mike to get an account number, password, and a telephone number to verify the account. On the first call, he could make a transfer and validate the account.

Mike called the old man back and agreed to his terms. However, he didn't want to go to the dock in New York City for the departure. Mike suggested that he meet them at National Airport tomorrow. The old man would get his daughter and Mike would get the account information. It moved up their departure by one day but so what? The family could afford an extra night in the big city. Mike was intending to do some serious partying during their absence. He was anxious to start.

Sandford met the family in the Red Carpet Club at the airport. Daddy was a big shot and belonged to several private clubs. When Mike received the account information, he went to a telephone and made the first transfer. It was easy. This was great. One telephone call and one password made $10,000. Fantastic! This was the life for him. The bookie suggested making a transfer every other day to a different account in the states. No problem. He waved goodbye to them as he left the club and said, "Bon Voyage!" with a sneer.

Since the big night at SCT that resulted in the death of Jonathan Claggett at the hands of Jack Carter, the surveillance effort had been scaled down dramatically. Clay and Joe wanted to keep a low-scale effort in place as a precaution. It was not realistic to tap the company telephone lines. It was much easier to tap Carter's home line. It was easy to review the tapes every few days and note any significant activity

As the Christmas season approached, the telephone logs reported that Carter's wife and kids would be departing on December 15 for Albany, New York. They would stay with the wife's parents through the holidays. Carter was supposed to join them on Christmas Eve and stay through the New Year.

The surveillance reports on Arthur Goodman, Assistant Vice President at Visorex Systems, Inc., indicated a dull, fastidious individual with few outside interests. He was married but he had no children. Mrs. Goodman was a Vice President at a local bank. Arthur did not have a girlfriend. Mrs. Goodman did not have a boyfriend. On the surface, they appeared to have a sterile existence. Neither of them had any local family members. There were no family pets. He did not belong to any clubs. If Goodman was not at VSI, he was working in his home office. The guy was a dull tool. The one opening was a two-mile walk in the morning and another one in the evening.

Clay had resigned himself to killing Goodman during the evening walk. He would try to get close enough to use a knife but, if necessary, he would use a pistol. He hated to risk alarming the neighborhood with the noise but it might be necessary.

The new situation with SCT gave Clay some new options. He had delayed killing Goodman because it would tie his name to yet another assassination in the local area. Four killings with one common name in the data bank was stretching his luck a bit too far. Jack Carter's decision to violate his "parole" could prove to be a fortuitous event for Clay and Joe.

*   *   *

By the time Mike Sandford's wife had been gone a week, he had transferred $40,000 from the offshore account. He had paid off his debt to the bookie and reclaimed his Rolex watch from the pawnshop. He had purchased a load of new clothes and shoes. Life was looking and feeling very good. Tomorrow would be another transfer day for money.

Tonight was another magic night with a new girlfriend. She was a cocktail waitress at the fancy lounge in the new Sheraton Hotel near the D. C. line. He had heard a few of the guys talking about the gal with the twin milking mounds but when he gazed at her tits for the first time, he wanted to post a "No Trespassing" sign. He wanted those tits as his private property. The lady was aware of her talents and, at the Sheraton, she did not lack for admiration or offers for either a short time or a long-term engagement.

Currently, Mike Sandford was the boyfriend du jour because of the size of his bankroll. She would be true to him as long as his money held out. When the money ran low or the boyfriend's generosity dried up, she would dump him.

For the past three days, Mike Sandford's schedule was to arrive at the lounge around 10 PM. He would nurse a drink or two until 1 AM when the lounge closed. Mike kept a sharp eye on any would-be poachers for his girlfriend. If a customer got a little bit too amorous or aggressive, Mike would warn him off. Most of the customers were traveling salesmen. They were not fighters; they were businessmen looking for a little action on a trip away from home. Mike looked like a construction worker wearing a suit. Usually a word from Mike was sufficient to cool the desires of these amateur Romeos.

Tonight was a little bit different. One of the customers was very aggressive with Mike's girlfriend. She never discouraged any proposition because she wanted to maintain her options for selecting the most profitable arrangement. When the new customer gave her a twenty-dollar tip for delivering one drink to his table, she gave him a big smile. When he tipped her a second twenty, she leaned over to give him an unlimited view of her tits. The customer showed his appreciation by flashing a roll of green bills and pulling off a fifty for her.

Sandford watched the action and began to fume. He didn't blame the girlfriend as much as he blamed the customer. On a trip to the men's room, he leaned over the customer's table and whispered a warning.

"Back off, pal! That's private property! You don't want to get hurt, do you?" Mike growled.

"Hey, don't get all bent out of shape. There's enough woman there for both of us. Tell me what room you're in and I'll send her over to you when I'm finished. If she can walk, that is. They don't call me Big Joe for nothing." The customer laughed.

"I'm going into the men's room for a leak; you'd better be gone when I come out." Mike turned around and walked away from the table.

Mike took his time in the john. He washed his hands and combed his hair. He wanted to give the stupid bastard time to think over his warning. If he wasn't gone when Mike came out, it was going to be a bloody scene.

When Mike opened the door of the men's room, he was met by the bartender/manager.

"I don't want any trouble in here. If you got a beef, take it outside. If you even raise your voice, you'll spend the night in the cooler. I've already alerted security. Got it?" The bartender was no midget.

"Yeah, I got it. Did you give that asshole the same good news?" Mike asked.

"He's not causing a problem. He's drinking quietly and playing a little grab-ass with Linda. That's her job. You're the one with an attitude. Maybe you should call it an early night." The bartender suggested.

"No way! I'm staying until Linda gets off work. If that asshole makes another play for Linda, I'll invite him outside. Okay with you?" Mike sneered and walked around him. As he focused in on the customer's table, he saw him tuck a one hundred-dollar bill into Linda's cleavage. The stupid bitch was smiling from ear to ear and letting him feel her tits. It was too much. He walked over to the table.

"I gave you fair warning, you fucking wop. Now I'm going to stomp your greasy ass. Meet me outside if you got the balls. I'm walking out now. If you don't show up in five minutes, I'm coming back in for you. I'll drag your ass across the lobby." Mike turned and left the lounge.

Big Joe Colissimo got up from the table and walked over to the bar. He motioned for the bartender. When the guy came over, he started to apologize. Joe held up his hand to stop him.

"There's no problem here. I think I'll get a breath of air and stretch my legs. You look like an intelligent guy with extremely poor eyesight. I wanted to contribute a few bucks to your medical fund." Joe counted out five hundred dollars and gave it to him. The bartender smiled.

Joe left the lounge and headed for the parking lot. When he exited the front door, he headed for the darkest corner. He didn't bother looking for Mike Sandford. He knew Mike would follow him.

"Hey, wait up! You're not going to get out of this, asshole." Mike was walking fast to catch up. He was surprised when the Italian-looking guy turned on his heel and waited for him. The guy looked a little bigger when he was standing up. Mike began to have second thoughts but he was committed now. If he backed down, the guy would return to the bar and claim his prize. Mike couldn't stand the thought of someone else fondling Linda's twin nipples and mounting her for the ride of a lifetime.

Mike was glad the guy had parked in a dark corner of the parking lot. He didn't intend to use any rules when he put him down. He would kick him in the balls for a start. When he got him on the ground, he intended to stomp him. If the big wop lived, he would remember this night for a long while.

Mike was within three steps of the guy when he started his run to launch a kick. When he threw his leg into the air, he was surprised to see the asshole sidestep. The next move was a blur that Mike felt more than saw. The guy grabbed his ankle in midair and pushed it straight up. The result was that Mike fell on his back. The fall knocked the air from his lungs. Then he felt something cold in his stomach. Then he turned hot all over his body. He was trying to get his breath when the big bastard stood up. He was holding a bloody knife and wiping it off with his handkerchief. He was looking around to see if anyone had witnessed the encounter. Mike started to scream at him. It was unfair to use a knife. It was against the rules. But he couldn't get his breath so he couldn't scream. And he was hurting all over now. Mike realized he was dying and it was really unfair. He had all the money in the world and Linda was waiting for him. The last thing Mike saw in his life was Big Joe Colissimo walking away.

When the hotel security patrol found Mike's body at dawn, they called the County Police. Later in the day, Detectives questioned the entire staff including the bartender and Linda, the cocktail waitress. Mike was identified as an occasional customer. No one remembered him meeting or talking to anyone.

30 - No Forgiveness

On December 15th, Jack Carter left the office at noon. He was driving his wife and kids to National Airport for their Christmas trip to New York. His wife was anxious to see her parents. The kids were anxious to see "Gramps and Lolly" as the old folks were called. The trip gave him an opportunity to drive the new Mercedes Benz Sedan. The new model was an absolute delight to drive. It was roomy on the inside and everyone was comfortable. The luxury car gave him a bit of an edge when he double-parked at National Airport. The airport police force was the most politically aware law enforcement group in the world. It seemed like a politician could park an RV in front of the main terminal for the duration of a thirty-day trip if desired. The only reason a politician wouldn't use the loading zone as long-term parking was that they had a special, no-charge private lot immediately adjacent to the main terminal. On the flip side, a passenger driving a Ford or Chevrolet could barely coast to a stop near a terminal building before being warned off. Such is life in the nation's capital.

On the way to the airport, Carter's wife was oohing and ahhing over the Christmas decorations. The kids were fighting in the backseat and wondering what presents they would receive for Christmas. Carter was wondering if he could wrangle a congressional license plate from their congressman. The company's contributions to the political war chests had increased dramatically over the past five years. It seemed to Jack that you ought to get something for your money. None of the passengers paid any attention to any of the others. Carter dropped them off in front of the terminal and turned the luggage over to a redcap. He was anxious to return home. It was the height of the football season and the Washington Redskins were riding high. Carter was betting a ton of money on every game. The girlfriend would be in town tomorrow.

Joe Colissimo and Clayton Matthews watched the big Mercedes exit the Carter driveway. They waited thirty minutes to see if the family might return for some forgotten item. When it looked clear, Clay drove into the driveway. Joe pushed open an unlocked window in the garage and crawled through the opening. Joe pushed a button to open the garage bay that housed the familiar Chevrolet Suburban. He entered the house through the garage entry door and immediately heard the alarm system beep and relay instructions. "Disarm system now!" Joe punched in the PIN number as reported in the surveillance reports. The alarm system dutifully reported that the system was disarmed.

Joe found the key rack inside the pantry door and lifted the keys to the Suburban. He backed the Suburban belonging to Jack Carter from the garage and drove off to complete his mission.

Clay pulled the rental Suburban into the garage. He exited the vehicle and closed the garage door from the wall button. Then he entered the home and settled down to wait on Jack Carter. Clay spent part of the waiting time reviewing his plan. It still seemed good and everything was working. So far!

Arthur Goodman pulled on his jogging clothes and put on his Nike shoes. He was preparing for his nightly two-mile jog/walk. The nightly ritual was almost sacred at this point. If he didn't do it for some reason, it threw his system completely out of balance. He hated to travel on business trips because it disrupted his routine. Mostly, he was senior enough so that he could assign business travel to an underling. Also, he felt that promotions were won at the home office not on field trips. He was so tired of the "Assistant" in front of his title. He felt that his promotion was long overdue. Well, he would think about it on his walk tonight. Perhaps he could come up with a solution.

Goodman left through the front door and headed down the driveway. He increased his pace slowly and controlled his breathing. Later in the walk, he would pay closer attention to his heart rate monitor. He tried to maintain a steady 130 beats during the last half of the walk.

Less than half a mile from his driveway, he was startled to see a dark-colored Chevrolet Suburban headed directly for him. Crazy drivers! What the hell was he thinking of? He was even more startled when the big vehicle stopped beside him. The driver rolled down the window on the passenger side and addressed him.

"Are you Arthur Goodman?" The driver demanded.

"Yes, I am. Who are you?" Goodman was apprehensive. He could not imagine what this was all about or who the dark, heavy-set driver could be.

"I'm from Visorex. I have an urgent communiqué for you. Hop in!" The driver was holding up a business size envelope.

"Just give it to me." Goodman stretched his hand through the window.

"No way, pal. You have to sign for it. If it's bad news, you may deny receipt later. Like I said, hop in!" Joe Colissimo held up a clipboard for his signature.

Although somewhat leery of the entire scene, Goodman opened the passenger door and climbed into the vehicle. He thought he might know what the contents of the envelope were. It could be his promotion. God, it was time. His wife never said anything directly but it galled him that she was a Vice President and he was an Assistant Vice President.

Colissimo looked around when Goodman closed the door. There was no one in sight and the nearest house was over a hundred yards away. He closed the electric window from his side of the vehicle. Then he turned to Goodman and pulled the.32 caliber revolver from his pocket.

"Due to the NAFTA agreement, Visorex has decided to terminate your employment." Joe shot him two times in the chest. Death was immediate but Goodman had time to be startled by his termination.

Joe pushed the body down on the floor and drove out of the area. He maintained a legal rate of speed as he headed towards the Carter house.

When Jack Carter pulled into his driveway, he scanned the house and grounds. He was a careful man after the trouble with those two madmen. He blamed Jon Claggett for the entire mess. Stealing the invention from them was a major error. But it was Claggett who made the error – not him. Claggett deserved just what he got. Carter couldn't believe the way they coerced him into killing Claggett. He had watched the tape and was horrified. However, he believed that if any intelligent law enforcement officer should ever view the tape, the coercion would be obvious. No one would believe that he killed Claggett except under extreme duress. It was sort of a justifiable homicide. Like self-defense. If he hadn't killed Claggett, they would have killed him. Oh, sure, they made it sound like it was about money – like he did it to reduce the payment from ten million dollars to two million dollars. But he knew better. He knew they would have killed him if he hadn't killed Claggett,

They would not get away with it. Carter knew that he had too much money and power. And the Germans were behind him. He hadn't told them the complete story. Certainly not the part about the invention or the killing of Claggett. The Germans did not need to know the details. When he explained the need to upgrade the entire security system and locate the perpetrators, they approved a huge budget to get the job done. Finding John Higgins, the homicide detective, was a stroke of luck. With his investigative experience, he would be able to find Clayton Matthews and Joe Colissimo. Once Higgins was on the payroll, he would be able to control him. The man was desperate for money so that he could care for his son. The whole thing was coming together.

Everything looked normal at the house so he actuated the garage door opener. As he pulled in, he glanced around. The Porsche was in the stall next to his Mercedes. The Suburban was next to the Porsche and his wife's station wagon was in the fourth stall. He closed the garage door before he exited the Mercedes. When the door was fully closed, he unlocked the Mercedes door and exited the vehicle. He hurried towards the house door while the light was on. He was rushing for the door to beat the light timer when he realized that something was wrong. Something troubled him.

He opened the entry door to the house and turned towards the alarm panel to deactivate it. It was not armed. Oh, shit! His wife must not have set the alarm system when she left the house. She was the last one out. He'd kick her ass up between her shoulder blades for being so goddamn stupid. He headed for the family room trying to figure out what else was troubling him.

When he turned on the lights in the family room, two things leaped into his mind – that wasn't his Suburban parked in the garage and Clay Matthews was sitting in his recliner chair. Fear flooded Carter's body. He felt weak. He started to shake. He tried to speak but only stammered.

"Why are you here?" Carter managed to ask. "I did everything you asked. Didn't you get the money? I wired it into the account number written on the paper. If you didn't get it, it's not my fault. I still have the piece of paper you gave me. I carry it in my wallet." He pulled out his billfold and removed the piece of paper. He waved it at Matthews.

"That's interesting. I wondered if you would save that piece of paper. Let me see it." Clay stretched out his hand towards Carter. Reluctantly, Carter surrendered the paper. To his dismay, Matthews stuck it in his shirt pocket.

"I thought you were an intelligent guy." Clay said as he continued holding the .45 caliber automatic pistol on Carter. "I thought you understood what would happen if you didn't follow instructions. I was convinced that Claggett was the primary thief of our invention."

"I did everything just as you instructed." Carter had to sit down. His entire body was shaking. He could not take his eyes off the gun. He remembered the loudness of the warning shot Clay had fired at him.

"No. You didn't drop the matter and chalk it up to experience. Your arrogance and stupidity led you to planning some revenge on us." Clay accused him in a quiet voice.

"As far as I'm concerned, the whole thing is history. I've learned my lesson. I'll never cheat anyone again. That one time was Claggett's idea. What else can I say to convince you?" Carter was pleading.

"Why did you hire Lieutenant John Higgins of the homicide department to head up your new security detail? Why did you tell him you wanted to track down the perpetrators who destroyed your computer system? Why did you tell him you wanted some payback?" Clay looked at the startled man sitting in front of him.

"Did you think we would go away without keeping tabs on you? The only place I don't have a wiretap is up your ass." Clay continued with an increasingly angry voice. He cocked the pistol and raised his arm towards Carter.

"No! Please No! I won't make another mistake. Please don't." Carter was crying. "I can get you some more money. I have a new budget with some discretionary funds. No one will ever know. I'll do anything."

Both men raised their heads at the sound of a garage door opening. A minute later, Joe Colissimo entered the room. Joe seemed startled to see Carter.

"We gotta get going, Clay. Why is this piece of shit still alive? I thought you were going to waste him?" Joe seemed indignant. Carter was horrified. These thugs really did mean to kill him.

"Did you pick up the other package?" Clay asked.

"Yeah, sure, he's in the car." Joe answered.

"Carter says he is willing to pay us more money and he's willing to do anything we ask. How about that?" Clay looked at Colissimo. Everything was going as planned.

"Yeah, right. And you're willing to trust this asshole again? He's had his chance. Drop him and let's hit the road." Joe sneered.

"No, wait! It's true. I can get you another two million dollars. That's good, isn't it?" Carter clasped his hands together in an effort to control the shaking.

"It's not enough to save your life." Clay spoke quietly and menacingly. "But I'll tell you what I'll do. There's another piece of shit in the car that betrayed us. He's going to die tonight regardless. If you'll take care of him for me and wire us two million dollars again, I'll give you another chance."

"Okay! Anything you say." There was no hesitation this time. "Give me the pistol."

"Not so fast. What about Higgins? I don't want him hired to track us down." Clay looked at him.

"I won't hire him. I promise." Carter crossed his heart with the fingers of his right hand.

"You've already sent him a written offer. How can you rescind it?" Clay asked.

"Easy! I'll send him a letter and explain that there's been a change of plans. I'll offer to reimburse him for any financial damage he may have suffered. There won't be any problem." Carter tried to reassure these madmen.

"I don't know." Clay hesitated. He looked around the room. "I don't trust you to send out the letter when you return to the office. Do you have a computer here?"

"Yes. I have my laptop computer in the bag on the floor. I have some letterhead stationery. I'll print it out and you can mail it. How's that?" Carter realized he was on trial for his life. He was trying to be sincere. He was remembering how it felt when he killed Claggett. Now he was going to have to kill again in order to save his own life. Would it be easier to kill a stranger? His stomach was churning. He swallowed hard to keep everything down.

"Well, let's try it and see how it looks. Go ahead and type out a letter." Clay motioned towards the computer.

Carter jumped up and ran towards the computer case. He opened the case and removed the computer. He set it up on the table and ran a cable to the printer while the computer was booting up. When the computer was ready, Carter typed quickly. He read what he had typed onto the screen and saved the document to a file. Then he printed out a copy and handed it to Clay.

Clay took the letter slowly with a look of doubt in his eyes. He wasn't going to make it too easy on Carter. He didn't want to seem like he was letting him off the hook too quickly. He looked at Joe and Carter followed his eyes. Colissimo looked even more doubtful but he seemed to indicate that it was up to Clay. Carter swallowed again. These lunatics did not seem to be in a hurry. No wonder! They seemed to know everything in his life. They probably knew he wasn't expecting anyone tonight.

December 15, 1992
Lt. John Higgins
110 Onyx Road
Rockville, MD 20852
Dear Lieutenant Higgins:
Due to a change in plans, I am forced to rescind the recent offer of employment. I apologize for this inconvenience. I am instructing the payroll department to forward a check equal to three months pay as a severance package.
If you feel that you have incurred any further financial damage, please call me.
Very sincerely,
Jackson Carter
Chief Executive Officer

"Well, that might work." Clay conceded. "Go ahead and sign it."

When Carter signed the document, he handed it to Clay.

"I noticed that you called up another document before you started this one. What was it? The original offer of employment to Higgins?" Clay hoped that he had guessed correctly.

"That's right. I needed the address for Higgins." Carter was starting to breathe normally again.

"The man you're going to kill for me is named Arthur

Goodman. Does the name mean anything to you?" Clay asked him.

"No. I've never heard the name." Carter answered firmly.

"He works for Visorex Systems. You know them, don't you?"

"Yes, of course. We do some business with them. They're one of our customers." Carter was puzzled.

"I want you to substitute Arthur Goodman's name on the letter you sent to Higgins. I'll dictate the address. Then print it out." Clay directed.

"Why? I don't understand! I have no intentions of hiring him and besides, he'll be dead." Carter protested loudly.

"Why? Because I want you to. This is one of those things you promised when you said, "I'll do anything!" Remember?" Clay leveled the pistol again.

"Dammit, Clay! Quit screwing around with him. He's not worth it. Do him and let's go." Colissimo interjected.

"No! Wait a minute. I didn't mean I wouldn't do it. I just meant I didn't understand. Give me the address and I'll do it. Okay?" Carter turned to the computer and prepared to type. Clay dictated the name and address. When he finished the typing, Carter printed the document and handed it to Clay.

December 15, 1992
Mr. Arthur Goodman:
2913 Mailers Path
Gaithersburg, MD 20944
Dear Arthur:

In accordance with our discussions, I am confirming my offer of employment as Vice President – Internal Security for our Company.

The salary will be $96,000 per year payable semi-monthly. You are entitled to a company car and country club membership plus other benefits standard for an officer of the company.

I have attached a special rider to your medical benefits package that will address your special concerns.

I hope this offer is acceptable. We're looking forward to having you aboard. Please let me know as soon as possible.
Very sincerely,
Jackson Carter
Chief Executive Officer

"Very good. Sign it and we'll be on our way." Clay waited for the signature and return of the document. He motioned for Carter to stand up and pointed towards the garage.

The three men went through the garage to the driveway. Carter saw his Chevrolet Suburban standing there. Joe got into the Suburban and drove down the driveway towards the road. Clay motioned for Carter to start walking down the driveway.

"We're going to meet Joe down the driveway a bit. You can take care of this business for me and we'll bury his ass in the woods on your property. Ain't that a gas?" Clay laughed.

Carter was thinking furiously. Obviously, these two killers had set him up again. They had the whole thing planned out. There were no spur-of-the-moment decisions taking place. This was a carefully planned operation. Regardless of what it was, he could not see any way out of it. At least for the moment. He had to do whatever was necessary to live.

It didn't matter what he had to do. He had enough money to hire the best lawyers available. But first, he had to survive. He gritted his teeth.

Joe was standing next to the big Suburban on the passenger side. The door was open and he could see a pile of something on the floor. Carter was sickened when he heard Joe's words.

"I had to put a slug in him to keep him quiet. Looks like the asshole is unconscious. You better hurry up and plug him or he'll die of old age." Joe grinned at him and held out a .32 caliber revolver. Clay moved up behind him and jabbed him with his .45 automatic.

"Take the gun and keep it pointed towards Goodman. Fire one bullet into him. Keep the gun extended towards him and I'll take it from your hand. If you deviate one inch, I'll kill you. Got it?" Clay jabbed him again with the pistol.

Carter grunted his understanding. He took the gun from Colissimo and pointed it towards the hump on the floor of the vehicle. He pulled the trigger and was startled by the explosion. He kept the gun extended until Clay took it from his hand.

Colissimo moved forward and dragged the body from the vehicle. He pulled it into the woods. Carter was surprised to see the beginnings of a hole in the ground. Beside the hole in the dirt was a videotape. He wondered what…. ?

Clay held the .32 caliber revolver next to the right temple of Jackson Carter and pulled the trigger. It took less than a second. Carter's body dropped to the ground. He was dead.

Joe drove the Suburban back to the house and switched it for the rental Suburban. Then he drove back and picked up Clay. While Joe was switching the vehicles, Clay was arranging the crime scene. He planted the two letters in Carter's coat pocket. Due to the fallen leaves, there were few identifiable footprints. The videotape was next to Carter's outstretched hand. He nodded to himself and joined Joe.

The two men were silent during the drive to Clay's home. They were physically and mentally exhausted. The only good thing about the gruesome events of the day was that all of the loose ends were tied up. Clay had completed his mission of demanding retribution for past injustices. Visorex, SCT, the Insurance Company, and the Landlord. It was all done. And along the way, he had engineered a solution for an abused wife and worried father.

Now Clay was anxious to get home to Stanley.

31 – The Day After

The day after the murders was a depressing mess. Clay didn't see or hear from anyone. He knew Joe intended to return the rental Suburban and spend the day with Sylvia.

The weather was dark and overcast. It looked as if the Washington area might get its first snowfall of the season. The house felt cold even though the thermostat was cranked up to a toasty seventy-six degrees.

Stanley stayed close to Clay and followed him from room to room. At one point, Clay scooped him up into his arms and hugged the little guy.

On Thursday the 17th, John Higgins called. He wanted to visit Clay at his house.

When Higgins arrived, he was puzzled and a little bit shook up. On the one hand, he wanted to know everything about everything. An inner voice was whispering that it would be better not to know too much. A lie detector cannot detect a lie if the person under test doesn't know any details.

Clay invited him into the house and offered him a beer. They stared at each other waiting to see who would break the silence. Finally, Higgins spoke.

"The police discovered the body of Mike Sandford. They are completely stymied. He was stabbed in a parking lot. There were no witnesses. Not even a whisper of a clue. The body was not discovered for at least eight hours after death." It appeared that Higgins was struggling to determine how he felt about all of this stuff. Was he admiring? Disgusted? Scared? What?

"By a strange coincidence, I received information that an

offshore bank account that I control has been credited with half a million dollars. I took the liberty of setting up a fund for Billy in the amount of $250,000. You are the executor of the fund. You may draw out any amount of money at any time for any purpose. The mission statement of the fund says that the money is to be used for anything that will improve Billy's quality of life. It states that you are the sole arbiter of what will improve his life. Here are the papers with the account numbers and the procedure for withdrawing funds. If anyone checks on the source of the funds, it will look like Billy's grandparents set up the fund." Clay stopped to let Higgins absorb the information.

Higgins was staring at him with an open mouth and glazed eyes.

"I didn't know you were going to do that. I don't know what to do or say. My God, Clay! What should I do?" Higgins was dumbfounded.

"Well, I suggest that you start spending some money to improve Billy's life. I suggest that you do so discreetly and quietly. There's no need to raise any alarm bells. Okay?" Clay smiled. "For instance, I suggest a full-time housekeeper for you and Billy. Also, he needs a full computer system at home. You should consider some modifications to your house to accommodate Billy's wheelchair. How's that for a start?"

"I'm staggered, Clay. This will change our lives but I have mixed emotions on several fronts. I'm supposed to be a police officer. I'm sworn to protect all of the people – not just the ones I like or approve of. And now I'm benefiting from the death of a citizen. It's a lot to absorb." He looked at Clay searching for answers.

"Well, let me summarize the situation. A girl's life has been saved. A father is grateful to have a daughter to love for his few remaining years. Billy's life has been improved. Your life has been improved. I'm richer by a goodly sum of money. And the world population of violent psychopaths has been decreased by one. Does that sum it up?" Clay smiled.

"Yeah, I guess it does. Now I have only one other situation to be resolved. I wrote a letter of acceptance to SCT and a letter of

resignation to my boss. I need to withdraw both of those letters."
Higgins was scratching his head.

"I suggest that you do nothing on either item for a few days. I
believe they will be resolved. You need to keep your wits about
you and use your cunning. You have done no wrong. Nothing
can be proven even if something is alleged." Clay looked the
younger man in the eye.

"Clay, I will do anything for you that I can but please
understand that my first thought must be of Billy." John had a
sad look on his face.

"I understand. I would have it no other way. Tell the truth at
all times and stand tall. You have nothing to be ashamed of and
you are guilty of no crime." Clay smiled.

After Higgins left, Clay sat in the living room staring at the
bird feeders. He knew Higgins was apprehensive but, in Clay's
opinion, there was minimal danger of detection. During the
planning phase, Clay had researched the crime statistics for the
nation, several metropolitan areas and Montgomery County
in particular. The so-called "closure" rate on homicide cases
was abysmally low. Nationwide, murder cases had a slightly
higher than 50% solution factor. Some cities were as low as
23%. Montgomery County had 102 murders during the last year
reported. Their solution rate was 63% - one of the highest in the
nation. In other words, they solved approximately 2 out of every
3 murders. An in-depth analysis showed a different picture.
Most murders are done by a member of the family or a close
friend. Usually the police had a good theory about the murder
within 24 hours. The chances of a solution diminished greatly
when a stranger or distant acquaintance committed the murder.
Particularly if the murder weapon was not recovered. In cases of
murder for hire, money trails or telephone records would lead
the police to the family member who benefited the most. Clay
avoided these mistakes. He created an alibi for the time of the
crime. The only concern in his mind was a preponderance of
circumstantial evidence pointing to him because of his presence
in several cases over a relatively short time.

In the case of Mike Sandford's execution, Clay had attended a lecture at the local Wild Bird Center store. He signed the register, asked several questions during the lecture and purchased several items on his credit card. He had not made any contact with Sandford, the wife or the father. The money had been paid into an untraceable offshore bank account. He had similar alibis for the times of the Nagel, Farthington, and Taylor murders. For the raid at the SCT facility, he could prove that he was with Joe Colissimo and his family at a family celebration.

On Friday the 18th day of December, the nation's capital awoke to a new layer of snow. Most of the schools closed and the government announced a generous leave policy. Those employed by industry crowded the highways and cursed the delays. State highway workers smiled and dreamed of the many ways to spend the overtime pay. Airlines delayed flights at every airport East of Chicago.

And the Internal Affairs Department of the County Police Department rang John Higgins' doorbell at 7 AM. He was already dressed and preparing to leave for work. The two officers showed their identification and asked if they could enter the house. Higgins replied that they could enter if they agreed to have a cup of coffee with him. They smiled and agreed. Higgins put on a fresh pot to brew. He removed some homemade Banana Nut bread from the refrigerator and set up the toaster. One of the nurses at the hospital had made it for him yesterday. She had mentioned that she was almost as good a cook as her mother and smiled.

Over coffee and snacks, the two officers questioned John Higgins about his relationship with Jackson Carter and Signal Control Technology, Inc. John told the truth, the whole truth, and nothing but the truth. He explained the offer of employment and showed them the letter confirming the offer. Mr. Carter had asked the officers investigating a major break-in and fire at the plant for a recommendation of an officer with a background in investigative techniques. Higgins' name had been mentioned.

After two interviews, an offer of employment was made at an attractive salary. Higgins had accepted.

Did he know the nature of the break-in and fire at SCT? Only the bare essentials, Higgins assured them. It was not his case and he had enough cases without being curious. They laughed. Perhaps it should have been his case, suggested one of the Internal Affairs Officers. What about the missing sales manager, Jon Claggett? To the best of Higgins' memory, Claggett was listed as a missing person. Higgins reminded them that he was in the homicide department.

What was the attraction of being employed at SCT? "Money," confided Higgins. "No one knows better than us that the county is not a generous taskmaster. Right? Better hours. How many times have you failed to show up at a special dinner? Oh, yeah, we've all been there. Right?"

"Now what's this all about? Am I so valuable to the county that my resignation is the subject of an internal investigation?" Higgins asked.

"Late in the evening on the 16th a young lady of Mr. Carter's acquaintance drove to his house to meet him. Mrs. Carter and the children were out of town. When she pulled into the driveway, the garage was open and many lights were on. She stopped to see if something unexpected had occurred. Like maybe the wife had returned. She noticed something in the woods near the driveway and turned the car to shine some light on the object. It turned out to be Mr. Carter. He was dead. She called 911. Because of some of the crime scene evidence, we were called in to investigate." The IAD Detective finished the narrative.

"Since it was a homicide, I'm surprised I wasn't notified." Higgins looked at him.

"The evidence at the crime scene involved you so you were isolated from the case."

"Aha! The plot thickens. What was the evidence?"

"A letter addressed to you and signed by Mr. Carter."

"Well, the only letter I have ever received from Mr. Carter is the one I showed you."

"This was a different letter dated on the 15th of December and signed by Carter. It rescinded the offer of employment to you. Any comment?"

"The first one that comes to mind is SHIT! I think I'm unemployed." John looked disgusted.

"Do you know a Mr. Arthur Goodman, Detective?"

"Not in connection with SCT or Carter. I have met and interviewed a Mr. Arthur Goodman at a company called Visorex Systems. He's the supervisor of a Mr. Steve Johnson. Johnson was murdered a few months ago and I'm the primary detective on the case."

"Mr. Goodman of Visorex Systems was found beside Mr. Carter. He had been shot three times and was very dead."

"Jesus! What's the connection? Have you found out?"

"A second letter at the scene was addressed to Goodman and signed by Carter. The wording is identical to the letter offering you a job. He was offering your job to Goodman."

"What? No way! The Goodman that I interviewed would not be a good candidate for a Security job. The guy was an office type that would faint at the sight of a gun."

"Where were you on the night of December 15th, Detective?"

"I checked out of the bureau about 4 PM. I got to Holy Cross Hospital about 4:30. I was at the hospital until about 10 PM. I drove directly home and watched the 11 PM news. Then I turned in." Higgins answered after giving the question some thought.

"Can anybody verify your presence at the hospital?" One of the IAD Detectives asked.

"Yeah, several people. I waved to Mrs. Pryor in the gift shop and also to Mrs. Griffee who was at the reception desk. There's a nurse on my son's floor that shared some conversation with me on and off throughout the evening." John smiled at the thought of the conversation. He and Susan were starting to form an attachment.

"Are you involved with the nurse?" The Detective had not missed the little smile.

"Not yet. Is there anything else?" John started to stand up.

"Yes. Have you ever met a Jonathan Claggett?" Neither of the Detectives showed any indication of being in a hurry.

"No, but I know the name. He's the missing sales manager. What about him?"

"The ground seemed to be disturbed around the crime scene. We called in the dogs and followed their lead. We dug up the body of Jonathan Claggett."

"Jesus, it sounds like a massacre out there. Were there any other bodies?" Higgins returned to his seat.

"No, but there was some interesting evidence. As a homicide detective, you'll be fascinated. There was a .32 caliber revolver at the scene. It had been fired four times and the ballistics matched the three bullets in Mr. Goodman's body. The gun had Mr. Carter's fingerprints on the handle. There's more. Carter had gunpowder residue on his hands. Also, there was a .38 caliber revolver in the hole with Mr. Claggett's body. Claggett was killed with a bullet from it. The handle was covered with Carter's fingerprints. Lastly, Carter was killed by a .32 caliber bullet to the right temple. The bullet was from the same gun. There were no other foreign prints at the scene or in the house. And the crowning gift – are you ready for this? – We found a videotape showing Carter executing Claggett in the computer lab at SCT. The time and date stamp on the tape is the same date as the fire at SCT."

"Sounds like a TV show. You didn't happen to find a coil of small diameter rope in Carter's pocket, did you?"

"No. Why?"

"Steve Johnson was strangled with a small rope. A garrote. I thought maybe you might solve one of my cases for me. Just wishful thinking."

"Sorry, Lieutenant. No garrote. There was only one strange inconsistency." The Detective paused and scratched his head. "The bullets in the two revolvers were hand loads. Neither Carter nor Goodman had any hand-loading equipment or any other weapons in their homes. Both of the wives deny that their husbands had any interest in weapons."

"Thanks for your cooperation, Lieutenant. We'll write this up but I don't see anything for you to worry about. Have a good day!"

*   *   *

John Higgins drove to the station house deep in thought. When he walked into the squad room, he was summoned by his supervisor.

"John, I'd like for you to meet Mr. Robert Maxton and Mr. Allen Stark. They are attorneys representing the Eastern Mutual Insurance Company. They are here to discuss the cases of Mr. Nagel and Mr. Farthington. Gentlemen, this is Lieutenant John Higgins. He is the primary detective on both cases. "

"Lieutenant Higgins, have you made any progress on the cases?" Mr. Maxton's question was asked in an offensive tone of voice.

"If you're asking if we've solved the cases, the answer is no." John answered.

"Why not? It's been long enough. Do you think the cases will be solved?"

"We're doing our best. We certainly haven't given up." Higgins answered calmly.

"We have a press conference scheduled for 3 PM this afternoon. Can you be there to answer some questions from the reporters or would you like for us to quote you?"

"I'll be there and ready to answer questions for the reporters. You said 3 PM? Where is the conference being held? Would you like to use our conference room?" Higgins was eager and ready.

"I'm surprised, Lieutenant. I wouldn't think you'd want to tell a bunch of reporters that you haven't made any progress on solving the murders of our two employees."

"I didn't say I hadn't made any progress. I said we haven't solved the cases. We have made some progress. We have discovered that the two employees were involved in numerous cases of fraud. They would pressure families that suffered a severe loss into taking a reduced settlement. I have a list of fifty people that feel they deserved to die. It seems that your company offers a bonus to agents and adjusters who secure reduced settlements without incurring a lawsuit. I have documented evidence of more than twenty cases over the past three years. I suspect that the fraud reaches back further than three years and involves other agents and adjusters."

"You can't say that. That's libelous."

"No, it's the truth. I suggest that you review your position on the press conference, gentlemen."

"I'd like to see the evidence of this fraud."

"I'm not in the habit of showing my case file to an insurance company lawyer. You'll see it when we go to court to prosecute the murderer or if we decide to prosecute your company for fraud."

"What?" Maxton and Stark screamed in unison.

"I'll be forwarding my files on the short settlements to the District Attorney. It will be up to them about any prosecution." John looked at the two weasels. They would think twice before they threatened him with a press conference again.

"Someone from our office will be in touch with you. In the meantime, we appreciate the information and your cooperation." Maxton said coldly. The two men left.

"John, you are a piece of work." The Captain laughed. "I'm going to miss you."

"Well, Captain, I was hoping we might talk about that little thing."

John cleared his throat nervously. This was not going to be easy.

"What 'little thing' would that be, Lieutenant?" The Captain leaned back in his chair. He knew what was coming and he intended to enjoy it.

"My resignation letter. I've been having some second thoughts, you know?" John felt a nervous sweat on his brow.

"Are you referring to the letter written in ink and boldly signed with a flourish? The one that was thrown down on my desk like a gauntlet? Is that the one you're having second thoughts about, Lieutenant?" The Captain looked at him sternly.

"The very one." John knew he would pay and pay and pay for his indiscretion. He sighed.

"What would you suggest I do with the letter, Lieutenant? I

mean, other than the obvious?" The Captain enjoyed watching Higgins squirm. This was great.

"I was hoping you might find your way clear to tearing up the letter, Captain, Sir." John felt like he now knew the true meaning of groveling.

"Why would I even consider such a thing, Lieutenant?" The Captain looked at him in amazement. Like he would never consider such an action.

"It would be an opportunity for you to retain the services of an Ace Detective, Sir." John was sitting up straight in the uncomfortable side chair.

"Hmm. There's a lot of Ace Detectives around here. They solve murder cases and perform other functions." The Captain smiled fiendishly.

"What other functions are you referring to, Captain, Sir?" John was inwardly groaning.

"The important things in life, Lieutenant. Like washing the Captain's car. Like shining the Captain's shoes. Like supplying the Captain with a beautiful virgin from time to time. Those kinds of things, Lieutenant."

Both men were laughing loudly by this time. The captain stood up and offered his hand to John. "Welcome back! Now get the hell out of my office and do some work for a change."

As he left the Boss Man's office, John thanked his lucky stars. He enjoyed being a Police Officer. There was a lot of bureaucratic bullshit and some politics but he loved it. He believed that it was truly an opportunity "To Serve and Protect" his community. He was proud of the job and his part of it. The homicide department was charged with the responsibility of speaking for the dead. Many people did not understand the importance of or even the need for someone to speak for the dead. Lieutenant John Higgins did.

"Joe, I think we need to have a long lunch at the Crab Shack across the bay. But this time, you're going to have to park on the bridge – not just slow down." Clay was disgusted with himself.

"Why? What's up, Clay?" Joe was puzzled. He knew of no reason to dump anything over the bridge railing.

"A little bird told me that the cops are puzzled about the hand-loaded ammunition used in the Carter-Claggett-Goodman deaths. Since my name is in the computer, I think it would be a good idea to dispose of the remainder of my weapons and the hand-loading equipment. Damn, I hate to do it. My father spent years collecting this stuff. And I enjoy messing around with it. It's restful for me. And a lot of the equipment isn't manufactured anymore. I hate to get rid of it and, even worse, I hate to think of destroying it." Clay looked miserable. "On the other hand, I don't want the stuff around here in case the cops show up with a search warrant."

Joe thought about the situation for a minute. Then he hit on an idea.

"I know. Let's rent a van and drive the stuff up to New Jersey. You can store it at my cousin's place. He has his own workshop and does hand loading of ammunition. He'll enjoy storing it for you. And when you're ready to get it back, it'll be there for you." Joe was proud of coming up with a solution.

Clay smiled. It was the perfect solution. He put his arm around his friend's shoulder. "I didn't know you had a cousin in New Jersey."

Both men laughed until the tears came.

At 2 PM on Christmas Eve, John Higgins handed an envelope to each of the Conner sisters. The envelopes contained a Christmas card and a hundred-dollar bill. John had hired the sisters to care for the house and do some cooking. They had prepared a beautiful dinner for John and his guests who were due to start arriving at any time now.

"It's time for you ladies to skedaddle and care for your own families. I can do the rest. Thank you so much for your help." John helped them with their coats. "The turkey looks beautiful and the pies smell wonderful. I may have to sample everything before my guests arrive." Everyone laughed. The sisters were delighted with their new job. It was close to their homes and Lieutenant Higgins seemed like such a nice man. And a Police Officer, too. It was such a shame about his son but they would see that father and son had a clean, comfortable home to enjoy.

The first guest to arrive was Susan Heche, a nurse from Holy Cross Hospital. "Am I too early?"

"Nope. Just right. The other guests aren't here yet and Billy is taking a nap. He wants to stay up late tonight." John loved the smell of her. "Let me have your coat."

"Are you sure you want me here tonight? Christmas Eve is traditionally for family and close friends." Susan was feeling insecure.

"Having you here is the rightest thing I've done in a long while." He put his arms around her and kissed her on the forehead. "Come on in and help me set up for dinner."

At 4 PM, the doorbell rang again. It was Joe and Sylvia Colissimo. Standing behind them on the porch was Clayton Matthews and Stanley. Everyone had a big smile on their faces. Coats were collected and introductions were made. Billy heard the noise and rang his bell. He wanted some help with his wheelchair so that he could join the group. He heard his new best friend let out a big "Aarf!"

The evening revolved around Billy. He was the action center – the pivot point. Billy was so excited that he didn't know what to do first. Stanley demanded first attention from Billy so the adults had a chance to settle into a comfortable level with each other. John was beginning to realize how far he was committed to Clay and Joe. At first, it was a little scary but he was becoming more comfortable. They were partners. He trusted them. And one of the reasons that he did trust them was that they gave him their trust first – even before he realized the full scope of their relationship.

Billy was eager to show "Uncle" Clay his new computer system.

"It's just like yours, Uncle Clay, except that I got the color ink-jet printer. You don't mind that I got the same system, do you?" The thought had suddenly occurred to him. "Can you show me what they mean in this manual on writing software in C language? I'm really stuck."

Higgins looked over the group and knew the real meaning of the Christmas spirit. These people were his family. They were a group of misfits who depended on each other. Clay had lost his wife and daughter. Even Higgins, the hardened homicide cop, had to shake his head in frustration when he heard the story of Clay's daughter and the added blow of the breast cancer that claimed his wife. And there was Joe and Sylvia. They were from large families but they were on the fringes of their families. For whatever strange chemical imbalance, they didn't quite fit the New Jersey Italian Mafia mold. Somehow they had managed to find each other but now they had an expanded family with Clay and Billy and himself.

The big question on this chilly Christmas Eve was Susan. Was she the soul mate that he was missing in his life? They were moving closer to each other with every conversation, every touch and every kiss. She was going to be sleeping over tonight. He had made up the guest bedroom but he hoped she would share his bed. In the meantime, there was Billy and his friends to share a Christmas Eve dinner.

Everyone was happy and in good spirits when they sat down for dinner. Everyone was laughing. John started to carve the turkey and Billy grabbed his arm.

"Dad, we haven't said the blessing yet." Billy was insistent.

"Okay, son, do you want to do the honors?"

Billy nodded and bowed his head. He raised his head just enough to make sure that everyone else complied.

"Thank you, God, for our many blessings. Thank you for our food and our home and my Dad. Thank you for Stanley and Uncle Clay. Thank you for Uncle Joe and Aunt Sylvia." He stopped and hesitated. He raised his head a notch and peeked. Everyone else was peeking, too. They were looking at him when he added, "And Dad and I both thank you for Susan. I'm the luckiest kid in the world. Amen." And the little boy in the wheelchair raised his head and said, "Let's eat."

Billy was amazed to see that every one of the adults was crying big tears. Go figure.

"Lieutenant, please summarize your cases for the group and share your conclusions. Maybe we can learn something or add something." The Captain sat down and turned the floor over to John Higgins. It was the monthly departmental review session.

"We've had some bizarre developments since the last departmental meeting. Some of the items are still being sorted out. Here's what we know:

Jack Carter, the CEO of Signal Control Technology, shot and killed Jonathan Claggett, the Sales Manager of SCT. Apparently, he shot him in the computer lab at SCT. He transported the body to his estate in his Chevrolet Suburban. We found hair and blood evidence in the vehicle. He buried the body on the grounds. In the hole with the body, we found the murder weapon – a .38 caliber revolver. The weapon had Carter's fingerprints on the handle and barrel. There is a ballistics match between the weapon and the bullets recovered from Claggett's body. We found a videotape showing Carter shooting Claggett. There was a copy on the ground near the burial site and another copy in Carter's home office. The tapes were made on two different video cameras. The date stamps on the recordings coincide with the date of a fire at SCT that destroyed the computer lab and a great deal of equipment. We don't know the who or the why on the arson. There is no explanation about why he recorded the killing. We have not recovered the cameras. The ammunition used in the revolver was hand-loaded. We have not located the site of the reloading.

Jack Carter abducted and killed a man named Arthur Goodman, an Assistant Vice President at Visorex Systems, Inc. According to the Medical Examiner, Goodman was killed by two bullets from a .32 caliber revolver. Sometime after occurrence of death, Goodman was shot a third time with the same gun. We believe the third shot is an indication of the anger and frustration of the killer. Carter transported the body in the same Chevrolet Suburban to the same spot on his estate. Apparently, he intended to bury Goodman's body next to that of Claggett. We recovered the .32 caliber revolver at the burial site. Carter's fingerprints were all over the weapon and he had gunpowder residue on his hands consistent with the loads in the revolver. Once again, the ammunition was hand-loaded.

Jack Carter probably committed suicide. We found his body at the burial site for Claggett and the intended burial site for Goodman. Carter died from a .32 caliber bullet entering the right temple. Carter was right-handed and, as I mentioned, he had gunpowder residue on his right hand. The angle of the bullet path is consistent with a self-administered wound.

Steve Johnson was an employee at Visorex Systems who worked for Arthur Goodman. He was murdered at his home in Upper Montgomery County. He was garroted with a small diameter rope. We have not been able to establish a link between Jack Carter and Steve Johnson except that they both knew Goodman. We found a coil of clothesline in the Carter garage consistent with the size of rope used to garrote Johnson. The ME was not able to recover enough fibers from the wound on Johnson's neck to match the clothesline in the garage. In Carter's library, we found a much-read, dog-eared copy of "The Godfather" and several murder mysteries. None of this is enough evidence for court but it is enough to convince me that Carter probably killed Steve Johnson in addition to Claggett and Goodman.

Our status report to the District Attorney currently stands as listing Carter as a suicide and the murderer of Claggett and Goodman. Our report will say that Carter is the probable killer of Johnson.

On other cases, we have the open cases of Jerry Nagel and Walter Farthington. Both men were employees of The Eastern Mutual Insurance Company. Our investigation shows that these men were pressuring insurance claimants to accept short settlements. They usually offered 50% of the claim as a settlement.

They received a substantial bonus from the company for each settlement. The bonus program was open to all employees but not widely touted. Nagel and Farthington discovered the incentive a few years ago and ran with it. The insurance company has discontinued the program. We have referred the matter to the District Attorney for their decision about prosecution of the company. We know that the company is sending representatives to victims of the program in an effort to compensate them. They are hoping to limit the lawsuits. The chances of clearing these two homicides are remote. We have very little evidence. There are probably 50 to 100 people with reason to kill them. Any one of them could have done it or hired it done.

Lastly, we have the open case of William Taylor, a tax accountant, landlord, and retired government IRS tax auditor. Taylor kept a large sum of money in his office. That was probably the reason for his murder. He was hated by his tenants and probably by every citizen he ever audited. He had no will and no living relatives. The State will inherit his assets. Chances of clearing this case are remote.

That's all I have, Captain. Any questions? Any suggestions will be gratefully received."

"John, is there any information about the amount of money in the Taylor case?" The question came from one of the police officers in the audience.

"It was definitely in the thousands, maybe even a hundred thousand or more. Taylor used to collect the rents from his eight-unit building every Saturday. He warned them that if they didn't pay on Saturday, he would evict on Monday. We found his bank statements and he did not deposit those receipts. He must have been hoarding the money in the old safe in his office. It was open and ransacked." Higgins reported.

"The guy sounds like a real sweetheart. The world is really going to miss him."

"Now, now, gentlemen," joked the Captain, "Let's not talk about justifiable homicide of civil servants and assholes. The police department is already shorthanded."

Everybody laughed and filed from the room.

32 - The Settlements

In mid-February of 1993, Clay Matthews was sipping a cup of coffee and watching the bird feeders when the two well-dressed men walked up to his front door. They didn't look like cops but.....

Clay answered the door and the older one introduced himself and his associate as being from Eastern Mutual Insurance Company. Could they come in?

After some hesitation, Clay invited them into the house and indicated a couch. He was not openly unfriendly. He adapted a neutral attitude. He did not offer them a cup of coffee.

"Mr. Matthews, the company has been reviewing your case file and the claim you filed when your house burned down. I'm sure you remember the incident." The agent started.

"I do have some vague recollection of the "incident" as you call it." Clay said coldly.

"I apologize, Sir. I didn't mean to trivialize your loss. I understand how you feel, believe me." The agent stammered.

"When did your house burn down?" Clay asked.

"Sir?"

"Well, you said that I could believe you know how I feel. When did your house burn down?"

"Ah, no, sir. I didn't mean it in the literal sense. I'm sorry." The agent was desperately trying to recover.

"Why don't you just say what you came for and quit shuffling your feet." Clay was out of patience.

"Sir, during a review of your case, we noted that you received $140,000 against a claim of $280,000. Our review board feels the settlement was too low. I'm authorized to pay you the remainder of your claim." The agent smiled. Surely the man would be a little friendlier now.

"So you're here to do what? And in return for what?" Clay asked.

"I'm here to pay you the balance of $140,000 on your claim. Naturally, we would require a release from future claims." The agent smiled nervously. This visit wasn't going real smooth.

"My claim was for a replacement value which was estimated to be $280,000 last year. Not this year. I also claimed $4500 for reimbursement of living expenses." Clay was beginning to take a real dislike towards this pipsqueak.

"Oh, yes, I see now that the file does include a claim for the $4500. We can include that amount today. I suppose we can make an adjustment on the amount in view of the elapsed time. Let me see. ... if I figure 8% per year and.... " The agent was scribbling on his notepad.

"Will you want my wife's signature on the release?" Clay asked.

"Yes, of course, Sir. Your wife is listed on the claim." The agent smiled.

"She's in Frederick, Maryland now." Clay said.

"Is she living up there, sir?" The agent was puzzled.

"No, she's dead up there." Clay looked at the agent with distaste.

"I'm very sorry, Sir. The file didn't list her death. According to my report, there were no injuries in the fire." Now the agent was sweating. Of all the cases in the area, how in the hell did he end up with this nut?

"She died of cancer. Her death was accelerated due to the stress of the fire and dealing with your company." Clay accused.

"Sir, I am very sorry for your losses. I feel like we have intruded on your grief. I would like to settle this matter. Suppose we round off the amount to $200,000 to cover the living expenses and the delay. I believe that's more than fair. Would that be satisfactory to you?" The agent was thinking that this guy was really bad news.

"You guys never learn, do you? You had an opportunity to make an equitable settlement but you came out here prepared to screw me out of the $4500 living expenses if you could. No wonder life is so dangerous for insurance agents." Clay smiled grimly.

"Sir, if you could give me a figure that would represent an equitable figure for you, maybe I could do something." The agent realized that trying to overlook the $4500 was a major mistake on his part. He was going to get a severe reprimand if it got back to his office.

"Take a deep breath and adjust your thinking to seven figures!" Clay said quickly.

"Sir, I am authorized to go to $500,000. That's our limit." The agent couldn't believe it. The day had started out so well. The first family had been so agreeable and willing to settle.

"It's not going to happen, sonny. Tell your boss to send out the seven-figure adjuster or plan on meeting me in court. By the way, how's the fraud investigation going?" Clay set the hook.

At the same time on the following day, an older man approached the front door and rang the bell. Clay invited him in and offered a chair. He asked him if he would like a cup of coffee. The man accepted.

"I'm sorry if our representative riled you yesterday, Mr. Matthews." The older agent opened the conversation.

"I gather that you're a seven-figure man?" Clay smiled.

"Well, let's say that I am authorized to be as fair as possible." The agent returned the smile.

"Five million dollars." Clay said.

"Excuse me?" He gawked at the man in front of him. He must have heard it wrong.

"Five million dollars." Clay repeated the number quietly.

"Sir, I'm prepared to offer up to one million dollars."

"That won't do. I thought you wanted to settle everything. The material loss, living expenses, stress, effect on my wife, delay in settlement, fraudulent actions, etc." Clay offered.

"We would require a release on all matters. In view of your loss, we will go as high as two million dollars." The agent bartered.

"I would have thought that you would want a confidentiality agreement, too." Clay smiled again.

"Yes, we would want a confidentiality agreement. I believe three million dollars could be arranged." The older man intended to fire the young agent as soon as he returned to the office.

"I will accept three million dollars if you can offer a check right now. If there has to be a delay, you'll have to negotiate with my attorney. I'm meeting him this afternoon so I can give him your card." Clay sat back and looked out at the bird feeders. Mr. and Mrs. Cardinal were back but he hadn't seen the woodpecker in several days. He started thinking about the cardinals. He sort of remembered reading that they mated for life. Why weren't humans like that? That's the way it should be. Clay was startled when the man touched his arm.

"Excuse me, Mr. Matthews. Are you okay? I have your check for you and the release papers are ready to sign." The agent handed him a pen.

Clay looked at the check. It was typed out to him and the amount was three million dollars. The guy must have made it out in advance. Clay wondered how many checks he had in his briefcase. Clay figured there were two more checks – one for four million and one for five million dollars. Oh, well. He leaned back in his chair and began to read the agreement carefully.

After he signed the agreement, the agent packed up his papers and prepared to leave. As he offered his hand, he remarked, "Well, I guess you won't have to see your lawyer today, will you?"

"Actually, I was seeing him on another matter. I'm buying some property in Frederick County. I had no intention of talking to him about your company." Clay smiled.

The agent paled. He couldn't wait to return to the office and fire that young asshole.

After the man left, Clay looked at his watch. John and Billy were picking him up in a few minutes. They were looking at property suitable for a camp for handicapped kids. He felt a pressure on his leg and looked down. "Come on, Stanley. You're invited, too."

During the drive to Frederick, John Higgins mentioned that he had received telephone calls from almost all of the families that he had interviewed during the investigation of the Nagel and Farthington deaths. All of them had received settlements on their claims.

"You should feel good that your investigation led to a settlement for them." Clay observed.

"It wasn't my investigation that led to their settlements. Those swindlers would have continued cheating people until they died of old age. Someone stopped them cold and gave the police an opportunity to shed some light on their schemes. Occasionally the law needs a helping hand." He smiled at Clay. "By the way, did you settle with them?"

"Can't say." Clay smiled.

"Can't? Because of a confidentiality agreement? Hmmm." Higgins thought for a minute. Then he asked, "When we talked about this camp for the kids, you said you would put a million dollars into the fund. How much would you consider putting up today?"

"I could go as high as four million dollars today." Clay answered.

"That was a nice settlement." Higgins whistled aloud.

"No wonder they call you a detective." Clay laughed.

33 - New Faces

Kurt Steiner stepped off the mobile lounge and into the customs area at Dulles International Airport serving the Washington, D. C. area. It felt good to stretch his legs and be off the airplane. He grabbed a luggage cart and collected his bags. He joined the shortest line and waited patiently. When it was his turn, he presented his papers to the immigration officer. They were completed meticulously. Kurt Steiner was a patient and meticulous man.

"How long will you be in the United States?" The officer asked.

"Four months." Actually, Steiner was not completely sure. He was here to take control of their subsidiary company, Signal Control Technology, Inc. He knew that the immigration officer was not interested in the details. He simply needed an answer to write down to prove that he had asked the question."

"Tourist or business?"

"Business."

"You're in sales?"

"Yes." Close enough, thought Steiner.

"Your forms indicate that you have nothing to declare. Is that correct?"

"Yes."

"Open the small bag, please." Steiner complied. The officer poked around and indicated that the bag could be closed. Then he turned and started stamping the passport and visa.

"Have a nice stay, Mr. Steiner." The officer turned towards the next passenger.

Steiner exited the customs area and walked directly to the rental car desks. At National Rent-A-Car he signed for a Volkswagen Jetta. He received maps of the local area and directions to his hotel in Rockville, MD.

On Monday morning, Kurt Steiner drove to the SCT building. He was pleased to see that the reserved parking place for the CEO was unoccupied. He parked and entered the building. After establishing his identity, the Chief Financial Officer was called. The CFO escorted him to the large corner office that would be home.

Kurt Steiner was a Managing Director at the large International Systems, Inc. building near Munich, Germany. He was one of many holding this position. It was the equivalent of Vice President. After weeks of meetings and discussions, Kurt was selected to take control of SCT. The US subsidiary represented ten percent of their gross sales and over twelve percent of their profits. In the past year, SCT had been the fastest-growing segment of the company. It was important for the home office to feel confident that the profitability would continue. Steiner felt that he had to understand the reasons for the growth and the reasons for the recent tragic events. Kurt had met Jack Carter on numerous occasions at the company headquarters in Munich. Although his exposure to Carter was limited, he found it difficult to believe that Carter would kill two, maybe three, men and then commit suicide. He was determined to find out the truth. He summoned the CFO to his office.

"I've reviewed the financial performance of SCT for the past fiscal year. A growth rate of 8% plus the reported profitability is very impressive. Now I would like to have the story behind the numbers. In the face of a declining international economy, how did SCT manage to grow and be profitable?" Steiner asked the CFO.

"Mr. Carter and Mr. Claggett made a good team. They planned an aggressive effort and worked hard. They motivated the rest of the work force and we responded to their efforts. I'm not sure what else there is to say." The CFO was extremely nervous.

"I'm going to visit the washroom. I'll be a few minutes. I

recommend that you take the time to review your position with the company. I am the CEO of SCT now. You work for me. When I ask you a question, I demand the complete truth. When I return, you have an opportunity to start again. If you ever hesitate to answer me or lie to me again, you will be summarily dismissed." Steiner left the room.

When Steiner returned, he took his chair behind the large executive desk. He straightened a few things on the desktop and then looked at the pencil-pushing bean counter in front of him. He raised his eyebrows in a silent question and nodded for him to begin.

"A few years ago, we were facing a downturn in our traditional product sales. The outlook was bleak and I anticipated some layoffs. I prepared a business plan and a projected earnings report for Mr. Carter. He was very upset and called Mr. Claggett to his office. They were in a meeting for four hours. I don't know what transpired. I was told to delay my report for a few weeks." The CFO was sweating. He had dreaded this day of reckoning.

"Mr. Claggett gave some drawings to our engineering and production departments for a new product within two weeks of their meeting. They launched an advertising campaign and the product was rushed into production. Sales of the Model 900 High Voltage Control System exceeded our expectations. The product accounted for almost 20% of our total sales. That's about all I know of the matter." The CFO collapsed back into the chair.

"Was Mr. Claggett an engineer by education?" Steiner wanted to know.

"No."

"How did he come up with the design of a new and revolutionary product?"

"I'm not sure. I heard one of the secretaries describe a meeting with two gentlemen about a product that SCT evaluated. There was an argument and Mr. Claggett told them to leave the building." He was searching his memory for details. The CFO had a good salary and a company car. He had four daughters approaching college. He could not afford to be without a job.

"Is there a possibility that the new product was pirated from these two gentlemen?" Steiner was incredulous.

"I believe the possibility exists. It has happened on an earlier occasion."

"So Claggett had a history of pirating ideas and Carter had a history of approving the action?"

"Yes, Sir."

"What do you know about the fire in the computer lab and the recovery of the backup tapes? I thought you had custody of the backup tapes?" This question had been bothering Steiner since he heard the original story of the fire.

"It was my job to take the backup tapes to the bank each night for safekeeping. I would pick them up in the morning. Due to a heavy workload during the last quarter of the fiscal year, I was unable to leave my office before the bank closed. I explained my problem to Mr. Carter and he approved leaving the tapes in my car overnight." This was a bad news scene and the CFO was nervous.

"And?" Steiner prompted.

"On the night of the fire, the tapes were stolen from my car. I had arrived home from the office very late and my daughters had used the spaces in the garage. I parked my car in the driveway." Now it was all out on the table.

"So it was the tapes stolen from your car that Carter ransomed?"

"Yes Sir."

"Who do you think stole the tapes and received the ransom money?"

"I don't know. My best guess would be the two gentlemen who suffered the loss of their stolen product. But my guess doesn't agree with the police evidence on the murders and suicides."

"What about those two men from Visorex Systems?"

"I have no idea or even a wild guess. The whole thing was so violent and complicated that I am at a loss."

Steiner swiveled his chair and looked out of the window for a few minutes of deep thought. When he turned around, he riveted the CFO with his eyes.

"I want the names of the two individuals in the meeting with Claggett. You are not to discuss the matter with anyone else but me. Do you understand completely?" Steiner demanded.

"Yes Sir." The CFO stood up and left the room.

Clay Matthews had added a new ritual to his morning routine. Now he read the Washington Post. He started with the Metro section followed by the Business section, then the Front or A section, then Sports and lastly the Style section with the crossword puzzle. He was a fast reader and the whole ritual did not take long.

Of course, the first thing he had to do when he woke up was to feed Stanley. Then he started the coffee and fed the birds. Then he could read the newspaper.

A short article in the Business section caught his eye. A Mr. Kurt Steiner of Munich, Germany, was the acting CEO of Signal Control Technology, Inc. Clay wondered how this appointment might affect him and his friends.

On the spur of the moment, Clay reached for the telephone. He called Gino, Joe's brother in New Jersey who ran the investigative service. Clay asked Gino to keep an eye out for Steiner and SCT. He asked him to sort of keep in touch with the situation by maintaining a loose vigil on the place. Gino understood.

Gino Colissimo called a data service and ordered a subscription to any PR releases or articles about SCT. Next, he called his man in the Washington, D. C. area and explained the situation. He wanted feelers put out gently that would report any unusual activity at SCT. What constituted "unusual?" Hmm. Anything that caused attention from an outside source. Anything that involved the police. Layoffs. Hirings. Accidents. Fires. Burglaries.

Okay was the response. Understood.

The Washington, D. C. man saw an opportunity to star in the boss' eyes. He went to work. The first series of calls were to snitches that he had cultivated at the other investigative services.

He promised to mail each of them a hundred-dollar bill just to remember his request about SCT. If they learned anything, it would be very profitable for them.

Kurt Steiner located a Penthouse apartment close to the company building. It was perfect for him. The building had a maid service and several businesses on the ground floor. There was a dry cleaners/laundry, deli, coffee shop, and a full restaurant on the third floor. Most important, it had a full gym with steam, sauna, and massage service. Steiner pushed himself into a daily exercise period. He would rise early and have one cup of coffee with the morning paper – New York Times not the local rag – and then go to the gym. After a spirited workout and a jog on the indoor track, he had a massage. He would return to his apartment for a breakfast prepared by room service and look over his paperwork for the day. Steiner was proud of his physical condition. He could do an impressive number of push-ups and sit-ups. He could run a mile easily. Steiner had never been in the military service. He had managed to avoid his obligation because of the intervention of his boss, Dr. Gernot Kohl, the Chairman of International Systems, Inc. It was just as well. He found all weapons distasteful. For that matter, he found all forms of combat ridiculous and unnecessary. Negotiation and financial strength could solve everything. He was secure and confident in his life. He had never known hunger, want, or hardship. He realized that he had a good life but he knew he deserved a good life. It was a matter of intelligence, education, and breeding.

Steiner avoided any show of weakness. He was firm with subordinates. Steiner did not tolerate mistakes or suffer fools. He avoided friendships and maintained a cool distance from everyone except Dr. Gernot Kohl. Even with his boss and mentor, the relationship was at arm's length. One of his missions at SCT was to enforce a chain of command and restore dignity. The use of first names at all levels in the company was offensive to him. Company picnics and other social gatherings would be discontinued. He was eager to fire the first few people to set an example of discipline. Much to his chagrin, he realized that he could not fire the CFO. The man was too critical at this time. However, the CFO didn't know this so he could lean on the man.

The CFO sat at his desk in the fancy corner office and studied the situation. He was in a ticklish spot. He knew Steiner was going to be a long-term problem. There was no other replacement CEO on the horizon. He had no illusions about his own capabilities. He decided to start a quiet search for another job. In the meantime, he would kiss Steiner's ass at every opportunity. He would jump at every command. He would anticipate his needs and have the information available in advance. As a first task, he had to locate the names of the two individuals that Claggett cheated.

Claggett's position had been filled by his assistant on an interim basis. The man stayed in his old office waiting and hoping that the position would be finalized as permanent. Thus, Claggett's office was unoccupied. The information requested by Mr. Steiner was probably in Claggett's files. He worked late that evening going through the boxes, file drawers and desk drawers in Claggett's office. It took less than two hours to find the names of Clayton Matthews and Joseph Colissimo. Unfortunately, he could not find street addresses or telephone numbers. A call to information was not productive. Yes, there was a telephone but, at the customer's request, the number was unlisted. It was not surprising. No one had a listed number in the D. C. area except merchants and lawyers. Fortunately, there was an easy alternative. The CFO picked up the telephone and dialed the night number for the investigative service used by SCT. Rarely a day passed that SCT did not need a credit check or security background on someone. Then he would have the information available when Mr. Steiner asked for it. When the manager of the investigative service returned the call, the CFO tasked him with finding out the telephone numbers and addresses of a Mr. Clayton Matthews and Mr. Joseph Colissimo. The CFO emphasized the need for confidentiality and asked him to limit the costs to the requested information. This request was not for a security check. A deep background would not be necessary.

"Clay? It's Gino. Sorry to tell you this, pal, but your instincts were right on target. SCT tasked their investigative service with the job of finding telephone numbers and addresses for you and Joe. My information is less than twenty-four hours old."

Clay sighed and studied the ceiling for a few minutes. Then he started asking questions and giving instructions.

"Do you have an international associate, Gino?"

"Yes, we do. It is based in Italy as you might imagine but they have offices in most of the major European countries. I assume your question is about Germany?"

"Yes. How secure would any inquiry be, Gino? You have information on SCT's question about us. Would they know of our inquiry about them?"

"Clay, I'm not going to shit you and use words like never or impossible. I can promise that I will take extra personal precautions and tell you that I believe your inquiries will be confidential. If there is a leak, I will mail you the testicles of the squealer."

"Okay. Fair enough. We have quite a bit of information on SCT locally with the exception of this Steiner. Let's get a full file on him and move our inquiries to Munich. Let's find out everything there is to know about Steiner's boss – personal and professional life plus a lot of pictures. Okay?"

"Okay. We're rolling." Gino didn't have to discuss fees. He knew Clay would mail him a retainer as soon as he hung up the telephone. Clay was his single best customer. He paid well and promptly. Plus, he was Joe's best friend. There was no higher recommendation.

*   *   *

The CFO stood in the outer chambers of Mr. Steiner's office. The new executive secretary was truly a battleaxe. When he requested an appointment with Mr. Steiner, she wanted to know the purpose and how long the meeting would last. Mr. Steiner was a busy man.

At precisely 10 AM, the CFO was told to knock on the door two times and enter. Mr. Steiner was signing some documents so he waited inside the door until he was invited to advance and be seated.

"Sir, I have the information you requested on the two individuals that Claggett cheated. I've written them down for you." He handed a piece of paper to Mr. Steiner. "The files bear out your suspicion. There are copies of a receipt acknowledging the product samples and several memos dealing with the copying of the product. Apparently, the samples were encapsulated. Considerable time and money were spent removing the epoxy."

"There are only names on this paper. What about addresses and telephone numbers?" Steiner demanded in a stern voice.

"Sir, there were no addresses or telephone numbers in the files. Mr. Claggett's telephone book seems to be missing. However, we have an excellent investigative service that..."

"You didn't contact an agency, did you? I told you not to discuss this matter with anyone except me. Didn't you understand? Well, did you call an agency?" Steiner had jumped up from his chair and was turning red. The CFO was terrified.

"Uh, uh, uh, no, sir." The CFO lied. "I didn't call the agency or tell anyone else of your inquiry." The CFO was feeling sick to his stomach. He couldn't wait to leave Steiner's office. He would have to call the agency and cancel the request. He would tell the man that he would pay any charges personally but, please, don't let anyone know of the inquiry. It would be okay. No one would ever know. Oh, God!

At midnight, Steiner went out to the balcony of his penthouse. He was holding a special satellite telephone with an encryption device. Dr. Kohl had obtained the unit from a German General who hoped to work for International Systems when he retired.

Steiner dialed Dr. Kohl's home telephone number and waited. When he heard the familiar, gruff voice, he suggested enabling the encryption device. After several clicks, they continued their conversation. Steiner reported the names as he had been instructed to do before he left Munich. He reported the lack of addresses and telephone numbers and assured Dr. Kohl that their inquiry was completely confidential.

Dr. Kohl advised Steiner that a senior agent would be sent to Washington to handle the investigation. The agent had special contacts at the Pentagon and FBI. He would be able to obtain the information without alerting the individuals.

Three weeks later, a file folder was delivered to Steiner via Fedex that contained full information on Matthews and Colissimo. There were photographs of the subjects, their families, and their friends. Steiner was impressed with the thoroughness of the report. He was in awe of the power of Dr. Kohl.

Steiner was not sure of the approach that would be made to the two commoners but he knew that Dr. Kohl would insure the future safety and stability of SCT. And he, Kurt Steiner, would do his part with loyalty and accuracy.

Clay Matthews was restless and could not fall asleep. Stanley had no such problem. The little guy was almost snoring. Clay looked at him with affection. It was incredible that such a little creature had made such a difference in his life.

And Billy. He was a marvel to see and talk to and work with on the computer. Billy was so intelligent that it was scary. He grasped even the most advanced concepts so quickly that Clay had to study hard between visits.

And Higgins. Clay felt like he had found a gold mine in John. He was a friend and partner rolled into one dynamic person.

And Susan. She brought so much sunshine into John's life. He knew the exact night they consummated their love. He could see it in their eyes. Clay wondered if he had looked like Higgins when he and Lydia returned from their honeymoon. Probably. It was the look of love.

And Joe and Sylvia. My God, who ever could have guessed that such fierce friends existed in this cynical world? They would lay down their lives for him as he would for them. Their friendship had been tested in combat and forged in blood. The three of them had been tested by a cruel and unforgiving society. If they had bowed their heads, their lives would have withered. But the three of them had stood tall and fought side-by-side. And they had won. True – they had violated a few commandments and they would have to answer for their sins. They had thumbed their noses at the law and walked away from the masses.

Clay was not happy in the same way that he was when Lydia was alive and Kathryn Ann was at home. He had a difficult time accepting his losses. But those losses were facts and they could not be changed. He had to accept them.

Clay was happy in a much different way. It was not necessarily a better way or a worse way. It was different. He remembered the night that he woke up with the idea of establishing a camp for kids like Billy. In his dream, he envisioned a computer learning center with the buildings constructed to ease the burden of the handicapped youngsters. There would have to be a large nursing staff to care for their needs. Special buses would be required for transportation. Clay had reached for a notebook and started scribbling notes as fast as he could write.

The cost estimates were much higher than Clay had forecast. He was willing to use every dollar in his possession but it wouldn't be enough. Then Eastern Mutual Insurance Company had shown up on his doorstep. After the agent left, Clay looked skyward and apologized for doubting him.

Now the camp was a reality. Clay had purchased twenty-five acres in Frederick County, Maryland. It was named Camp Lydia. When Joe, Sylvia, John, Susan, and Billy presented him with the suggestion of naming the camp for his wife, Clay wept. His friends surrounded him and held him until the tears stopped. Alfred Levits had handled the paperwork and set up a trust fund to insure perpetual operation and care.

So Clay was happy. He had a life. He felt productive. There was no sex type love in his life but he did not miss it. He figured that some people were like the cardinals. They mated for life.

Now his way of life was threatened. Apparently, SCT was not going to let matters lie. Like Jack Carter, they would have to be stopped.

Clay did not consider himself a genius. He could never be the President of the United States or Federal Reserve Chairman or a doctor or a lot of things. But he was smarter and better than anything SCT and International Systems could put into the field. If they wanted a round three – so be it. Round three was coming up.

The information from Gino was rolling in everyday. Gino had gone to Italy and personally taken charge of the case. He went to Munich to supervise the efforts and explain why it would be dangerous for anyone to leak the case. Gino was able to explain matters so that it was easy to understand. There were many pictures of the company headquarters in Munich and the personal homes of the corporate officers including Dr. Kohl.

Clay did not have a plan as yet. One of the reasons for the lack of direction was that he had not defined his goals. Did he simply want them to leave him alone? Yes, but something more. Was it money? Maybe. Was it more justice for the original act of piracy? Yes. If they were not going to leave him alone then they would pay the price.

On this go-around, SCT would cease to exist.

What about International Systems, Inc.? What about Mr. Kurt Steiner and Dr. Gernot Kohl?

Clay decided to see how the intelligence developed before making a final decision on the extent of the upcoming battle.

*   *   *

Edward "Big Ed" Thomson was the owner and manager of The Left Guard Investigative Services, Inc. Big Ed had spent 12 years as a Washington Redskin playing Left Guard. At 6 feet 5 inches and 290 pounds, Big Ed resembled a tank to the average person. When he retired from the NFL, Big Ed started his own business. Originally, he envisioned the business would be a protective service but when he wrote out the name it sounded like a mob outfit. And Big Ed was on the up and up. From his Redskin days, he knew a lot of people from all walks of life. The business thrived from the beginning. He had an office manager, Rita, who set up the computer and accounting systems. She ran the office with an iron hand. No one, not even Big Ed would dare to deviate from standard procedures.

When Big Ed talked to Albert Tillis, the CFO of SCT, about obtaining the addresses and telephone numbers of Clayton Matthews and Joe Colissimo, he opened a computer case file and entered the known data. SCT and Tillis were the requesting company and individual. The computer filled in their address and billing data automatically from the customer database. Ed answered one of the computer "prompts" by affirming that he wanted the addresses manually verified. When he told the computer he was finished, the computer prompted for distribution list. Ed typed in ALL. Rita was automatically copied on all information. Ed's command meant that his three field investigators would be copied. If anyone on the copy list had any information on the subjects, he or she would enter the info into the case file.

Unbeknownst to Big Ed, one of his three investigators had received a one hundred-dollar retainer to be on the lookout for this inquiry. The investigator downloaded the case file to a 3.5-inch disk and slipped it into his shirt pocket. After dinner, he e-mailed the file to Gino Colissimo from his home computer. He added that he would be verifying the addresses when the data search reported the addresses and numbers. He received one thousand dollars for the tip. He was a happy man.

Two days later, the investigator approached the house of Clayton Matthews. He walked boldly around the house to the gas meter. After making some notations on his clipboards, he cocked his hardhat at a jaunty angle and rang the doorbell.

"Good Morning, Sir. I hope I'm not disturbing you. As you

can see from my identification, I'm from Washington Gas and Electric. I was sent out to double-check the reading on your meter. Our computer shows a slight increase in your gas usage. We wanted to be sure there was no problem. Have you noticed any smell or anything unusual?" The investigator paused and looked at his clipboard. "Are you Mr. Clayton Matthews? I hope I'm not at the wrong house. May I get your telephone number and verify the data on our records?"

"You're at the right house. I'm Matthews. And I haven't noticed any problem." Clay smiled.

"Okay, sorry I bothered you, sir. Have a nice day." The investigator turned and left.

Clay closed the door and smiled. He crossed over to the telephone and dialed a number for Joe Colissimo who lived a mile away.

"Joe, I just had a visitor. He was a meter reader for Washington Gas and Electric. He verified my name, address, and telephone number." Clay reported.

An hour later, the investigator used the same routine at the Colissimo house. He was surprised at the friendliness at this house. They invited him inside for a cold drink of water. Such a hard job on a hot day, they sympathized. And could he help them with a little problem? Could he take a picture of the Colissimo couple standing together with their new camera? Here, just put your hard hat on the table. Just look through here and press this button.

When the investigator accommodated them with their innocent request, he handed the camera to Sylvia. Joe thanked him and offered his hand. The investigator automatically shook the offered hand and Sylvia snapped their picture. The investigator protested but the deed was done. What was he going to do? Rip the camera from her hands and expose the roll of film? Not hardly. Another thing that he wasn't going to do was to tell the office about this embarrassing event.

On the following day, Big Ed noticed with satisfaction that a field investigator had verified the addresses and telephone numbers for Matthews and Colissimo. He was less pleased to see that it was his least competent field investigator. The guy was slower and dumber than a turkey reporting for work on Thanksgiving. Big Ed was acutely aware of SCT's status as a large client. Also, Tillis was the guy who wrote the check. Big Ed decided to double-check the information and keep his eyes peeled for anything unusual.

Big Ed pulled up to the curb across the street from Clay Matthews' house. He was looking it over very carefully when a voice made him jump. Big Ed cracked his head on the roof and got a headache. Damn! He rubbed his head.

"Can I help you? I noticed you looking at my house. I'm Clayton Matthews and I live there." Clay smiled.

"Uh, uh, I'm with, uh, Long & Foster Real Estate. I was just cruising around looking at houses. We always want more listings, you know? You wouldn't be interested in selling your house, would you?" Big Ed smiled. He had some phony business cards in his briefcase and he was trying to find one.

"Well, gosh, I don't know. Come on over and take a look at my house. Maybe you can estimate what a selling price might be?" Clay opened the door for him. Big Ed had little choice but to follow through on his role.

"Come on into the house. You're Big Ed Thomson, aren't you? Used to play left Guard for the Redskins? I'm a big Redskins fan. Hey, I want you to meet some friends of mine. They've been waiting for me to finish walking the dog." Clay guided the big man into the house by the arm. Stanley trotted in behind them.

"Hey, Joe? Sylvia? Come out and say hello to my visitor. I want you to meet Big Ed Thomson. Remember him? He's in real estate now. He wants to list my house. How about that?" Clay was digging around in the end table drawer.

"Ed, these are some friends of mine, Sylvia and Joe Colissimo. They live pretty close to me. Hey, Joe, why don't you give Ed your address and telephone number so he can look at your house?"

Joe walked up to Big Ed and shook hands with him. When he shook hands, he held onto Big Ed's hand and turned towards Clay.

Clay raised the camera and quickly aimed. The flash was

blinding in the small house. Stanley jumped. Big Ed blinked. And Joe smiled.

"Hey, I'm coming up in the world. Yesterday I got my picture taken with a gas meter reader and today I'm getting mugged with Big Ed Thomson. This is great. Isn't this great, Sylvia?" Joe was really smiling.

Sylvia handed a piece of paper to Big Ed and said, "Here's our home address and telephone number. Drop by and see us. I've wanted a bigger house. I don't have enough housework to keep me busy."

Big Ed had the distinct feeling that he was the brunt of something or other. Whatever was going on here was not good. It was time for him to boogie.

"Well, it was nice meeting all of you folks but I gotta hit the road. Thanks for the hospitality." Ed turned and quick-stepped towards the car.

Joe, Sylvia, and Clay were laughing so hard they had to sit down.

In a few minutes, the laughing subsided and the serious side took over.

"I guess there is no longer any question about SCT's intentions, is there?" Clay asked.

"Not in my mind." Joe answered. "Let's move on those fuckers." Sylvia punched him on the arm.

"Watch your language." Sylvia admonished.

"So – when you were verifying the addresses on Matthews and Colissimo, did anyone see you?" Big Ed had the investigator on the mat.

"Uh, no, Boss."

"You're sure?"

"Positively, Boss."

Big Ed grimaced as the man left his office. Now he knew the guy was a liar as well. What a schmuck. Letting the target get pictures of the investigator posing with another target.

*   *   *

"Yes, Mr. Tillis? How can I help you?" Big Ed answered the telephone.

"Look, Ed, I was a bit hasty in asking you to run down those addresses and telephone numbers on Matthews and Colissimo. I was jumping the gun a little bit, you know? You haven't done anything on that matter, have you?" Tillis held his breath.

"Uh no. No, I haven't. We've been pretty busy around here and since you didn't say it was urgent, I didn't get to it yesterday." Ed felt like someone had run an end play on him.

"Well, that's good. That's real good. But, the thing is, I want to be absolutely sure. Because if you did do any work, I'd want to be sure you got paid." Tillis probed.

"No, we didn't do anything on it." Big Ed felt like he was really learning how to lie in this business. It was a lot easier to lie on the telephone.

"Okay, well, I'll let you go. Is everything else okay? Are we up-to-date on your invoices?" Tillis joked.

"Everything is okay. Thanks for calling."

Tillis hung up and rushed into the bathroom. He had an urgent need to urinate.

"Joe, are you carrying anything?" Clay asked.

"You bet. I've got a 9mm automatic in my shoulder holster and a .32 caliber revolver in an ankle holster. I always carry my six-inch switchblade. How about you?" Joe asked.

"Yeah, I have a .45 automatic in my shoulder holster and a .38 caliber revolver in my rear belt holster." Clay responded.

"Well, what's the plan, Clay?" Joe looked to Clay for leadership.

"This time, we are going to put SCT out of business. I'm waiting on some more Intel from Gino. In the meantime, I want you to stock up on incendiary grenades. We'll need twice as many as we had on the first visit. I want to make sure that the computer room and the software records are completely destroyed. Then we will need some explosives to set around the building supports. When we blow it, I want to reduce the place to a pile of rubble."

"What about the backup computer tapes? If we don't get the backups, they can be back in business as soon as they buy new machines and lease a building." Joe reminded him.

"We'll get the backup stuff from the CFO. I'll explain to him how much I want those records. He'll be glad to cooperate." Clay smiled.

"Sounds like you have a plan in mind?" Joe wanted to hear the details.

"Just about. It depends on what Gino finds out in Munich. Let's decide how much money we want on this round. You got a figure in mind?" Clay wanted to know.

"Well, I haven't thought a lot about it. Inflation has been pretty bad during the last two years. And the stock market has been a little weak. I know that you want some more money for Camp Lydia. How about five million?" Joe raised his eyebrows.

"Sounds good to me." Clay agreed. And the die was cast.

John Higgins asked Clay to go to lunch with him. Normally, things were not so formal so Clay was puzzled by the exactness of the time and location.

"Clay, I've got some news for you. I don't know how bad the news might be since we haven't discussed this issue for a long time." John was apprehensive.

"Just give it to me straight, John." Clay braced himself.

"I've kept tabs on a Mr. Hugh Nolan through my Virginia police contacts. Since your problems started with his attack on Kathryn Ann, I figured it would be good to keep track of him. He's being paroled next week. I tried to stop the parole but without success." John looked at him with concern.

Clay sat back and looked at the ceiling. He remembered every detail of the days leading up to the sentencing of Hugh Nolan for assault and battery on his daughter. Then he responded.

"Well, he's served the time that the State of Virginia decreed that he serve for his crime. It wasn't up to me to set his punishment. Unless he causes me or Kathryn Ann a problem, I guess we'll let the matter die." Clay looked at John Higgins calmly.

Later, over a glass of Chianti Classico, Clay told Joe Colissimo about the conversation. To his surprise, Joe already knew about the parole.

"It's taken care of, Clay. Don't worry about it." Joe assured him.

So Clay put the matter from his mind. He wanted to concentrate on SCT.

Stanley was excited. He loved riding in the car. An hour's ride was perfect but if the ride went to two hours, Stanley needed a stop. It was an hour's ride to Frederick so today was perfect. Instead of turning off the main road towards Camp Lydia, Clay drove directly to Resthaven Memorial Gardens. He had not visited Lydia's grave for some time.

Clay pulled onto the shoulder of the narrow road that wound through the cemetery. He let Stanley exit the car and walked over to Lydia's marker. Lydia had been gone for almost five years now. So much had happened to the world and to Clay during that time. He knelt down beside the marker. Stanley was by his side.

"I'm sorry I haven't been by for awhile. I've been spending a lot of time with Joe and Sylvia. The Camp is really doing well. We can handle ten kids at a time now. Really fifteen if necessary but ten is the ideal number. Susan and John – I told you about them – got married last month. It was a small quiet wedding. You'd like them. And Billy – he's a miracle. His condition is not any better but on the bright side, it isn't any worse. I told you that Susan is a nurse, didn't I? That makes it a lot easier. Did I tell you that I've been promoted? I'm not just Uncle Clay to Billy. I'm Uncle Clay that gets a hug on every visit. Isn't that great? I got a letter from Kathryn Ann the other day. She and her husband are doing great according to the note."

Stanley nuzzled his hand and he realized that he had been daydreaming. He looked at his watch and saw that they had been here for an hour. He stood up and stretched his legs. He looked around and saw that they were alone in the cemetery. Well, it was usually quiet during the week. Most people visited their loved ones on the weekends.

"Hang on, Stanley. I need to talk to Lydia for a few more minutes."

"Look, it's going to be awhile before I can come out here again. Joe and I are going to be pretty busy for the next few weeks. I know you don't approve of all this stuff with SCT but I think it's the right thing to do. It's not just what they did to us. I've evened out the score for the piracy. But they won't let it go. I have to eliminate the threat – not just to me but to Joe and Sylvia and the Camp. And they're not good people, Lydia. They're arrogant and much too powerful. They run roughshod over people. I intend to shut them down permanently this time. If it doesn't work, I won't just be coming out here for visits. I'll be next to you. And that wouldn't be so bad. I still miss you. See you later."

34 – Jimmy's Bones

James A. "Little Jimmy" Colissimo was ready to take his place in the family. He had planned his act of manhood with his older brothers – Joe and John. Every detail had been reviewed and rehearsed a thousand times. Little Jimmy was ready. He was not anxious; he was eager. And when the deed was done, the "Little" would be permanently removed from his name. Then the answer to the age-old question of "What's black and blue and laying on the ground?" would be "The first asshole that addresses me as "Little Jimmy."

Joe Colissimo was nervous and a little upset about the plan. It was his daughter, Josephine that had been wronged. He should be the one to mete out justice. But the head of the family, older brother John, had decreed that Little Jimmy should have the opportunity to make his bones. After all, it was Jimmy's niece, argued John.

Little Jimmy was the youngest of the four brothers and the smallest one. Life had not been easy for him. It was like he had three extra fathers. To compensate, Jimmy had worked diligently at physical development and fighting skills. He joined the high school boxing team but was dismissed for being too rough in the ring. He was proud of his dismissal. Almost since he could walk, he had received lessons from "Pug" Wilson, a family retainer for physical fitness. Pug ran a gym and Jimmy was his favorite student. Pug thought of Jimmy as a Godson. He taught him boxing but then Pug elevated him to street fighting techniques. Jimmy blossomed under Pug's tutelage. On the pistol range, Jimmy's extraordinary eyesight and reflexes made him a natural marksman. Pug introduced him to the knife and Jimmy smiled. The final step was the instrument of the artists – the garrote.

Hugh Nolan was a bitter, angry man. He had served his sentence in Virginia State Prison but he was not rehabilitated. Hugh's trial and conviction was a big frame-up in his mind. It was a political shitpot. Who ever heard of going to jail for trying to screw a secretary? Just trying, for chrissake! He didn't even get close to getting into her pants. The whole goddamn thing was unfair. And prison was brutal. How in the hell can someone go so long without a decent drink? He had some grain alcohol diluted with water and flavoring in prison but he was afraid of the side effects. But, God, he ached for a drink of scotch or bourbon. A boilermaker was his favorite drink. Straight bourbon with a beer chaser was a man's drink. It put hair on the chest and lead in the pencil. And that was the other thing – no women in prison. He wouldn't have anything to do with the fairies – he was terrified of AIDS.

Now he was back in Northern Virginia. Back to his old stomping grounds. Back to the land of bourbon, beer, scotch, and pussy. He intended to satisfy his appetites to the max. Except that there was the little problem of money. As a convicted felon, he could not get a security clearance. Working for one of the beltway bandits was out of the question. After making the rounds, he was about convinced that nearly every company was out of the question. Finally he got a job in a food distributor's warehouse. He was loading boxes and sweeping floors for ten goddamn dollars an hour. After paying rent for a room and buying a little bit of food, it didn't leave much for booze and broads. He needed a steady girlfriend. With his money, he couldn't afford to buy sex. He needed sex but more than anything he needed booze. When he was sober, Hugh Nolan was surly and morose. When he was drunk, Nolan was a loud, boisterous bully. At six-foot two inches and 230 pounds, Nolan was a formidable chunk of beef on the warpath. Most men steered clear of him.

Hugh Nolan's job was near the rail yards in Southwest Alexandria. Since he didn't have a car, he was forced to live and drink as close to the job as he could get. He rented a one-room apartment with a hotplate and shared a bathroom with three other rooms. He did all of his drinking at "Bud's Place" because it was close and cheap. On weeknights, he was careful to get a buzz on and keep it until bedtime. He needed to be able to work on the following day and it was all that he could afford. But Friday, blessed Friday, was payday. He would cash his check and hide part of his money in the room. The rest of the money he kept for his Friday night drunk. Friday night was boilermaker night.

On this Friday night, Nolan cashed his check and rushed to his room. He was anxious to shower and shave and dress for the night. He owned two sets of work clothes and one set of slacks, sport shirt, and a windbreaker. Hugh had some furniture and a lot of clothes in storage but he couldn't afford to get his things out of storage. When he came out of his room and headed for the shower, he saw that it was occupied. Goddamn it! Now there won't be enough hot water to shave and shower. Would he rather shower in hot water and shave in cold water? Or the other way around? Goddamn it, it was time to get another job.

Finally he was ready to go. He was practically running by the time he got to the front door of Bud's place. He jerked open the door and headed for the bar.

Bud, the owner and operator of the joint bearing his name, winced when he saw the newcomer. Hugh Nolan was a pain in the ass. Bud knew there would come a day when he would have to tell Nolan to get out and stay out. Nolan tried to run a tab every night. He tried to get free drinks by suggesting that the bar should treat. Nolan tried to borrow money from everybody. For now, Bud sighed and reached for the bar bourbon – some nights it was *Early Times* but tonight it was *Old Guckenheimer*. He poured a shot glass full to the brim and set out a cold Budweiser for Nolan at the bar. He stood waiting for the three dollars.

Forget about any tip.

"Good man, Bud." Nolan said as he reached for the shot glass.

Before the nectar reached his lips, someone bumped his elbow and the shot glass went flying across the bar. Sonofabitch! Nolan whirled around and glared at the man behind him. He had to lower his eyes because the guy was six inches shorter. He had black hair and was wearing horn-rimmed glasses. He looked like a Dago that might weigh 150 or 160. A fucking wimp.

"You clumsy cocksucker. Pull out your money. You're going to pay for another drink or I'm going to kick your ass." Nolan was hurting now. He needed that drink.

"A fat pig like you ought to be able to lick up the spilled drink. Then you'll learn not to be so careless." The kid spoke quietly but everybody in the bar heard him. No one had ever seen the kid before tonight but they knew Nolan. The smart thing to do was back away from the action. This might be a good show.

Nolan whipped a fast right hand towards the kid that would have torn his head off - except that the kid wasn't standing there anymore. The force of the swing turned Nolan around and the kid hit him in the kidney. It hurt like a bitch but he turned around and rushed the kid. If he got his hands on the kid, he would squeeze him until every zit erupted.

The kid sidestepped again and buried his fist in Nolan's gut. Nolan fell to his hands and knees trying to get his breath. It took an eternity but Nolan started breathing again. He stood up and looked around for the kid. The asshole was leaning against the bar cleaning his glasses. He was smiling at Nolan.

"I told you to lick up the spilled drink. A smart man would do as he was told but you don't look too smart." The kid spoke quietly and was breathing normally. The fight hadn't even raised a sweat on his forehead yet. Nolan was too far gone to notice these things and he barely heard the words.

Nolan took a deep breath and walked towards the kid. He raised his right arm high and started a fist towards the kid. It was a feint to cover the kick headed towards the kid's groin.

The kid moved like a lightning bolt and twisted inside the

kick. He rammed a fist into Nolan's balls and stood back. Nolan fell to the floor and vomited. Nolan's only set of dress clothes was torn and bloody. He smelled like a toilet and he was humiliated. He would never be able to visit Bud's Place again and the story would spread to the warehouse.

Nolan reached into his front pocket and took out the switchblade knife. When he snapped it open the blade was six inches long. The one skill he had learned in prison was how to use a knife. He intended to slice the kid up into strips of fettuccine.

When he made eye contact with the kid, he was surprised at the calmness. There was no fear. He thought he saw a kind of anticipation. The kid looked pleased. Then he noticed that he wasn't wearing his glasses anymore. Apparently, the kid was right-handed, too. Nolan figured that out because that was the hand holding his knife. Oh, shit! Things weren't going too well for Hugh Nolan.

The two men circled around the floor looking for an opening in each other's defense. Nolan began to wish there was some way to stop this madness and he would buy his own replacement drink. Nolan knew it wasn't going to happen. This fight was going to the finish regardless of what he wanted. The thought entered his mind that he had been set up. And it wasn't fair. All he wanted to do was to get drunk. He didn't want to die. Even when the kid pushed Nolan's knife arm to the side and stepped towards him, he was still hoping to live. Maybe the kid would be satisfied with a cut or two and a show of blood. Hugh had figured out that he was outclassed. Then he felt the icy hardness of the knife enter his stomach and he knew the end was near. He felt the kid pull out the knife and start another blow towards his chest. He heard the kid say, "This is for Josephine, you scumbag."

As the life left his body on the barroom floor, Hugh Nolan was trying to tell the kid that he didn't know any Josephine. It was all a big mistake. But he died before he could tell the kid.

Jimmy Colissimo folded his knife and put it away. He walked over to the bar and pulled a roll of money from his pocket. He peeled off five one hundred-dollar bills and handed the money to Bud. "This ought to cover the bar for the night. You gentlemen can discuss what story to tell the police."

Bud locked the front door when the kid left. The three guys in the bar were friends since high school. He set up drinks for everybody and they talked about the fight. Eventually two of them went home before Bud called the police. Bud and the remaining customer told the cops about the huge black man who had stabbed poor Hugh Nolan.

35 - *The Set-Up*

Clay and Gino met at Joe and Sylvia's house. Gino was exhausted. He had made two round trip transatlantic flights within the last month. Even flying first class on the jumbo 747s was tiring because of the time change and the effects of jet lag. Gino had to admit that he was getting older and it rankled.

Sylvia set out the wine, bread and sausage for the ritualistic sustenance. Joe and Gino reached for the comfort-giving food without a second thought. Clay sipped lightly at his wine.

"It looks like you have everything in your report, Gino. Good work. I guess we've got our work cut out for us, Joe." Clay looked at his partner thoughtfully.

"If there's a question in that statement, Clay, I have the answer. Sylvia and I have talked about it. We know that we could drop out of this round if we wanted to. We don't want to. We're up for this. Now let's move on. What's next?" Joe clamped his mouth shut. Clay knew the matter was decided.

"How about you, Gino? This is a convenient stopping point for you. You've gotten the information that I requested. If I need anymore, I can call you. I mean no offense but I hate to see you get caught up in this mess." Clay looked at Joe's older brother.

"I know what you mean and I don't take offense. So I won't have to cut your heart out in accordance with the Sicilian custom." Gino smiled. "It's your show, Clay. But I'm ready to carry out my part and if the family knows the plan, we might be able to make a suggestion or two. We can be on standby if you need some assistance in an emergency."

"Great! " Clay said sincerely. "Here's what I have in mind."

"Do you remember the service company in Greenbelt that put in the computer system for SCT?" Clay asked.

"Yeah, sure. We got you the information on their system from an old acquaintance that worked for them. The guy had run out on a couple thousand dollars of gambling markers. He was very glad to help us." Gino smiled.

"Is he still working there?"

"I'm sure he is. We told him to let us know if he decided to move. I'm sure he understood us." Gino rolled his eyes.

"Okay. I want him to get us some duplicate tape reels like the ones SCT use for their backup tapes. We'll need eight reels. I want to pay for them. We don't want him hauled up on a petty theft charge and point to us. We'll give him the money and demand a receipt from the company." Clay was speaking rapidly.

"No problem." Said Gino.

"According to your notes, the CFO – what's his name? Tillis? – Still takes the backup tapes from the plant every night but now he goes to the bank. Right?"

"Yeah. He leaves the plant at 4 PM sharp and arrives at the bank before 4:30. He rings the night bell and they let him in the side door. He comes out in five minutes. Sometimes he goes back to SCT and other times he goes home. There's no pattern except on Friday afternoon when he always goes home." Gino related. "In the mornings, he leaves home at 7:45 AM and goes directly to the bank. He rings the night bell at 8:00. They let him in and he comes out in five minutes with the tapes. He always drives directly to the plant."

"Okay, I figure we'll hit him on the way to the plant in the morning. I've looked at the street map and I think we'll have a small fender bender with Mr. Tillis. We'll have a little talk with Mr. Tillis and exchange the tapes. Mr. Tillis will report to work with the blank tapes and perform a couple of chores for us." Clay smiled.

"How do you know he won't report the theft to Steiner and call the cops?" Gino asked.

"Joe and I will work out a routine to convince Tillis that he should cooperate. From your reports, we are not dealing with a man of strength. I don't anticipate a problem." Clay dismissed the CFO with the offhand comments.

"Dr. Gernot Kohl and Kurt Steiner are a different matter. The one point in our favor is that Steiner is untested. He hasn't felt pain or tasted blood. In that regard, he is an unknown. He will hesitate when he faces the first test. Everyone does." Clay said.

"Dr. Kohl must be assumed to be a dangerous adversary. We must assume that Kohl has resources that we have not encountered as yet. The Head of Security at International Systems, Inc., is a retired military officer named Max Krug. He has an impressive background. He has been tested. We must assume that Kohl is deploying his forces against us as we speak." Clay continued.

"My friends, this will be a tougher battle than we had on the earlier encounters. Our chances are not nearly as good. I fear that we will shed blood in our ranks. As you know, I asked Gino to increase his men on our surveillance team when we first learned of their interest in us. Gino reports that we have been followed on several occasions. They are keeping a loose tail on us to see if we change our pattern of behavior. There is no doubt that we are targeted." Clay had everyone's attention now.

"Tomorrow we will go operational. We will start our offensive. Sylvia will go to California on the early flight. She will stay with Josephine and command a detail of men hired to protect Josephine, Kathryn Ann and her husband. The men under her command will be instructed to kill anyone they find observing the girls. They will be in radio contact with Sylvia and explain their observations to her. If she concurs, they will act immediately." Everyone nodded. Sylvia hated to leave Joe and Clay but she agreed on the necessity of protecting the girls.

"There is a complete team of men backing Joe and me. They have pictures of the Head of Security and the three individuals that have followed Joe and me at times during the past few months. From now, if they spot any of them, they will shoot to kill." Clay's voice was growing steadily more serious.

"I've alerted John Higgins. He's taking Susan and Billy to Camp Lydia. He's going to take Stanley with him, too. He will have three cops with him to maintain security." Clay continued briefing them. "He has a copy of the pictures. John wanted to know the truth so I told him the whole program. I didn't want to do that but he insisted."

"Gino goes back to Germany tonight on the red-eye flight. He has a team waiting for him. He'll be prepared to move on Kohl as the situation develops."

"We cannot allow Steiner, Kohl, or Krug to survive. If one of them lives, we'll always be looking over our shoulders. If everything goes according to plan, Steiner and Krug will be eliminated within a few days. Kohl will be eliminated within a week. If one of us falls, remember the plan. Those three guys have to go. We can't leave our families to their mercy. Got it?" Clay looked at each one of them. He felt a terrible responsibility on his shoulders.

"Any questions? Okay. Gino, you better head for the airport. Sylvia, try to get some sleep before your early flight. Joe, let's go over some details." Clay looked at his old friend. "Think we can dream up some words to scare the shit out of Tillis?"

"No problem." Joe smiled.

Albert Tillis pulled out of the driveway at precisely 7:45 AM. Some mornings were a hassle but this was a smooth morning for a change. The four girls were in their teens and any one of them would have been a handful. The four of them together constituted a conservative definition of chaos. He knew all of this but he did not regret having four daughters. Each one of them was a precious angel in his eyes. He and his wife had known each other since they were six years old. He loved her and worshiped her. She had worked as a secretary to help get him through school. When he graduated from Wharton, he felt they had the world at their feet. It was true that they were moderately wealthy now. They had the house in Potomac, Maryland and several cars. The girls' college funds were assured. They had a modest portfolio and an emergency savings fund.

The problem was his unhappiness at SCT. Tillis felt as though there were a lot of undercurrent activities at the company. Things had started to deteriorate after Carter sold the majority of the stock to the German Company. Tillis felt that the recent acts of violence were outgrowths of the German activities. Basically, he wanted out. He had started putting out feelers several months ago. If he had his way, they would move to California. There were a lot of opportunities. His wife pointed out the hardship of uprooting the girls. He promised to try to find a job locally but it wasn't looking real good.

Tillis pulled up to the side door of the bank in downtown Rockville at 8 AM. He parked in the loading zone and exited the car. When he rang the night bell, the guard smiled at him and unlocked the door. He went through and headed for the vault. The cases were ready and he smiled at everyone when he grabbed them.

Traffic was comparatively light as he left the downtown area headed East on Route 28. As he approached the I-270 interchange, there was a brief delay but he crossed over the superhighway and headed for the SCT building. He slowed for the traffic light at Research Boulevard and looked to see if he could turn right on red without any danger.

Tillis was startled to feel the incredible jolt and loud noise when the large SUV struck the right rear fender of his Cadillac. He felt a rush of adrenaline followed by a surge of anger and outrage. He looked in his rear-view mirror and saw the driver signaling to him. He turned around on the seat to get a better view. He did not intend to exit the vehicle until he felt safe with the situation. There were too many stories about road rage in this area.

Tillis saw the driver of the car behind him stick his arm out of the side window and motion for him to pull over. Tillis completed the turn onto Research Boulevard and pulled over to the shoulder area. He stayed in his car while he evaluated the situation. It looked okay. There were two guys in the car and they were wearing suits. They looked respectable and in control. The driver was exiting the vehicle and walking towards him.

He left his car in gear and opened his window far enough to hear the man speak to him.

"Hey, I'm really sorry. That was my fault. I thought you were going through the light and I was in a hurry. You were right to stop and clear the way. I have my driver's license and insurance card in my wallet. I guess we better exchange information so that the insurance companies can earn their pay. Again, I'm sorry."

"Okay. I guess accidents happen. You're right. We should exchange information." Tillis was assured. He felt himself calm down and prided himself on maintaining control.

"Do you mind if I get into the passenger side? It's a little dangerous for me to stand here with the traffic going by me so close." The stranger smiled and shrugged his shoulders.

The guy sounded reasonable and calm so Tillis agreed. He unlocked the door and the stranger entered the car. He closed the door behind him.

"Tell you what." Said the stranger. "There's a motel up the street. Let's drive up there and exchange information. It's a lot quieter in their parking lot. My buddy will drive my car and follow us."

"Uh, no, I don't have time. Let's exchange information and I need to get to the office." Tillis responded.

"Let me put it another way, Mr. Tillis. Drive up to the motel parking lot or I'll shoot you right now." The stranger cocked the .45 automatic pistol in his right hand.

Albert Tillis felt a deep, cold fear in his stomach. The stranger had addressed him by name. It was a setup. The first thing that entered his mind was that he had waited too long to change jobs. He had no doubt that this was related to SCT.

"I'll do whatever you say. I don't want to get hurt." Tillis shifted into drive and pulled out onto the road. The vehicle behind him was right on his tail.

As they approached the motel, the stranger motioned for him to turn into the lot. He directed him towards the rear of the lot and pointed out a parking place. He nosed into the space. The SUV behind him backed into the adjacent space. Then the second man left the SUV and entered the back seat of Tillis' car.

"Well, Mr. Albert Tillis, here we are. I'll bet you've been doing some thinking during our short drive, haven't you?" The stranger smiled.

"A little. Obviously you know my name and my regular morning route. You must want something from me or you could have killed me earlier. I don't want to get hurt or killed. I'll do whatever you tell me to do." Tillis tried to control his breathing and remain calm.

"Very good, Mr. Tillis. Well, you will have the opportunity to avoid death and probably even pain. More importantly, you will have the opportunity to keep your family alive and well." The stranger waited to judge the effect on Tillis.

"My family has nothing to do with SCT. I've told you I'll do anything you ask. I don't give a damn what happens to SCT but if anyone of my family is hurt or even scared, I'll be your enemy as long as I live. Don't even look at them." Tillis was turning red in the face.

"Very admirable, Mr. Tillis. Now tell me why I can't stalk and hurt your family but you can stalk me and my family." Clay's voice deepened to a threatening growl.

"I haven't done anything to your family. I don't even know you." Tillis protested.

"Lying is a poor way to approach me. Didn't you order Big Ed Thomson of the Left Guard Investigative Services to find my address and telephone number and that of my friend in the backseat? Here's a picture of Big Ed and me and another picture of Joe and one of Big Ed's investigators. Weren't you preparing to take some action against us? Maybe kill us?" Clay drilled in on the man. "You're looking a little pale, Mr. Tillis."

"Yes, I ordered Big Ed to find your telephone numbers and addresses because I thought Mr. Steiner would want them. I was trying to be prepared. But Steiner got upset when I mentioned an investigative service so I called Big Ed and canceled the request. He told me that he had not taken any action towards finding you. Obviously, he lied. I had no intention of harming either of you in any way." Now Tillis knew his assailants. Matthews and Colissimo. And he knew they were the ones that SCT had cheated out of an invention.

"So Steiner didn't order you to get our names and addresses?" Clay was thinking hard.

"No. He ordered me to find your names and addresses in the information on file at the company. When I could only find the names, I called Big Ed. We use his service for personnel security checks and minor administrative matters. Then I reported to Mr. Steiner with the names. When I explained that the addresses were not in the file, I offered to have Big Ed find the information. Steiner got very agitated and jumped up from his desk. He asked me if I had already called Ed. I lied and said that I hadn't. He ordered me to forget about the entire matter. When I returned to my office, I called Ed to cancel the request. He assured me that he had not taken any action. I asked him twice." Tillis was trying to remember every word of the conversation.

"So Big Ed lied to you and you lied to Steiner? Why do you think Steiner told you to forget about the whole thing?" Clay asked. Inwardly, Clay was elated. This could prove to be a significant edge in their battle.

Tillis thought about it for a few minutes. He stared out of the windshield and considered all angles. Then he turned towards Clay. "I think he intended to use his own resources to find out everything he wanted to know about the two of you."

"Do you think he intends to take some action against us?" Clay studied the man next to him. He was impressed with the man so far.

"Yes. He questioned me about the earlier events with Carter and Claggett. He figured out that the tapes Carter ransomed were the backup tapes from my car." Tillis was speaking calmly now.

"Do you think Steiner is capable of violence?" Clay sensed that the conversation had turned in a favorable direction. Tillis was trying to cooperate. Joe was sitting quietly in the rear seat listening to the dialogue.

"Absolutely! Between him and the other German, they're poster boys for a new Nazi movement." Tillis left no doubt about his convictions.

"What other German?" Clay asked immediately.

"I think his name is Krug or something like that – he's head of security for the parent firm in Germany." Tillis answered.

"Is this the man?" Joe spoke for the first time and held up a picture.

"Yes." Tillis confirmed the identity.

"Have you seen or heard of any other Germans over here on a trip?" Joe asked.

"No."

"Have you met Dr. Gernot Kohl?" Clay took over the questioning.

"No. Dr. Kohl has been to the SCT building but I was on a business trip. I've never been to Germany." Tillis explained.

"Okay. Do you have the computer backup tapes in the trunk of your car now?" Clay tested him.

"Yes."

"Are they the only backup tapes in existence?"

"No, there is a set of backup tapes in Mr. Steiner's office that is updated weekly."

"I want the tapes from your trunk. Is that okay with you?"

"Absolutely."

"I have two jobs I want you to do for me. Then I want your silence on these matters forever. Regardless who asks. The law or anybody. Are you willing to cooperate?" Clay demanded harshly.

"If it is humanly possible, I will do it. What are the two jobs?" Tillis asked.

"I am going to take the tapes that are in your trunk. I'm going to give you a replacement set of blank tapes. When you return to the plant, I want you to reprogram the main frame computer so that it will never make another set of duplicate tapes regardless of which user types in the command Can you do that?" Clay waited.

"Yes, I can do it. I'm the computer manager. All changes have to be made by me. I can lock out all other users. I'm willing to do it. The tapes will run but the data will not be transferred to the tapes. What else?" Tillis was committed.

"I want you to make me a copy of every piece of data that exists on the Model 900 High Voltage Switch products. I want a copy of the patent, schematics, wiring diagrams, parts lists, manuals, and software. Also, I want a list of customers and their addresses for the product line. Can you do it?" Clay challenged.

"Yes, I can do it. It will take me about two hours. I can get the information from the computer and have the printouts routed to my private printer in my office." Tillis was feeling better. He saw a little daylight in front of him. "Is that it?"

"Don't forget the most important part. You are not to discuss this matter with anyone at any time. Do you understand?" Clay looked at him with flat eyes.

"I understand." And Tillis did understand.

"What do you think would happen if you did say something to somebody?"

"I think I would be endangering my family and myself. I wouldn't be so stupid." Tillis declared vehemently.

"You know, Mr. Tillis, I am constantly amazed at how stupid and greedy people are. Do you know that this whole thing started because Claggett decided to steal our invention? He could have bought it for a hundred thousand dollars. Hell, probably less. For one hundred thousand, Joe and I would have taken turns kissing him on all four cheeks. But he chose to steal it and Carter approved. In seeking justice, I made Carter kill Claggett and pay us two million dollars. I have a videotape of the murder. Carter shot him in the head with a revolver. Can you believe that? And I told him the score was even. I warned him not to take any further action. And do you know what he did? He started setting up a team to get some payback. So now he's dead. And now Dr. Kohl, Kurt Steiner and Max Krug have decided to get some payback. People are stupid and greedy, Mr. Tillis. How stupid and greedy are you?"

Clay looked at the man and tried to judge him. Tillis had listened to the story with wide eyes. Now he swallowed hard and tried to talk.

"I'm smart enough to know that I don't want to be a part of this mess. I had no part in any of the previous dealings. The only mistake I have made is to make the one telephone call to Big Ed Thomson. I won't make another mistake and I will do everything you asked of me. I've been looking for a job so I could quit SCT. But as soon as I have helped you, I am quitting whether I have a job or not. Please leave my family and me alone. Please!" He looked at Clay and prayed.

"If you quit right now, you'll draw attention to yourself. Do the jobs that I have asked you do and keep your head low. Don't work any overtime. Don't do anything out of the norm. Don't tell anyone. Not even your wife Got it?"

"I've got it. What do you want me to do with the Model 900 data when I have it collected?" Tillis asked.

"I want you to wrap it up in plastic and leave it in the trunk of your car. Park your car outside for the next few nights. I'll have someone pick it up some night."

"Do you need a key to my trunk? I have an extra." Tillis was eager to help.

"That's okay. We have a key to your car." Clay smiled. "I want you to look over these papers."

Tillis took the packet of papers and started reading. As he did so, he started to feel sick again. "My God, this is a complete report on my family. My daughters and my wife."

"Did we leave anything out? Let's see, date and place of birth, school data, class schedule, extracurricular activities, doctors' names, car descriptions, looks like it's all there. By the way, Mr. Tillis, you're a lucky man. I can assure you that your wife doesn't have a lover."

"But....But what are you going to do with all this information?"

"Nothing if you live up to your end of the bargain. But if any of those schedules change like a sudden vacation to see the grandparents or something, it will be a different story. "

"I don't trust this asshole." Joe growled from the back seat. "He's just like the rest of the SCT crowd. Why don't we keep a hostage to make sure?"

"Ah, come on, Joe. I think he's okay." Clay said.

"You think he's okay and you're willing to risk your ass on him. The problem is that you're risking my ass, too." Joe argued.

"Well, I don't want to take one of his daughters or his wife as a hostage. That's final. I'll listen if you have some other suggestion." Clay glanced at Tillis who was looking positively sick as he followed the conversation.

"How about the Japanese Yakuza thing? When they want someone to pledge loyalty, they ask him to chop off a little finger. I like that approach." Joe sounded gleeful.

"No! No! I can't do that!" Tillis screamed.

Joe whipped out a switchblade and snapped it open. It was a good six inches long and looked like a razor. "I'll do it for you." Joe offered.

"You'll cripple me and I won't be able to do your jobs for you. Besides, everyone will notice. Particularly Mr. Steiner." Tillis was thinking rapidly and grasping at straws.

"I know what we can do." Joe smiled. "We had this same problem up in Jersey last year so we cut off the guy's little toe."

"Joe, I think you're being a little too cautious. Let's give Mr. Tillis the benefit of the doubt. I think he's going to come through for us. Won't you, Mr. Tillis?" Clay raised his eyebrows in question.

"Yes. Yes, I will. I most certainly will. I will program the main frame so that backup tapes cannot be made and I will make up a data package on the model 900. It will be in my trunk when I leave tonight. The tapes that I leave at the bank tonight will be blank. I promise. And I won't ever tell anybody about any of this. Not my wife or anybody. That's the God's truth." Clay was amused to see that he actually crossed his heart.

"Okay. Let's exchange the tapes and we'll be on our way." Clay opened the door.

"Oh, yeah, did you want to file an insurance claim for the fender damage?" Clay asked innocuously.

"Uh, no. Uh, that won't be necessary. But thanks." Tillis stammered.

*   *   *

After the encounter with Albert Tillis, Clay was driving and heading towards his house. Neither man had spoken any words since they left the motel parking lot. Suddenly Joe started laughing and looked at Clay.

"I thought he was going to wet his pants when you asked him if he wanted to press the insurance claim. He would have given you his car if you had asked for it." Joe chuckled. "But what was that comment about "kissing Claggett on all four cheeks" if he had offered us one hundred thousand dollars?"

"Are you saying that you wouldn't have given him at least a little peck on the ass? Remember, we were pretty close to being broke?" Clay laughed as he asked the question.

"Well, maybe a little kiss. But I'd have to get more than one half of a hundred large before I got into something really kinky." Joe bantered.

"Okay, as long as I know you have a price, we'll save the negotiation for the next opportunity. And I won't mention your availability to Sylvia." Clay threatened him.

"Come on, Stanley, jump up here on my lap. Atta boy. How are you doing? How was dinner? Okay, we'll go for a walk in a minute but I want to talk to you for a minute. John and Billy will be by here in a little while. I want you to go with them. I'm going to be pretty busy for a few days and I want you to be safe. Also, I want you to help take care of Billy. Can you do that?" Clay petted him and gave him a hug.

The little dog looked at Clay and cocked his head to one side. It was almost as if he was asking, "What's going on?"

"There are some bad guys that intend to hurt us and our friends, Stanley. I'm not going to wait for them. I'm going to hurt them first. But, the thing is, there's a possibility that I might not make it through this battle. If I don't make it, I want you to live with Billy and John and Susan. They love you and it will be a good home for you."

The little dog emitted a long moan as if he understood. He

twisted around on Clay's lap.

"Ouch! You need a nail trim."

"Look, if things go bad, I'll bet you anything that John and Billy will bring you out to visit Lydia and me at Resthaven. I'll miss you, buddy, but I'll be with Lydia and you'll be with Billy. So we'll be okay until we meet again. I'll keep an eye out for you when you cross over to us. I'm not real sure how it works on the other side. I've been working on that bible study book but it doesn't go into those details. It seems to concentrate on a lot of things not to do. It seems that the ten commandants are not suggestions but more like holy laws. I might have a little trouble explaining some of my actions but I'm sure I'll get a fair hearing. And Lydia will be there to help me. It'll work out."

"Okay, let's go for a walk."

"Yes, we'll stop at every telephone pole and fire hydrant. Hold still while I clip on the leash."

Gino Colissimo waited in the departure lounge at Dulles Airport for his flight to Munich, Germany. He wanted a drink but there was no booze until this operation was over. He expected things to get rough during the next few days.

Gino expected two of his Italian cousins to meet his flight. On earlier visits, they had used some people from their German associates to help them with surveillance and gathering of intelligence. On this trip, they would not use or meet the Germans. The three members of the Colissimo Family would carry out the operations.

Gino intended to set up surveillance on Dr. Kohl and his grandson. He would also try to determine if Max Krug was in Germany or in the United States. As soon as he received the command from Joe or Clay, his team would take out Dr. Kohl and Max Krug. If possible, they were going to try to reason with the grandson. It might not be possible.

*   *   *

Sylvia Colissimo was apprehensive as she exited the United Airlines jumbo jet at San Francisco International Airport. She scanned the crowd of people meeting passengers at the gate and spotted Josephine. They waved at each other across the waiting area. Sylvia was relieved to see Kathryn Ann and her husband beside Josephine.

Sylvia had called Josephine on the previous evening and explained the bare minimums of the situation. Basically, she said that the family was in danger and they were concerned for the safety of the daughters. She told Josephine her arrival flight number and time. Sylvia said that Little Jimmy Colissimo would be with her and reminded Josephine not to call him Little Jimmy. He should be referred to as James. Sylvia said that Alfred Levits would be calling Kathryn to explain the situation. Josephine was to pick up Kathryn and her husband on the way to the airport.

Sylvia hugged the two girls and tried to reassure them. She hustled them out of the terminal and towards Josephine's car after asking about its location. James would pick up their luggage and rent a car for his use during their stay. They would meet at Josephine's condominium in Santa Clara. When Sylvia asked James if he wanted to follow them, he rolled his eyes.

In the baggage area, James was joined by a tall, dark Italian man in his late twenties. They hugged each other in the manner of family members after a long absence. They spoke in Italian. He helped James carry the luggage to the rental car area. As they exited the airport, he directed James to a local service station where they met two other men in a van. The two vehicles proceeded to Santa Clara.

"I have a briefcase full of hardware for you in the van. Everything you requested is in the case." The man said.

James had ordered a .32 caliber automatic for Sylvia. He would give it to her when they met at the condo. For himself, he had ordered two .45 caliber automatics and four extra magazines. One weapon was in a shoulder holster; the other gun was in a belt holster. He had requested a six-inch switchblade and a garrote rope.

"I have a set of pictures for everybody. If you see any one

of these individuals, kill him. Try to do it quietly but, if that's not possible, kill him anyway you can. The only reason any one of these four men would be in this area would be to kill one of the girls. We have to stop them. You should consider each of them as being armed and dangerous. One of them, Max Krug, is particularly dangerous. Anyone who taps any of these guys gets a ten thousand dollars bonus. If you get Krug, it's worth twenty-five thousand. Any questions?" James concluded his briefing.

"Tell us about communications and the patrol pattern." James ordered the tall man.

"These condos are not like the ones on the East Coast. They are one-story units. Your niece lives in one of the sixteen units in this complex." He pointed to a diagram in his hands. "There is a duplicate complex on the back side of this one. The units are arranged in a square-sided figure eight. As you instructed, we will rely on your sister-in-law to handle security inside the unit. We will have one man in the van at all times monitoring the radio. He will run to assist anyone who spots trouble. That will put three of us on foot. We will rotate positions every hour. Each man has a portable radio with a lapel microphone. They are voice actuated. I've marked the patrol path on the diagram. The front door will be in full view of at least one man at all times. That's it."

"Okay, we're operational. Let's do our job. I'm giving ten-to-one odds that I score first. Any takers?" James challenged.

"Yeah, I'll put down a thousand on those odds." The tall man smiled.

"You're on." James agreed to the bet.

At midnight, Clay drove past the driveway of the Tillis home in North Potomac. Everything looked okay so he turned around at the next intersection. When he pulled up at the entrance off the side street, Joe jumped out of the car and ran up the driveway. This time he opened the trunk with the first key. There was a box with two plastic-wrapped bundles inside. Joe scooped up the box and closed the trunk. He strolled casually down the driveway and got into the car. He smiled at Clay.

"Looks like our man gave us two copies."

"Good. I told you he was a convert." Clay laughed.

Lieutenant John Higgins of the Montgomery County, Maryland Homicide Squad pulled up to the main building of Camp Lydia a few minutes before 8 PM. In the handicap-accessible van with him were his wife, Susan, and son, Billy. Stanley was on the front seat looking out of the front windshield. He recognized the place and gave a small bark.

In the vehicle behind him were three police officers. They were old friends who had gone through the police academy with him nearly twenty years ago. Two of them had transferred to the D. C. Police Department. One of them had transferred to Baltimore. Each of them had requested and received a one-week emergency leave. Tonight they were dressed in hunting clothes.

John worked the lift controls and lowered Billy's wheelchair to the ground. He wheeled him into the main headquarters building. Susan and Stanley followed them. John ordered his brother officers to check the perimeter of the building and the grounds. Two days ago, he had met with the main groundskeeper who lived in Thurmont. He ordered him to dig four oversize foxholes and marked the location. He explained that he expected a publicity crew to shoot some film of the camp. Digging the holes was not a lot of work because the camp owned a lot of power equipment including a backhoe. The man did not seem the least bit curious at the request. John was one of the Directors of the camp and he had the authority to give orders. Good jobs were scarce in the Thurmont area. Working at Camp Lydia was a plum job. It paid top wages. The only job better than this one would have been Camp David but it was all civil service jobs. They did not employ locals.

After Billy and Susan were settled, John came outside to talk with the men.

"Look, guys, I hope this is a false alarm but I can't take any chances. As I explained, we received a threat against the families that own and run Camp Lydia. If we do have visitors, they will be armed and dangerous. They will be here to do harm to my family. Load up on supplies before you go to the foxhole. Take a bottle of water, box lunch, rifle and a box of ammo with you. Take an empty jar for relief. There are four foxholes to cover three hundred and sixty degrees. Each of us will have a forty-five degree quadrant on each side of our hole. We have a clear field of fire. " John looked at each one of them in turn. He was asking a lot of them.

"Each of us has a radio. If you spot any movement, whisper into the radio. Identify yourself and give the angular location of the movement relative to your hole. If we are attacked, I'd prefer that you nail the intruder with your pistol. It will be easier to explain to the local authorities later. The reason for the rifle is that I have no idea how many intruders to expect. We may need the firepower. Any questions or problems?" John waited for a response.

"Did you bring any extra batteries? The damn things have a habit of failing at the worst time."

"Yeah, they're on the floor of the van. Help yourself."

"Okay, let's make a pit stop and be in position by 11 PM. I don't think anything will happen before then. We'll stay in position until the first light of dawn about 4:30 AM. Tomorrow we'll have one man on roving guard while the others sleep and eat. I don't know how long this will last but certainly no more than a week." John finished and they headed for the restrooms.

36 – Action

"Well, Joe, it's about time to start the final round. Are you up for this?" Clay looked at his closest friend.

"Play the music, Clay. I'll dance." Joe smiled.

Both of them were joking to relieve the tension. The truth was that it was far too late to stop or back out. They were committed. Both of them knew it.

"It's 11 AM now. Let's get some sleep this afternoon and have an early dinner at my house. We'll pick up Steiner about 7 PM and take him to SCT." Clay yawned. He was tired.

"Okay, catch you later." Joe said. He left the car and headed for his house. Clay drove off towards his place.

As Clay drove off, Joe was looking around while trying not to swivel his head and be obvious. He pulled out his billfold and pretended to remove a card but dropped the wallet in the dirt. As he stooped to retrieve the wallet, he took a good look at the area. When he stood up, he went into his house. Once inside, he called Clay on his cell phone.

"Yes." Clay answered his cell phone and continued driving.

"Clay, I have a stakeout near my front door. I saw him duck down when you drove off. I stalled a little bit and saw him rise up. Do you want to take him now or wait a bit?"

"It would be difficult to do in daylight, Joe. Where is he parked exactly?" Clay was thinking furiously.

"As you drove away from my house, he was parked on your left – almost in front of where the Hanrahans used to live." Joe was visualizing the location of the vehicle.

"Is he one of the guys in our pictures?" Clay asked.

"I don't know. I didn't get a real good look and he's too far away to see his features. It was his quick duck below the dash that caught my attention." Joe explained.

"Let me walk out my front door and check the mail. I'll see if I have a tail. I'll call you back." Clay hung up the telephone.

Clay walked through his front door and towards the street to the mailbox. He scanned the street in both directions for any movement or anyone sitting in a car. He recognized most of the cars. He returned to the house and called Joe.

"I don't see anyone at my house. I hate to try to take this guy during daylight but I don't think we have a choice. It will still be daylight when we leave tonight. I don't want him following us tonight."

"How do you want to do it?" Joe asked.

"I can walk over to your house in fifteen minutes easily. Let's synchronize our time. In fifteen minutes, you walk out to your mailbox with an envelope in your hand. Take your time and put the envelope in the box and raise the flag. While he's watching you, I'll come up behind him. Let's hope there's no one else on the street. When you see me brace him, come down to the car. Okay?" Clay was planning by the seat of his pants.

"Okay. Give me a countdown for a time hack and I'll exit the house in exactly fifteen minutes."

"One, two, three, mark!" Both of them hung up their phones.

Clay left his house via the rear door and crossed through his neighbor's yard to an adjacent street. He walked rapidly towards Joe's house. When he neared Joe's street, he slowed and looked towards the old Hanrahan house. He saw the car that Joe must have been referring to and then saw the top of the guy's head. Two minutes later, he saw Joe walk out towards his mailbox. The guy sat up a little straighter.

Clay crossed the sidewalk and walked down the street staying close to the line of parked cars. He had a .357 caliber Magnum revolver in his right hand. He held it down along his pants leg. He was hoping that the guy would not see him in the side mirror.

As Clay neared the front driver's door, a shadow of movement alerted the man at the wheel. He turned quickly towards Clay who raised the gun and pointed it at him. The guy looked confused and indecisive as Clay jerked open the door. Clay was surprised that the door was unlocked. It was a lucky break.

"Keep your hands down and slide over to the other side. Do it now or I'll kill you." Clay threatened him.

The man moved over the seat towards the passenger side. Joe came up on the passenger side and opened the door. They had the man boxed between them.

The keys were in the ignition so Clay started the car. He drove quickly but carefully to his house. He pulled into the driveway and motioned to the man to go into the house.

"How many are there in your team?" Clay asked.

"I don't know what you're talking about. You can't kidnap someone on a public street. It's against the law." The man protested in a heavily accented voice.

"Is this your picture?" Clay showed him his photo collection. "Is Krug with you?"

"I don't know any Krug or what you are talking about." The man sputtered.

"You have one chance to live. Tell me everything about your surveillance team and I'll tie you up for a day or two. Refuse to answer and I'll shoot you." Clay said calmly.

"I don't know what you're talking about." He did not believe the threat.

Clay shot him in the heart.

"Dumb bastard." Joe uttered the man's epitaph.

"Let's put him in the trunk of his car and clean up the mess. We'll dump him at the SCT building later tonight."

"I can't believe how easy it was to set up Old Steiner. He was like a fish jumping out of the water asking, "Where's the hook?" Joe laughed.

Three weeks earlier.

"Oh, Mr. Steiner? This is Gertrude Talbot. I'm Executive Assistant to Mr. Melvin Dougherty, Montgomery County

Executive. Mr. Dougherty intended to call you today but his flight has been delayed in Chicago due to weather. I hope you don't mind that I'm calling you in his place?" Sylvia paused for a response.

"How can I help you, Mrs. Talbot?" Kurt Steiner asked. When his secretary told him the name of the calling party, she had reminded him that "County Executive" was the highest ranking civil government official in the county. Above the county, one would be talking to the Maryland Governor.

"Well, actually, it's Miss Talbot, but that's not important, is it? I mean, except to me." Sylvia actually giggled. "Mr. Dougherty wanted to invite you to a meeting of Montgomery County businessmen. He has such a meeting once each year. There is a social hour at the Bethesda Country Club. You will have an opportunity to meet other Corporation Presidents located in Montgomery County. After the social hour, limousines will transport the group to the Kennedy Center for a night of Opera. Do you enjoy the Opera, Mr. Steiner?" Sylvia stretched the word "Opera" by trilling the middle syllable.

"Oh, I'm so glad to hear you say so. So many men today do not understand the Opera. So, if you are free on the twelfth of next month, I will have a limousine meet you at your residence at 6:30 PM. Oh, I almost forgot. The dress is formal evening attire. I hope that isn't a problem?" Sylvia paused on an upbeat note.

"Oh, good! Well, I am the coordinator for the evening's activities. If you have any questions, please call me on my private number. Let me give it to you. Now I will call you or your secretary two days before the event to review the schedule. Thank you so much for accepting the Governor's, oops! I mean Mr. Dougherty's invitation." Sylvia hung up.

"So which one of you is going to be the chauffeur?" Sylvia wanted to know.

They reached into their pockets for a coin and flipped for it.

True to her promise, Sylvia had called on the tenth to confirm Mr. Steiner's acceptance of an evening at the Opera with Mr. Dougherty. Yes, it is correct that a limousine will meet Mr. Steiner at his residence at 6:30 PM.

On the last day, Clay decided that it was dangerous for either he or Joe to drive the limousine. Steiner might have seen a picture of them in his intelligence data. Lacking any other solution, Sylvia purchased an actor's kit at a local hobby shop and pasted a mustache on Joe. With his dark complexion, it looked natural – even attractive. With the chauffeur's cap pulled low, there was little chance of recognition.

Joe pulled up to the Regency House in a rented Lincoln Continental. He exited the car and approached the middle-aged gentleman in the tuxedo.

"Excuse me, sir. Are you Mr. Kurt Steiner? Thank you, sir. I'm your driver for the evening, sir. My name is Joseph, sir. May I open the door for you, sir?" Joe opened the rear door on the passenger side for Kurt Steiner. He closed the door and went around to the driver's door. He drove sedately from the grounds of the prestigious residence.

As Joe pulled up to the front door of the Sheraton Hotel, he turned and said, "I hope Miss Talbot told you that you would be sharing the limousine with another guest tonight?"

"No, she did not." Steiner said in a disapproving tone.

"I'm sorry, sir. Bear with me on this segment of the trip and I'll see that you have a private limousine for the remainder of the evening.

"Very well." Steiner huffed and looked out the window.

Joe exited the car and opened the rear door for Clay. As he entered the car, he kept his head down until the car was moving. Then he turned to the other passenger. "Good evening, I understand your name is Kurt Steiner. My name is Matthews."

Steiner recognized the name and the face simultaneously. He drew back into the seat.

"Mein Gott! What's going on here? I demand that you leave this vehicle at once. Driver, pull over!" Steiner demanded in a scream.

"No chance, Asshole." Joe threw over his shoulder.

Clay pulled his .45 caliber automatic pistol from his shoulder holster and told Steiner to shut up and concentrate on remaining alive.

During the drive to the SCT building, Clay attempted to find out the location of Max Krug, the security chief. Steiner maintained a sullen silence.

At the SCT building, Joe pulled up to the front door.

Clay cocked the revolver and jammed the barrel into Steiner's side. "There is one thing that you need to know and remember for the remainder of the evening. When I ask you a question or tell you to do something, I will do so only once. If you do not respond, I will shoot you. Is your American fluent enough to understand, Herr Steiner?"

"Good." Clay said when Steiner nodded. "Now hand me your wallet."

When he opened the wallet, he extracted Steiner's identification card for entering the SCT building. He had his fingers crossed on this point. It was entirely possible that Steiner might leave the card at home. Fortune smiled.

"Now get out of the car. We're going into the building." Clay ordered.

Joe went to the rear of the vehicle and opened the trunk. He removed two large suitcases. He would come back later for the body of the man Clay shot earlier.

After they entered the building, Clay directed Steiner to the Computer Lab. He ordered Steiner to sit down on a chair and secured his hands behind him with a plastic tie strip.

Joe returned to the car and retrieved the body from the trunk. He carried it inside the building and dumped it at Steiner's feet.

"What have you done?" Steiner cried out. "That man is an employee of International Systems. Are you mad?"

"The poor man had a heart attack when he was visiting my house. He was so young, too. Maybe he was a smoker?" Clay joked.

Joe opened the suitcases and began removing the incendiary grenades. He attached a grenade to every piece of equipment and on each side of the software and file cabinets. He set the timers for one hour. Clay retrieved the second set of backup computer tapes from the closet in Steiner's office and added them to the pile of software programs wired for destruction.

Joe went to the first floor of the building. This floor was constructed as an open bay with only the support pillars marring the openness. It was the manufacturing level. Joe attached a powerful explosive device to each pillar. Then he placed the remainder of his grenades at each of the four building corners. He set the timers for one hour and ten minutes. He returned to the second floor and told Clay, "All set."

Clay turned to Steiner and raised the pistol. "Where's Max Krug?"

Steiner bit his lip.

"Did you think we were going to wait for you to kill us?" Clay demanded.

Clay shot Steiner through the heart.

Clay and Joe were watching television and sipping a glass of wine when the "Breaking News" interrupted regular broadcasting.

"Fire and Police are at the scene of an inferno on Research Boulevard in Rockville, Maryland. Witnesses reported a loud explosion or multiple explosions. A towering flame followed. There were no cars in the parking lot and police believe the building was empty. Stay tuned for the 11 O' Clock news."

Joe and Clay touched their glasses in a toast.

It was the third night of sentry duty at Camp Lydia. Everyone was exhausted despite the rest periods during the day.

Nights are very long when you are on guard duty. Every

person with military experience remembers the long hours of sentry duty. Although boring, the day tours are not so bad because there is always some form of activity in the area. At night, everything is still. Normal people are sleeping. Nights are darker and quieter. If you are a little bit nervous, every noise is magnified a hundred times. You feel like you're going to jump out of your skin. At this point, some people break and start screaming or get up and run.

Glenn Halverson, the cop from Baltimore, was almost at the end of his rope. If that goddamn grasshopper in front of him farted one more time, he was going to blow his fuzzy legs off! He sneaked a peek at his watch and was disgusted when he realized it was less than thirty minutes since he checked it the last time. The only way the night could be more miserable would be if it started to rain.

Then everything seemed to happen at once. He saw some movement at the tree line about fifty yards away. Adrenaline shot through his body and the boredom was forgotten. He reached for his radio to report the movement when he heard John Higgins report movement directly in front of his position. Glenn realized it was a second intruder – not the one he saw. He keyed the mike.

"Halverson. Movement at the tree line straight ahead. Fifty yards. Out."

"Higgins. Let them move in close. There might be more than two. Let's flush all of them. Out."

"Halverson. My man is in the open. Estimate forty yards. Out."

"Higgins. My man is in the open. Estimate sixty yards. Out."

Neither of the other two cops reported any movement.

"Higgins. Brace your man before he gets closer than twenty yards. Challenge him one time. If he raises a weapon or runs, put him down. Remember that he might have explosives. Out."

"Higgins. Lou and Bud. Hold your positions unless Glenn or I ask for help. We can handle one man. Keep your quadrants secure. Out."

"Higgins. Keep your head low, Glenn. Out."

"Halverson. Here we go. Out."

Everyone heard Glenn Halverson shout at the intruder. "Stop! Don't move! Stand up and raise your hands! Drop your weapons!"

Everyone heard the rapid fire of an automatic weapon. They knew it wasn't Halverson's gun.

Then they heard the cannon-like roar of a .357 Magnum challenge the night.

John Higgins saw his man freeze and hug the ground. He shouted directly towards the man. "Stand up! Drop your weapon!"

John saw the man raise his weapon. Without waiting for the shot, John fired at the man and saw him reel backwards. The man discharged his weapon into the air.

"Halverson. My intruder is down. There is no movement. Out."

"Higgins. My intruder is down. No movement. I think we should hold our positions until first light. We don't know if they had anyone covering for them from the trees. Out."

"Roger that! Out."

At 4:30 AM it was light enough to see more detail of the lifeless hulks lying in the field. Higgins and Halverson advanced on their individual forms with revolvers cocked and pointed. Neither form moved. Both cops moved back from the scene until the local cops could give their blessing on the shooting. The rifles were collected so they could be stashed inside the cabin. There was no need to confuse the local police with the rifles.

John Higgins hurried to the main cabin to assure Susan and Billy that everything was okay.

James Colissimo was pleased that no one had made the mistake of calling him Little Jimmy. Apparently, the story of his graduation to the senior level of the family had made it out to the West Coast. This branch of the family was a bunch of weird ducks in James' estimation. They were his mother's side of the family. The tall man that met him at the airport was Elliot, his cousin. Whoever heard of an Italian named Elliot?

However, from everything James had heard, Elliot was hard as nails. He had made his bones early in life and enjoyed a senior position in the family. Although it was a long distance contest, James and Elliot were sort of competitive because each of them was the youngest brother.

On a previous trip to California, Elliot had taken him surfing. He said it would be good training for reflexes and smiled. James had busted his ass on the first wave and swallowed enough saltwater to qualify as a pickle. Elliot seemed to enjoy the afternoon just a little too much to suit James.

This was the third day of their stakeout in front of Josephine's California style condominium. James was tired and bored but he wasn't about to admit it. Elliot looked as fresh as he did on the first day. The bastard always seemed to have a smile on his face.

During the day, James holed up inside the condo with Sylvia and the others. Elliot and his crew were holed up in a motel about two blocks away. Each of them took a three-hour shift in the van during the day. Everybody kept his radio turned on.

As the third day rolled into the fourth day, James was beginning to believe that the girls were safe. It was highly unlikely that they were even targeted in the first place. It was 2 AM when his cell phone vibrated in his pocket.

"Yeah." James grunted into the mouthpiece. He figured it was Sylvia.

"It's Joe. How's it going? Any action?"

"No, nothing. Absolutely quiet. How's it out there?"

"We've had some excitement here. They attempted a hit at the Camp. John Higgins and his crew took out two of them. One of them was in our photo collection. Clay and I had a visitor. He was in front of my house when we introduced ourselves. He was in our photo collection, too. Clay and I threw a party in Rockville and everything went okay. Keep your eyes open. This thing isn't over. We haven't found Max Krug yet. He's the toughest one of the bunch. Watch yourself."

"Okay, we'll keep alert but it sounds like you guys had all of the fun." James voiced the resentment of the young.

"Talk to you later. Call me if anything happens." Joe laughed and hung up.

James keyed his radio mike and alerted his crew. "Stay alert. They had some action in the East. Out."

At 3 AM, Elliot alerted everyone. "Here comes a maroon Ford Crown Vic. He's been by here earlier. There are two men in the front seat. He looks like he's slowing down. Yes, he's stopping. One man is getting out. The car is taking off. The other guy is in the shrubs next to the sign. James, do you see him?"

"Yeah, I think so. Let's try to handle this quietly if we can. The car will probably circle the block and swing around to pick this guy up. Let's get the driver of the car when he comes around." James ordered.

James knelt in the darkened shadows of the corner unit and watched the shrub intently. Yes, there was a movement. He waited. Then the assassin bolted from the greenery and towards his target. James ran at him from an angle with his knife held low. The assassin saw James only a second before the collision. He tried to raise his arm but James deflected it upwards. James plunged his knife into the rib cage of the doomed man. He opened his mouth to scream and James used the edge of his hand to crush his larynx. When the assassin fell to the ground, James followed him down to deliver the deathblow.

Simultaneous with the fight between James and the assassin, the maroon Ford rounded the corner to pick up his partner. The driver was peering intently towards the passenger's side to locate his friend. He did not see the arm of Elliot enter the open window on the driver's side with the knife aimed for his throat. Elliot cut his throat while the car was still moving. The car crawled forward slowly with a dead man at the wheel. It hit a parked car and came to rest.

In reviewing the action, the eager band of guards swore that James and Elliot killed their man at the same moment of time. The contest was a draw.

Since James and Elliot were splattered with blood, one of the other men reported the results of the encounter to Sylvia. She came outside to hug the men and send them to the motel for cleanup.

The bodies were deposited in the van. One of the men drove the Ford Crown Victoria and they disappeared into the night.

En route to the motel in Elliot's car, James dialed the number of Joe's cell phone.

"Joe, this is James. They made their try. We got them. There were two of them. One of the guys is in our photo collection. Neither of these guys is Max Krug. What do you want me to do?" James waited.

"Were you able to get everything cleaned up?" Joe wanted to know.

"Yeah. Elliot's men are taking care of the trash dump. Everything is quiet here." James reported.

"Sylvia and the girls are okay?"

"Absolutely."

"Okay, get some rest and head back here as soon as possible. Have Elliot keep his crew around you until you get on the plane. Okay?"

"Okay, we'll let you know our flight number."

"Hello?" Gino answered his cell phone.

"It's Clay, Gino."

"How are you guys doing? Any developments?" Gino was a little apprehensive.

"Yeah, we've been busy. Joe and I had a visitor. One of the guys is in our art gallery. It was good to meet him in person. It was a short visit. He didn't seem to know the location of the other guys so we sent him on his way." Clay was trying to get the message across without being too specific on an open cellular telephone line.

"I understand. How are you and Joe doing? Feeling okay? No problems?" Gino was hoping that they were not wounded in the encounter.

"Oh, we're doing fine. No problems with our health. We were

able to make the big dinner party and night at the opera. After a lively social hour, we visited the shop to review the latest inventions. We had a roaring good time. And you know Joe, he had a booming reunion." Clay chuckled.

"How about the other guys? How are they getting along?" Gino asked.

"Well, James and Elliot met some more of the guys from the art gallery. They made a brief visit to Josephine's place. James was disappointed that he didn't get to talk to them in detail but their stay was extremely brief." Clay chuckled again.

"Also," Clay continued, "Remember our old friend John Higgins? He spent the weekend up in the mountains and they had some visitors. I guess they had a really good time and the visitors liked the area so much that they decided to stay permanently. How about that?"

"Well, I guess that pretty well wraps everything up on your end. I'll get busy on my agenda." Gino was so pissed he was clenching his jaw. Those guys actually made a pass at Josephine and Kathryn Ann. He was going to enjoy doing his part here in Munich.

"Not quite," Clay interrupted his thoughts. "We haven't seen our old friend Max. I'm a little worried about him. Be sure and be on the lookout for him. Okay?"

"Gotcha! I'll add that to my program. I'd better run. The music is about to start." Gino clicked the END button on his cell phone.

"How's Gino doing? " Asked Joe.

"He's okay. He's starting his show now. He'll call us later. All we can do is wait and see how it goes. Glass of wine?" Clay was every bit as nervous as Joe was. He wasn't afraid for himself but everybody else was married or had someone. It mattered whether they lived or died or got hurt.

"What's the latest with John Higgins and his party? " Joe was pacing the floor.

"Come on, Joe. Have a seat and pour us a glass of wine. I talked to John earlier. Everything is going okay. The local cops were not happy about having two bodies on their doorstep. Having a note made up showing a threat to the camp and alerting the cops in advance helped a lot. The fact that John and his buddies are cops was the finishing touch. They'll do a routine investigation and present the facts to the Grand Jury. The whole thing will be done." Clay was trying to calm Joe.

"Everything is okay with James and Elliot. Those two young guys are faster than a bolt of lightning. They kept everything quiet and took the bodies into the mountains for burial." Clay reassured him.

"Sylvia and Josephine are fine. Josephine and Kathryn were never close to any of the action. They're just barely aware that there was a problem." Clay continued.

"What about Max Krug? What are we going to do about him?" Joe asked.

"Higgins is going to put out a bulletin for him. The cops want to talk to him about the fire at SCT. Krug is an employee for the parent company. They have proof that he was in the country and they want to talk to him. When John finds him, we got him."

"What? John is going to turn him over to us?" Joe asked doubtfully.

"No. He's going to question him and turn him loose – after he calls me. We'll pick him up after he leaves police custody."

"So the loose ends right now are Max Krug and Gino's operation in Munich?"

"You got it."

37 - The German Connection

Dr. Gernot Kohl was a happy man. He had celebrated his 75th birthday a few weeks ago. At the party, he had announced his retirement. He had introduced his grandson as the new head of International Systems, Inc.. He had led a successful, exciting and rewarding life. He had built the company from scratch with only the dregs of a family fortune devastated by World War II.

He lost his wife in the late forties during the birth of their second child – a daughter. Neither of them survived. He was left with an eight-year-old son to raise. Dr. Kohl hired the best governess for his son and made sure he spent an adequate amount of time with the boy. His son received the best education that money could buy. In truth, Dr. Kohl did not completely agree with his son's choice of a wife but it turned out well. In 1964, he became a Grandfather. With the family line of secession guaranteed, Dr. Kohl decided to retire. His son would rule the corporate empire. Fate intervened in the form of a car accident. His son was killed by a drunk driver on the Autobahn. The drunk, an American Rock Musician in a new Porsche, was killed, too.

Although the Kohls were a wealthy family, the younger Kohl had a very modest estate. It was easy to convince his daughter-in-law to bring the grandson and live with him on his estate. Dr. Kohl began grooming the boy for his rightful place in German society as the Kohl heir. After completing his undergraduate work at Eton in England, the boy returned to Germany to complete post-graduate studies in electronic engineering. During the summers, he worked at International Systems, Inc. By working in different departments, he was able to gain valuable experience in the manufacturing and marketing of the firm's products. He was able to know and judge the people who would be working for him someday. When he completed his college studies, he went to work in the design-engineering department.

Now at the age of thirty-two, young Gustav Kohl was ready to take the helm of the very successful International Systems, Inc.

Over the years, young Gustav made several trips to the United States and spent some time at their American subsidiary, Signal Control Technology, Inc. He was fascinated with the company and the country. He traveled the United States from shore to shore and from Mexico to Canada. He would have preferred to take over SCT but he knew it wasn't possible. Gustav's grandfather was depending on him to lead the entire company not just one subsidiary. He knew and understood his grandfather's hatred towards the United States. His grandfather had served in the German Army at the end of World War II. He blamed the US for the rape of his country during the years of occupation. He blamed the entire country for the death of his son not just one driver. As a result, young Gustav had to be content with trips of a few weeks duration to the United States.

During those trips, Gustav was wined and dined by Jack Carter and Jon Claggett. He was a frequent guest at their homes and knew their families. He was on an extended trip to the United States when the Model 900 High Voltage Switch was introduced. He had read the patent application and, as a design engineer, he understood the concept and circuitry. The patent was filed in Jon Claggett's name and assigned to SCT.

When Gustav read the patent application, he was amazed at the technical complexity. He had not realized that Jon Claggett was such a gifted designer. However, after several conversations on the subject, he began to realize that Claggett had not designed the product. Gustav reasoned that the product was probably designed by a subordinate who let Claggett take the credit. It was a common practice in Germany.

It was on the same trip that Gustav met the most beautiful girl in the world. She was also the most intelligent and the most glamorous. He fell in love at their first meeting. Laura Brock was teaching German at SCT. The company encouraged their employees to learn German since they were a subsidiary of a German company. The classes were free to any SCT employee or dependent who wanted to learn the language. Laura was fluent because her parents had moved to the United States from Germany shortly before she was born. German was spoken in their home as a primary language. Laura's father, Dr. Werner Brock, worked for NASA in Greenbelt, Maryland. Laura's mother was a schoolteacher.

Gustav and Laura started dating during the early part of a one-month trip. When he returned to Germany, they corresponded and telephoned on a regular basis. Gustav managed another trip within three months and they became engaged. On his return to Germany, Gustav had to tell his grandfather of his intention to marry an American girl. It was not a pleasant conversation. However, as Gustav pointed out, he was twenty-four years old and did not need permission to marry. Or to immigrate to the United States if necessary. Dr. Kohl capitulated and gave his blessing on the union.

The wedding was very traditional and held in the United States at the expense of the bride's family. After a two-week honeymoon spent touring the United States, the newlyweds moved to Munich to establish their home. Dr. Kohl was relieved.

During the second year of their marriage, Gustav and Laura had a baby boy. During the fourth year of their marriage, they had twin boys. During the sixth year of their marriage, they had a baby girl. All of Dr. Kohl's reservations disappeared with the birth of his first great-grandson. He gave the couple a larger house located within a mile of his own house. And Gustav's career at International Systems was advanced to a faster pace in anticipation of Dr. Kohl's retirement. Young Gustav was headed for the exciting stratosphere of corporate management and Dr. Kohl was eager to be a full-time great-grandfather.

Dr. Kohl wanted to turn over the reins when the company was running smoothly. At the present time, there was one major problem remaining to be solved.

When the first sign of problems had developed at SCT, Dr. Kohl was startled at the violence of the scene. Jon Claggett disappeared and a major fire destroyed the computer lab. He was uneasy that there was no solution to the mystery of what had happened. When Jack Carter had to ransom the backup computer tapes for two million dollars, the motive for the violence was clear but Dr. Kohl was still uneasy. He discussed the matter with his head of security, Max Krug. They agreed that there were too many unanswered questions. Max was assigned to start investigating the scene quietly. Jack Carter was not informed of the investigation.

Max Krug had served under Lieutenant Gernot Kohl in the German Army at the close of World War II. He was a veteran of much combat when he was assigned to the young Lieutenant. The experience and strength of the grizzled sergeant combined with the intelligence and cunning of the young Lieutenant were enough to help them survive the war. In the final months of the humiliating rout of the German Army, they lost count of the number of times they saved each other's lives. Max went to work for the company as bodyguard, security chief and problem solver. There had not been many problems over the years but the few that occurred were solved instantly – sometimes violently.

Max Krug and Dr. Kohl would retire from the company at the same time. The criterion was solving the mystery at SCT. Neither wanted to leave a potential problem for young Gustav.

Before they were able to make any measurable progress, the second round of violence at SCT occurred. Jack Carter was proven to be the killer of Jon Claggett and another local man. Forensic evidence indicated that Carter committed suicide at the burial site of his two victims. Now Kohl and Krug were thoroughly confused. Neither of them believed that Carter would commit suicide. They accepted the fact that the suicide could have been staged. The mystery was the body of the local man – a Mr. Arthur Goodman of Visorex Systems. Who was he? What was the connection? The videotape showing Carter shooting Jon Claggett could have been faked but it had the feel of authenticity. The best explanation was that Carter discovered that Claggett was involved in some criminal act against the company. But, if that was the case, why not prosecute him or fire him or any number of other solutions? And, for God's sake, why make a video record of the killing? That was incredibly stupid. Both Krug and Kohl knew that Carter was not stupid. Thus, the best explanation was that Carter pulled the trigger in front of a camera while under duress. But from whom? And why?

Dr. Kohl was relieved when Kurt Steiner reported a possible solution that would explain all of the questions. Claggett must have stolen the design of the Model 900 High Voltage Switch from a couple of local men. Those individuals must have planned their revenge carefully to engineer the plot that took Claggett's life, implicated Carter in his killing, and resulted in a two million-dollar gain. Kohl admired their skill and courage.

And Kohl could understand that the whole thing must have enraged Jack Carter. He was a proud, arrogant man. He was confident to the point of foolishness. Carter must have been unable to live with the idea of being outsmarted. So the two men relieved Carter of the burden of living.

Dr. Kohl wished that the two men had never been cheated in the first place. If he had known of the situation, he would have ordered a different approach. And he admired the men for solving their problem. They set a price on the situation – Claggett's life and two million dollars – and they collected. All indications were that they were satisfied and posed no further danger. Jack Carter was stupid not to let the matter die a natural death.

Dr. Kohl was neither vindictive nor vengeful. He would have been happy to let matters stand as they were now. The problem was his retirement and leaving young Gustav with a situation that may arise at some future time. He didn't really think the two men would be any future problem but "think" wasn't good enough. He decided to eliminate the problem. The solution wasn't fair but no one is guaranteed a fair treatment in life. The men were simply unfortunate by being in the wrong place at the wrong time.

Now that Kurt Steiner had solved the mystery and identified

the men, Dr. Kohl turned the problem over to Max Krug. Max's instructions were to eliminate the two men without implicating SCT or International Systems. Steiner had assured Dr. Kohl that the men had not been alerted by some ill-advised inquiry. Krug could take his time and do a good job. He had an unlimited budget.

Max Krug was only one year older than Dr. Kohl was but he had led a much different life. Trained in the German Army during the time of war under Hitler's regime, Max learned the value of physical strength and ruthlessness early in life. As a Senior Sergeant, Max wanted to serve under a tough, intelligent officer. He had served under weaklings – the ones who received their commissions as a result of family connections or political influence. They died young in battle. Even with a tough sergeant to clean up behind them, the weaklings fell in combat. When Lieutenant Kohl arrived in his unit, Max knew he had a leader in front of him. Now he would help him survive the savagery of the battlefield.

After the war, Max labored in construction until young Gernot Kohl got the company established. In the intervening years, he had never regretted his decision to follow Dr. Kohl.

Max Krug had never married. For sex, he used prostitutes. He woke up each morning alone by choice. The thought of having the same woman around his apartment for years was repugnant to him. He preferred a Spartan life. Each day of his life contained a physical training regimen that few men could rival. It was true that he had slowed down as the years crept by – he jogged three miles each day now instead of running five miles. And he did one hundred slow push-ups rather than two hundred fast ones. His eyesight was still good. He required glasses only for reading small print but his target shooting was as accurate as ever.

The new assignment to locate and eliminate two Americans named Matthews and Colissimo was a bonus for him. He knew it would be his last assignment. Over the years, he had handled many such assignments. He had killed several competitors. Two politicians on the local level had tried to intimidate Dr. Kohl. Their deaths had been described in the newspapers as gruesome. One young scientist had tried to take some company designs to a competitor. Krug had eliminated the man and his family – a wife and teenage son. Max was not squeamish.

Max had cultivated many police contacts over the years. He used these contacts to extend his acquaintances to the international field. With the acquisition of Signal Control Technology, Inc., Max increased his efforts to meet law enforcement officials at the state and federal levels in the United States. There was always someone eager to earn a little extra money by supplying information. Krug used the time proven technique of paying too much for too little until the hook was set. Then he could get anything he wanted for a more reasonable price.

38 – Losses

During his investigation of Matthews and Colissimo, Krug discovered the underworld influence of the Colissimo family. Max decided that the four Colissimo brothers would have to be eliminated along with Clayton Matthews. In Joe Colissimo's family, Sylvia was an active part of the operation. She would have to be killed.

Surveillance of Clay Matthews revealed the existence of Camp Lydia. It was a fortuitous discovery because it exposed John Higgins. Now he knew the identity of Matthews' police informant. John Higgins was identified as another target.

A phone tap on the Colissimo and Matthews home revealed the existence of the two daughters in California. A credit check revealed the incredible wealth of the Matthews daughter. Krug deduced that Kathryn Ann's wealth was the result of their raids on SCT's treasury. She must be the convenient hiding place for the money. Thus, the two daughters were targeted for elimination.

Max Krug intended to enjoy his last assignment to the maximum. He planned to cast a wide net.

John Colissimo headed the Colissimo Family because he was the oldest brother. He was also the smartest and toughest brother. The Old Man had trained him for his role in life since he could walk. He made his bones before the age of eighteen and served as his father's right-hand man until the Old Man died. John took over the family at the age of thirty-five. Over the years, the family business had changed dramatically. Earning money was almost secondary to staying ahead of the various government agencies.

As distasteful as it was to him, John had concluded that it was easier and safer to earn an honest living than a dishonest living. It was a disgusting situation. Now he spent his days and nights worrying about various business enterprises that barely earned ten or fifteen percent return on investment. The only hope in the family for huge profits and the excitement of shady dealings was in teaming up with Clay Matthews. The man was brilliant. Clay was a gifted design engineer but he was also a remorseless avenger. If he had been born Italian, James figured the man would be an international crime boss.

The family had profited greatly by teaming up with Clay Matthews but this latest plot was the best one of all. Everybody's appetite for violence and excitement would be whetted and the money would flow in by the millions. Untaxed millions! The best kind of profits. John Colissimo had deployed his brothers on their assignments like a Roman General. Now he would monitor the battle.

It did not dawn on him that he would be a target.

Max Krug rated his targets by their degree of difficulty. The daughters would be the easiest so he sent his youngest associates to California to deal with them. He did not anticipate any trouble. The targets were not forewarned or so he had been told.

Camp Lydia was the next easiest target. True, John Higgins was a police officer and probably armed. But, at the camp, he would be relaxed and playing on the computer with his son. At night, he would be sleeping in the arms of his new wife. Again, there should be no problem. He instructed his associates to approach the camp at night. They were to kill all of the occupants.

Krug left one of his men to keep an eye on Colissimo and Matthews. He anticipated that the two men would have dinner together and return to their respective homes. The associate was to call him on a cell phone if the routine varied.

Krug intended to travel to New Jersey. He would personally dispatch John Colissimo. Max thought the wily family chieftain might present a problem to his junior associates. He knew the history of John Colissimo. He thought the element of surprise would prevail but the man probably had the instincts of an alley cat. If anything went wrong, it could endanger the entire operation. Max would take care of John and then return to the Washington area to deal with Clay Matthews and Joe Colissimo. The team from Camp Lydia would return to the local area to assist him.

The data reported on John Colissimo's schedule showed very few weaknesses. The man traveled with a chauffeur and a bodyguard. He had a mistress but apparently recognized the vulnerability. When he visited her, extra troops were on the alert. The Colissimo estate was an electronic marvel. Motion detectors would report the minute movements of mating mice. The best opportunity was during the day inside the office. John was surrounded by accountants and lawyers not guards. The elevator was disabled and a well-armed team at the ground entrance guarded the single stairway. However, it had been so long since there had been any trouble that they were not alert.

Max Krug approached the front entrance an hour after lunch. The two guards were drowsy. He saw their relaxed posture as he shuffled down the sidewalk like an old man. As he approached them, they lazily motioned him to go around the entrance. Max smiled and moved as if to obey. At the last possible moment, he lunged towards the two guards. He stabbed one of them in the chest with a bayonet. He swung a collapsible baton towards the head of the second guard and heard a loud squash. He mounted the stairs in a long stride.

Everyone in the room looked up when the door swung open. They saw Max with a 9mm automatic pistol in each hand. The group of accountants threw up their hands and kept their seats. Max rushed towards the corner office and saw John Colissimo reaching for a weapon in a drawer. He shot him one time in the chest. As he approached the body, he fired directly into the top of John's head. Then Max Krug turned and exited the offices. He was anxious to return to Washington.

Gino Colissimo was waiting in his rental car near the entrance to the Kohl estate. He was relaxing and finishing a cigarette when his cell phone vibrated. The call was from the chief accountant for the family.

Gino was shocked to hear of the death of his older brother. He knew why the call came to him. He was the next in line. It would be up to him to notify Joe and James. Before the man hung up, Gino gave some instructions and asked some questions.

"What did he look like?" Asked Gino.

"He was old. He looked like a piece of old shoe leather. He wore a hat and his clothes looked sort of foreign like a European cut to the suit."

"What kind of accent did he have?"

"I dunno. He didn't say a word."

Gino discontinued the call and used the speed dial to call his brother Joe.

After speaking to Joe for a few minutes, he called James.

After the calls, Gino remembered the last conversation with Clay Matthews. He had warned that this might be an expensive operation. He had reminded them that pain and death were two-way streets.

None of them had anticipated that John would be a target.

What else had they overlooked?

Max Krug had driven a rental car to New Jersey for the assassination of John Colissimo. Flying would have been more convenient but then he would have had to procure some weapons in the local area. In the Washington, D. C. and Northern Virginia areas, there were several places to buy any weapon known to man. The return drive to the D. C. area was tiresome because of the heavy traffic. Finally, he cleared the Baltimore beltway and started calling his associates. He wanted to know the location of Matthews and Colissimo. He was puzzled when there was no answer. Thirty minutes later, he tried to call the associate again. There was no answer. Max figured the operation had been compromised in some way.

Max exited the Washington I-495 Beltway at Wisconsin Avenue. He parked in The Marriott Hotel parking lot and located a bank of telephones. He dialed the cell phones of the Camp Lydia team and the California team. There was no answer.

Max entered the coffee shop on the main level for a sandwich and a cup of coffee. He had not eaten since breakfast and he needed a few minutes to think. He did not want to call Dr. Kohl until he had more information.

After eating, Max sat in the waiting area at the registration desk and read a newspaper. Occasionally, he would call the numbers of his associates. There was no answer. The only explanation was that they had been eliminated. Incredible! How could all of them have been captured or killed?

Max checked into the hotel for the night while he decided what to do. He was too restless to remain in the room so he adjourned to the bar for a Schnapps. He was starting to order a refill when the television in the corner reported the breaking news of the fire at SCT.

Max realized that he had received some faulty intelligence. The enemy had been alerted and was taking some offensive action. This was a worthy adversary. He needed to consult with Dr. Kohl about the next steps but Germany was six hours ahead in time. It was the wee hours of the morning in Munich. He could not call Dr. Kohl at 2 AM. It was unthinkable.

After his encounter with Matthews and Colissimo, Albert Tillis had followed his instructions to the letter. He disabled the "Backup Data" command at the computer. It could not be done by pre-programming or manually. The tapes would run and the indicator would report a completed operation but the tape reels would be empty of data.

Tillis, known as Ab by his friends, had made two copies of everything on the computer relating to the Model 900 High Voltage Switch product line. He wrapped each set in plastic and packed them in a box. Ab stored them in the trunk of his car and parked outside the garage. He didn't sleep very well. He was relieved to find the material missing from his car on the following morning.

On the following days, Ab stuck to his regular schedule and routine except that he went directly home after dropping the tapes by the bank. His wife asked him if there was anything wrong and he assured her that everything was okay. When she offered to skip her regular bowling night with the other ladies in order to keep him company, he nearly went ballistic. He insisted that everyone keep a normal schedule.

Ab's instincts told him that something was going to happen soon. He didn't know what it would be but it would probably be massive and catastrophic for SCT. Although he feared the insecurity of unemployment and the effect on the rank and file employees of the company, Ab felt that any action by Matthews and Colissimo was justified. He had been horrified to hear the details of the continuing feud between the parties. He prayed that he would never be so arrogant and greedy as to even contemplate those sorts of actions.

Despite a vivid imagination, Tillis was stunned to see the news flash on the explosions and fires at the SCT building. The two determined men had certainly solved the problem of SCT. Given the destruction reported on the television and the lack of backup data, SCT was out of business. It was mind-boggling. SCT was a thirty-two million-dollar per year corporation with a book asset value of nearly sixty million. If the owners had wanted to sell the company, they would have received a sum in the neighborhood of seventy-five million dollars. Now the value was zero. And all because two greedy employees decided to steal a hundred thousand dollars from two hardworking entrepreneurs.

And the second part of the lesson was that the two greedy

employees were dead. They had paid the ultimate penalty.

Ab's problem now was that the home office would soon discover that the backup data tape reels were empty. They would ask him to explain. What would he say?

Ab planned to say that he had no idea why the "Backup Data" function on the computer had failed. The daily backup had been pre-programmed. True, he was the computer manager but he could not be responsible for checking every function every day. Failures happen.

Their procedures called for a complete diagnostic checkup once per month. At the last checkup, everything had functioned normally. If you have any doubts, check the files. Oops! No files!

Albert Tillis pulled out a pad of paper and started making a list of things to do. First, he would update his resume. Next he would make a list of potential employers and start making calls. He would call a real estate agent and list the house. The Tillis family was moving to California. The head of the Tillis family had made a decision. On second thought, California might not be far enough away from Matthews and Colissimo. What were the job possibilities in Hawaii?

Gino Colissimo was talking to himself. He was telling himself to put his grief aside until the job was done. If John were here, he would tell him to straighten up and act like a man. Stand tall. The family expected it and John would demand it. There would be time for memories at the wake and time for tears at the funeral. He picked up his radio and made contact with his two Italian cousins. They were stationed at strategic locations around the Kohl estate.

"Gianni, report." Gino ordered.

"The limousine arrived and dropped Dr. Kohl at the front door. The chauffeur is parking the car in the garage now."

"Follow the plan." Gino reminded him unnecessarily. When the chauffeur closed the garage door and started for his apartment over the garage, Gianni would stop him. With a gun to his head, he would tie up the chauffeur until further instructions. If the chauffeur resisted, he would kill him.

"Peter, report." Gino ordered the other man.

"The guard is inside with Dr. Kohl."

Gino would wait until Peter secured the bodyguard. The normal procedure followed at the estate would be that the bodyguard would precede Dr. Kohl into the house. He would disarm the alarm system and clear the immediate area. Dr. Kohl would enter and they would proceed to the second floor master bedroom after locking the door. After clearing the second floor, the bodyguard would return to the ground level. He would exit the rear door of the house and make a check of the grounds. When the guard turned to lock the door behind him, Peter would kill him with a knife. They would make no attempt to subdue the guard. It was too dangerous.

When Peter reported his status, Gino would enter the house through the rear door. He would proceed to the master bedroom for a talk with the good doctor.

Clay and Joe were in high spirits as they traveled around the 495 Beltway towards home. Everything was going according to plan. The girls were safe. Sylvia and James would be home tomorrow. John and his family, including Stanley, were safe. They were returning from the law offices of Alfred Levits. They had left the documentation for the High Voltage Switch products with him. They had given him a cryptic explanation about the possibility of selling the material. They promised to explain the negotiation if they were successful.

Joe was laughing when his cell phone rang. He answered it and immediately went silent. When he hung up, he told Clay about the death of his older brother John.

After the initial shock, Joe did the same thing as Gino. He told himself to get the job done. It was necessary for the safety of the family. There would be time for grief later.

Now they knew that Max Krug was still in the United States.

They figured he would try to call his various associates. When he was unable to contact them, he would know what happened. They knew that Max Krug would see the television news report about the SCT building. When he was unable to find Kurt Steiner, he would understand the implications. The question was "What would he do next?" Would he call Dr. Kohl for instructions or proceed on his own initiative?

Clay picked up the telephone and called John Higgins. He explained the events of the evening. He told him that as long as Krug was on the loose, none of them was safe. He ordered John to load Billy, Susan, and Stanley into the van. He wanted him to depart Camp Lydia immediately. He suggested that he drive north towards Pennsylvania and get lost until the situation was resolved. He reminded him that damage to Camp Lydia could be repaired but their lives could not be replaced. John promised that they would be on the road within fifteen minutes.

Joe was talking to James on the other cell phone. After sharing their grief, Joe jolted him back to reality. Joe ordered him and Sylvia to remain in California. He wanted James and Elliot's family to move the girls and themselves to a new location. He was to pick something at random. He was to use cash not credit cards.

Clay and Joe decided to follow their own advice. They did not return home. As an interim measure, they headed for a busy shopping mall. That would be good for a few hours. In the meantime, they hoped to hear from Gino. If Max Krug called Dr. Kohl, they had a chance of closing this battle without further losses. If Krug proceeded on his own path of destruction, it would get bloody before the battle was over. Neither of them thought of a negotiation or compromise. The original plan was still operative. Steiner, Kohl, and Krug had to die. Steiner was gone. Gino would take care of Kohl tonight. Krug was the problem.

As Dr. Gernot Kohl prepared for bed, he reflected on the evening with his grandson and great-grandchildren. In his wildest dreams, he could not have imagined that he would know such happiness and pride. Gustav was the heir of his dreams. He was intelligent, handsome, strong, and honorable. He was a decent man without the weakness of a liberal. Although Dr. Kohl cringed a little every time he heard the American-corrupted accent of Laura's German, he knew she was the one soul mate for Gustav. The two youngsters were perfectly in tune with each other. He saw the glances that passed between the two of them as they silently communicated. He saw the little touches as they moved around the room.

It was approaching fifty years since his beloved wife had died in childbirth. She died in pain without adequate medication. At the time of her death, she was malnourished from the war years of deprivation. Time had dulled his pain and memory of the loss.

When Dr. Kohl heard the news of his son's death in an automobile accident, he cursed the Gods and screamed at the Heavens. In addition to the loss of his son, the other driver, a drunken rock and roll American singer, was killed. He was cheated of a revenge that would have been cruel and sweet. The passage of time rescued his sanity. Since his son's death in 1965, he was spared further pain and rewarded with financial success and another generation of Kohls.

He chuckled as he remembered the antics of little Karen earlier in the evening. She was an angel in disguise. When she hugged him and kissed his cheek, his heart would beat stronger with love and pride. He knew that Gustav's sons were the standard bearers for a continuation of the family line but Karen was the hidden treasure. When his eyes welled up during a hug from Karen, he looked up and saw the smile on Laura's face.

Dr. Kohl continued his reflections as he performed his nighttime ablutions. When he heard the bedroom door open, he assumed it was his bodyguard returning to report a secure perimeter. When he finished brushing his teeth and turned around, he froze in shock at the sight of a total stranger pointing a gun at him.

"Good evening, Dr. Kohl. My name is Gino Colissimo. I am here to discuss certain matters with you." Gino smiled but it was the smile of death.

Gernot Kohl drew himself to attention. He had always known that death would come one day. During the war years, he had seen many men die. Some died as weaklings while screaming in protest. Some died as brave heroes. During his infrequent prayers to the Gods whose presence he doubted, Gernot Kohl did not plea for mercy or salvation. He prayed for the strength to meet death as a man. As he looked into the eyes of Gino Colissimo, he knew that he would find out if his prayers would be answered. He knew in his heart that he would not survive the visit of this grim-faced man.

The next words from Gino Colissimo's mouth shattered any hope he may have harbored of a peaceful death. It reminded him of the depths of depravity that man could explore.

"I am here to kill you before I visit your grandson and his family. Tonight I will eliminate the Kohl family." Gino spoke in a low, calm voice.

"You are the brother of Joseph Colissimo?" Dr. Kohl asked in a desperate play for time. He knew the bodyguard must be dead. The chauffeur was probably dead.

"Yes. And I am the brother of John Colissimo who was slaughtered by Max Krug today." Gino threw the words at him.

"I ordered the deaths of Clayton Matthews and Joseph Colissimo. I did not order Max to kill your brother John. I am somewhat confused. Do you know the circumstances? Was Max confronted by your brother?"

"No! My brother was in his office in New Jersey. Max traveled from Washington, D. C. to kill him. It was not an accidental confrontation. And the attempt on the lives of my niece and sister-in-law was not an accident. Krug sent two assassins to California to search for them." Gino screamed at him in his grief.

"Even though I know nothing of these acts, I am responsible. I understand why you must kill me. What I don't understand is why you must murder my grandson and his family. You look like a man of honor not a crazed killer."

"I do what is necessary. As you intended to do." Gino retorted.

"I did not intend to kill your family. I wanted to eliminate Matthews and your brother Joseph as future threats to my family. It was the last act of an old man who wanted to protect his loved ones." Dr. Kohl tried to explain.

"You turned a mad dog loose to slaughter at will. Now you will pay the price. As will your family." Gino raised the pistol.

"Wait! What is your rush? You should enjoy your revenge more and I deserve a chance to present my case."

"Go ahead, Herr doctor. Beg to your heart's content. I will enjoy the spectacle. I will tell your grandson and great-grandsons of your pleas." Gino sneered.

"I do not beg. I do not cry. Do you see tears in my eyes? Do you see my body tremble? You are mistaken if you believe you can make me cringe. You are not nearly as cruel as a Russian soldier with a bayonet. I have faced much worse threats than you." Dr. Kohl laughed at his tormentor. Inwardly, he marshaled every ounce of strength and cunning to secure the survival of his family.

"Are you under the impression that you will die quickly, doctor?" Gino asked. "We have all night I can spend some time with you. It will not take long to dispatch your family into eternity. I will do them quickly. I will not enjoy it. It is a necessity not a joy." Gino decided it was time to throw him a hint of hope.

"You are mistaken. It is not a necessity. My grandson knows nothing of the problems with your family. You will debase yourself for nothing. Do you wish to face your God with the blood of innocents on your hands? He will not see you as a warrior but as a monster." Kohl screamed at Gino.

"Your grandson may not know anything about these matters now but he will in time. When he uses the resources of your financial empire to investigate your death, he will know the truth. Then he will seek revenge. He will disregard the safety of his children as you did. He will believe in the power of his inherited riches and he will act with arrogance." Gino accused.

"If you give me an opportunity to discuss the future with you, I can guarantee you that my grandson will not seek revenge. I can compensate your family for their losses. If you give me a chance to redeem myself, you will be welcomed by your God as a man of honor and compassion." Dr. Kohl saw a sliver of light and he pleaded without shame.

"I don't understand. What is this babble? Are you offering me money?" Gino laughed.

"No. I offer you safety and salvation and reparations." Dr. Kohl corrected him.

"Really? Tell me how you intend to protect my family from your rabid dog Krug." Gino challenged.

"It is evening time in the United States. Max will be sleeping. At 7 AM our time, he will call me to ask for instructions. I will order him home." Kohl promised.

"And what of this salvation?" Gino wanted to know.

"You speak of rabid dogs. What will you be if you carry out the orders of the madman Matthews and kill my grandchildren? Do you think for a moment that you will not spend an eternity in hell?" Kohl spoke in a thunderous voice as if calling down a judgment.

"Matthews? Do you think Matthews ordered me to kill your family?" Gino asked in a disbelieving voice. "Clayton Matthews is an honorable, compassionate man. He did not order me to kill your family. Matthews ordered me to make you take certain actions and then kill you quickly. I decided to kill you slowly and eliminate your family because you killed my brother and attempted to kill my niece." Gino shook his head in amazement at Kohl's ignorance.

"What did Matthews order you to do?" Kohl asked.

"He told me to tell you that Steiner was dead. Also, the SCT building has been completely destroyed. Clay has the backup computer tapes in his possession. There is no way that SCT can be restarted. He has a separate documentation package on the product that you stole from him. He wanted you to arrange a sale of the product to some American company and have the funds paid to him. He set a minimum price of seven million dollars on the product. We figured that the product could be sold quickly at such a low price." Gino related his instructions as if from some written page.

"I can do those things." Kohl stated quietly.

"Matthews was wrong on several things. He anticipated that Krug would be dead by now. He is still alive and we do not know his location. Obviously, we are in danger." Gino explained. "Also, Matthews did not know you would kill my brother and attempt to kill other members of my family when he gave me those instructions."

"So! If I understand you correctly, Matthews wanted Steiner and Krug dead and he wanted seven million dollars which would be raised by the sale of his product? "

"No, Herr doctor. You did not understand correctly. Matthews wanted Steiner, Krug, and you dead. And he wanted seven million dollars from the sale of the product line." Gino corrected Kohl.

"So be it. Steiner is dead already according to you. My death is assured by your swift hand. I can give Krug to you and arrange the seven million dollars. The product line is worth much more than such a paltry sum. Several American companies would jump at the chance to buy it. If we proceed along this line and you spare my family, you will have your salvation." Kohl was negotiating the most important deal of his life.

"How can you give Krug to us?" Gino asked.

"I believe that Max will call me at 7 AM and ask for instructions. I will tell him to stay at his location while I decide what to do. You can call Matthews with the information." Kohl made it sound simple.

"So you would betray your friend and subordinate?" Gino looked doubtful.

"No. I am executing him for disobeying my orders." Kohl spit out the words.

"And what about the product sale?" Gino wanted to know.

"I will make three telephone calls. I will tell the heads of three American companies that the first one to offer me seven million dollars for the product line will have a deal. I assume that Matthews gave you some instructions about the method of payment?"

"Clay has two copies of the complete documentation on the product line. He wants the buyer to travel to Bethesda, Maryland and meet at the office of our attorney. The buyer will transfer the money to an offshore account. He will receive a Bill of Sale from your company and the documentation from our attorney. You would have to prepare and certify a Bill of Sale and express ship it to our attorney in time for the settlement."

"These things can be done. What else do you need besides my death?" Dr. Kohl looked at Gino and waited.

"My family must be indemnified for the death of my brother. He had five children and a wife. Most importantly, you must devise a way to guarantee that your grandson will not seek revenge."

"How much will it cost to indemnify your family? I ask this of you with respect towards your brother." Kohl spoke with sincerity.

"Five million dollars."

"Done!"

Gino lowered the pistol. Both men breathed a sigh of relief.

Dr. Kohl knew he had won a reprieve for his family.

Gino knew he had carried out the mission assigned to him.

Clay's telephone startled him from a daydream. He was talking to Lydia in his mind and telling her about Billy's idea for a new software program. Clay was so proud of Billy.

Joe had been studying his partner quietly. He knew him so well that he could almost read his thoughts. He saw the little smile on Clay's lips and knew he was thinking of Lydia. He wondered what it would be like to love a woman so deeply. Joe loved Sylvia and could not imagine a life without her but he knew his love was different. Clay's love for Lydia was so devoted and eternal. He knew that Clay would never be able to love or touch another woman. He grieved for his friend.

Both of them stared at the telephone for a minute before Clay answered it.

"Clay, it's Gino. I'm with Dr. Kohl now. The good doctor has agreed to all of the terms that you suggested plus the ones that I added because of John and the girls. He says that he doesn't know the location of Max Krug or how to contact him. However he expects Krug to call at 7 AM Munich time. That's one hour from now. He will find out his location and tell him to stay there while he decides what to do. I'll call you with the location. Do you have a method of handling the matter on your end?"

"Yes. It's no problem. Let me know."

"Okay. Talk to you later."

Max Krug was restless. He was unable to sleep even though the room at the luxurious Marriot Hotel was very comfortable. He felt like he was in a cage. It was over an hour before he could call Dr. Kohl. He dreaded the conversation. He knew that he had botched the last mission he would ever have for his beloved leader. Max considered the possibility of suicide. If he killed himself now, he would not have to face the wrath of the one man he respected above all others. On the other hand, Dr. Kohl may have instructions for him that would allow him to serve again. He decided to postpone his demise.

When Max left the room, he intended to stretch his legs by taking a short walk. However, in the lobby, another idea occurred to him. There was one other thing he could do. Max headed for his car.

It was only a short drive to enter the 495 Beltway headed east – the inside loop as the Americans referred to it. He took the Beltway around to the New Hampshire Avenue exit. From the exit, he wound his way through the residential sections to Clay Matthews' house. As he drove past the house, he could not detect any sign of occupancy. The rental car that belonged to his associate was in the driveway so that explained one mystery. He made one turn around the block and parked in front of the Matthews house. As he exited his car, Max drew his pistol and held it down beside his leg. He walked towards the front door.

No one challenged him. He looked through the windows of a darkened and unoccupied house. Too bad. He would have preferred a shootout to settle the matter. Well, there was another way. Max reached into his pocket and extracted a small piece of C-4 plastic explosive and a contact detonator.

After wiring the front door of the Matthews house to the explosives, Max returned to his car and started for the hotel. He knew the route to the hotel. Unfortunately, there were an unbelievable number of eighteen-wheel trucks headed in the same direction. It seemed to take forever to travel the last mile to the exit for the hotel. He was running late for his telephone call to Dr. Kohl. On top of everything else, his superior would fault him for a lack of punctuality.

"No, Aunt Sylvia! I don't want to go into hiding. I want to return to Maryland and be with my Dad. If he's in trouble, I want to be with him. Tom and I want to help him in any way we can." They were in the car and headed for the airport. Elliot and his men were in the car behind them. They were driving fast in an effort to catch the early red-eye flight to Dulles Airport. Sylvia had been arguing against this move since Kathryn Ann had suggested it. Tom, Kathryn's husband, sat silently against the door. James was in the backseat. He was silent but he was cursing Kathryn as a stupid bitch under his breath.

Dr. Kohl and Gino were silently staring at the clock. It was past 7 AM and there was no call from Max Krug. Neither of them knew what to do. Dr. Kohl was afraid that Max's failure to call might release the fury of vengeance on his family. Gino knew that he did not intend to harm the Kohl family. He would never harm the children. But he was in the position of a poker player being caught bluffing. What's the next move? He had to keep up a front of cruelty and vengeance. Dr. Kohl had to be convinced that he would harm his family. Most of all, they had to find and kill Max Krug.

At twenty minutes past seven, Gino stood up as if he had reached a decision of some sort. He saw the dread in Dr. Kohl's eyes. He opened his mouth to speak and -- the phone rang. Dr. Kohl grabbed for the receiver.

"Hello."

"Max, speak English. I'm talking on two other lines in English and I can't think in German just now. Where are you and what's happening?"

Gino could only hear one side of the conversation. After several minutes, he heard Kohl ask, "Are you sure that Steiner is dead?"

Then he heard, "I saw pictures of the SCT building on CNN television. It appears to be a total loss. I am negotiating for the backup computer tapes now."

After a few minutes, Gino heard, "Max, I am negotiating some matters now. Then I will make some decisions and call you back. Did I understand you to say that you were at the Marriott Hotel in Bethesda? What room and what is the telephone number? Stay by the telephone in your room, I will need you quickly when I call. It may be several hours. Goodbye."

Dr. Kohl turned to Gino and handed him a sheet of paper. "Here is the telephone number and room number. You heard the location." He hung his head in defeat as he gave up his Sergeant to the enemy.

Gino took the paper and placed a call to Clay Matthews.

The noise of the telephone startled John Higgins. Susan had been dozing and she sat up straight. Billy and Stanley were sound asleep but John saw Stanley open one eye.

"Hello."

"John, this is Clay. How far away from the 495 Beltway are you now?"

"I'm on the south side of Harrisburg. About 65 or 70 miles.

Why?"

"Do the Montgomery County police still have a bulletin out for Max Krug?"

"Yes. As of a few hours ago, there was a "detain for questioning" bulletin out for him."

"I suggest that you head back this way and call in a tip. Maybe you could say that you received a tip on Krug's location?"

"I can make that work. Where is he?"

Clay told him the location and room number. They hung up so that John could call in the tip. John decided to get started and call it in from his cell phone. He told Susan and Billy that he would return as soon as possible.

John called his boss. "Captain, this is Higgins. I received a tip. I think I know where Max Krug is holed up. We may have caught a break here on the mess at SCT. A desk manager at The Marriott Hotel in Bethesda called me. He wants to remain anonymous. One of the bellboys reported escorting a foreigner to a room. He says the guy is German. He's registered under his name and showed his passport for identification. What caught the bellboy's attention is that the guy is heavily armed and acting nervous. I suggest that we approach the room with caution." Clay paused to pass a car.

"I'm less than an hour away from the Marriott now. I've got my light on and making good time." Clay added.

"Captain, we don't know what this guy's involvement is. We do know he is armed and nervous and in a crowded hotel. I suggest that we approach the room with about six men in helmets and vests. Let's use the bullhorn or call him on the telephone and tell him that he's wanted for questioning. We'll have him open the door and throw out his weapons. If he does it, no harm done. If he's slipped a notch out of the real world, we're prepared. At worst, we've embarrassed a visiting businessman. We are fully justified because of illegal possession of firearms." Clay reasoned.

"Sir, I'm in my personal van and I'm alone." John had left Susan and Billy at the motel. Stanley was on guard duty. "I'm south of Frederick and passing Urbana. I'm moving at 70 miles

per hour in the left lane with the red light on. There's very little
traffic at this time of night. I'll be there in less than thirty minutes.
This is my case, Captain. I think we may have caught a big break
on solving the whole SCT mess." John realized he was repeating
himself.

"John, Internal Affairs will be on the scene with you because
of your history with SCT. Watch yourself. Do it by the book. Do
you read me?"

"Yes sir!" John hung up and nudged the accelerator a little bit.
The speedometer moved up to 75 mph. At the exit for MD 109,
he passed the sign marking the boundary between Frederick
County and Montgomery County. He was on his home turf now.

"So where do we stand?" Joe wanted to know.

"Well, John says that Montgomery County has a "detain for
questioning" bulletin out on Krug. I gave him the location and
he's on his way to the hotel now. Presumably, he'll have a SWAT
team with him. I told him that Max is heavily armed." Clay
answered.

"Will John take him out?" Joe asked.

"John knows that this is the guy that ordered the hit on him
and his family at the camp. He believes, as I do, that Krug will
try again if he has the chance. So, yeah, if he has a chance, John
will take him out." Clay told him after a few minutes of thought.
Then he added, "John will have to be careful. He'll have to
assume that he's on national television plus internal affairs will
be looking over his shoulder."

"He'd be better off if he turned him over to us." Joe said.

"It might come to that yet." Clay said. "Max will either resist
or surrender so openly that John will have to arrest him instead
of killing him."

"So what happens if he surrenders?"

"He'll be arrested and transported to Rockville for questioning.
I hope John will let someone else do the interrogation and
stay in the background. Krug must know John's name and his

relationship with us. They'll book him on illegal possession of firearms but he'll be out in twenty-four hours. When he comes out, we'll be waiting." Clay smiled in anticipation.

Dr. Kohl telephoned his office and told them that he would be working at home today. He left a message for his grandson that he would call him later. He told his secretary that he did not want to be disturbed. He had several documents to prepare that were very important. By the time he finished with them, it would be late enough to place some calls to the United States and sell the product line.

Apparently Gino had decided to trust him because he was moving in and out of the room. Dr. Kohl had a pistol in his nightstand but he was not tempted. He knew it would only be a temporary reprieve and might endanger his family again.

Dr. Kohl overheard enough of the conversations between Gino and his men to know that the bodyguard and chauffeur were dead. They were discussing the disposal of the bodies. Well, that was their problem, not his. He had enough to worry about. Damn Krug to hell.

He began work on the Bill of Sale.

BILL OF SALE

I, Gernot R. Kohl, certify that I am the Chief Executive Officer of International Systems, Inc. On behalf of the

Company, I acknowledge receipt of $7,000,000.00 (Seven Million Dollars U. S.) as full payment for the exclusive proprietary rights to the Model 900 Series Product Line for High Voltage Switch Control.

The owner has full exclusive rights to sell and manufacture the products without competition from International Systems, Inc. to perpetuity. In addition to this document, the owner will receive a full documentation package.

The patent rights will be assigned to the owner by

registration with the U. S. Patent Office. With these actions, the sale of the product line is complete and no further action or payment is required by either company.

By:_____   Gernot R. Kohl

International Systems, Inc.

Although a simple and short document unlike the thick sheaf of paper normally generated in such a transaction, Dr. Kohl felt that the Bill of Sale was a defining and legally defensible document by both parties.

The second document was a suicide note that would be found by the police. He wanted the document to be lucid and leave no doubt in the minds of the readers as to the sincerity and responsibility of the act.

TO WHOM IT MAY CONCERN:

I, Dr. Gernot R. Kohl, have decided to commit suicide. I am of sound mind and I am not under duress. My reasons are private and are of no concern to legal authorities. My Last Will and Testament are held by my attorney. Please note the lack of any changes in more than a decade. My life has been full and rewarding. I bear ill will toward no man.

After some thought, Dr. Kohl signed the note with a flourish. Now it was time to prepare the most difficult document of all. He needed to write a letter to Gustav. The letter must convey his love and trust in his beloved grandson. He must tell him the truth and convince him not to pursue any path of investigation.

My dearest Gustav,

By now you know that I have committed suicide. Please believe me when I assure you that I am completely sane and under no duress. My love for you and Laura and my beloved great-grandchildren is boundless. I wish I could spend eternity with you but it is not to be. Now read and understand my reasons and obey my instructions. I committed an act of dishonor by allowing my subordinates at SCT to steal a design from a decent and honorable man. It was a despicable and cowardly act and I am shamed. Before I could rectify the mistake, several acts of violence were committed by him and us. I have determined that these repetitive acts of violence must stop. To this end, I have sold the product line and directed the proceeds to be paid to the injured party. During one engagement, Max Krug killed an innocent family member of one party. I have transferred five million dollars of my private funds to indemnify the wife and children. I have negotiated a truce with all parties. There will be peace as long as you do not take any action to change or avenge the steps I have taken. My decision to take my own life is because I cannot live with the dishonor of my actions. If you love me, please obey my last wishes. Do not do anything to endanger yourself or your family. I leave you now to join your Grandmother.

Love,

Dr. Kohl read the note several times and signed it with a bold stroke of the pen.

It was now 3 PM in Munich. It was 9 AM in the United States. He would make his telephone calls and finish this business. He was eager to be on his way. He was curious to see if his wife had aged as he had or if she retained her youthful beauty.

Max Krug was apprehensive when he answered the telephone in his hotel room. He knew that he had botched the entire affair and he dreaded the response from Dr. Kohl. If he had quickly and quietly dispatched Matthews and Colissimo on his arrival, this matter would have been settled long ago. In his desire to retire with a flourish, he expanded the affair beyond his instructions. The tone of Dr. Kohl's voice on the earlier telephone call was impatient. He had indicated that he was negotiating a settlement that was not favorable.

"Ja!" Max Krug answered the phone on the first ring.

"Mr. Krug, this is the Montgomery County police. We have a warrant to detain you for questioning about the fire at the SCT building in Rockville. We have been advised that you are armed. You are ordered to open your hotel room door slowly. Throw all of your weapons into the corridor. Then put your hands behind your head and back slowly from your room. You will not be harmed. We only want to question you. We are taking this approach because you were observed with firearms. Do you understand these instructions?" John Higgins waited for a response.

"I understand. I am willing to comply with your instructions. I ask only that I be allowed to make one telephone call before I leave the room." Max was thinking rapidly. He had registered under his own name because he did not realize that he was wanted by the police. He cursed himself for the carelessness that allowed a hotel employee to see his pistol. There was another possibility. An unthinkable possibility. He wanted to call Dr. Kohl for instructions. He did not want to make another mistake.

"You have ten minutes to complete your business and throw out your weapons." John was pretty sure that he knew whom Krug would call. It wasn't a lawyer.

Max dialed the number from memory and listened to the electronic crackling of the transatlantic carrier. "Hello?"

"Dr. Kohl, I apologize for this intrusion. I intended to wait for your call but the police are at my door. Do you have instructions for me? I am at your service." Max was standing at attention.

Dr. Kohl hesitated and considered his words carefully. Then he began to talk to his old comrade.

"Max, my dear friend and comrade, I fear that we have arrived at the end of the road. We have enjoyed a long and fruitful life. When we fought together on the Russian front, did you ever think that we would live to see the age of seventy? I certainly did not." He paused and then continued when Max did not respond.

"I believe that we survived because we were honorable men of courage. For these long years, we have served our country and advanced its place in the world. However, in this matter of Matthews and Colissimo, we have dishonored ourselves. It is not enough to say that we were ill-served by Carter and Claggett at SCT. The responsibility was mine and I have failed. At my age, I cannot live with this failure on my conscience. I know of only one way to end this circle of violence before it consumes more innocent people. I intend to do my duty. I release you from your pledge to me. You must make your own decision as I have made mine. Goodbye, old friend." Max heard the dial tone on the disconnected line.

Max Krug was not shocked. He was not even surprised. He realized that he had unconsciously expected something along this line. He was not disappointed. In fact, he was pleased to hear that he had been discharged from active service and was now free to make his own decision. He walked to the mirror and straightened his tie. He buttoned his coat and inspected his image.

Then he picked up his Walther 9mm automatic pistol and delivered a fatal wound to his right temple.

39 - Product Line Sale

Dr. Kohl dialed the first number in the United States after consulting his electronic telephone directory. Many men of his age rejected these new advancements in information technology. Dr. Kohl embraced them. He encouraged their use within the company and prided himself on staying abreast of new products.

When the telephone was answered, he identified himself by name, title and company. He asked for the Chief Executive Officer by name. He was connected to the executive secretary to the CEO. She explained that the personage in question was on a long distance call. He would be able to return Dr. Kohl's call within the hour. Dr. Kohl explained that he would hold the line for sixty seconds before he hung up. She should advise her superior that he would be missing an opportunity if he did not take this call.

"Dr. Kohl, this is an unexpected surprise. I hope you are calling to accept the lunch invitation that I extended to you at the European Business Council meeting last year." He paused and silently asked himself what in the world this old man could possibly want.

"I am sure that you have seen the news report about the loss of our facility in Rockville, Maryland. After some deliberation, I have decided not to rebuild the structure. In fact, I have decided to discontinue our business ventures in the United States. To this end, I have decided to sell our Model 900 High Voltage Switch product line. I assume that you are familiar with these products?" He paused and received a positive answer

"The price for the product line is seven million dollars. We will assign the patent and supply a complete set of documentation. Payment must be in full by way of an electronic transfer at the time of settlement. The place of settlement will be in Bethesda, Maryland and must be completed within the next five business days. I am making this offer to you and two other companies. None of these terms are negotiable. You will receive a fax in a few minutes giving you the address, telephone and fax numbers in Bethesda. The first one to fax an acceptance will be the successful bidder. Thank you for taking my call. Goodbye." And he hung up.

The CEO was stunned. He had never received such a proposition in his entire career. It reminded him of stories he had read about business transactions among the oil wildcatters. He was painfully aware of the SCT product line. It was considered to be a leader in the field. His company had been unable to compete successfully. Although he did not have exact figures, his analysts had estimated the annual sales at ten million dollars and growing. The product was on the verge of market domination. Seven million dollars was a very reasonable price. He wondered what had caused such a radical decision on the part of the old man. Surely it wasn't the fire at the Rockville facility. If he thought a fire could provoke such a reaction, he would have set the fire himself. He buzzed for his secretary and started writing out an acceptance fax. God, he hoped that he was the first one.

When the police squad in the hallway at the Marriott Hotel heard the gunshot, they poised to rush the door. Lieutenant John Higgins jumped up and ordered them to hold in place. He had a pretty good hunch what the single gunshot meant. He decided to wait a few minutes and try the door. When he pushed on the door, it was open. He entered with his gun drawn but, as he expected, it was unnecessary. Max Krug's body was sprawled on the floor.

*   *   *

Gino Colissimo read the two notes written by Dr. Kohl. He listened to the telephone call to Max Krug and the calls to the three executives. He heard the sincerity in the tone of the old man's voice. He was convinced that everything had proceeded as he directed. He trusted his adversary. He had holstered his pistol many hours earlier. Gino felt a strong surge of sympathy for the old man. He hoped that when his time came, he would be able to muster the same dignity and courage.

"Dr. Kohl, I will leave you now. It has been an honor and a privilege to meet you. I pledge to you that my family will honor the agreement that we made today." He bowed to the old man and left quickly.

Dr. Gernot Kohl realized that he had enjoyed many more of life's joys than most men. At seventy-five years of age, he had lived more years. He remembered the loyal love of a wife who had given him a son during the most difficult and darkest days of a bloody world war.

He had been given a remarkable grandson and four of the most loving great-grandchildren that a man could imagine.

In short, he had received much more than he had given.

Now it was time for him to give something in return for those many blessings. It was time for him to give his life. He had bargained his life in return for the lives of his grandson and his children.

On one level his mind was racing and reviewing the action steps of the past few hours and few days. Had he left anything undone or unsaid? Dr. Kohl could think of nothing else.

On another level, he was reminiscing and reliving his life. Max Krug had been his sergeant, comrade, friend, employee, and weapon. It was the latter category that brought both of them to this final day. He wished he had controlled Max and kept a tighter leash. And leash was the right word. Max was like an attack dog. He was loyal and loving to one master.

Dr. Kohl realized that he was stalling. He wasn't only trying to remember if everything was done; he was looking for a way out of this final commitment. And he was shamed. After all of these years, he wanted more. A young man might ask, "Who wants to be seventy-six years old?" and the answer would be "Anyone who is seventy-five."

One of the possible excuses for delay was the fact that he had left no mechanism to make sure that his enemies lived up to their part of the bargain. Would Gino Colissimo be able to convince Clay Matthews and his brother Joe to end their vendetta? After losing his older brother, would Gino be able to forego the final step of his vengeance?

In truth, Dr. Kohl did not know. There was no way to know. But, in seventy-five years of life, he had learned to judge men and act on that judgment. In this case, he believed Gino Colissimo would act as a man of honor. And Dr. Kohl believed to a certainty that if he did not carry out his final offering, the Colissimo Family and Clayton Matthews would annihilate the Kohl Family.

With determination, Dr. Gernot Kohl removed the 9mm automatic pistol from the nightstand drawer and placed the barrel firmly against his right temple.

40 – Memories Of A Hard Road

Kathryn Ann leaned against her husband's shoulder as the big jumbo jet descended towards Baltimore-Washington International Airport. On the one hand, she was excited at the prospect of returning home and facing the ghosts of the past. On the other hand, she was painfully aware that her weaknesses had caused a great deal of pain to her family. It was over five years now since her mother had died. On this trip, she would visit her mother's grave for the first time and place flowers at the base of the marker to show her love and respect. Her husband, Tom, would be with her and she would find the words to introduce the two of them.

What on earth was she going to say to her father? Sorry was such an inadequate word. She would try to convince her father how far she had traveled emotionally since she moved to California. She had moved during a crisis of fear because she let her emotions control her mind. Her mind knew she had been wronged at the Christmas party by her boss, Hugh Nolan. Her mind urged her to keep things in proportion. Her emotions told her that she had been raped. She had been sullied beyond repair. She felt that decent people would shun her. She felt that every man would know that she was an easy mark. She would be raped every time she dated. She flirted with the idea that the whole thing was her fault. It was the way she dressed or did her hair or blinked her eyes. If that was the case, she deserved to die as punishment for her crime.

Her mind screamed "NO" and demanded a recount of the events. If not her fault then whose? Who was responsible?

Someone must be held accountable. Her mind said that it was the fault of the predator Nolan. Her emotions said that Nolan was like a large truck. He ran down whoever was in his way. The reason that it happened to Kathryn Ann was that someone failed to keep her out of the way of the truck. Through a process of elimination, she concluded that it must be her father and mother. They were responsible for her. Why had they not warned her? So, if she did not wish to be ravished repeatedly and eternally, she must escape to an area beyond their control. California was as far away as her mind could comprehend.

She remembered Mr. Levits and Dr. Jacobs and their tender treatment of her during the dark days. They were solicitous but they tried to point out her strengths. Yes, a bad thing did happen but – nothing worse happened because she was strong and intelligent. She had protected herself because she was fortified with the strength of her parents and her background. She could not understand so she had fled. The first year in her sun-filled exile was interesting, fun, safe, and new. New as in a fresh start. New as in nobody knew of the Christmas Party. New as in nobody knew she was sullied. And everyone accepted her. No one asked any questions. She was treated respectfully. She found a job. She rented an apartment. Kathryn Ann's life stabilized and she matured.

Meeting her future husband was a scary experience. She knew she had met someone who was meant to be an important part of her life. But what if he didn't feel the same way towards her? But the magic worked in both directions and she found happiness. Then she began to realize how many blessings she had in her life. Josephine was a true friend. Josephine's parents, Aunt Sylvia and Uncle Joe, were absolute cornerstones. And her mother and father, they were …no, mom was gone. Blessings are not permanent. They are not guaranteed. Blessings must be nourished and allowed to grow. They must not be shut out or they will go away. Like mom.

But one blessing was still living and he needed her. If her father was in trouble, she would find a way to help. And he needed to meet her husband. They would like each other. She was sure of that. Maybe she could get her father to visit California. Whatever it took, they needed to find a way to spend more time together. She had so many questions about so many things. She wanted to know how her mother and father felt when they knew her mother was pregnant. Were they happy? Were they as happy as she was right now? Her father needed to know that he would soon be a grandfather. He would be needed to help raise the baby.

41 - Payday

As Head of the Colissimo Family, Gino felt as if he had a ton of responsibility on his shoulders. There were an unbelievable number of details that required his attention. He had received the five million dollars from Dr. Kohl's attorney. It was deposited directly into an offshore account. After deducting one million dollars for the general family fund, Gino set up accounts for John's wife and children. An education fund guaranteed their college years. John's family would never have to work for a living but they could not blow the money in a wild spending spree. John's wife had the freedom to live her life unless she remarried. In that event, the balance of her living fund reverted to the family. In other words, Gino controlled the purse strings.

The seven million dollars received from the sale of the Model 900 High Voltage Switch product line was disbursed in accordance with Clay's instructions. The Italian cousins and the California cousins received one-half million dollars each. Gino, Joe, and James received one million dollars each. Clay received one million dollars and the Camp Lydia account received one million dollars. The remaining million dollars was transferred to John Higgins. Clay assumed that John would take care of his cop buddies. He certainly wasn't going to approach any cops with cash in hand.

John Higgins could not believe how much his life had changed over the past few years. The changes started when he met Clayton

Matthews. John did not feel manipulated as much as he felt like he had been set free to pursue his destiny without the financial burdens imposed by the miserly pay of the police department. And, of course, Clay was not responsible for bringing Susan into his life.

Tonight was a celebratory dinner at his house with the three cops who had helped him protect his family at Camp Lydia. All three of them were married. Glenn and Lou had children. Bud and his wife were newlyweds – a second marriage for both of them.

Everybody was coming – kids and all. Billy was really looking forward to the party. It was a cookout with plenty of hamburgers, hot dogs, potato salad and cold drinks. Susan had made up a batch of mix and John picked up ice and salt at the store for cranking the ice cream freezer. The trick was not to tell the kids to crank the ice cream machine. If you waited for them to drift over and observe, they would want a turn. Then everyone would clamor for a turn at the crank.

Billy had some new games for his computer station and he was looking forward to comparing notes with Glenn's son on a new software language. They had discussed the project on the telephone and Billy had discussed it with his mentor Clay Matthews.

John Higgins had three envelopes in his pocket. Each envelope contained a checkbook. The names on the accounts were those of his three friends. Each account had been credited with one hundred thousand dollars. He knew that each of them would be floored. Then they would be suspicious. He would have to give a lengthy explanation to his square-shooter friends before they would accept the money. No problem. He intended to tell them the whole story working backward from the shoot-out at Camp Lydia. The source of the money was the settlement from Dr. Kohl and International Systems Inc. He did not think it was advisable or necessary to mention the Colissimo family. Actually there were several points that he would have to gloss over sort of lightly but everything was cool. The money would change their lives by permitting them to buy houses and assure a college fund for the kids. John was pleased with the disposition of the money. His conscience was clear. The good guys had won a round.

42 - Goodbye Clay

Clay decided to stop by the grocery store on his way home. For one thing, he was completely out of dog food. Stanley would not be a happy camper if he came home to an empty larder.

By the time he pulled into the driveway, it was dusk and the temperature was cooling. Clay was in a happy mood. Everything had happened pretty much to script and on schedule. No one could have foreseen the actions of Max Krug. The man was a throwback to the Stone Age. Clay did not want to encounter another Max Krug in his life. The loss of John Colissimo was a blow to the whole crew.

Clay exited the car and stood back to admire the house. It was in pretty good condition. He could afford a much larger house but he didn't want one. He didn't need it and it would be more housework. Besides, he had lived here with Lydia and it was easier to think about her as long as he lived here.

Clay did all of the housework such as vacuuming and dishes and routine laundry. He took his shirts to the laundry. Every weekend, he tried to do something from his list of home repairs. This weekend he intended to paint the shutters. The following weekend would be reserved for the garage door.

As he stepped up onto the porch, Clay had a bag of groceries on each arm. He had his key chain in his right hand and extended his hand towards the lock. For some reason that he could not explain, he hesitated. The thought occurred to him that he was forgetting something. Nothing came to mind so he figured that as long as he had food for Stanley, anything else could wait for tomorrow.

Clay inserted the key and turned it clockwise.

He felt the pain first and then heard the explosion.

His first thought was to warn Joe who was supposed to arrive in a few minutes.

When Joe arrived, he found his friend on the sidewalk. He had been thrown almost fifty feet. Most of his clothes had been blown off and he was a mass of blood. Clay's right arm had been severed at the shoulder. Joe called 911 on his cell phone and screamed for an ambulance. Then he knelt down to comfort his friend.

"Clay, can you hear me?"

"Joe, don't go near the house." Clay could only whisper.

"Okay, buddy, it's okay."

"Joe, I always heard that it wouldn't hurt because of the shock. That's not true. It really hurts, Joe."

"Take it easy, Clay. I called an ambulance. We'll get you some medical help." Joe knew his friend was dying.

"Joe, I don't need an ambulance. I think I'll go see Lydia. But would you check my right hand? It sure is burning. Maybe you could do something about that?"

"I'll try, pal."

"What happened, Joe? Can you tell?"

"It looks like an explosion, Clay. I think the front door was booby-trapped."

"I guess our old friend Max left a going away present for me, huh?"

"Sure looks like it."

"I think I'm dying, Joe. But there's no bright light. Everything is black. The pain is bad, Joe. This dying is a hurtful process."

"I'm sorry, Clay."

"Joe, would you leave me alone now. Go check on the ambulance or something. I don't want you to see me like this and I want to talk to God for a minute."

"If that's what you want, Clay." Joe said sadly.

"Do you think God will forgive me, Joe?"

"Yes, I do. I believe it with my whole heart, Clay. All you have to do is ask for forgiveness and mercy." Joe spoke to his friend sincerely and urgently. He didn't think his friend had much time.

"I'm not sure I was ever baptized, Joe. I asked Dad about it but he was overseas when I was born. Will that matter?" Clay asked with the simplicity of a child waiting for punishment.

"All that matters is that you accept God into your heart, Clay. Do that and everything will be okay." Joe knew that he would never resist Sylvia's efforts to get him into church on Sunday again.

"Goodbye, Joe."

"Goodbye, Clay."

43 - Facing The Future

Clayton Giles Matthews was laid to rest on a warm, sunny Monday afternoon. He was placed next to his beloved wife, Lydia, who had preceded him in death some five years earlier. The funeral service was held at graveside and attended by his closest friends. There would be a memorial service on Friday for a larger group of mourners.

One of the attendees was in a wheelchair. Billy Higgins was devastated that he would never see Uncle Clay again. He had made a big difference in Billy's life with his teachings on the computer and in electronics. Billy remembered the first time that he visited Uncle Clay's house and stared in awe at the elaborate computer system.

The second part of Billy's life that had been changed by Uncle Clay was sitting in Billy's lap. Stanley, the little Benji dog, was staring at the people and the confusion around the gravesite. He seemed to understand what was happening.

When the service ended, the people started talking to each other and moving towards their cars. Stanley jumped down from Billy's lap and ran to the grave. He sat down on his haunches and cried softly. John and Susan and Billy left him alone for a while. Then John picked him up gently and carried him to the van. John promised Stanley that they would come out to Resthaven and visit Clay often.

*　　　*　　　*

Kathryn Ann and her husband, Tom, drove to the local hotel after the service. Kathryn Ann was over four months pregnant and she needed some rest. She was exhausted after spending time with her father in the hospital. She had talked to him continuously for the three days of life. She tried to explain her feelings and understanding. She spoke of the coming birth of her child.

Clay's injuries were massive. The right arm had been severed close to the shoulder joint. The left arm and hand were lacerated and bones were broken. Both eyes were damaged. Several ribs were broken. Due to the severe chest damage, a ventilator was used for life support.

Because the pulse was strong and there was brain activity, the doctors continued their efforts to keep him alive. A large amount of morphine was used and injected intravenously to keep him calm. They tried to communicate with him and asked him to move his foot if he understood them. Most of the time, he responded. When Kathryn Ann asked him if he heard her, he moved his foot.

The doctors knew that he could not survive. On his Maryland driver's license, Clay had indicated that he was an organ donor. There was no decision for the family to make. The hospital staff prepared for the organ harvest. When death came for Clayton Giles Matthews, it was in the early hours of the morning before any friends or family had arrived for the daily vigil. By the time anyone arrived, the body had been removed to the operating room for the final donations.

The announcement of Dr. Gernot Kohl's death by his own hand made headlines in the business newspapers around the world. After a complete investigation, the Munich Police had confirmed the initial reports of suicide. Apparently, Dr. Kohl had called the police emergency desk and reported a shooting at his own residence. The theory was that he did not want his body to be discovered by his family.

Speculation on his health was the initial reason for the suicide. The autopsy proved that Dr. Kohl was in remarkably good health for a man of seventy-five years. Then the speculation turned to the recent events at the subsidiary firm in Rockville, Maryland as a possible reason for depression.

Press reports were beginning to surface that SCT did not have any computer backup data for the operation. On examination by company and insurance officials, the backup tapes stored at the bank were blank. An investigation was launched to determine how the data was erased from the tapes. Several wild theories were advanced by the more imaginative members of the press.

Mr. Albert Tillis, the Chief Financial Officer, was questioned extensively by the police and insurance company officials. He professed ignorance as to how the data disappeared. He reviewed the system procedures from memory and remembered the last monthly diagnostic checkup of the system as being three weeks before the fire.

The results of the fire were proving to be catastrophic for the parent company. Over three hundred people were unemployed. They were filing for unemployment benefits at the local office in Rockville. For most of them, the application for benefits followed a discussion with their lawyer. There were several class action suits being prepared against the parent company.

The insurance companies were withholding payment pending an investigation of the fire. Beyond that question was the more difficult one of assessing the value of the claim. For instance, in the property damage section, the machinery, furniture, and fixtures were insured for their replacement values. Well, how many file cabinets were there on the premises at the time of the fire? How many desks, chairs, rugs, fixtures, etc., were involved? The backup tapes had a complete list of the company assets but those tapes were blank. Did anyone think the insurance companies would volunteer a compilation?

SCT paid their bills to the various vendors promptly on a thirty days net basis. The monthly outgo added up to a cash outflow of an average 1.5. million dollars. Since all of the records were destroyed in the fire and the backup tapes were blank, there was no record of the unpaid invoices. Vendors understood their dilemma and sent duplicate invoices. However, in the first seven days following the fire, the parent company received a total of 7.2 million dollars in invoices. Clearly, the auditors would have a field day verifying the invoices. Accountants and attorneys benefited the most from any tragedy.

Until the invoices could be verified and paid, there were many small companies in danger of bankruptcy with the additional unemployment adding to the local problems.

A similar problem existed in the area of accounts receivable. SCT shipped and billed approximately three million dollars per month. Less than half of the invoices were acknowledged by their customers. Again, the accountants and attorneys would have to verify every transaction.

A police investigation had verified that Dr. Kohl had transferred five million dollars of the family assets to an offshore account prior to his death. No one could explain the reason for the payment.

Another mystery was the sudden sale of the Model 900 High Voltage Switch product line to a New York-based electronics company. The amount of the sale was seven million dollars. Industry speculation was that the product line was worth nearly twice that amount. The proceeds of the sale were transferred to an offshore account and the income did not appear on the income ledger of the parent company. The tax officials were most upset and still mulling over what action to take.

Customers around the world were reluctant to depend on International Systems, Inc. for future supplies of their components.

The company was facing a total collapse.

Alfred Levits had received several visits from the various insurance companies. In addition, he was visited by local, county, state, federal and international police investigators. Levits referred them to his attorney – another partner in the same firm. Some of the questions had to be answered as a matter of law or he would face criminal indictment. Other questions could be deflected on the basis of attorney-client confidentiality.

"What clients do you represent that are involved in the SCT investigation, Mr. Levits?"

"I am not at liberty to say." Levits responded.

"Who is the account holder where you transferred the funds for the sale of the product line?"

"I did not transfer any funds." Levits was vehement in his denial.

"You gave the information on the account to the company that purchased the product line, didn't you? You must know who owns the account."

"Did I? I'm not sure that I recall giving the information to the purchaser." Levits contemplated his answer carefully.

"Well, you did deliver the technical information on the product line to the purchaser, did you not?"

"Hmmm, I suppose I did." Levits conceded the point.

"Well, where did you get the information?"

"I assume it came from the owner of the information – SCT or International Systems, Inc." Levits was vague – again.

"Well, which one was it?"

"I'm not sure I recall at this time. I'll try to give the matter some thought." Levits was having fun but he reminded himself that this was serious business.

"How were the data packages delivered?"

"I believe a courier delivered the information to me." Levits nodded his head as if he were certain of the answer.

"What company was the courier from?"

"I really don't recall. It didn't seem important at the time." Surely the authorities did not expect a busy attorney like Alfred Levits to remember each courier delivery.

"According to the CEO of the firm that purchased the product line, you were rather dictatorial on the terms of the purchase. Is that correct?"

"Not at all. I believe Dr. Kohl told the man that the terms were not negotiable in a telephone call. He called two other CEOs and they have verified an identical conversation." This was a safe area and Levits hoped to keep the questions channeled down this avenue.

"But he says that you demanded his appearance at your office at 9 AM on the following day or you would cancel the sale. Is that true?"

"I had three faxes in my possession accepting the terms of sale that Dr. Kohl offered to them. I accepted the first one to arrive as specified by Dr. Kohl. When the CEO tried to stall on the payment, I simply informed him that the sale would be given to the second acceptance fax." Levits shrugged his shoulders.

"And what was his response?"

"He assured me that he would be here at 9 AM." Levits smiled.

"Well, how did that work?"

"The CEO came to my office with three or four attorneys in tow. They examined the Bill of Sale and the technical data package. They said that a simple Bill of Sale was inadequate and that they would have to study the technical data for a few days." Levits had enjoyed the exchange in his office and smiled with the memory.

"What was your response?"

"I asked them if they wanted my secretary to arrange transportation to the airport. I was dialing the number of the company with the second acceptance when the CEO decided that everything was in order and acceptable. Then he made a telephone call and transferred the funds to the specified account."

"What else?"

"I made a telephone call to verify receipt of the funds. The CEO signed the Bill of Sale. I distributed copies of the transaction and transferred the data packages. They left rather abruptly."

"And what did you conclude from their demeanor?"

"Well, I'm not sure. Like most attorneys, I always try to be friendly, helpful, honest, and forthcoming. I always charge reasonable rates and do a fair share of pro bono work. Frankly, I am always puzzled when I am faced with hostility." Levits looked puzzled.

"This is not a time for levity, Mr. Levits."

"I apologize. I realize that you're from the government and that you're here to help me."

Gino's wife, Florence, put some wine, bread and sausage on the table. Joe and Sylvia had driven up to New Jersey from Maryland. The two brothers had some business to discuss.

"I'm sorry I wasn't with you when Clay died, Joe. I was exhausted from my flight home from Germany and John's family needed my help." Gino explained.

"That's okay, Gino. I understand. There was nothing to be done. Sylvia and I sat with him at the hospital until the end." Joe shook his head in sadness and reached for Sylvia's hand.

"How on earth did he live for three days with those injuries?" Gino asked.

"I don't know. He was in a lot of pain despite the massive amount of morphine. Clay's right arm was amputated by the blast. The heat of the explosion cauterized the wound or he would have bled to death within minutes. The only good thing about those three days was that it gave the doctors a chance to set up for organ donation."

"Yeah? I didn't think of that. So he was an organ donor? How do you feel about that, Joe?"

"Well, in Clay's case, they were only able to use his kidneys. Everything else was damaged in the explosion. But there are two people that are very grateful for those kidneys."

"Clay felt very strongly about organ donation. He said it was a person's last chance to make a difference and do a good deed. For myself, I had not intended to be a donor but I've changed my mind."

"Did he say anything at the hospital?"

"No. He talked to me before the ambulance arrived but he didn't speak again."

"Did he know what happened?" Gino asked.

"Yeah, he asked me and I told him. I told him it was an

explosion and he figured out that it was Max Krug." Joe related admiringly. Clay was sharp at figuring things out.

"Damn that guy. Krug was a pile of bad news. I still can't believe that he got through to John." Gino had revamped the entire security arrangements at the family headquarters.

"Too bad he was cremated. I might be tempted to dig him up and kill him again." Joe hit the table with his fist.

"Well, let's get on with it. We have some decisions to make. Do you want to talk now or do you want to rest up and hit it tomorrow?" Gino gave him the option.

"Nah, we're okay. Let's get it done. We want to get back to Maryland and visit with Josephine."

"How's she doing with all of this?" Gino looked at them curiously. In many ways, Joe and Clay were closer than he and Joe.

"She's okay. She's helping out with Kathryn Ann. It turns out that Clay's daughter is four months pregnant." Sylvia chimed into the conversation. This was her bailiwick.

"Okay. Here's the reason I asked you to come to New Jersey for a sit-down. I've been following the financial news on International Systems, Inc. I don't think they're going to make it. I think the company may go down the tubes." Gino stated.

"How come? All we did was eliminate SCT. They were insured. I don't understand the problem." Joe protested.

"It's a lot more complex than that, Joe. The insurance company is holding up payment pending an investigation. Also, it's difficult to determine the extent of the loss without the records. And their customers and vendors are screwing them to the wall. The customers won't acknowledge their outstanding invoices and the vendors tripled the amount that SCT owed. Plus there are some companies that never did business with SCT that suddenly remembered some outstanding invoices. The attorneys are having a field day. The employees are claiming a lot of bogus vacation and sick pay. The list goes on and on."

"So what do you want to do about it? And why do we even care?" Joe asked.

"I care because Old Man Kohl carried out his end of the

bargain. He paid the five million for John and he sold the product line for the seven million like we asked. He committed suicide so that I didn't have to kill him. That way, there was no murder investigation and it guaranteed that his grandson would not be pissing around with some idea of getting even." Gino said.

"What I want to do is sell them the tapes." Gino continued and looked at Joe.

Joe didn't say anything. He simply stared at Gino. He knew what Gino would ask next. He was going to ask him about the tapes. He wasn't sure he wanted to tell him.

"The point is that we did not foresee that our actions would make the company vulnerable to every two-bit shyster that knows the way to the courthouse. We can stop most of it if we surrender the tapes." Gino continued.

"What if I tell you that the tapes were destroyed?" Joe asked.

"Then I will believe you. There is nothing we can do to help the grandson." Gino shrugged his shoulders. "Is that the case? Were the tapes destroyed?"

"No." Joe confessed. "But they should have been. I understand your desire to stop the damage. There was no way for us to foresee these events. But giving up the tapes opens the door for SCT reopening in the United States. That was one of our goals." Joe argued.

"We can keep it as one of our goals. And I'm not talking about giving the tapes to them. I'm talking about selling the tapes to them. And we can attach as many strings as we want. If we don't want them in the United States, we can make it a part of the bargain." Gino argued.

"It's a downhill slide, Gino. The grandson will start to wonder where the tapes came from and how they got there. He'll start to connect the dots. From what I hear about him, he's a bright guy. We've lost John and Clay. There are you, James and me left against the world, Gino. Why do we want to create a future problem? So they go out of business. So what? Screw 'em." Joe sat back in his chair emotionally exhausted.

"Joe, the family is going to need the money that we can get out of the tapes. Before we teamed up with Clay, we were almost broke. Every racket we touched went sour for awhile. We got our heads above water and then we started recouping our lost territories in Jersey. We need some more funding to set our position in concrete." Gino pleaded.

"There's no law that says there has to be a Colissimo crime family. The only thing we need to do is earn a living for ourselves and secure the future for our children." Joe argued. "The three of us have enough to live our lives in luxury and secure our children with education and safety. Let's do it that way." Joe wasn't about to give up.

"No! I don't want to do it that way. I don't want to play it safe and just get by. I'm the head of the family and I want the family to be a powerful presence." Gino thundered and stood up.

"Tell me, Godfather. How do you intend to approach the grandson? How do you intend to explain having the tapes?" Joe asked derisively.

"I think we can use the Chief Financial Officer Albert Tillis. He can be our negotiator. He can carry the terms and be the middleman." Gino had given the matter a lot of thought.

"I don't want to do this, Gino. Doesn't that count for something?" Joe raised his voice.

Sylvia and Florence were sitting silently while the two brothers argued. Florence clasped her hands in her lap and silently prayed for peace. She had never argued with Gino on any important matter. He was the head of the family and she had been conditioned since childhood to accept these terms. Sylvia knew that it was best to let the two brothers vent their disagreement but she was not going to accept their decision before she had an input. She had received the same conditioning as Florence but she rejected the passive wife role. She and Joe were partners. She stood beside him in combat and she expected to have a voice in the decisions.

"It counts for a lot. I will always want your counsel on these matters. But after we have discussed an issue, I must make a decision. Then I expect you to support my decision. The family is not a democracy. We do not count votes. You know this as well as I do. And you know the reasons for it. You learned it in the same way and at the same place that I did." Gino was flushed. "Now let's set the matter aside for the night. Let's finish our wine and get some rest. Think about what I have said. In the morning, I want to know the location of the tapes and we will make our plans." Gino came around the table and embraced his brother.

In the guest room, Joe and Sylvia prepared for bed. They were tired after the trip from Maryland and the heated discussion with Gino. Sylvia wanted to discuss the matter some more but she could tell that Joe was tired of talking for a while. She started kneading and massaging his shoulder muscles. He closed his eyes and smiled. "That feels good."

"Just remember that I'm the one that gives the massages. If I ever hear of you getting a massage somewhere else, you're going to be singing soprano in the choir. Got it?"

"Oh, yeah. I got it." Joe chuckled. Then he grew serious. "What do you think of Gino's plan to sell the tapes to the Kohl family?"

"Well, I understand that there is a large profit to be gained from the sale. It looks like the tapes might make the difference between the company failing or surviving. Gino has a good point about using the money to strengthen the family. I think Gino was greatly impressed by the Old Man when he leaned on him in Germany. Obviously, he feels like the Old Man did everything we asked and he doesn't want to see the grandson punished any more." Sylvia summarized.

"I understand your view, too. You think that we'll expose ourselves too much to the grandson and he might have some ideas a few years from now. Is that it?" Sylvia continued.

"Yeah, I suppose so. I want to get as much distance as we can get from the Kohl family. If their business fails, it will make us safer because they won't have the resources to come after us." Joe was still enjoying the neck massage with his eyes closed.

"But, honey, I heard something else in your discussion with Gino. I heard a message in your voice that said you wanted out of the family business. Am I reading you right?" Sylvia sat down on the bed beside him and looked into his eyes.

"I hadn't thought about it before tonight but, yeah, I think it's what I want to do." Joe looked at her with a question in his eyes. "What about you? How do you feel about it?"

"I've thought about it a lot. I think we would be happier and safer if we went our own way. It was different when your Papa ran the family. Or even with John when he was alive. But times have changed. Our family is changing, too. Did you know that Josephine has a serious boyfriend? I think there are wedding bells in her future and grandchildren in our future! How about them apples, old man?" Sylvia was smiling from ear to ear.

"News to me. I hope the wedding bells come before the grandchildren. How come I haven't met this guy yet? What if I don't approve of him?" Joe started worrying. It was difficult for him to think of his little girl as a wife and mother.

"Don't worry. We'll meet him soon. From what Josephine tells me, he's a very nice young man. And there won't be any shotgun wedding. I've done my job." She smiled.

"What does that mean? He's not messing around, is he? I mean, well, you know what I mean." Joe turned red in the face.

"Did we mess around before we got married? Did everything work out okay? Do you want her to marry some guy without trying him out? What if he's a dud in the sack?" She was laughing uproariously now when she looked at Joe. "Calm down. Everything's okay."

"Is he Italian?" Joe wanted to know.

"Well, he's taking Italian lessons. Does that count?" Sylvia joked.

"What's his last name?" Joe asked cautiously.

"I can't remember. It starts with an R – something like Rostakovsky or Rothstein or Rembrandt or something. Why?" Sylvia had a blank deadpan expression.

"Jesus, Sylvia! Be serious. You know I'm not a bigot but life is more difficult when you start mixing things up, you know?" Joe was sweating.

"I know what you mean, Joe. But this is for Josephine to decide and for us to accept. We'll take it a step at a time. Okay?" Then she switched the subject back to the matter at hand. "But may I put an oar in the water on the tapes and other stuff?"

"Yeah, sure." Joe looked at her.

"Give him the tapes but ask him to impose the condition that neither the Kohl family nor International Systems, Inc. do business in the United States again. Also, tell him that you would like to retire and I think we should move to California. You can open a small business of some sort or stay home and make love to me all day. We can live close to Josephine and enjoy our grandchildren. Tell him that whatever he decides on the amount of your share of the tapes is okay with you. Then we can be on our way." Sylvia sat back to see his reaction.

"Sounds good to me. All of it. Let's go to bed and get started on the loving part of my retirement." Joe smiled.

"Does Mr. Big want to come out and play? Is he feeling frisky tonight?" Sylvia laughed.

Albert Tillis reached for the telephone and caught the second ring. He was annoyed at the interruption. He was working in his home office. Gustav Kohl had asked him to write down as many of the accounts receivables shipments as he could remember. He was flying to California on Monday for a job interview. He grunted into the receiver.

"Mr. Tillis, this is Joe Colissimo. How are you doing?"

Tillis almost swallowed his tongue. After a fit of coughing, he responded. "Uh, I'm okay. I mean I guess I'm okay. Is everything okay with you?"

"Yeah, sure. No problems on my end. I've been reading the papers and I thought it might be time for us to meet. How about meeting me in the same spot we had our last meeting?" Joe proposed.

"Well, okay. I'm not sure what you have in mind. I'm pretty much finished at SCT. I'm clearing up some paperwork and I have a job interview next Monday. Are you sure I can be of service? When did you have in mind?" Tillis stammered.

"How about we see you in ten minutes?" Then Joe hung up.

Albert Tillis did not hesitate. He picked up his sweater and headed out the door. It was a ten-minute drive to the motel on Research Boulevard in Rockville. He did not want to be late.

When Ab turned into the motel parking lot, he headed for the rear part. He pulled into the same space. As he turned off the ignition, a Ford Explorer pulled into the adjacent space. Two men got out of the vehicle and walked towards him. He recognized one of them as being Joe Colissimo. He didn't recognize the second man but there was a strong family resemblance. Joe entered the front door on the passenger side and the other guy got into the back seat.

Joe offered his hand in friendship and smiled at him. "Thanks for coming over to meet us. This is my brother, Gino." Joe nodded towards the back seat.

Ab Tillis was a little taken back by the friendly approach. He remembered the last visit vividly. Joe was the one who wanted to cut off his little finger or a toe. He waited to hear about the purpose of this meeting.

"You mentioned that you were doing a little paperwork for SCT. How are they doing?" Joe asked.

"Not too good. The lawyers are raking them over the coals. The vendors are trying to overcharge them. The customers are trying to stiff them. SCT is definitely out of business. I suspect that International Systems will be out of business soon." Ab stated the obvious facts.

"Would it help them to have the backup tapes?" Joe asked.

"Oh, yes. Most definitely. They would be able to collect on their invoices and pay only the fair billing from the vendors. More than anything, it would negate most of the employee suits if they had the time records. Those records would be able to document their insurance claims. It would mean the survival of the company." Ab fairly gushed.

"We have the records. It was not our intent to sell the records back to International Systems but we don't want them to go out of business. I would like for you to be the middleman and help us sell the records to the grandson. Would you be willing to do me this favor?" Joe looked at him sincerely.

"Well, I'm willing to do whatever I can. What should I say? I'm not sure how to approach Mr. Kohl." Ab stammered some more.

Joe handed him an envelope. "Here's five thousand dollars for expense money. Give the grandson a call and tell him you know how to recover the tapes. Ask him for an appointment. I'll bet he'll jump at the chance. Fly over in the First Class cabin. That way you won't be so tired when you arrive. I want you to lay out a complete package for him. Would you like to take some notes or do you have a good memory?" Joe smiled.

"Here's the deal. We're willing to sell the tapes back to him. It was not our original intent but we don't want to see the company fail. Our original intent was to put SCT out of business not the parent company. The price of the tapes is five million dollars. We know he's short on cash now so he doesn't have to pay for six months. At the end of that time, if the company survives, he should deposit the money into this account." Joe handed him a slip of paper. "He must agree that neither the Kohl family nor International Systems will ever have a place of business in the United States again. If the company fails, extend our apologies and he owes nothing. What do you think of the deal?" Joe paused and looked at him.

"I think it will save the company. Otherwise, I think the company will fail. Allowing a six-month grace period is a gentlemanly thing to do. I'm sure he will appreciate it. He has already announced that International Systems will cease doing business in the United States so that's no problem. The Model 900 High Voltage Switch product line has been sold. I gather that you don't care what he does with the other SCT products as long as he doesn't do it in the United States?" Tillis was thinking out loud and asking the question.

"That's right. He can manufacture the other SCT products in Germany or wherever except in the U. S. If you get the opportunity, I would like for you to explain as much as you can to him. Most of it you know from what Clay told you during our last visit. What you may not know is that Max Krug killed my partner, Clay Matthews, after we talked to you. Also, he killed our older brother. He tried to kill my daughter and Clay's daughter."

"We want this feud to stop. We're taking a chance and offering him a hand by returning the tapes and waiting six months for payment. We don't want to fight anymore but we will if we have to." Joe waited a moment and then he continued.

"I have another suggestion. When you present it, be sure to tell him it is only a suggestion and only if the two of you are comfortable with the arrangement." Joe looked at him for a minute. "The easiest place to run those tapes is at the vendor location in Greenbelt. Technically, that is a violation of my instructions. I'm willing to allow it if he hires you to do it. If that is acceptable to him, tell him that we can communicate through you if the need arises. If you do it, tell him you want to be an independent contractor rather than an employee. I suggest you ask for at least twice what you've been making. How does that sound to you?"

"I'll tell him everything you said. If he's willing to do that, it's acceptable to me. How can I call you when I return with his answer?" Tillis asked.

"Oh, I'll call you. We'll know when you return." Joe smiled.

Gustav H. Kohl, newly elected Chairman of the Board of Directors and Chief Executive Officer, was a worried man. He couldn't cope with the many emergencies and lawsuits being thrown at his beloved and beleaguered company. There were not enough resources and time to meet the challenges. He had come to a decision to liquidate the company. He was writing out instructions to the attorneys when he received the telephone call from Albert Tillis. The man threw him a lifeline.

Gustav told his secretary to show Tillis into his office as soon as he arrived. He had met Tillis on many occasions during his frequent trips to SCT. He believed the man was competent so their relationship had been friendly. While he was grateful for the opportunity to obtain the tapes, he was puzzled about Tillis' involvement. It was Tillis' job to generate the tapes in the first place. When the tapes turned up blank, he accepted the story of a computer failure. Now it appeared that the tapes had been stolen and blank tapes substituted for the data reels. He was prepared to give the man the benefit of the doubt but the circumstances were strange. He had questions.

When Albert Tillis arrived at the airport, there was a company limousine to meet him. The chauffeur carried his luggage. When the vehicle arrived at the Headquarters building, there was a secretary to escort him to the top floor executive office.

"Albert. Please come in." Gustav came around the desk and extended his hand.

"Thanks for seeing me, Mr. Kohl." Tillis responded over the vigorous handshake.

"Please call me Gustav. I am still the same man who came to your house for dinner and helped your daughters with their German lessons." Gustav smiled and motioned him towards a chair.

"Your call was most unexpected. But it was also most welcome. Don't keep me in suspense; tell me what you have. Are the tapes intact? What do we have to do to retrieve them?" Kohl was excited at the possibility of having so many problems solved in one stroke. Not all of the problems but a good share.

"Two days ago, I received a call at home. A man told me he had the tapes and was willing to sell them. He directed me to leave my house immediately and drive to the parking lot of a motel in Rockville. When I arrived, two men entered my car." Tillis paused. This was going to be a sticky conversation. He knew that Gustav was extraordinarily intelligent. He was fast and sharp.

"They told me they had the tapes. They said that they did not intend to sell them originally. They intended to destroy the tapes to guarantee the destruction of SCT. Now they were reconsidering because they read of the difficulties. They did not intend to destroy you or International Systems." Tillis continued.

"So what do they propose?" Gustav asked.

"They want five million dollars and your promise not to open another business in the United States. You can defer the payment for six months. If the company doesn't survive, there is no obligation. They are prepared to deliver the tapes when I return with your agreement." Tillis closed his statement with a shrug.

"How long is the ban they propose against International Systems doing business in the United States?" Gustav wanted to know.

"The ban is against you personally and your family and International Systems. It is forever." Tillis tried to analyze the question. Did this guy think he was negotiating? Surely he was smarter than that. And he used the word "propose" in asking about the situation. These people weren't "proposing" anything. They were dictating.

"I'm not sure that is realistic. After all, my wife and children are American citizens. But, anyway, please continue. I need to know the complete situation with these individuals." Gustav said. Tillis had a sinking feeling in his stomach.

"I believe they were very serious about the ban, sir. I urge you to take the matter very seriously. If you agree to do this, you must live up to everything in your part of the bargain. It would be very dangerous not to do so " Tillis was alarmed.

"You use the word "bargain" which is the same as a deal or agreement. Have they prepared a piece of paper for me to sign or should I prepare a contract defining the terms?" Gustav asked seriously.

"No, sir. There is no paper or contract. If you agree, it will be verbally. I will carry your word to them. I'm not sure you understand the situation. They made you an offer. You have the option of accepting or not accepting their terms. That is the only freedom that you have. Yes or no. If you say yes and later renege, I believe it would be very dangerous for you and your family." Tillis tried to convey the deadly seriousness of the situation.

"You say that you will carry my decision to them. That implies that you know their names and location or telephone numbers." Kohl picked up a pen as if prepared to write down the information.

"They're going to call me when I return. I don't have any way to contact them." Tillis said truthfully.

"Do you know their names?" Kohl asked.

After a long pause, Tillis answered. "Yes, I know their names but I don't have their permission to divulge the information to you. Therefore, I cannot tell you."

"Look, Albert, we have been associates and, I believe, friends for several years. I'd like to think that we have a certain level of mutual respect and trust. You have had a good career at SCT and you have many good years remaining. This is a problem for the two of us to solve together. We need those tapes to survive now. After we recover, we will need to expand the company and the United States is the largest and most lucrative marketplace. We cannot exclude it from our business plans. Lastly, if these people have our tapes, they were obtained illegally. There are laws to protect us. Now, let us be reasonable and work through these problems." Gustav Kohl thought that he had presented the situation in a reasonable manner that even an accountant could understand.

Albert Tillis looked at him aghast. He could not believe his ears. This could not be happening to him. How could he have gotten into the middle of a situation so potentially deadly?

"Sir, you are refusing to understand the situation. I refuse to be a part of your destruction. I intend to return to the United States. I will tell them that you do not understand enough to make a rational decision. If they want to contact you again, it will not be through me." Tillis stood up and reached for his briefcase.

"Sit down, Albert. You're not going anywhere! If I have to restrain you, I will. If you think that I don't understand the situation, then it is your job to explain it to me." Kohl's voice had lowered and seemed somehow threatening. Tillis almost laughed. This naïve nincompoop didn't know the meaning of the word except in the theatrical sense. It was too bad that Joe Colissimo wasn't here to ask him for a finger or a toe to prove his sincerity. Then he would understand the seriousness of a threat.

"I will sit down and I will continue to discuss the situation with you. But things have changed since I entered the room. If you want me to tell them that you accept their deal, then you will have to convince me that you understand it and intend to live up to the terms. And I don't have any remaining years in my career at your company. I resign. Right now. For the remaining few hours before my return flight, I suggest that you try to understand your predicament. You are at a crossroads in your life. What you do now will determine your future and that of your family." Tillis felt better now that he had made a decision.

"Very well. I accept your resignation. I will listen to everything you have to tell me. In particular, I want to hear about your involvement with these people. You were the computer system manager at SCT. I want to know why they have those tapes and we do not. As I understand it, we lost the tapes once before in some sort of mix-up. Why was the system not corrected? Can you enlighten me on this matter?" Gustav sat back and actually crossed his arms on his chest. It was such a pompous gesture that Tillis actually chuckled and shook his head.

"You're right. The tapes were stolen on a previous occasion. Jack Carter and I made some changes in our backup arrangements. Previously, we had a habit of taking the tapes off the premises every night. The plan was to take the tapes to the bank for overnight storage. However, if we were busy, either Jack or I would simply store the tapes in the trunk of our car overnight. Our main fear was that the computer system at the plant would be destroyed in a fire." Tillis paused as he remembered the world as they once knew it.

"Following the theft of the tapes and payment of a ransom, Jack changed our emphasis. I was instructed to take the tapes to the bank every night and pick them up every morning. There was a second set of backup tapes kept in the closet in Jack's office. He figured that two sets would guard against any eventuality. In the event of fire, we had the tapes at the bank. In the event of theft, we had the set in his office. As you know, the entire building was destroyed in the fire and explosion including the contents of Jack's or Steiner's office. The bank tapes were worthless because of a computer failure. Our computer company analyzed the tapes. They said the tapes had been run but the data output channel was inoperative. Does that answer your question?"

"Very well. How did these people get a copy of the backup tapes?" Kohl asked coldly.

"I don't know. You may get an opportunity to ask them someday." Tillis retorted. "If I had to guess, I'd say that they may have the ones from Steiner's office."

"You know that the police have verified that Steiner was killed in the fire? Also, one of our security personnel was killed in the fire. What you're saying is that the people that have the tapes probably killed Steiner and the other man?"

"I don't know. I'm an accountant and computer systems manager. I'm not an investigator. I'll leave those speculations to the police."

"We seem to have gotten started down an adversarial path, Albert. I regret that. Perhaps if you started at the beginning, we can put our heads together and make some sense of this mess. Apparently, all of these events are connected. Where did this start? How did everything get out of control?" Gustav asked.

"I know a few facts. I know a few rumors and I have some theories. If you wish, I'll tell you what I think. But my decision to resign is final. I will be leaving on the return flight." Tillis set his jaw firmly.

He saw Gustav nod in assent.

"I know for a fact that Jon Claggett pirated the Model 900 product line from the two guys who designed the basic unit. Jack Carter knew of the theft and approved it. They treated the inventors with contempt and ordered them out of the SCT building. The patent was filed in Claggett's name and assigned to SCT. I don't know if you knew this story." Tillis paused.

"I suspected that Claggett didn't design the product. He wasn't a good design engineer. I talked to him about the circuit on one occasion and he didn't know much about the details. I assumed one of the junior engineers at SCT designed it and Claggett took the credit." Gustav mused. "Go on."

"SCT put the product into production and advertised heavily. Our sales soared and we avoided a downturn and a layoff because of it. I don't know if the inventors ever talked to a lawyer or contacted Claggett again. Apparently, they raided the plant one night and captured Claggett and Carter. The story I heard was that they promised to let Carter live if he would shoot Claggett and pay them two million dollars. They videotaped the shooting. The police have a copy of the tape. They warned Carter to drop the matter. They said they were satisfied with the payment and there would be no further trouble." Tillis waited for Kohl. He saw on the man's face that he had a question.

"How much would it have cost to buy the product in the first place?" Kohl asked.

"I heard that they would have been happy with one hundred thousand dollars. Probably less." Tillis answered.

"Incredible! So they saved one hundred thousand dollars and it cost them two million dollars and Claggett's life? Did they realize these two men were gangsters?" Gustav was fascinated with the story.

"I don't think they were gangsters. I think they were average men who were cheated and lied to by two men who acted on the part of a large corporation. They didn't have the money to sue so they chose violence to rectify the wrong." Tillis explained.

"But why would Claggett and Carter cheat them out of a hundred thousand dollars? The product was worth much more. It would have been a bargain and there wouldn't have been any trouble." Gustav was puzzled.

"Claggett was promoted to Vice President of Sales. He got a bonus, a raise and a stock option. Carter received praise and rewards from your grandfather and the Board of Directors." Tillis understood the reasons for the piracy. "They had stolen products in the past and got away with it. This time they paid with their lives."

"I thought you said that they let Carter go free and told him the trouble was over." Kohl reminded him.

"They did but Carter wouldn't let it drop. He hired a homicide detective to head up a new security force at SCT. One of his jobs was to hunt down the two guys who made him pay." Tillis had given the matter a lot of thought.

"How did these men find out about Carter's efforts to find them?" Kohl asked.

"I don't know. They must have had some kind of surveillance or phone tap on Carter."

"So they killed Carter?"

"The police are not sure. The evidence indicates that Carter killed himself and another individual from a local company. The location of the suicide was the place that Claggett was buried. They found the videotape showing Claggett's death. The murder weapon had Carter's fingerprints on it." Tillis recited.

"Who was the other guy from the local company? How was he connected to all of this?" Gustav asked.

"I don't know and the police have no theory."

"But you have a theory?"

"I have a wild guess. There was a second man from the same company who was killed earlier. I think they might have cheated these two guys. They simply decided to get even with everyone at the same time." Both men contemplated the sheer violence of these actions. It was unbelievable in a civilized society.

"Did they get any money out of us?" Gustav wanted to know.

"I don't think so. I think they were defending themselves against Carter."

"So what happened with Steiner? Why did they destroy the SCT building? Where did my grandfather and Max Krug figure in the picture? I can't believe my grandfather knew of the product piracy." Kohl was trying to make the pieces fit.

"I don't think your grandfather knew of the product piracy but I think he figured out the rest of the action. I am guessing that he sent Max Krug to the United States to find these guys. Possibly because he was retiring and he didn't want you to inherit a problem."

"And it's possible that they found out about Max's mission and made a preemptive strike? How would they find out?"

"Steiner ordered me to find the names and addresses of the two men that Claggett cheated. I contacted the investigative service that SCT used for credit checks and personnel security. I think they found out about the inquiry."

"These men sound like gangsters to me. Killing Steiner and one of our men and these other actions seem very drastic."

"Did you know that Max Krug killed one of the men and the brother of the other one? Did you know that he tried to kill the wife and daughter of one of them and the daughter of the other one? The Montgomery County Police cornered Max Krug in a local motel room and he committed suicide. They describe him as a rabid dog." Tillis kept trying to shock Gustav into some level of understanding.

"And you think my grandfather ordered these actions?" Gustav wanted to know.

"No. But I think he was responsible and I think he accepted the responsibility for Krug's actions. That must have been the reason for selling the product line and paying the proceeds into an offshore account. I read a news account that said your grandfather paid an additional five million dollars into an offshore account. It must be related."

"And now they want another five million dollars plus my exile from the United States."

"I think they would prefer to destroy the tapes. They are willing to sell the tapes if it will help you save the company from bankruptcy.

"What if the tapes are blank?"

"Then you won't be able to save the company and you won't owe them five million dollars in six months." Tillis thought the logic was irrefutable.

"So your recommendation is what? That I should accept their offer and pay them the money in six months and stay out of the United States?"

"No! My recommendation is that you decline the offer and liquidate the company. You have enough personal assets to live a life of luxury. You could be a consultant or design products for someone else or even take a government position."

"And you don't think these animals would take any further action against me or my family?" Kohl asked.

"That's right. I think the feud will be over." Tillis said with conviction.

"What if I accept the tapes and don't pay the money?" Kohl explored.

"I think you'll be killed." Tillis responded animatedly.

"What if I take this whole thing to the police after I get the tapes?" Kohl asked.

"At some point, you will endanger your wife and children as well as yourself." Tillis said sadly.

"Well, I hope you don't think I would endanger my family?" Kohl said with surprise.

"Yesterday, I would have defended your intelligence and acumen. Today I am remembering what a man told me one time. He said that it was amazing how stupid and greedy men are. So, yes, I think you will probably endanger your wife, your sons, and your daughter. You will justify it in your own mind so that you cannot blame yourself. But you'll do it." Tillis accused.

"Well, I think we differ on that point. Tell me. At some point, why didn't these men go to court? Surely they can see the reason and logic of the judicial system?" Kohl asked.

"They did not have the experience, education or financial resources to employ the judicial system. In every country, the party with the most resources will win a court case. They simply didn't have the money." He paused and decided to try one last time.

"I have a background similar to you. My family was moderately wealthy. I went to Duke for my undergraduate degree and to Wharton for my Master's degree. I have never known pain, hunger, helplessness, or real fear. Until recently, I would have hired a lawyer if I felt wronged. A few months ago, I had a glimpse of the other side. My family was threatened and I realized that I was powerless to protect them. They are as precious to me as your wife and children are to you. I tasted fear so powerful that I vomited and shook so violently that I could not move for an hour. I hope you never experience these feelings. But I think you will." Tillis concluded with an air of resignation.

"I'm leaving for the airport now. I wish I knew what else to say but I don't. Good luck. May God guide you." Tillis headed for the door.

"Wait! What will you tell them about my answer?" Kohl stammered.

"Whatever you tell me." Tillis shrugged and looked at the carpet.

"What else will you tell them?" Kohl wanted to know as he stared at Tillis.

"The truth to any question they ask me." Tillis raised his head and looked him in the eye.

"Tell them that my answer is yes." Kohl said as he turned his back on the departing Tillis.

Gustav was not quite as inexperienced as Tillis was led to believe. He knew a bit more about the situation after he read his grandfather's final note to him. The note had been placed in the secret wall safe. He and his grandfather were the only ones with access. After the police departed, he opened the safe and read the final note.

It would take a lot of time and care but Gustav vowed that his grandfather would be avenged. If he trusted no one, then he could not be betrayed. He would be careful and discreet. If he needed information, there would be several layers between him and the source.

But there would be a day of reckoning for the commoners. Power and resources did count for something. They would learn a bitter lesson.

He had six months to act.

44 – An Expensive Recovery

Ab Tillis had returned from Munich emotionally depressed and physically exhausted. Flying first class was a treat and helped with the fatigue but not with the time lag. He went to bed early in the evening and slept late but fitfully. He knew the reason for his inability to relax. He was waiting for a telephone call. He stayed home to be sure that he didn't miss it.

"Good morning, Mr. Tillis. How are you? Rested up from your flight yet?" The voice of Joe Colissimo was unmistakable.

"I'm afraid it will take more than a couple of days. I'm not a very good traveler." He responded.

"I would like to meet with you and discuss your meetings on the trip. Would this be a convenient time?" Tillis felt like he had been promoted. He wasn't being ordered to leave the house immediately and proceed to the parking lot. However, he wanted to get the meeting over and get on with his life.

"Now would be a convenient time. Should I go to the same place?"

"No. I would like to suggest a different location. Do you know a small park on Nelson Street in Rockville? It's pretty close to the old SCT building. If you were going to SCT from the bank, it is the last right turn before you get to the 270 interchange. Take a right on Nelson and go a few blocks. There's a strip mall on the left and the park is across the street. I'll meet you in the park. Okay? Thanks a lot."

Tillis dressed hastily and headed for his car. He remembered passing the park on his trips to the main post office in Rockville. It sounded like a better location for this type of meeting. It was more open and there were probably some people walking around the park. It should be safer for him.

Two minutes after he nosed into a parking place, the Ford Explorer SUV pulled in next to him. Joe Colissimo entered the front seat and Gino entered the rear seat. Joe offered his hand. Ab felt relieved that the meeting was starting out on a friendly note.

"Your eyes look a little red. You didn't let the airlines talk you into trying the champagne, did you?" Joe laughed.

"I'm afraid I could get accustomed to traveling first class." Ab confessed.

"I gather that you had no difficulty in getting in to see Mr. Kohl?" Joe asked.

"No. Not at all. He was quite pleased to see me." Tillis remembered.

"And you explained our offer to him?" Joe prompted. He didn't like the troubled look that he detected on Tillis' face.

"Yes. Yes, I did." Tillis answered.

"Did he give you an answer?" Joe knew how a dentist must feel. The information was coming out a tooth at a time.

"He told me to tell you that the answer is yes." Tillis was looking straight ahead through the windshield at a pickup ballgame. He wasn't looking at Joe.

"He understood the complete offer? The terms and everything?" Joe raised his voice enough to prompt Ab's attention.

"Yes, he understood the complete offer. He said to tell you that his answer was yes."

"Did he specifically say that he accepted the terms or did he say to tell me the answer was yes?"

"He said to tell you the answer was yes."

"Did he ask you for our names?"

"Yes."

"Did you tell him?"

"No."

"Why do you think he wanted to know our names?"

"I don't know. He didn't say and I didn't ask."

"Was he irritated that you wouldn't tell him?"

"Yes."

"Do you think he will pay the money in six months?"

"I don't know."

"But you're not sure that he will?"

"I guess I'm not sure he will pay."

"Would it be safe to assume that he is upset over the loss of his grandfather?" Gino joined in the conversation.

"Yes, it would be accurate to assume that he is mourning the loss deeply." Tillis confirmed.

"How does he intend to process the tapes? Are you going to be doing it for him as a consultant?" Joe asked.

"I don't know how he intends to extract the information from the tapes. I am no longer affiliated with the Kohl family or International Systems. Gustav and I were unable to agree on many things. We agreed that I would sever my ties with the company."

"Does he think you were involved in the disappearance of the tapes?"

"He thinks that I know more about the situation than an innocent man would know. He would never trust me again."

"That's too bad. He doesn't know you as well as we do. We trust you."

"Thank you. I think." Tillis said hesitantly.

"When we met you earlier, we weren't sure of you but you've been honest and straightforward with us. We appreciate it. I hope there's no hard feeling?" Joe was sincere.

"No. I understand a lot more now than I did earlier." Tillis was equally sincere.

"So I guess we should ship the tapes to Kohl in Munich rather than give them to you?"

"That's probably the best arrangement."

"Here's a telephone number that you can reach me at if you ever want to contact me. Call if I can help you in any way." Joe handed him a card.

"Thank you. I will keep this confidential. I hope everything works out okay." Tillis said.

*   *   *

When Joe and Gino returned to the house, Sylvia set out a snack and opened a bottle of Chianti Classico. She could see that Joe was unhappy so she didn't ask any questions. She knew she would hear all about it in short order.

"What do you think, Joe?"

"I think the grandson is going to be a heap of trouble."

"You don't think he'll pay?"

"I don't think he'll pay plus I think he's going to come after us."

"So what do you think we should do?"

"I think we should destroy the tapes and let the company fail. There's no point in giving him the financial resources to mount an operation against us. If he's broke, he'll have other things to think about."

"Well, that would mean that we won't get paid anything for the tapes. And I think the company would go broke not the grandson. The grandson has his own wealth outside the company. And I think he's going to come after us in either event. The trick is for us to get the money before we have to take him out." Gino explained.

"Shit! Isn't this crap ever going to stop? I'm tired of living like this. We've lost John and Clay. We've gone through some moments of terror. Isn't there some way to end this nightmare? Clay and I did not envision this recurring horror or we would not have started the first operation." Joe pounded the table with his big fist.

"Well, I guess twenty-twenty hindsight has a purpose. It ranks alongside the would-haves, could-haves, and should-haves. You'll be able to remember them on future decisions. But on this operation, the decisions were made when they pirated the product design." Gino lamented.

"So there's no way to end this shit? I want to retire. I'm almost fifty-five years old. You're almost sixty. I want to be able to watch my grandchildren grow up without having to look over my shoulder. Eventually, we're going to encounter another Max Krug and who knows how much damage we'll have to endure. I mean it, Gino. We have to find a way to end this shit." Joe fumed.

"Joe, you have to calm down and be patient. There are no instant cures and answers. We have to be smarter than the enemy. If we lose our temper or confine ourselves to some arbitrary time scale, we're dead and maybe our families, too. Retirement and grandchildren have to come second. This is first! Now stand beside me on this and help me win." Gino reached out and grabbed Joe's shoulder as if to shake him into some level of consciousness.

"Okay. I understand. I truly do. But, Gino, how can we win so that it doesn't keep coming back at us?" Joe almost wailed. It was a strange sound of desperation from such a big man.

"One way is to annihilate the Kohl family. You know that as well as I do. It's what our old man would have done in his time." Gino looked at him so that he could read his response whether in words or body language.

"That was another time. We can't do that and you know it. We wouldn't be able to live with ourselves. Our wives and kids would be sick of us. Do you think John Higgins wouldn't be able to figure it out?" Joe retorted.

Gino found it interesting that his brother did not shrink from facing the possibility of a massacre as a solution. Instead, he had pointed out the consequences and the danger.

Four days after Albert Tillis returned to the United States, Gernot Kohl received a heavy package via Lufthansa Air Lines freight. It contained the backup computer tapes. There were eight reels. Each reel was almost twelve inches in diameter and approximately one inch thick. One reel inside a thin aluminum case weighed almost ten pounds. The eight reels plus packing and outer container tipped the scales at one hundred pounds.

Gustav summoned his computer systems manager. He instructed him to make two copies of the tapes. Gustav ordered him to do it personally and report back to him on completion. He had located a system inside Germany that was identical to the system at the SCT subsidiary. Gustav leased the system for one month. The tapes would be transported to the leased facility for processing. They would download the information and re-create the business condition of SCT on the day of the fire. They would know how many invoices were outstanding and how many vendors were owed a payment. They would know the status of each employee's vacation and sick leave status. The insurance company would not be happy to know that there was a complete list of assets by serial number and asset tag number.

As soon as the tapes were verified to contain the data, Gustav released a statement to the business press. Basically, the business community was informed that the tapes had been found. As the data was printed out, each invoice would be paid or collected as appropriate. Lawsuits would be filed on companies that had issued bogus invoices. As each employee's record was reviewed, vacation and sick pay would be paid. Those employees who had filed false claims would be sued. The result would be that their names would be published. Although blacklists were illegal, the result would be the same. What company is going to hire an employee who filed a false claim on a previous employer?

International Systems, Inc. filed a lawsuit against the insurance company. ISG wanted the full amount of the replacement value of the furniture, machinery, equipment, and fixtures paid in full. They wanted interest pro-rated from the day of loss to the day of payment. They wanted compensation in the amount of ten million dollars for damages caused by the delay in payment. The attorneys stated in open court that a lack of cooperation by the insurance company prevented the resumption of business by SCT in a timely manner. The insurance company released a public statement refuting the claim. At the time of the press release, the insurance attorneys were negotiating a settlement with International Systems.

All of the employee lawsuits were dropped. The employees were told that they could avoid a lawsuit by forfeiting all claims to any back pay and vacation and sick leave. The vendors who had issued invoices claiming payment for goods that were not shipped were offered a settlement figure of one hundred thousand to one million dollars depending on the size of their bogus claim.

ISG issued a notice that there would be no severance pay for the former SCT employees. Due to the nature of the catastrophe that destroyed the SCT building, the company did not feel responsible. However, any former SCT employee who wanted a job would be welcomed at the Munich plant. Fluency in the German language was a requirement for employment.

The technical information on the tapes allowed International Systems to resume production of most of SCT's products in the Munich plant. Some of the product lines were sold to competitors.

Gustav ordered the attorneys to study the sale of the Model 900 High Voltage Switch product line. He wanted the sale voided if at all possible. The computer tapes had yielded a complete data package on the line.

Three months after the return of the tapes, the computer systems manager asked for a special appointment with Gustav. He had struck gold. Gustav had ordered the man to research the Model 900 files for any information pertaining to the original design of the product. He had ordered the man to maintain complete confidentiality during the investigation. He promised not to say or write one word about his inquiry.

When Jonathan Claggett received the original samples from Joe Colissimo and Clayton Matthews, they were encased in a hard epoxy. In the parlance of the electronics industry, the products were potted. Clay had used a special epoxy enforced with carbide chips.

Claggett had sent the products to a special laboratory to have the epoxy removed. As each layer was removed, the company took a digital photograph of the part. One picture in particular was of interest in the quest for information. On the main printed circuit board, Joe and Clay had etched their names like schoolboys scratching in fresh cement in front of the schoolhouse. The boards were labeled -

Colissimo/Matthews 0001

Colissimo/Matthews 0002

Colissimo/Matthews 0003

Now Gustav had the last names of his grandfather's killers.

It did not occur to him that he had uncovered irrefutable proof that his company had stolen the product from Clay Matthews and Joe Colissimo.

"I don't understand, Gustav. It has been five months since your grandfather died. You are more upset today over his death than you were at the time it happened. You're having trouble sleeping and you seem obsessed with security. What's going on?" Laura spoke to her husband in English when they were at home. It was part of the training for the children. They heard and spoke German all day so English at home was a way of encouraging their fluency in English.

"Don't worry about it. I've had some difficulty at the company but I believe the worst is behind me. We've settled with the insurance company and most of the lawsuits have been settled to our satisfaction and gain. The company will show an extraordinary gain during this fiscal year of nearly forty million dollars. It will be the same as if we had sold SCT for that amount." Gustav explained.

"If everything is going so well, why the sleepless nights and the long faces?" She would never mention it directly but they hadn't had sex for three months. Something was seriously wrong but she could not figure it out unless Gustav confided in her.

"I have another problem on the horizon. I haven't decided what to do about it." Gustav said. "Until I have settled the problem, I want you and the children to be extra careful. I don't think there is any danger but it is difficult to tell with these crazy cowboy Americans."

Then he caught himself and smiled. "I'm sorry, liebchen. You know I love Americans. I just don't understand their attitude sometimes."

45 – Strategic Planning

"Dr. Brock? Dr. Werner Brock? It's good to see you, sir. Do you remember me? I used to go to school with your daughter, Laura." The young man offered his hand and Dr. Brock automatically shook it. In truth, the young man was not even vaguely familiar to him. However, he had to admit that he hadn't paid a lot of attention to some of Laura's friends.

"I'm sorry. I don't seem to remember your name. It seems so long ago. I guess you know that Laura is married and living in Germany now?" Dr. Brock hoped that this guy wasn't some brokenhearted lover carrying a torch for Laura.

Montgomery Mall in Rockville, Maryland was especially crowded on the weekends. Dr. Brock was doing some shopping for his wife's birthday. He hoped this young man wasn't going to delay him very long.

"Sir, I wonder if I could talk to you for a minute? I have some information that Laura will want to know and I hope you can tell her about it."

"Well, I'm in a bit of a rush." Dr. Brock hesitated. He hated to be rude and the young man was very well dressed. "Perhaps I can spare a few minutes but then I have to leave."

"Thank you, sir. I think you'll be glad that we met."

"I'm sorry. I still don't remember your name. Maybe you can start by refreshing my memory." Dr. Brock looked at the young man closely.

"My name is James Colissimo. They used to call me "Little Jimmy." He steered Laura's father towards a sitting area.

"Now what's so important that you need to tell me about

Laura?" He was starting to get a little irritated.

"She is in some danger, sir. I wanted to tell you about it in hopes that you could help her." James said.

"In danger? What do you mean?" Dr. Brock started to rise in alarm.

"Please, sir. Be seated and let me talk to you. Everything is going to be okay." James put his hand on the older man's shoulder and tried to calm him down.

"If Laura is in danger, you'd better start talking before I call a policeman."

"Sir, please calm down and give me a chance to explain." James was beginning to think that this was a bad idea. Gino was not as good at this type of planning as Clay or his older brother, John, had been.

"If I don't hear a good explanation from you in thirty seconds, I'm going to start yelling." Dr. Brock threatened.

The next sound that passed between them was the distinct and sharp swish of a knife blade being extended. James pushed the sharp tip against the old man's ribs and whispered, "If you even start to yell, I'll cut your heart out. Now shut up. Sit down. And listen to me. No one wants to hurt you or your daughter. That's why I'm here. We don't want to see her or your grandchildren get hurt."

Dr. Brock sat down and shut up. It had been many years since he had been threatened with violence. He remembered the taste of fear too well. He thought these feelings were past now that he was in the United States.

"Your son-in-law, Gustav, owes my family a considerable sum of money. The payment is due in less than a month. We believe he is going to default on the payment. He has been warned that his life is forfeit if he doesn't pay." James paused to measure the effect of his words.

"I don't understand. Gustav has done very well financially for the past several months. He turned the SCT mess around to an enormous profit. I don't believe he's short on money. If he owes you some money, I'm sure he will pay you."

"My family recovered the computer tapes that allowed him

to recover from the SCT mess. We agreed on a price for the recovery and we gave him six months to pay. The date is close now and the information that we have indicates that he does not intend to honor the debt."

"I assume you have a contract for the work that you did. All you have to do is file a lawsuit." Dr. Brock made it sound so simple. James sighed.

"Are you calm enough now that I can put away my fingernail file?" James asked. He collapsed the switchblade knife and put it away. "I'd like to tell you a story. Then I'd like to have your help. If you decide to help, it will guarantee the safety of your daughter and grandchildren and it will help us collect our money."

Dr. Brock looked at the sincere young man and nodded his head in assent.

James began telling him the story of SCT and the wronged inventors.

When the telephone rang in the middle of the afternoon, Laura Kohl's first thought was that it was a call from the United States. It would be 8 AM at home – she still thought of Maryland as home – and her father sometimes called before he left for his office. As these thoughts ran through her mind, she automatically answered in English.

"Hi, honey, it's Dad! How are you doing?"

"We're fine, Dad." Laura answered automatically. "How are things at home?"

She winced as she recognized the word she used and the tone in her voice. It was more than wistfulness. It was homesickness. She missed the easy informality of the United States. In Germany, conversation and friendship were so formal.

"Well, it's not bad but it would be better if you and the grandkids lived a few thousand miles closer."

"I know, Dad. Sometimes it seems to be light years away, doesn't it?" Laura sighed.

"Seriously, honey, how are things going for you? We worry

about you, you know?"

"Oh, we're okay. The twins are a handful. So what's new about that?" She laughed.

"The reason I called is that I met an interesting young man yesterday. As you know, I'm more into scientific matters than I am in history and politics but he had some interesting views on some matters. As it turns out, he is traveling to Europe and will be in Munich soon. I asked him to contact you."

"Sounds mysterious. Should I invite him out to the house for dinner? Gustav has been working some strange hours recently but I'm sure he can take one evening out of his schedule." Laura was puzzled at the tone of her Dad's voice.

"Well, I'd like for you to wait until he contacts you. I don't quite know when that will be or even how he might contact you but, when he does, please remember that I vouched for him."

"Is there anything wrong, Dad?"

"I'll let him explain some things to you, honey. I have to leave for the office now. Kiss the kids for me, okay?"

"Goodbye, Dad."

"Bye, honey."

After she hung up the telephone, Laura sat at the desk and reflected on the strange nature of the conversation. Finally, she stirred herself and started making a shopping list. Today was her weekly trip to the market and she had a few things to purchase at the department store for the children. The twins were especially hard on clothes. They seemed to be roughhousing all of the time.

James Colissimo was sitting at the curb two blocks from the Kohl house. When Laura passed him in her Mercedes Coupe, he pulled out and maintained a cautious distance from her. He had one of the associates from the Munich office with him. When Laura pulled into a parking space, he double-parked and exited the car. He told the associate to slide over and find a place to park in the vicinity.

Laura was walking into the department store as James was

exiting the car. He had to rush in order to keep her in sight. As he passed through the revolving door, he caught a glimpse of her dark blue blouse heading for the elevators. This could be a perfect opportunity if they could share an elevator without any other observers.

The elevator doors were closing but James was able to insert a hand to re-open them. He smiled in apology at the beautiful lady in blue. It was his first live view of Laura Kohl. She was captivating. James had never experienced a first impression quite so strong. He had to remind himself to keep his attention focused on the business at hand. He entered the elevator and looked at the control panel. Laura had punched in a request for the fourth floor. He smiled and nodded to her. "That's the same floor I'm going to." James saw her register the strong American accent.

"I assume you're shopping for children's clothes." Laura reasoned.

"No. Actually, I'm looking for someone – a young lady. I don't have a picture of her but I have one of her father. Have you ever seen this man?" James extended a picture of Laura's father and himself sitting in a restaurant in Montgomery Mall.

Laura was completely off-guard and, because she was so totally surprised, she felt a rising feeling of fear. James saw the look on her face.

"Please don't be alarmed. Your father gave me several pictures and a note because he is convinced that you should talk to me." He handed her several pictures and a letter.

Laura glanced at the pictures but kept a wary eye on the stranger. She was uncomfortably aware of his presence in the small, enclosed room. She was relieved when the elevator reached the fourth floor and the door opened. She hurried through the door and then turned to confront the young American beside her.

"I don't understand why you chose to confront me in the elevator. My father called me and told me of your trip to Germany. However, I expected a telephone call." Laura paused with the expectation of an explanation.

"I'm truly sorry. I hated to alarm you but I thought it was urgent that I contact you and your father agreed with me. He agreed that I should try to talk to you in private." James let the inference dangle between them.

"You mean that you wanted to talk to me without my husband's presence?" She observed.

"Yes. That's exactly what I mean. And I thought it would be less distressing to you if I contacted you in a public area so you would not feel threatened." James explained.

"Well, you have my attention. And I am curious. I can't imagine what you said to my father to get his approval of such a maneuver."

"Could we sit down in the coffee shop or somewhere? This is going to take a few minutes." James looked around.

"Okay, there's a coffee shop on the second floor." Laura pushed the elevator call button. Then she asked, "When did you see my father?"

"Those pictures were taken two days ago. I think he called you this morning. Is that correct?"

"Yes, it is. And he sounded as mysterious as you are sounding now. And I notice that both of you are avoiding mention of Gustav. Why is that?" Laura demanded.

"Because the discussion is about Gustav and it is not flattering." James warned her.

"Then I don't want to hear it." Laura was adamant.

"Not even if it involved the safety of your children?" James challenged.

Before she could answer, the receptionist guided them to a table and James pulled out a chair for her. It was the first time in his life that he had offered such a courtesy to a lady.

A waitress approached the table with a menu. Laura spoke to her in German and ordered two coffees.

"Okay, we're seated. You have your audience. What is it?"

James looked at her and thought about his next words for a few minutes. "I'm willing to bet that Gustav has been acting different recently. Perhaps it seems that he is under pressure or worried about something. Despite the fact that the financial problems have been solved at International Systems, he probably isn't happy. Is that true?"

Laura did not respond. She simply looked at James with a neutral expression on her face.

"Okay. I think the answer is yes. I would like to tell you a story about how events came to the point that they are today." James promised.

James Colissimo proceeded to tell Laura the complete story from the beginning. He started with the situation of two guys with very little money. Each of them had a wife and daughter. Both of them worked two jobs to make ends meet. Then they designed a new product and made the mistake of letting SCT evaluate it. He told her of the piracy and how both men decided to let it go. They were going to chalk it up to experience. But one of them was a proud man from a large family. They would not let him forget the piracy and the affront to his pride. The other man was a quiet, law-abiding man who would not join his partner in seeking revenge.

But then the second man suffered several other strokes of ill fortune including the death of his wife and the estrangement of his daughter. He decided to commit suicide but before he checked out he decided to exact justice against every stroke of bad luck caused by his fellow man.

James described the death and destruction at SCT and then the second visit when Jack Carter would not let the matter rest. He described the revenge on Visorex and the hated Form 1556. He told her of the insurance scam and the resulting deaths of the adjuster and agent. Finally, he came to the part where Dr. Kohl decided to eliminate the two men because he was retiring. James described the massacre planned by Max Krug and the partial success. The death of his oldest brother and the attempt on his niece Josephine were difficult for him.

Finally James came to the part where the family had to decide to let International Systems fail or sell the tapes back to Gustav. He told of the trip by Albert Tillis to offer the deal to Gustav and the six months of payment terms. He described the financial gains of International Systems and Gustav personally as a result of the returned tapes.

Finally he detailed their conclusions about Gustav's recent actions. They felt that Gustav would default on the payment for the tapes and that he would mount some action against them.

Laura passed through several emotional states during the telling of the story. She experienced disbelief, horror, revulsion and finally acceptance. She realized that her father must have heard the same story and believed it. Now she knew the reason that her father had asked her to talk to James.

James had one more point to cover and it was the most difficult. Since Laura had been born in the United States, he started with a review of the famous Hatfield and McCoy feud. He continued with the old European view of feuds. The violence extended down to the youngest members of the families. The most recent evidence was Max Krug's bloody battles during his attempts to wipe out the Colissimo and Matthews families.

James waited while the impact of his words penetrated her consciousness.

Tears came to her eyes and she cried, "No! No!" so loudly that the other customers looked up and the waitress came to check on them.

When she had regained her composure, she looked at James. "But my children and I are not a part of Gustav's plan." She protested.

"Yes, you are. You are as long as you are living with him. He is your husband and the father of the children." James looked her in the eyes and did not flinch. He granted no mercy or leeway.

"You're telling me that if Gustav takes some action against your family then my children and I are in mortal danger?" She asked aghast.

"If Gustav comes after us, he will come after everybody in our family. We will have to retaliate. Both families will believe that they have to eliminate any future threat."

"But you're only guessing. How can you be sure that he isn't going to pay on time? How do you know that he is planning some action against your family?"

"Because we have him under surveillance and we have tapped

his phones." James explained quietly and conclusively.

"So why are you telling me? What can I do?" Laura wailed.

"You have an opportunity to leave the field of battle. You can take your children and walk away. I'm not talking about spending a weekend with your parents or going to the beach for a few days. You have a choice of either standing with Gustav or abandoning him forever." James would have given anything he owned for the right to hold her in his arms now. She was in pain and he wanted to comfort her. He knew he could not weaken if he wished to save her life.

"Did he discuss this situation with you? Did he explain that he could not live with the punishment meted out to his grandfather? Did he say that he was willing to risk his life, your life, and the children's lives to avenge his grandfather? Did he tell you that he had decided it was more important than your marriage?" James spoke quietly as in the drumbeat of the march to the gallows.

"I have to go now. Please let me take you to a taxi. You are upset and should not be driving." He offered.

"No. I'm okay. I'm going to sit here for awhile and think about these things. Thank you for talking to me. At least, I have a choice now." She stood up and offered her hand.

James found the car and driver a few spaces down and across the street from the front entrance of the department store. He jumped into the passenger's side and put out his hand to restrain the driver from starting the car.

"Do we have a tail?" James was looking for a yes or a no. Anything else would have been unacceptable to him.

"Yes. There is only one guy. He followed her into the store and he followed you out of the store." The driver grinned. He knew James demanded a high level of professionalism. Actually, James was much more demanding than Gino. "He's about eight parking spaces behind us on the opposite side of the street."

"Go ahead and pull out. Let's see if he follows us." James

ordered. He turned his attention to the rear-view mirror.

"He's going to stay with us and see who we are. He's holding about three cars in the rear." The driver observed. "What do you want to do?"

James did not answer immediately. He reviewed his options and thought about the consequences of each step. He did not know what Laura Kohl would do and that was a big factor in determining his course of action here. Finally, he decided to be optimistic. He would assume that she would do what he wanted her to do. She would find a way to return to the United States. In that event, she did not need the handicap of Gustav finding out that she had met and talked with an American. So the answer of what to do now was simple. He had to eliminate the driver of the car following them.

"Drive down towards the industrial section. Find an area that we can get ahead of him far enough that I can exit the car. Then go around the next corner and stop. When he stops behind you, I'll take him." James explained.

"And do what with him?" The associate wanted to know.

James considered the man beside him. He was not family but he had been associated with them for many years. He was willing to gamble on the man. "Does it matter to you?"

"Sometimes these things go wrong. I will back you to the limit. As I expect you to protect me. If I get hurt or killed, I need to know that my family will be protected and supported." The man turned his head and looked at him.

"You have my promise." James swore.

The driver made a right turn around the corner of a four-story warehouse. James jumped out of the car and into a recessed doorway. The driver accelerated and was disappearing around the next corner when the other car appeared. As soon as the car passed the doorway, James sprinted out and gave chase. He remained close to the building in the afternoon shadows. He hoped to avoid attracting the man's attention in the rear-view mirror.

The driver accelerated because he saw his prey disappearing around the next corner. He was not prepared when he rounded the corner and was confronted with a stopped car. He stomped on the brakes and was startled to see James standing beside the driver's window with a gun pointed at him.

James and his associate forced the driver from the car. They searched him and confiscated the small automatic pistol from the shoulder holster. Walking around behind the man, he clipped him behind the ear with his gun butt. The man fell to the ground unconscious. James said a silent thanks to his trainer Pug Wilson for his training. For now, they carried the man to the rear of the car and put his limp body in the trunk.

"Let's take him out to the airport. We'll pull into the long-term parking lot and park this car in a far corner. Hopefully no one will find him for ten or twelve hours." James said.

"I thought you were going to kill him and we would have to dispose of the body."

"I don't want to kill him if it isn't necessary. I want to give Laura time to exit the country. After that, I don't care if he's found or what he does." James explained.

Laura Kohl sat in the coffee shop for a long time. After the second visit to the table by the waitress, she ordered a sandwich in order to buy some time. She was thinking rapidly and forming some undesirable conclusions. She knew that Gustav had involved her and the children in this trouble without discussing it or getting her input. She felt betrayed. She could not understand how or why he decided to do this monstrous thing. But then she did know. Gustav loved his grandfather more than anything or anybody on earth. It would appear that he worshiped the memory of his grandfather more than the lives of her and the children. She had to protect her children. They were more important than her marriage.

Once she made the decision about what was more important, she had to decide what to do. That was easy – return to the United States with the children to her father's house. Now the next step was to decide when and how. She felt the danger was very real so action was required now. Would Gustav try to stop her? Yesterday she would have said "no." Today things were different. An idea began to form in her mind.

"Dad?" Laura had placed a collect telephone call to her father from a pay station in the basement of the department store.

"Yes, honey?" Her father was terrified at the prospect of his daughter and grandchildren being in danger.

"I guess you talked to James and you're aware of the situation?" Laura asked.

"Yes, I am. I'm scared for you and the kids, honey."

"I'm coming home, Dad. And I'm bringing the kids. I don't know if Gustav will try to stop me or not but I don't want to take any chances. Here's what I would like for you to do." Laura began to outline a plan.

When Gustav arrived home at 5 PM, Laura was packing suitcases for her and the children. She had called Lufthansa Airlines and reserved five first-class seats for New York and a connecting flight on US Air to Washington National Airport near Washington, D. C. She had their passports in her purse.

"What's up?" Gustav demanded. He was alarmed at the packing scene.

"Darling, Mom's had a heart attack. She's in the hospital. They have her stabilized now but she is going to have a bypass operation in two days. I want to see her and be with her. She's asked to see the kids. I tried to call you at the office but they said you had left."

"This is very sudden."

"Yes, it is. Heart attacks are like that – very sudden."

"Have you called the airport? How do you know you can get a reservation on such a short notice?"

"I've called and they have seats for us. If I had not been able to get seats, I would have asked you to use some influence." Laura smiled.

As Gustav started to ask some questions and protest the trip, the telephone rang. He scooped up the receiver and answered with some impatience.

"Gustav? This is Dad. I guess Laura has told you about the emergency that we have here. I wanted to talk to her and see if she has made any arrangements for a visit. Is she there?" Laura's father waited to hear a response.

"Laura was telling me about it. She has made some reservations and I'll let her tell you about the arrival times. I'm wondering if it is a good idea for the children to accompany her. I believe it may be too much of a burden on you during this emergency. We have a nurse who is perfectly capable of caring for the children." Gustav was thinking over the situation while he talked.

""I hope the kids will be coming with Laura. It is very important to Mother. She wants to see the children so much before her operation. We'll be able to care for them. Please remember our neighbor who is a nurse. She is semi-retired and has plenty of time. "

"Well, we'll see. Here's Laura for you." Gustav handed the telephone to Laura.

"Hi, Dad. Yes, we have reservations. We're on Lufthansa flight 680 arriving at JFK in New York at 6 PM – the same time we leave Munich due to the time change. Neat, huh? We will connect with US Air 412 arriving at National Airport at 7:45 PM. The travel agent has arranged for a limo to meet us. " Laura listened for a minute and then said, "Dad, Gustav loves you and Mom as much as I do. Don't be silly! He's concerned for your welfare. Yes, I'll tell him! See you later! " Laura hung up.

Laura turned to Gustav with a question for him. "What's going on? You've never been hesitant in the past about me or the kids visiting my parents. Even on short notice! Lately you've been nervous and preoccupied. You haven't paid the least bit of attention to the kids or me. Now all of a sudden you don't want us to visit Mom after a heart attack? I would think you would want to have a little space if you're having a problem that you can't share with me. "

"I don't know what's wrong. I am having a few work-related problems. I didn't want to bother you with them. Go ahead and visit your parents. Be sure to let me know how everything is going. Okay?" Gustav surrendered.

By 11:30 PM Munich Time, Gustav had heard the report of the guard detailed to follow Laura. He knew she met with an American for more than an hour in the department store. Obviously the heart attack story was a hoax. She wanted to remove the children from his protective custody. The bottom line was that she must have believed whatever the American had to say. It also meant that the Americans were active in Germany and probably had him under surveillance.

The five million-dollar payment was due tomorrow.

The telephone rang in Albert Tillis' home at 5 PM. Tillis had walked through the door only ten minutes earlier. He had returned from a trip to the West Coast for a job interview. He was tired and rumpled from the flight. He did not expect his wife and daughters to return for at least an hour. He intended to collapse for fifteen minutes and then shower and shave for a dinner date with his wife. He wanted to describe the community in Northern California that might be their future home.

"Hello."

"Albert? This is Gustav Kohl. How are you?" The man sounded cheerful.

"Fine. I just returned from a trip. Your call is well timed. How are you?"

"Well, I have a bit of a problem. I was hoping you could help me."

"I guess it depends on the problem. What's up?"

"Well, as you know, I accepted the terms of the deal when the tapes were returned. Tomorrow I am supposed to pay out the five million dollars. As it turns out, some of our cash flow was delayed and it will be impossible for me to meet the deadline. I wonder if you can get in touch with the other party and request an extension on my behalf?" Gustav paused.

"I'm not sure I can reach them. I have one avenue I can try but it may not work. I believe that you should do everything in your power to meet the terms, Gustav."

"I understand but it is a lot of money and cash is tight. I would appreciate your help on this matter. Would you please try?" Gustav sounded a little stressed.

"Yes, I will try. Should I telephone you if I make contact?"

"Yes, please call the company switchboard and they will track me down. Call me as soon as you can."

"Very well." Both men hung up their receivers.

Joe Colissimo answered his cell phone on the first ring.

"Er, ah, this is Albert Tillis. To whom am I speaking, please?"

"This is Joe Colissimo, Mr. Tillis. How are you? It's been six months since I spoke to you and, yet, I had a hunch that I might hear from you today. I guess I'm just psychic."

"Perhaps you are a better judge of men than you are a psychic. And please call me Ab."

"Well, thank you, Ab. I would like it if you called me Joe. May I assume that you had a call from Germany?"

"Yes, I did. Our friend was inquiring about the possibility of an extension on his payment terms. I told him I would do my best to contact you."

"Did he use my name when he asked you to contact me?"

"No. He referred to you as "the other party" and wondered if I had a way to contact you."

"Did he state a reason for the request?"

"He said that he had a delay in his cash flow."

"Did you believe him?"

"I'm not sure. I didn't really think about it."

"I thought six months was a generous concession on our part. And from what I read, he has been very successful in the use of the tapes."

"I agree with you on both counts." Tillis said.

"What would you do in my position? "

Albert Tillis laughed. "You wouldn't try to put an innocent bean counter in a difficult position, would you?"

"Not at all. I was just wondering what a senior financial consultant would tell a client that asked for an extension on an interest-free five million dollar loan?"

"I'm afraid that my charity does not extend past my family and my church."

"My sentiments exactly. Please tell your caller the answer is no."

"What if he wants to speak to you directly?"

"Tell him that you have not been authorized to give out my number. Better yet – tell him it was a one-time number that is now disconnected."

"Okay."

"Thanks for your help, Ab. I hope everything goes well for you. There is no problem between us." Joe hung up.

"Gustav? This is Albert Tillis."

"Yes, Albert. How did it go? Were you able to make contact with the other party?"

"Yes, I was. Unfortunately, the answer is no. They made the observation that six months was a reasonable period of time. They observed that the business news continue to report your huge success in turning around a difficult situation following the destruction of the SCT plant. They said the deadline is firm." Tillis reported.

"I don't think they have considered all of the factors. I would like to talk to the party directly. Please give me a telephone number." Gustav's voice was authoritative. The "Boss" had spoken.

"I'm sorry I can't grant your request. I have been instructed not to give out any information. Also, they said that it was a one-time number that would not be functional in the future. Apparently, they do not wish to hear from me again." Tillis explained.

"Well, go ahead and give me the number anyway. Maybe I can find the new number." Gustav was not accustomed to receiving negative answers to his requests.

"I'm sorry, Gustav. As I said, I have been ordered not to divulge a confidential piece of information."

"You don't take your orders from them. You take orders from me." Gustav fumed.

"You're wrong. I don't take orders from either of you, I haven't been on your payroll since I left your office six months ago." Tillis hung up the telephone.

Gustav Kohl failed to make the payment to the Colissimo family for the return of the computer tapes. He had the money. He could have made the payment early. A little voice was screaming at him to do the smart thing. The voice cautioned him to do the safe thing. It argued that it was the fair thing. After all, he had agreed to pay the money for the tapes. If the tapes had not been returned the company would have been forced into bankruptcy. The result would be a multi-year recovery from the financial disaster. The voice argued that the Colissimo family did not have to return the tapes. The return of the tapes could be viewed as a good faith gesture to end the feud and limit the damage caused by the death of his grandfather and the destruction of SCT.

Somewhere deep in the soul of Gustav Kohl, there was a stubborn fist of fortitude that argued against the payment. The tapes belonged to International Systems and the Kohl family. Why should he have to buy them back from these criminals? Why should he surrender to blackmail? These were the men responsible for the death of his grandfather. How could he bring himself to pay these commoners for the return of stolen property? The commoner theme was rampant in his mind. These people were not on his social level. Gustav had delayed his decision about paying the money until the last hour but, basically, he had known that he would not pay from the beginning.

Albert Tillis had gone to great lengths to make it clear that he had a choice. He could accept the tapes and the payment terms or he could decline the offer. If he declined, there were no penalties and no future option. If he accepted the offer and the terms, it would be an affair of honor. There was no contract or lien to enforce a legal claim against him. Tillis had told him that if he defaulted on the terms, he would place himself and his family in danger. However, the terms were brutal and savage. The payment was five million dollars but the added levy was that International Systems and he personally could not do business in the United States. The criminals from the common masses were dictating a course to the Kohl family. Gustav knew that his grandfather would never have permitted such an onerous burden.

The loss of his grandfather had left a permanent scar on Gustav. He adored the man. He respected him. Everything he was today was the gift of his grandfather. He could not reward the killers of such a great man.

Although he believed the danger to be quite real, Gustav did not believe that his family was at risk. If anything happened to them, the entire world would revolt and pursue the criminals. No! The threat to his family was empty. For his own safety, Gustav had engaged a private security firm.

"Yes?" Gustav answered the intercom summons of his secretary with some annoyance.

"You have a call from a law firm in the United States. They want to discuss some legal papers that were served on them this morning."

"Herr Kohl here!" Gustav barked into the telephone.

"Yes, sir. This is Mark Zimmer of Schmidt and Schmidt in Rockville, Maryland. I haven't had the pleasure of meeting or speaking to you in the past. I appreciate your taking my call."

"What is it, Mr. Zimmer? I have a meeting in five minutes." Gustav was brusque.

"Sir, we were served with court papers this morning because we are your attorney of record with the local courts. Were you aware that you were about to be named in these papers?"

"I have no idea what you are talking about. What papers?"

"Sir, you are being sued for divorce. Further, there is a protective order prohibiting the physical presence of you or your representatives within one mile of your wife and children. There is a complex formula of financial demands by your wife. Do you want me to review them?"

"No!" Gustav hung up the telephone. The sting of betrayal brought tears to his eyes.

When Laura Kohl made her decision to return to the United States with the children, she knew it would end her marriage. It tore her heart at the foundation. She loved Gustav. He was the father of her children. He would always be a part of her life – the past life not the future life. She was bitter about the undeniable fact that Gustav had chosen to endanger the children and her for five million dollars. She knew the pain he suffered over the loss of his grandfather. And she was willing to grant him the tolerance that his motive was not solely for the money. She knew that Gustav would never forgive her for abandoning him. He would see it as a betrayal.

"Laura?"

"Yes, Dad?"

"Telephone for you, honey." Her father came into the room. "Do you remember the man you met in Munich in the department store? I think you should talk to him."

"Hello?"

"Laura, this is James Colissimo. Thanks for taking my call. I wanted to say that I'm sorry you were caught in the middle of this controversy. I know that you have filed for divorce. I wanted to tell you – to reassure you that my family has no problem with you. You're out of the picture as far as we are concerned."

"So you're assuring me that we are not in any danger?"

"Not from us. You'll have to decide if you are in danger from your husband. I suggest that you think it over carefully before you decide. If you want protection, we can offer it to you." James promised.

"How would you do that? I have a protective order from the courts. My husband or his representatives are ordered to remain one mile from the children and me."

"Well, what that means is that if your husband or a representative actually does come within a mile, they will be arrested if the courts can find them. Our protection will guarantee that they will not be permitted close enough to do you harm."

"And what would you do if they attempted to approach me?"

"We would assume that they intend to harm you. We would harm them first. Many men are willing to commit an act for money and take a chance that they will not be apprehended. And if they are arrested, they have a chance of no punishment or a light punishment. Most men will not endanger their own lives for money when there is a high degree of certainty of death or serious injury."

"I don't want my children surrounded by a squad of gunmen."

"No ma'am. These men and women are licensed private investigators. They are authorized to carry a weapon. Most of them are former police officers."

"I see. And do you think we need this protection?"

"I don't know. But what can it hurt? Better to have it and not need it than the reverse."

"Good point. I'd like to discuss this with my father. Is there a number that I call to reach you?" Laura asked.

"Absolutely. Copy down this number. It will reach me at any time. I live alone. I'm at your service at any time." James' voice was soft as he gave her the information.

Laura chuckled as she copied down the number. It had been a long time since anyone had made a pass at her. But she still recognized the signals and the vibes.

Laura's father made a sobering input. He did not feel there was a danger of injury or death. He thought the greatest danger was child abduction. If Gustav took the kids to Germany, it would be nearly impossible to have the children returned by the German courts.

The next telephone call was to James Colissimo. She accepted the offer of protection. When Laura asked about the costs, he said they would discuss the details at a later date.

"Listen to me, Gino! It's an investment. Damn it, can't you see? We need to thwart this guy's every move. We need to do everything but kill him. If we kill him, we can't get the payment."

"James, I understand that we can't kill him. I understand that we need to scare the shit out of him. At least we need to scare five million dollars worth of shit out of him. What's that got to do with running a full protection detail on his wife and kids?"

"It has everything to do with it. I'm convinced that he will try to recover his kids. If we stop him dead in his tracks, we'll have shown him some muscle. If he is personally present during a kidnap attempt, we'll have him in our hands. Then I guarantee you he'll fork over five million clams. He will pay more if you want it."

"What else is there, James? Is there something else I need to know?"

"Need to know? No. But I'll tell you something else. In total confidence. Capische? Don't make me slice the balls off my older brother because he got diarrhea of the mouth. But the truth is that this is the greatest gal I've ever met. I haven't even held hands with her and I'd like to marry her."

"Holy shit, James! Are you out of your mind? She's married with four kids. How are you going to do that? You're talking like a teenager. Wise up. Keep your eye on the ball." Gino advised forcefully.

"I've got my eye on the ball. We're going to collect our money. Then she is going to get a divorce. Then she's going to fall in love with me. Then we'll get married. What could be simpler?" James laughed. "Lighten up, big brother."

"Tell me about the collection first. What's the next step?" Gino asked.

"We have to get inside this asshole's mind. We have to figure out what makes him tick. How can we make him do what we want him to do?" James murmured as if thinking aloud.

"Right now he has to be pissed at us because of his wife and kids. That's counterproductive. It adds to his feeling about his grandfather. What we have to do is scare him so badly that he wants to pay rather than endure what we will do to him. Threatening his life is not enough. Few people can envision death until the last few minutes of life. It has to be something of dread --of horror." Gino said.

"The scariest thing next to death is loss of manhood. But again, a threat is not enough. He would have to feel the knife on his scrotum." James gripped his fist as if holding a knife.

"Getting to him is going to be a problem now because of the bodyguards." Gino observed.

"Hmmm. I suggest that we take out one of those bodyguards. It might intimidate the others and impress on Gustav that welching is a lethal offense."

"How about a car bomb for the chauffeur/bodyguard?" James asked.

"So be it!" Gino agreed.

46 – Debt Collection

Gino Colissimo reclined the seat in the first class section of the United Airlines Jumbo 747. He reached for the glass tumbler filled with shaved ice and a generous serving of Jack Daniels Black Label Bourbon whiskey. Life was good. Very good!

A life of luxury and comfort was the dream that occupied his mind during dark days and times of stress. He had used the escape mechanism since his teen years. During high school, Gino was a handful of trouble for the school officials and the police. Gino's father had kicked his butt on a frequent schedule until he realized that it had no effect.

Finally, a District Court Judge solved the problem for all of them when he gave Gino a choice of prison or the Marine Corps. North Korea had crossed over the 38th Parallel and the Korean War was on the front page of every newspaper in the land. The word had gone out to all of the courts to send men into the military service not into prison. Gino elected to serve in the Marines rather than Attica prison. He enlisted for four years. Since he was not eighteen, he would be released on his twenty-first birthday. It was called a "Kiddie Cruise."

From boot camp, Gino had a ten-day leave before reporting for shipment to Korea. He was a part of the Inchon landing that preceded the Chinese invasion. Although military experts hailed the landing as a strategic masterstroke, the Marines called it a bloody mess. Casualties were high in terms of killed and wounded. The enemy was stopped and the rear echelon brass called it a turning point in the war. McArthur was hailed as a military genius. It was an often repeated description of the legendary general except in the White House or the Pentagon.

Most of Gino's buddies were killed. The rest were wounded in some way. Gino lost two toes to frostbite and took a shrapnel round in the shoulder.

Gino was four months past his seventeenth birthday when he entered the Marine Corps. He was nine months past his seventeenth birthday when he landed in Korea. He was in a hospital in Japan on his eighteenth birthday. He spent the rest of his hitch training recruits at Camp Pendleton. He was discharged on his twenty-first birthday.

On his return to New Jersey, Gino applied to the Newark Police Department. He had several buddies from High school on the force and he thought he would like it. After marine boot camp and Korea, the police academy training was a piece of cake. The icing on the cake was that his military time counted towards his seniority on the police force.

Papa Colissimo insured that Gino was never involved in any family business. In the 1950s era, it was not unusual – particularly in Italian and Irish families – for one son to choose the priesthood and another one choose the police force while the eldest son worked in the rackets at some level. They were all part of the family at reunions, weddings and funerals.

Police work was satisfying to Gino. He liked the uniform, gun and discipline as much as he liked the same things in the Marine Corps. On the police force, he had more individual freedom and the advantage of working in his hometown. Gino knew the ropes and was popular with his fellow officers. He never volunteered, kissed ass or ratted out a fellow officer. More importantly, he never backed off from a confrontation or fight. He was a stand-up guy. He was a pal. He was trusted by his buddies.

Many policemen serve out their twenty years and never draw their weapon. The primary reason is that the average policeman serves five or six years on the front line and moves into a staff job. Gino almost made it to the staff job without incident. During a routine patrol in the warehouse district, he left the patrol car to check out a door. It was ajar. Before the significance of the event had registered, the door was jerked out of his hands and he was bowled over by two fleeing felons. As he picked himself up from the ground, he yelled, "Stop! Or I'll shoot!" At the time, he had not drawn his weapon. One of the felons turned and fired. Gino was hit in the right upper leg and knocked down again. This time he drew his weapon and fired from the ground level. One of the perps had rounded the corner and was forever free. The other one died instantly when Gino's bullet entered his forehead between his eyes.

The distance of the shot was measured at 150 feet or 50 yards – an astounding distance for the conditions, time of day, Gino's position on the ground, stress level, type of weapon, etc. Gino's fellow officers congratulated him on his good luck. Gino said that luck had nothing to do with it. He was aiming at a pimple on the guy's forehead and he hit it. Gino was not smiling when he made the claim.

The liberal press lamented the age of the deceased felon. He was only twenty-one years old, they wrote. When asked for a comment, Gino answered that the deceased had attempted the murder of a police officer and was punished with death. End of story! Gino's lieutenant observed that Gino would never have a career in public relations.

The bullet fired by the fleeing felon damaged the bone structure in Gino's leg. The doctors advised the use of stainless steel pins as the best method for avoiding a permanent limp. It would have worked perfectly except for the infection around one of the pins. As a result, Gino spent over eight months in the hospital and had a slight permanent limp.

The permanent damage to his leg coupled with the loss of two toes in Korea limited Gino's fitness for duty. He was offered a choice of permanent administrative duty or a medical retirement on a 75% disability. Gino elected to retire at the ripe old age of twenty-nine years.

The hospital stay yielded a major benefit in that he met Florence – his future wife. She was a nurse on his floor. Following his retirement, the happy couple was married in St. John's Cathedral. They traveled to Italy for their honeymoon.

During his convalescence, Gino spent a considerable amount

of time planning a future career. He decided to open a private investigative service. He would employ a full time secretary/ bookkeeper and himself. All other manpower requirements would be fulfilled by current or former police officers as needed. Gino's prediction that he would receive a large amount of business from various family members and friends was very true.

Within five years, Gino had a thriving practice. He had operated in most of the states in the union and expanded to several countries in Europe. He had become an expert on the international movement of money and tax laws. He was becoming a very wealthy man.

The range of customers was surprising. Although many men, or women, wanted to know if their spouse, fiancée, or lover was cheating, few could afford the services of an investigative service. Some wealthy individuals could afford a background check on a future son- or daughter-in-law. Many corporations wanted a background check on men or women slated for the upper echelons. Most of them had endured an expensive or embarrassing situation over the years.

Tracking the movements of an individual was a tricky situation. Gino determined that he did not want to set up a murder for the simple reason that most of the individuals would be apprehended. The first piece of information given up would be the role of the investigative firm. When Clayton Matthews tasked them with the movement profiling of certain individuals, the request came through his younger brother Joe. It would have been difficult to refuse the assignment. On the other hand, Gino had met Clayton on a few occasions and sensed an inner strength or resolve that formed an unusual independence. It was impossible to imagine Clayton talking to the police as a result of a failed operation. And, lastly, working with Clayton always resulted in an unusual amount of profit for the family.

*   *   *

Gino knew that Clayton would have approved of the current trip to Germany. Clayton always planned his operations so that some street justice was combined with profits. At the very least, young Gustav the frigging fourth would learn the value of honoring his agreements. He would also taste a little pain and pay out some money. Gino knew that if Clayton were watching, he would be smiling.

After clearing customs, Gino picked up a reserved rental car and proceeded to do some local shopping. At one automobile parts store, he purchased a five-liter gasoline can. At a hardware store, he purchased some hand tools including a pair of pliers and a box knife. With these items in hand, he checked into a hotel for some rest before beginning the attack on Gernot Gustav Kohl IV.

At 1 AM, Gino drove out to the Kohl estate. He parked about one-half mile from the main driveway and walked the rest of the way. Staying next to the shrubs and trees, he was able to approach the garage with confidence. The structure was designed to accommodate three vehicles and had living quarters on the second floor. There was a side door entering a stairway access to the upper floor. The door had a simple doorknob lock that took less than one minute to enter.

Inside the garage, Gino selected the large Mercedes-Benz sedan for a target. He deposited his tools on the concrete floor under the rear bumper and quickly crawled under the vehicle. With the aid of a pocket flashlight, he located the gasoline line leading from the tank towards the engine compartment. At the juncture of the metal line from the tank with the neoprene rubber line to the engine, he shredded the line with the knife until it began to seep gasoline.

Gino emptied the gas container onto the floor of the garage and headed for the door. He laid a book of paper matches in the path of the slowly spreading gasoline. At the last minute, he ignited the book of matches and ran for the door. Over his shoulder, he saw the structure being consumed by the flames. He made it to his car before the explosion.

The morning TV news programs covered the fire in great

detail. Although Gino's German was limited, he was able to follow the gist of the story. The chauffeur was killed in the explosion and the property damage was extensive. The garage structure was completely destroyed and the main house was damaged. The cause of the fire was under investigation. It was believed that the fire started under the family sedan. There may have been a gasoline leak.

Gino ordered breakfast from room service and asked for a copy of the International Herald Tribune. He was already homesick.

There was no doubt in Gustav's mind about the origin of the fire. For the first time, he began to think that he might have to pay the five million dollars. He called the bank and had them prepare a wire transfer for his authorization. He thought he would hold off for a few days and see if there was any contact. He had a faint hope that he may think of an idea about some way to incriminate these thugs in the garage fire.

Gustav's life had a new complication with the filing of the divorce papers by Laura in Montgomery County, Maryland. He did not oppose the divorce. In fact, he would never allow her to return to his house. He felt betrayed. Even worse, she had betrayed the memory of his grandfather. In retrospect, he could not remember loving her or having sex with her.

But Gustav would never give up his children. They must be trained and educated to carry on the family name. Gustav had interviewed and hired a firm that specialized in child recovery. The attorney told him that the German courts almost never returned children to a foreign country. In three days, he intended to fly to the United States in a private charter jet for the purpose of recovering his children. There would be four members of the detective agency with him. He would identify the children and they would seize the children. Once in the limousine, he would calm the children and have a reunion with them. He did not anticipate any resistance from the children when he explained that they were going to take an airplane ride. If they encountered opposition from Laura or any bystanders, the private detectives were prepared to handle it. One of the reasons for the private jet was so that they could carry arms into the United States.

Prior to Gino's departure for Munich, he worked with James to set up a security detail for Laura and the children. They were living with Laura's parents. All of the children were enjoying the unexpected visit with their grandparents. Dr. Brock had taken an extended leave from NASA and the family was ecstatic with the reunion. Gino wanted to station one agent in front of the house and one in the rear. James wanted an additional agent on the front porch and a roving agent. James prevailed.

James realized that the manpower requirements for keeping four guards around the family on a twenty-four hour schedule were expensive. In fact, they did not have access to enough personnel to continue the schedule for a very long time. Both men agreed to review the manpower level after Gino returned from Germany.

On the second day after setting the garage fire, Gino was waiting in the bushes near the front entrance of the Kohl home as dawn arrived. He was neither sleepy nor tired. He was alert and fully prepared for his mission. He estimated that he was within fifteen paces of the Mercedes-Benz sedan parked at the front entrance. Heavy dew had settled on the area including the windows of the automobile.

Gino tensed as the front door opened and a man exited closing the door behind him. It was not Gustav so he relaxed. The man proceeded to unlock the car. He started the engine and then started to clean the windows while the car warmed up. Finally, he opened the front and rear doors on the driver's side that was the closest to the front door. Then he turned to the entrance as

Gustav Kohl left the house.

Gino sprang from the bushes with gun in hand. Both men whirled to face him and the bodyguard started to draw his weapon. Gino ordered him to raise his hands and the man complied rather than risk death from the gunman with the crazed eyes.

Gino ordered Gustav to tie the guard's hands behind his back with a plastic tie that he handed to him. Grumbling and cursing the guard for his cowardice, Gustav obeyed. Gino pushed him aside and checked the security of the binding. Satisfied, he ordered both men back into the house.

Inside the house, Gino ordered the handcuffed guard into the hall closet. He warned him that any noise would result in a gunshot through the door. Gino ordered Gustav to lay down on his stomach while he tied his hands behind his back. Gustav snarled but he obeyed.

Gino jerked the smaller man to his feet and pushed him towards the kitchen area. Gino backhanded him viciously and directed him towards a chair. Gino pulled a coil of thin rope from his pocket and tied him securely. He was unable to move his arms or legs. Gustav began to curse him loudly but subsided when he saw the smile on Gino's face. As he realized his predicament, fear started to course through his body and he was barely able to control his bowels.

"So, Mr. Kohl, it seems that we have a disagreement about a five million dollar payment that is past due. I thought we would talk it over this morning. Any comment?"

Gustav glared at him and tried to speak but his mouth was too dry.

"No comment, huh? Too bad, I thought you might tell me that the check was in the mail." Gino chuckled as he looked through the kitchen drawers. He found the linen drawer and pulled out some hand towels. Then Gino turned swiftly and grabbed Gustav's hair. He tilted his head back violently and stuffed a towel in his mouth. Gustav twisted his head and grunted but to no avail.

Gino kneeled down in front of Gustav and began to remove

his shoes and socks. Gustav was grunting loudly and trying to twist away. When Gustav was completely barefooted, Gino rose up and removed a switchblade knife from his pocket. He smiled sorrowfully at Gustav.

"This is going to be really painful. You will not be able to contain your screams. There is no one around to hear or help you but I dislike the noise. I have found in past instances that high-pitched screams actually hurt my ears." Gino started to remove his own shoes and socks. When he was barefoot, Gino raised his foot in the air and showed it to Gustav. The foot was missing two toes.

"I lost these two toes when I was only eighteen years old. I can still feel them every day. I remember the loss every morning when I treat the area before putting on my socks. Still, I am grateful that it wasn't my fingers or an arm. I'm sure you will feel the same way in the years to come." Gino spoke calmly.

Gustav was crying softly and the tears rolled down his face.

"Your grandfather was a braver man in the face of defeat, Gustav. He conducted himself with courage and dignity. I think he would be disappointed with your tears." Gino paused to let the words register.

"I intend to amputate two toes on your left foot. Then we will have something in common." Gino continued in a conversational tone. "You'll probably lose consciousness for awhile so I'll have a chance to rest up. I didn't get much sleep last night."

"When you come around and the pain subsides a little bit, I'll remove the gag and we can discuss our situation. You may have a completely different outlook after this experience. I remember how I felt at the time." Gino reached down and touched the tip of the knife blade against the smallest toe.

Gustav began jerking around and having spasms. His stomach was heaving as he tried to hold back the vomit. Gino yanked the towel from his mouth in time to keep him from choking on his own discharge.

When he finished spitting, Gustav began to talk before Gino could insert the gag again.

"I'll pay you the money! I'll pay! I have the money ready

for transfer now. I intended to pay today. Please don't do this. Please!" He sobbed and let his head fall on his chest in exhaustion.

"I gave you six months to transfer the money that you agreed to pay for the tapes. You failed to honor your word. Now you want me to believe that you intended to pay the money today?" Gino scoffed and stared at the man's toes.

Gustav started vomiting again. When he had a chance to breathe, he remembered Albert Tillis' words about fear and the stupidity of man. He blamed Tillis for not warning him in a way that he could understand. He blamed Laura for not explaining the American mentality to him so he would understand. He blamed his grandfather for not teaching him how to deal with these situations. Then, in a flush of shame, a spark of courage erupted from some inner core of strength in a testament to his heritage. He remembered Tillis saying that he would find a way to justify his actions. Gustav raised his head and spoke to Gino.

"Whatever you do to me today, I will pay the five million dollars as soon as I am released. I gave you my word when I agreed to the terms laid out by Tillis. I am shamed that I reneged. My grandfather would not approve. If you look in my briefcase, you will see a statement of a special account with a five million-dollar balance. Your original transfer instructions are stapled to the sheet. I can make the transfer with a single telephone call to the computer access using the account number and password." Gustav started to calm down as he spoke and seemed to draw strength into his voice.

"I cannot explain my actions nor justify them. I guess I felt that the tapes were the property of my company. I resented having to pay a ransom for them. Now, in this situation, I understand your position and regret my actions. I understand why the violence started when the product was stolen from your family. So I will pay the money and I will forego any further action against your family. Now do what you have to do quickly and leave me!" Gustav hung his head and closed his eyes in anticipation of the pain to come.

Gino stared at him. In his mind, Gino remembered the dignity of the grandfather as he faced death. He knew that he must do his part to end the feud now or it would haunt the families in the future.

Gino turned his back on the young man and stared out the window. He did not want Gustav to see the relief on his face. He did not want to amputate the boy's toes but he would have carried out the threat if it were necessary.

Gino waited for a few minutes to let the fear do its work. Then he turned around. "Okay, I believe you. I will release you without any further violence. I felt like I heard your grandfather speak now. But heed my words. Do not fail again." He stepped behind Gustav and used the knife to cut his bonds. Then he turned and left the house.

Gino drove back to his hotel and laid down for a nap. When he woke, he took a walk through a nearby park and ate an early dinner. He retired early and slept soundly. When he woke early the next morning, he used the telephone to check the balance in the offshore account. The five million dollars had been paid.

Gino packed quickly and departed for the airport. He was anxious to get home. In the airport lounge, he had time to call James and Joe.

47 - Custody Battle

Gustav freed the bodyguard after Gino's departure. He told him to leave the premises. His services were no longer required. Then he went to his office and transferred the money to settle accounts with the Colissimo family.

The telephone rang and he accepted a call from the head of the investigative service hired to recover the Kohl children. The man confirmed that an advance team was in place with the children and their mother under surveillance in the United States. The charter airplane was due to depart at 3AM the following morning. Did Herr Kohl intend to accompany the team on the recovery mission? The answer was yes.

James was relieved when he talked to Gino. It was good to have matters settled with Gustav. Now if the divorce went smoothly, he intended to pursue his case with Laura. He knew it would take time but he was deeply in love.

Grandpapa Brock was taking Laura and the kids to the Montgomery County Fair in Gaithersburg, Maryland. He had taken them to the Fair on a previous trip and they remembered the event with squeals of delight. There were farm animals and carnival rides and exhibits and candy and everything was fun.

James agreed with Dr. Brock that the complete security detail was not necessary. They talked it over and agreed that James and one other guard would accompany the family. James was a little bit reluctant but, after all, the Fair was crowded with people and there were many policemen in attendance. What could happen?

On the other hand, there was a way to play it safe and accomplish another step in his long term plan. He wanted Gino and Florence to meet Laura and the kids. He wanted Gino to spend some time with Dr. Brock. The man had some great ideas for some businesses after his retirement from NASA. Gino would be another able body on the reduced security team.

The charter aircraft flew from Munich to Baltimore without refueling. It had been equipped with long range fuel tanks during a previous outfitting. On the ground in Baltimore, they checked through customs without any trouble. The aircraft was not searched since it was from a western European nation. After refueling, the aircraft departed for Frederick, Maryland. The runways were adequate for the business jets without the bother of a control tower. Aircraft movements were not monitored or recorded.

From Frederick, the head of the security established contact with his advance element. He was informed that the family, including Laura and the four children, were visiting the County Fair. They rented two vehicles and drove the thirty miles to Gaithersburg. They rendezvoused with the advance team within an hour of landing in Frederick.

At the fairgrounds, the recovery team gathered for a briefing. Each member was assigned a role and an escape route was planned. They had three vehicles. Gustav and the four children would be put into one of the large Chevrolet Suburbans. He would be able to calm the children. The other two vehicles and personnel would cover their departure. If they did not encounter any resistance, everyone would proceed to the aircraft and they would return to Germany. If the rear guard was delayed, Gustav and the children would return on the aircraft. The recovery team would disperse in different directions and get lost in the urban sprawl of Washington, D. C. They had sufficient cash and credit cards to make their way back to Germany via commercial flights.

At the Montgomery County Fair, everyone was having fun. It was a warm August day so every hot dog required a generous-sized coke. James bought straw hats for everyone and they pretended to be farmers. Gernot, the oldest at nine, was enjoying the Ferris wheel with James. Grandpapa Brock had the seven-year old twins in tow on the merry-go-round and Laura was holding a sleeping five-year old Karen.

When Gino and Florence arrived, James made the introductions to Dr. Brock, Laura and the kids. Florence took the twins by their hands as the men started talking shop. James and Gernot headed for the Ferris Wheel.

After the recovery team parked the three vehicles, the leader distributed automatic pistols with extra magazines to the members. He handed one to Gustav without even thinking about it. Gustav accepted the weapon. He had never held or fired a weapon in his life. He stared at the lethal object and remembered television programs. He located the safety lever and knew enough to charge the weapon with a bullet in the chamber.

As James and Gernot stepped off the Ferris wheel, Gernot pleaded with James for one more ride. James laughed and turned to the ticket booth to purchase the tickets. Gernot turned to find his mother and wave. Instead he spotted his father.

"Papa! Papa! Did you see me on the Ferris wheel?" Gernot cried.

James whirled to see the recovery team rushing towards Laura and the children. Gino tried to block the rush of the recovery team and was quickly knocked to the ground. He was not licensed to carry a firearm in Maryland so he was unarmed.

James drew his weapon and ran to protect Laura.

Gernot knew something was wrong and he followed the instincts of every child. When in danger, run to Mama. Laura gathered him into her arms along with Karen, the baby. Grandpapa Brock clutched the twins tightly and held his ground. Florence helped a dazed Gino to his feet. The two of them stood in front of Grandpa Brock and the twins.

The leader of the team reached Laura and knocked her to the

ground. She lost her grip on the two children. James reached the group and pistol-whipped the leader into unconsciousness. James turned to help Laura and the two children. When he saw the other team members converging on him, he realized they were greatly outnumbered. James looked around for help and saw that the spectators had scattered when the screaming started. There was not one policeman in sight.

In desperation, James thumbed off the safety of his pistol and fired the first shots. He dropped two members of the recovery team before they reached Laura and the children. Gustav saw the scene develop and panicked. He raised the pistol and pointed it towards James. He didn't intend to fire it. He wanted to tell this unknown stranger to take his hands off his children and wife. Unfortunately, Gustav squeezed the trigger and the automatic weapon began to fire. He was not prepared for the recoil and the shots went wild. The entire magazine of fifteen bullets was fired.

At this point, several policemen were beginning to converge on the scene. The remaining recovery team members saw the police and began an orderly withdrawal towards the vehicles. The police saw Gustav holding and firing a weapon.

James was struck by two bullets. Although the wounds were serious, they were not fatal. James was on the ground and out of the battle.

Laura was struck by one bullet. She fell to the ground unconscious. She would recover.

Gino was struck by three bullets. Any one of the wounds would have been fatal. Florence fell on top of Gino to shield him from further wounds but it was too late.

Grandpa Brock was struck by one bullet to the head. It was fatal but he had managed to shield the twins long enough for the police to kill Gustav.

Three Montgomery County Police Officers fired at Gustav almost simultaneously. They each fired two shots and every bullet hit the target. Gustav was dead at the scene.

The leader of the recovery team was taken into custody at the scene. After treatment of his wounds, he was charged with four counts of attempted kidnapping. The remainder of the charges would wait for forensic evidence. The police had the weapons and would be able to determine which weapon killed Dr. Brock and Gino.

James and Joe Colissimo went to the county morgue to perform the official identification of Gino Colissimo. Both brothers were devastated. The family had lost their oldest brother, John, at the hands of Max Krug and now they had lost Gino.

Gino was the one that insisted on selling the computer tapes to Gustav and started the latest chain of events. He paid the ultimate price. Gino's death would be the end of the Colissimo crime family. Neither Joe nor James had any desire to continue the family activities.

48 – Conclusion

The police investigation concluded that James Colissimo acted as an employee of the family-owned security service. He was licensed to carry a firearm in the states of Maryland and New Jersey. They confirmed that the company was under contract to provide protective services for Laura Kohl and her children. There was a restraining order that had been issued by the court forbidding Gustav Kohl or his representatives from approaching Laura and the children. The deaths of the two recovery team members were ruled justifiable homicides.

The leader of the child recovery team was convicted of all charges. He was sentenced to serve two consecutive terms of twenty-five years in Maryland State prison. None of the other members of the team were apprehended.

Laura Brock Kohl was awarded permanent custody of Gernot, the twins Herman and Peter, plus the youngest child, Karen. The court action protected Laura and the children from any suit that may arise out of Germany. In addition, Mrs. Brock sued the Kohl estate for the wrongful death of her husband, Dr. Werner Brock.

The German High Court appointed an executor to manage International Systems, Inc. pending the outcome of the legal action and the distribution of the estate.

Gustav Kohl was buried next to his grandfather in Germany. Dr. Werner Brock was buried in the family plot in Laurel, Maryland. Gino Colissimo was returned to New Jersey and buried next to his older brother, John, and his parents in the Colissimo family plot.

Joe Colissimo was devastated over the loss of his brother. He felt guilty about his less-than-enthusiastic support during the last few months. After the funeral service for Gino, he turned the remaining family business over to his next-in-line subordinate. Joe made a settlement with Gino's widow and John's widow for the benefit of the children. Joe and James Colissimo never spoke again during their lifetime.

Joe and Sylvia Colissimo moved to California to be near their daughter and son-in-law and future grandchildren. Joe continued as an active member of the family trust for Kathryn and her children and he served on the Board of Directors for Camp Lydia.

James Colissimo and Laura Brock were married within six months of their recovery from their wounds.

Kathryn Ann and Thomas Phillips announced the birth of a baby boy. Eight pounds six ounces. Twenty inches long. His name was Clayton Lee Phillips. He was named after his two grandfathers.

Joseph and Sylvia Colissimo announced the forthcoming marriage of their daughter Josephine to Mr. Stephan Rossini. The ceremony will be held in the Fair Oaks Catholic Church.

John Higgins retired from the Montgomery County Police Force to become the full-time Director of Camp Lydia. He and Susan, plus Billy and the new baby and Stanley moved into the permanent quarters at the Camp.

Susan Higgins resigned her job at Holy Cross Hospital. She intended to spend full time taking care of Billy and the new baby due in four months.

Camp Lydia received an award from the Governor of Maryland for accomplishments in teaching computer literacy to handicapped children. The Governor praised the camp as an example of focused private sector charitable efforts.

Everyone remembered Clayton Matthews. He was discussed frequently by the various parties. No one doubted that he got his revenge on the parties that hurt him and his family. There was no consensus about whether the price was worth the satisfaction.

And no one ever said they would take the same course of action again.

Father, forgive us our trespasses as we forgive those who trespass against us.

THE END

Acknowledgements

There are three good friends who helped guide me through stops and starts on my books. I started writing short stories about various family members and my military service years ago. The effort was enjoyable and therapeutic. Getting to a full length novel was a whole nuther staircase of ups and downs.

Beth Mende Conny is a friend and neighbor. She is also a professional and successful author with over forty published books. She teaches classes and writes a blog – all of her waking hours are dedicated to writing, teaching and helping people express themselves. When I gave Beth a first sample of Nothing To Lose to review, she asked me one question that caused me to re-write the ending. In a later critique, I was able to see the book through her eyes. I could see the effect of each visual detail that formed the complete portrait and story. She shared her experience in printing and publishing generously.

As we progressed, Beth introduced Alyssa Fowler to the team. Alyssa's knowledge of graphic design was immediately helpful. Her enthusiasm and personality were bonuses.

Constance Pryor is also a friend and neighbor. She is a college teacher, choir singer and pianist. She is a problem analyst and solver of uncanny ability. Connie listens, analyzes and then asks questions that go to the heart of the problem. Connie's experienced eye for detail catches every error in spelling, punctuation and formatting. She explains the reason you should do it this way rather than that way.

Ernest Hodge came into my life via a letter out of the blue.

He introduced himself as a half brother to one of my many first cousins. He was looking for family information. He wanted names, dates, and places. More importantly, he wanted stories and anecdotes. As he read the stories, he asked if I had ever published a book. No, but I had written several books over the years. When I sent him the first book to read, I was apprehensive waiting for the judgment. When I got his comments, I was a happy author. He liked it and praised many parts.

Then I encountered the page that started – "BTW, I noticed a few things that might be helpful." The following "comments" were over twenty pages and covered structure plus words not in my normal vocabulary – protaganist, 1st person and 3rd person perspective. There were block diagrams and flow charts. He covered the importance of character descriptions and character movements during dialogue.

Over a few months and many e-mail exchanges, he showed me how to turn an enjoyable hobby into marketable products. Ernie is a retired U.S. Marine with over twenty years of service. Since retirement, he has worked in several fields including advice to authors. He has retained his skills in leadership and motivation. In short, there would not have been a book without Ernie's inputs. It would have been an enjoyable hobby.

As you can see, the common denominator of my friends is their willingness and ability to help and encourage people.

About the Author

Jimmie Toms grew up in Northeast Oklahoma — home of hard-rock ore mines, hard work and Mickey Mantle. He enlisted in the Air Force after High School graduation. After boot camp, he completed Electronics A and B schools and volunteered for flight duty. He served as tail gunner on a SAC B-36 Bomber crew for three years.

After military service he worked on KC-135, B-52 and X-15 aircraft as Field Engineer on navigation and autopilot systems at military bases, airlines, and aircraft manufacturers.

He is a certificated General Aviation pilot with commercial and instrument rating in single engine, land, light aircraft.

Currently he writes and lives with his family in the Washington D.C. area. *Nothing To Lose* is his first novel.